*

The
SECRET
HEALER

*

*

The
SECRET
HEALER

*

ELLIN CARSTA
TRANSLATED BY TERRY LASTER

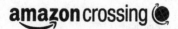

Text copyright © 2015 Ellin Carsta

Translation copyright © 2016 Terry Laster

Previously published as *Die heimliche Heilerin* by Amazon Publishing in Germany in 2015. Translated from German by Terry Laster. First published in English by AmazonCrossing in 2016.

Published by AmazonCrossing, Seattle

www.apub.com

Amazon, the Amazon logo, and AmazonCrossing are trademarks of Amazon.com, Inc., or its affiliates.

ISBN-13: 9781503953864
ISBN-10: 1503953866

Cover design by Rachel Adam

Printed in the United States of America

Prologue

A scream tore through the night. "Hush now. Here." The terrified Madlen, barely thirteen years old, grabbed a cloth and pressed it into the woman's hand. "Use this when all else fails."

The laboring mother writhed in pain, arching her back. It seemed as though the unborn child was fighting its mother, as her movements became increasingly erratic, every muscle taut.

"Pick up the candle and give me some light!" Clara ordered as she reached deep between the woman's legs. "A little higher, please."

Madlen held the candle over Clara's head, in the hope that Clara would be able to see well enough to finally bring the baby into the world.

"Agnes," Clara said to the laboring woman, as calmly as possible. "Please don't push any more for the moment, do you hear me? The baby hasn't turned yet, and I think its umbilical cord may be wrapped around its neck. If you keep on pushing, the baby will choke to death."

"Please get it out!" groaned Agnes, completely exhausted. "I need to push; I just want to get it out."

Clara threw Madlen a helpless look. It had been a long time, and they weren't making any progress. Another contraction came, and again, Agnes arched her back to push the child from her womb.

"We've got to calm her down somehow," Clara whispered anxiously. She tried to reach inside the woman's womb again to turn the baby, but it was no use. Agnes was much too tense. Clara couldn't penetrate the birth canal if Agnes kept fighting her. "She will die if we can't calm her down, and the baby will, too."

Agnes seemed to have heard Clara, as she began to cry and beg them not to let her die. Madlen gave her a sympathetic look as she held the candle high so that Clara could at least save one of their lives. Agnes settled down as the severity of the situation sunk in.

"The baby can't turn. She's too tense." Clara shook her head in despair.

Agnes stared at the candle in Madlen's hand, her eyelids fluttering and the corners of her mouth twitching from exhaustion. Madlen noticed that the dancing candlelight seemed to mesmerize her and slowly moved the candle back and forth behind Clara, who still squatted in front of Agnes's legs, hoping for a miracle. Agnes's eyes followed the light, right to left, then back again. Madlen knelt down and continued to move the candle ever so gently, back and forth.

"That's good," said Madlen, taking a deep breath. She thought about the calm voices of the priests at Sunday Mass and tried to imitate them. "The light is warm and peaceful; the monastery nuns made these candles and prayed to God that their flames would bring you light and give you peace. You are calm and your legs are relaxed. Hail Mary, full of grace, the Lord is with thee." Her lips formed the words of the Mass, as if they'd taken on a life of their own. "Blessed art thou among women and blessed be the fruit of thy womb, Jesus." She paused for a second and saw Agnes's eyelids continue to flutter. She turned to Clara and, with a nod, gestured for her to keep going. Madlen turned again to the woman and noticed that her eyelids now grew restless. "Hail

Mary, Mother of God, pray for us sinners now and in the hour of our death. May Almighty God have mercy on us. He leads us away from temptation and to eternal life. The Almighty and merciful Lord grants us forgiveness for all our sins."

Clara shoved her hand inside the woman's womb and gave the baby a full turn. Madlen tried to concentrate, but it was if her mind had been swept clean of any more prayers or psalms. She swayed the candle to and fro and looked at Clara, who indicated that she should keep on praying. "But I trust you, Lord. You are my God. Our destiny lies in your hands; deliver me from the hands of my enemies and persecutors! Let your light shine upon your servants, help us in our hour of need! Lord, I call on you to not let us fail, because failing would be . . ."

With a rapid, violent movement, Clara turned her arm and pulled the baby, slipping it out of the womb. Agnes arched her back and screamed in agony, as Madlen dropped the candle in fright. She hastily beat out the flames with her apron. Everything went quiet.

Madlen looked anxiously over Clara's shoulders as she placed her hand over the infant's nose and eyes and blew into its mouth with all her might. After a terrifying few moments, the child began to cry lustily. Agnes's lips quivered. She was too exhausted to focus on her newborn. Elated, Clara shrouded the little boy in fresh sheets and pressed him close to her body. Then she got up and showed the child to Madlen with a thankful grin. "You saved this baby's life with your calming voice and prayers. Now we must take care of Agnes so that we can lay the baby on her breast."

Madlen stood and pulled up Agnes's seemingly lifeless body with one arm, the other wrapping around the back of her neck. She rearranged a stack of cushions before gently letting the new mother sink back against them. Weakened, Agnes could barely open her eyes as Madlen situated her.

Clara laid the baby boy on Agnes's breast and held him tight until the newborn latched onto his mother's nipple. Agnes slowly came to and smiled gratefully when she felt his tiny lips at her breast. She embraced her son for the first time as he suckled peacefully. The wondrous feeling of birth made the difficult labor and threat of death seem like a hundred years in the past. Deep happiness coursed through her body. Madlen could have remained there for hours, just to admire the peaceful image of mother and child, alive and well.

"You have a beautiful son. What will you call him?"

"Felix," Agnes answered, after considering the question briefly.

"That means 'happy,' doesn't it?" Madlen asked.

"Yes," Agnes said. "It's fitting. It's a happy miracle that he and I survived. I'll never forget you both, as long as I live."

Clara smiled. Hundreds if not thousands of women had said the same, though they didn't seem to remember when Clara struggled to survive the harsh winter months. She looked at Madlen, whose earnest expression suggested she believed Agnes's words. Still, Clara wouldn't say anything. It was Madlen's first time assisting with a birth. Sooner or later, the thirteen-year-old would learn that women promised a lot in the afterglow of a successful childbirth. But they forgot those promises just as quickly. Life was like that.

Chapter One

Three years later. Heidelberg, in the year of our Lord, 1387

Madlen strolled around the market with her basket. She should have been dead tired since she'd barely slept a wink last night after helping Clara with yet another birth. Everything went off without a hitch. No wonder, as this was the woman's eighth child. Finally, after seven boys, she'd been blessed with a little girl. Madlen had been thrilled with the outcome, assuming the mother must have ardently longed for a girl. But she didn't seem to care whether it was a boy or a girl. Nevertheless, no matter how many times Madlen attended a birth, she always felt as though she had witnessed a miracle.

At this particular birth, it wasn't even necessary for her to light a candle or speak softly as usual. Clara had warned Madlen many times that her work could be interpreted as some sort of witchcraft. She may very well be called to account for it. But Madlen remained firmly convinced that women appreciated the calming effect that she provided in the special hours of childbirth—these women would never dream of speaking ill of her. On the contrary, she'd already worked with many women who had several births behind them, and she'd expertly calmed them down during labor. This spared them undue pain and increased their chances of survival. But Clara had her doubts. She'd often experienced the women's elation and gratitude, but those moments didn't last long. Still, everything had gone pretty well so far. Even Clara was forced to admit that many difficult births only went well because of Madlen's ability to deal calmly with the women, putting them into a kind of a reverie. Clara couldn't say how her young friend did what she did. In some ways, she didn't want to know, for the influence of the devil couldn't be entirely ruled out.

It was now autumn. The farmers had begun to harvest their crops a few weeks back. Madlen loved this time of abundance, when fresh vegetables were available without having to pay a king's ransom. Madlen bought cabbages, onions, beets, and leeks. She'd already baked bread early in the morning. As soon as she got home, she'd prepare soup before making her way to Clara's place.

"Madlen!"

She turned and saw Leonard, the obese butcher, his bald head crimson red as he hurried toward her. His face looked puffy and swollen. He'd probably stayed at the tavern too late last night. Madlen rolled her eyes. She knew what he wanted. Just yesterday, her father had scolded him for ordering two more tables without paying for the previous delivery. Jerg wouldn't give him one more piece of furniture if he didn't settle the outstanding debt. By the time the bald man had reached her, he was already out of breath.

"Your father was supposed to bring me new tables two days ago," he said angrily. "The old one broke under the weight of a pig and all the meat fell into the dirt where the dogs got ahold of it. Jerg needs to reimburse me for that loss." He stood with his hands on his hips.

"I'll tell my father. If he promised to bring the tables, then he'll do it." She hesitated before straightening her back and lifting her head. "Have you paid for the goods already delivered?"

The butcher's head got even redder. "Who said I didn't pay, huh?"

She shrugged. "Nobody. I only know that my father always delivers his contracts on time. That is, unless someone is very past due."

Leonard chomped at the bit to reply, but Madlen continued. "However, if indeed you paid on time, as you imply, then the guilt must lie with my father. I'll speak to him as soon as I get home."

The butcher started to look uncomfortable. "You do that. And if there is an unpaid bill, tell him he'll get his money as soon as he brings me the tables."

"Indeed I will." She nodded politely. "Good day to you, butcher." With that, she turned and walked away quickly so that he couldn't see the smile forming on her lips. She strolled farther but bought nothing; it was simply a pleasure to admire nature's treasures during these autumn months. Soon the ships wouldn't be able to sail, the ice too thick over the winter months. Everyone had to manage to get through the winter with what they had. Those who could afford it stocked up. This luxury wasn't available to Madlen or her family. She lived with her father, Jerg, and her older brother by two years, Kilian, in a small cottage at the edge of the settlement. Her father and Kilian did carpentry work in the barn, where the family had once kept cows.

Madlen never knew her mother. She'd given up her life to give life to Madlen. Everyone said that Madlen looked exactly like her: light-blue eyes that Kilian also inherited, long dark hair, and delicately carved features. The only difference was a small mole above her lip, which made her beautiful face even more distinctive. To this day, Madlen was plagued with guilt about causing her mother's death and taking her away from her brother and father. She often wondered if her mother could have been saved by an experienced birth assistant or even a midwife. She was sure that someone like Clara could have helped and had dreamed about it a hundred times.

In her dreams, Madlen saw Juliana, her mother, in Clara's cottage, her pregnant belly sticking out, the birth imminent. Even though it was impossible, Madlen saw herself next to Juliana, holding a candle in her hand and letting it sway back and forth. She heard Clara say that it would be a difficult birth, that something was wrong. In the dream, Madlen saw sweat running down Clara's face. She heard herself recite psalms in a comforting voice, one after another, as she calmly moved the candle and watched her own birth. Finally, the time came and she saw the light. Juliana lost all strength and wanted to give up, but Madlen continued to pray that her mother would not die. Miraculously, she opened her eyes and took the newborn tenderly in her arms. Madlen felt her mother's warmth as she held her, just before waking up. It was all just a dream. Her mother died without ever taking her newborn daughter in her arms.

Despite the endless guilt, Madlen knew that whatever she did or thought, nothing would bring her mother back. So, she did her best to make up for it, cooking for her brother and father and keeping everything neat and tidy, always trying to imagine everything that her mother would have done if she'd lived. When she was nine or ten years old, she would sometimes get so tired that she would fall asleep while eating and her father would carry her to bed. It had gotten better as she grew older. She was stronger now and could do a lot more. She also earned a coin or two helping Clara and could contribute to her family's overall earnings.

As she approached their small cottage, she could hear her father and Kilian arguing loudly in the woodshop.

"He's a scoundrel," her brother yelled. "Besides, who's going to help us with the household when she's gone?"

"We'll just have to take care of everything by ourselves."

Madlen paused before sneaking a bit closer to the workshop. Her heart pounded wildly. They were talking about her, of that she was sure. Who did her father want her to marry?

"Mother would never have allowed this," said Kilian, his voice suddenly calm.

"Mother isn't here!" her father shouted. "She is dead, dead, dead! I have to make sure both of you have a roof over your head and something to eat."

"At least let me speak to her," Kilian said so softly that Madlen could hardly hear him. She swallowed hard, not daring to breathe as she waited for her father to change his mind or for Kilian to say that they would find another solution. But they didn't. She stood as if frozen in place. Kilian opened the door and walked out of the workshop. Their eyes met, and Madlen knew she'd been caught eavesdropping. Her brother took her by the arm; she stumbled as she walked beside him.

"So, you heard us talking?" he asked softly as they reached their cottage.

She nodded. "Who?"

"A spice merchant named Heinfried. He's already had two wives, but neither could bear him children."

Madlen could barely choke out a short sentence. "I've never heard of him. Does he live in Heidelberg?"

Kilian sighed. "No. He lives in Heilbronn and only passes through here on business. He wants to take you there with him."

"When?"

"In two weeks."

"So soon?" Madlen said, her eyes wide. "Did he pay well?"

"Very well. I don't think we can talk Father out of it."

"How old is he?" Madlen's voice broke as a chill ran through her body. Kilian looked at her sympathetically but dodged the question.

"I can't remember."

She imagined what her future husband looked like: a fat pig, probably older than her father. She shuddered. Kilian opened the door, and she followed him inside, then set down the basket. She immediately started to chop vegetables. Her hands cut mechanically through the cabbage; she could hardly see through the tears in her eyes.

When her father finally came in, the soup was ready. Without a word, she filled up the plates with food and placed them on the table. During the meal, nobody said anything. It was as if Madlen was already gone.

Chapter Two

"It's the same old tale." Clara sounded angry, yet resigned. "The fat rich man takes a fresh young maiden to bed without a thought to her soul." She settled into a chair.

Madlen could no longer hold back her tears. "I don't want to leave home, but what can I do? My father needs the money. As soon as the spice merchant, this Heinfried fellow comes, he'll pay my father. And he'll pay him again if I give him a son."

"Heinfried." Clara rolled her eyes. "I wish I had the money to pay your father, but I just don't."

Madlen grabbed Clara's hand. "I know. Anyway, it won't be so terrible. But I'll miss you and Kilian desperately." She hesitated. "And my father, too," she added softly.

"You're so brave, sweet girl." Clara patted Madlen's hand tenderly. "I think of you as my own daughter."

Madlen hesitated to ask the next question. She often wondered why Clara had never married or had children of her own, like most women her age. She had to be at least forty, the age that fertility started to wane. She'd known Clara since she was a little girl, because her little cottage wasn't far from home. She couldn't think of a time when Clara wasn't in her life, although she knew that the midwife had moved here when Madlen was six or seven years old. Even then, Madlen had been immediately attracted to Clara's amiable nature. In many ways, she was the mother that Madlen had always wanted. Clara had even helped her when she had her first bleed. But Madlen had never dared to ask Clara why she lived alone. Since the midwife had brought it up, Madlen mustered the courage to ask, "Why didn't you ever have your own children?"

Clara lifted her head and looked at Madlen sadly. "I did have a daughter once. A wonderful girl. She would be two years older than you are now."

"What happened?" Madlen whispered, imagining a gruesome story.

Clara swallowed hard. "It's been almost eleven years now. An eternity. Even so, I can remember everything exactly as it happened." She took a deep breath. "My husband's name was Jobst. He struck out to chop and gather wood despite the freezing air. It was the coldest winter I can remember. At that time, we lived in Ulm. Have you ever been there?"

"No, but I've heard the name before."

"It's more than five days away from here," Clara continued. "Our home was right next to the river. My Marie was with me in the cottage. We baked together until she fell asleep. She was four years old at the time. I laid her down on her bed." Clara paused. Madlen silently held her hand. The pain of the memory was written all over her friend's face. "Suddenly, somebody knocked very hard at the door, and I answered to find my next-door neighbor. Her husband had hurt himself very badly, and she begged me to help her. I threw on my cloak, wrote Jobst a note, and followed her to their barn. There, I was met with a horrific scene. Fritz had slipped from the top of the ladder onto the hard frozen ground. His head was bleeding profusely, and his whole face was swollen and distorted. We did everything possible to stem the bleeding, but he finally closed his eyes, never to open them again." Clara's hand shook. "I went back to my cottage, but Jobst was nowhere in sight. The ax was stuck in the post, so I thought he was probably back in the house with Marie. But he wasn't."

"Where were they?"

"I searched and searched for them. Finally, overcome by dread, I ran down to the river. Marie liked the water. We always made sure that she didn't get too close."

Clara's voice became hoarse. "I called and called for Marie, then for Jobst. I didn't see either of them on the river. But then I saw the hole."

"What kind of hole?" Madlen said, stroking her friend's hand.

"A hole in the ice. The river was frozen over, but the ice wasn't very strong, due to the strong current. Then I saw something."

"Marie?"

Clara nodded, now sobbing. "And Jobst. Marie must have broken through the ice, and her father must have run to save her. They were both under the ice, and the current had dragged them close to shore. Jobst's eyes were still open as he held Marie in his arms. He seemed to look at me through the ice."

"I'm so sorry."

"I screamed until a neighbor finally came to help me. We broke through the ice, but it was too late." Clara cried as she leaned on Madlen, still grief-stricken. It was a while before she could speak again. "I couldn't bear to live alone in that cottage without them. So I moved away. But there's never a day that goes by that I don't think of them both."

"I'm so terribly sorry," Madlen said again. It was all she could think to say.

Clara shook her head. "Afterward, I drifted for a long time until I finally came to this village and had the feeling that I could stay." She sniffed. "Do you know why?"

"No."

Clara gave Madlen a tiny smile. "You had no mother, and I had no child. I thought that God had sent you to me so that we could bear our grief together."

She fell again into bitter sobs. Clara had been just like a mother to her over the years. Madlen felt safe and secure in her presence. Clara taught her how to cook, how to sew, and the best way to manage the household. She'd been by Clara's side for four years to help women in childbirth. And now she would be separated from Clara to marry some old pig? It drove them both to the depths of despair.

"What can I do?" Madlen asked.

Clara was about to respond when someone started pounding on the door. "Open up!" a deep, masculine voice threatened. Clara and Madlen looked at each other with fear in their eyes. The midwife finally rose from her chair, wiped the tears from her eyes, and went to the door as the pounding resumed.

"What is this all about?" Clara demanded as she opened the door to two men, their faces grim.

"Are you Clara, the midwife?"

Clara stood straight and tall. "I am." Madlen noticed a slight tremor in her voice.

"You will appear tomorrow morning at ten o'clock for an interrogation."

"Why?" Clara put her hands on her hips in indignation.

"You are responsible for the death of a baby."

Madlen hurried to her friend's side. "This doesn't make any sense. Who?"

"The ferryman's daughter. She claims you gave her herbs that led to a miscarriage."

Clara went pale as she groped for Madlen's hand.

"Let us in," the constable said. "We need to find these herbs."

Clara threw Madlen an anxious look. Subtly, her gaze moved over the jars of angelica, lovage, sage, and wormwood. Quickly, Madlen grabbed her abdomen and yelped.

"What's the matter?" The constable looked past Clara and raised his eyebrows as Madlen held her stomach.

"Please, I've got woman's problems. If Clara doesn't help me immediately, I don't know what will happen." She limped over to the bed and fell facedown on it. The men gazed at each other nervously. Madlen yelped again, as if in excruciating pain.

"Take care of her," the officer ordered Clara. "But we will be back, you can be sure of that."

Clara nodded hurriedly and quickly locked the door. "Thanks," she said to Madlen, completely drained and leaning back against the door she'd just closed.

"We need to hurry," Madlen warned. "They mustn't find anything here." She pointed to the jars.

"You're right." Clara hurried over to the table. "The constables wouldn't listen if I explained they only alleviate cramps and pains." She looked at the herbs with regret. It had taken her days and weeks to collect, dry, and process them. It hurt her very soul to destroy them, but she had no other choice.

"The ferryman's daughter?" Madlen looked at Clara. "But if you've helped her, why does she turn you in now?"

"I really don't know, my darling. But that's not important now. I have no other choice but to explain that I gave her nothing but a harmless brew. We can only pray to God that they believe me. Come on." She grabbed some jars and small bowls filled with finely ground herbs before rolling them up in a large cloth. "Light the torch. It will be dark soon, and we must go deep into the forest."

Without a word, Madlen obeyed. She grabbed the last two jars, lit the torch, and followed her friend out of the cottage. Although evening wouldn't arrive for a few hours, it was the time of year in which darkness moved earlier and earlier over the hilly landscape. Madlen had to hurry. She wanted to get home so that she wouldn't incur her father's wrath. But first, she had to help Clara bury every last bit of the herbs.

The women walked a good way into the forest when Clara finally stopped. "This should do it." She spread out the cloth and knelt down on the forest floor to dig a hole with her hands. When she'd finished, she stood up. "That's deep enough. Light the torch—"

"We've caught you red-handed!"

Madlen let out a frightened yelp, and Clara gasped. "We only, only wanted to . . . ," she stammered.

"We know exactly what you wanted," the constable said. "You ripped the baby right out of her womb—a wicked old wives' trick!"

"She didn't know what we gave her," Clara explained quickly as she looked at Madlen. "I lied to help her. She thought—"

"Silence, you wretched woman!" The constable gave Clara a resounding slap across the face, and she hit the ground, falling onto the jars, which broke into a thousand pieces. Clara lay unconscious, and Madlen cried out when she saw her head bleeding. She fell on her knees to help, but the constable grabbed her arm and she dropped the torch.

"Let me go!" roared Madlen as she tried to wrench herself away from his iron grip.

"Damn!" yelled the other constable, who had not yet taken part in the action. Madlen soon understood what he meant. The torch's flame had reached Clara's dress, and the fire was quickly consuming the highly flammable fibers of her multilayered skirt. The constable jumped on the flames, but they blazed higher and higher.

"Help me," the constable yelled, and his sidekick let Madlen go. They tried to smother the flames as Clara regained consciousness. She screamed like a tortured animal and tried to tear the burning dress away from her body, floundering as the fabric burned into her skin. Madlen could only watch in horror as the smell of burnt hair and flesh took her breath away. Two strong hands pulled her back with a jolt. Madlen's own dress had started to burn. The constable threw her to the ground and beat out the remaining glow with the palms of his hands. Madlen wanted to rush back over to Clara, but he held her down. "You can't do anything more for her, girl." His voice was tinged with regret, and he threw a furious glance at his counterpart. "Was it worth it?" he roared.

The other officer was too shocked to say anything. He gazed at Clara's still burning body, now motionless.

Madlen's arms began to shake, then her legs. Soon her entire torso shook like a leaf. The constable held her tight. "It's in God's hands now, girl. Shh, shh, it's in God's hands."

She opened her eyes as something within her snapped. She rose and turned on him, kicking and yelling until she had no voice left. Suddenly, she felt so sick that she bent over and threw up. He held her protectively to keep her from losing her balance. Bile continued to rise in her throat and she collapsed limply. Everything went dark. When she awoke, she was lying in bed in her father's cottage. A new day had dawned. She knew after this, nothing would ever be the same.

Chapter Three

The interrogation lasted only a few moments. The sheriff himself came to her father's modest cottage to gently ask Madlen about the accusations against Clara. Madlen shook her head to each question, and it only took him a short time to deduce that Clara was innocent. His verdict was likely influenced by the fact that one of the constables had caused Clara's death. Madlen felt nothing but emptiness; she was weak and barely able to put together a few short sentences.

As he walked away, the sheriff wished her a full recovery and then muttered something to her father as he patted him amiably on the shoulder. Then he was gone. Madlen pulled the blanket over her head and went back to sleep.

It took almost four days before she was strong enough to get out of bed. Her father and Kilian were in the workshop. She could hear the clamor of their saws and hammers. Madlen dragged herself to the doorway and inhaled the fresh air. It was cold out, but she wasn't ready to return to the warmth of the cottage. She thought about Clara. Over and over again, she dreamed of her friend's twitching body as it was engulfed in flames. Even now, Madlen was able to smell the stench of burnt flesh and hair. It made her sick. She quickly turned around, went back inside, and closed the door behind her. She started to pant, her chest rising and falling rapidly as she stumbled back to her bed.

An hour later, Kilian came in to check on her. She was sleeping deeply so he closed the door very quietly as he stepped out of the house again. He had never been this worried about his sister. But ever since this terrible accident with Clara, Madlen seemed like a completely different person. Even when she opened her eyes, it was as if she wasn't aware of her surroundings. Yesterday evening, when he lay down on his own bed, his concern for his sister's sanity rose to considerable heights; maybe Madlen had gone crazy. Kilian had heard of such things. People who had experienced something so horrific that they could no longer get ahold of reality. Kilian prayed that God would spare his sister this terrible fate. In less than ten days, Heinfried, her future husband, would come to pick her up. Kilian almost broke into a smile at the thought of the old goat being repulsed by his sister's condition.

However, there was a chance that Heinfried would feel betrayed and demand the reversal of the marriage contract. On the one hand, Kilian would take this as a blessing because he was convinced the spice merchant was a bad match for his sister. On the other hand, it was clear that his father, Jerg, depended on this money since so many customers had yet to pay their debts to him. A cancellation of the contract could mean his ruin. Neither Kilian nor his father knew how they'd survive the winter without Heinfried's marital contract funds. Kilian prayed for a miracle. But miracles seldom came to pass for him.

Pensively, he was headed back to the workshop when he heard someone call his name. Kilian turned to see Barbara. He'd known her since they were children. About five years ago, she'd gone to serve as a maid for the Trauenstein family. He knew that she didn't have it easy. Matthias Trauenstein, the head of the family, was known for being rough and unfair. There were rumors that he disciplined his servants with a whip. Kilian sometimes asked Barbara about her bruised swollen cheek or black eye, but she always claimed that she was just clumsy.

Although Kilian never believed a word of this, it wasn't up to him to interfere. It would probably make things much worse for her in the long run.

"Kilian," Barbara gasped, out of breath. "Is Madlen home? How is she? I heard what happened with Clara."

He nodded in the direction of the cottage. "She's sleeping. She hasn't done much else since Clara's death."

Barbara pressed her lips together. "But I need her. Can you wake her up for me?"

"Go inside and see for yourself," he offered. "Believe me, Madlen's in no condition to help you or anybody." He cocked his head slightly and scrutinized her. She was pretty, if somewhat pale, and timid as a deer hiding in the forest, ready to flee at the slightest snap of a twig or the crack of a dry leaf.

"What do you want from her anyway?"

"It's my mistress," she stammered, her despair evident. "She's in trouble."

"Yes, Madlen told me about this. Clara took care of your mistress, right?"

"That's right. Her body isn't strong enough to carry another life."

"And what do you want from Madlen?"

Again, Barbara bit her lip, weighing exactly what she wanted to say next. "She is . . . well, she can . . . do something about this," she stammered.

"What do you mean?" Kilian asked, as Barbara did her best to avoid his gaze.

"It's women's business," she explained breathlessly.

"Go on in." Kilian pointed at the cottage. "But you'll see it won't do any good." He turned to go. "I have to go back to work. It was nice to see you again."

"You, too," she said, picking up her skirt and hurrying into the cottage. At first, she knocked timidly, listening carefully. No one answered.

She knocked again, this time much harder. Again, no response. She gathered up her courage and opened the door.

"Madlen?" Her voice trembled. The cottage was furnished modestly. It was, by far, much smaller than the Trauenstein house, where the brick walls were almost two men high and included windows, wall hangings, and rugs. Madlen's house was simple and bare. On the left was the fireplace where a large black pot hung from a chain. Next to it, small kegs and jugs were set on top of a stone slab. A bit farther on were two knives. Three chairs surrounding a wooden table stood in front of the fireplace. Behind it were three small beds, two pushed close to each other and a third a bit farther away. On the right side of the room, a chest with two blankets on top was pushed up against the wall.

"Madlen," Barbara repeated carefully. She went a little bit farther and could easily make out a person on the third bed.

"Madlen," she said louder and more forcefully. This seemed to do the trick. Madlen moved slowly, pushing the blanket down a little. She blinked sleepily at the housemaid.

"Barbara? What are you doing here?"

"Madlen. Thank the Lord. You're awake."

The girl looked at her friend blankly. "What are you doing here?" she repeated.

Barbara sat on the edge of the bed. "Please, you have to help us."

Madlen yawned. "Help you?" she asked. "Why?"

"My mistress. She's bleeding." Barbara swallowed hard. "And now she has a high fever. I don't know what to do."

"Go fetch the doctor," Madlen suggested, not a hint of compassion in her voice.

"He's not in town right now. You're the only one that can help her."

"How can I possibly help her?" Madlen sat up. "I'm sorry you've come all this way, but Clara was the midwife. She's dead. I advise you to pray for your mistress. There's nothing I can do for her."

Barbara sucked in a deep breath. "My God, Madlen. What's wrong with you? It may make no difference to you if my mistress dies, but I know you can help her. You worked by Clara's side for years as she stirred up her herbal concoctions. I know that she would be ashamed to see you act and talk like this." The maid was beside herself.

Her last comment cut Madlen like a knife. She knew in her heart of hearts that Barbara was right. She had learned a lot from Clara over the years. She knew how to prepare herbal medicines better than an apothecary. Still, she couldn't muster the strength to take advantage of that knowledge. Just a few weeks ago, she dreamed of healing and educating people whenever and wherever possible. But now, after Clara's grisly death, it all seemed pointless.

"Madlen!" Barbara said, ripping her from her thoughts. "She's dying!" The maid broke out in tears.

Madlen looked at her. She wanted to tell this uninvited guest to get up, turn around, and get out of her house. But she couldn't find the right words. It was almost as though she could hear Clara's voice, urging her to help.

"I can take a look." Slowly, she pulled the blankets off and put her feet on the cold floor to stand. She staggered, and Barbara grabbed her arm to steady her. Madlen took her hand away with a grateful smile and went over to her chest. She opened it and selected a long wool dress. When dressed, she brushed her long hair and plaited it into a long braid.

"I need to go to the workshop to tell them where I'm going." She patted her braided hair back, picked up her long skirt, and stepped past Barbara through the open door. Where her sudden surge of energy had come from, the maid couldn't say. Barbara followed her. Speed was of the essence now. Hopefully, it wasn't too late.

The women hurried along the best they could. The crisp autumn wind blew into their faces; Barbara had to wipe her watering eyes with her dress sleeve in order to see. When they were almost halfway there, sudden rainfall hampered their trek even more.

"Come on, Barbara," Madlen said to the maid. "The rain's only going to get worse. Pretty soon, we'll both be soaked to the bone."

Barbara did her best to comply. She stumbled over a bump in the road, grabbing Madlen's arm so as not to lose her footing. They both kept running and were soaked when they reached the grandiose estate on the market square. Madlen stopped for a moment to gaze at the high-walled facade looming over her; she shook away a feeling of intimidation. She'd never had a soft spot for such pomp. This kind of wealth didn't make people any happier or more valuable to society. But she could not deny the Trauenstein home left a lasting impression.

"Come on!" Barbara urged, as one of the guards opened the gate and Madlen climbed the stairs to enter the house. "She's lying upstairs in her bedroom."

Madlen gathered up her skirt and climbed until she reached the top floor, Barbara right behind her. "Straight ahead, the second door," she said, pointing the way.

Madlen knocked on the door lightly and stepped in without waiting for an answer. The room was dark and she needed a moment for her eyes to adjust.

"Mistress," Barbara whispered.

"I'm awake." She sounded distressed. For a moment, Madlen was overcome by fear when she realized that Clara wouldn't be by her side.

"I've brought someone with me, mistress. You know Madlen. She's going to try to help you."

The sickly woman held out her arms. Madlen peered at the silhouette as she approached the bed. "Thank God you've come." Adelhaid Trauenstein's voice cracked, and she began to sob.

"Now, now. I'm here," she said, reassuring the noblewoman. "I'll do everything I can to help you and your unborn child." She touched her forehead and patted her cheek. Adelhaid was burning up with fever.

"I heard about what happened to Clara. I'm so very sorry."

Madlen nodded, but didn't say anything; the thought of her dear deceased friend was too much to bear right now. She knew that Clara had tended to Adelhaid Trauenstein many times before. Yet Adelhaid, well past thirty years old, was far beyond her prime. Twelve years ago, she'd given birth to a daughter. The infant was only a few days old when one morning she simply did not wake. Since then, the mistress had suffered four miscarriages. Madlen knew that Adelhaid was under pressure to bear a male heir for her husband. This child could very well be her last chance at motherhood.

"I need a washbasin and more light," Madlen commanded. Barbara nodded and left the chamber at once, returning just a few moments later with the basin and a few towels. Madlen washed her hands thoroughly; she had learned this from Clara. When treating a pregnant woman, proper sanitation was of the utmost importance so as not to endanger the child.

As Madlen washed up, Barbara brought over a dozen candles, which she set all around the bed. When Madlen turned, she could see Adelhaid's face. In the dim light, she hadn't noticed the massive bruising, swelling, and contusions covering the gentlewoman's face.

"Dear Lord. What happened?" Madlen sat on the bed right next to the woman to take a closer look; Adelhaid turned her face to the side and wept. "I fell," she said unconvincingly. All three women knew that only a man's fists could disfigure an otherwise beautiful face this way.

Madlen closed her eyes for a moment to gather her thoughts. "I'm going to examine you now. Did he hurt your stomach?" Adelhaid nodded silently.

"Help me," Madlen urged Barbara as she shoved the bedding aside in order to examine her mistress. "Take the candle and hold it like this so I can see."

Barbara did exactly as she was told, and Madlen looked at Adelhaid's pale body, covered with bruises. She lay on a stack of towels, the upper layers stained with blood.

"Did she lose much blood?" Madlen asked Barbara.

She nodded. "Yesterday evening, shortly after the fight . . ." Her eyes opened wide with fright when she realized that she'd slipped. "After the fall," she corrected, "the bleeding began. I did everything I could to stop it. And it did stop for a bit. But then she started cramping again."

"I understand." Madlen examined Adelhaid again. Right above her navel, there was a strip of blue and red veins under her skin, forming scar tissue. Madlen didn't see any bruises on her belly, and she sighed in relief. However, as she continued to scan the woman's body, something knocked the wind out of her. The entire pubic area was red, green, and blue. Her inner thighs were swollen and bruised. "Did somebody do this to you?"

Adelhaid nodded again, sobbing despondently. Madlen laid her head on her stomach to listen for the baby's heartbeat. She strained, changing her position again and again. But she couldn't hear anything. All of a sudden, Adelhaid's stomach contracted. Madlen knew exactly what these contractions meant. Adelhaid grabbed a pillow and bit into it to suppress her cries of agony.

Madlen covered Adelhaid's belly with her hands and started to massage it on the side. "Do you have arnica, sage, artemisia, oil, and honey in the house?"

"I'll look and see."

"And chamomile," Madlen called as Barbara picked up a candle and left the bedchamber. Madlen continued to massage Adelhaid's stomach, exerting a little pressure and speaking reassuringly to her until the contraction finally subsided and blood streamed out of her body. Barbara returned.

"We don't have any artemisia. I brought everything else."

"Good. Now I need a mortar and pestle to grind up the herbs."

"I'll get it." Barbara disappeared. Madlen guessed that the maid was relieved to avoid the horrific sight of her tortured mistress.

"Adelhaid," Madlen said calmly, in the softest voice she could muster. "Your baby is dead. You know that, right?" At first, the noblewoman didn't react at all. After Madlen stroked her belly softly, she nodded quickly.

"I'm so sorry." Madlen was tempted to say that by viciously beating and raping his wife, Adelhaid's husband had blotted out the life of their child before it even started. But it wasn't the right time. Madlen fervently hoped that Adelhaid would prosecute her husband for what he had done to her and their unborn child, but deep inside, she knew it was a lost cause. Clara had seen many abused women but had never heard of their abusers facing charges for their crimes. Madlen wondered whether Barbara was also a victim of Matthias Trauenstein's abuse. At that precise moment, the maid entered the bedchamber.

Madlen took the herbs and ground them into a pulpy mass. She rubbed the mixture on her patient's belly, gently massaging until she felt another contraction.

"Adelhaid, your body wants to expel the child, and we have to help it or you'll die, too."

Adelhaid sobbed loudly. "Let the baby stay. I don't want to live anymore. Let it stay, and we can die together."

Barbara became wide-eyed with fright. "My lady, it's a sin to say such things."

"Be still," Madlen ordered. She turned again to Adelhaid, speaking in a soft, comforting voice. "I understand. But this isn't our decision. Your body will bleed as it expels the dead body. By that time, the pain will become unbearable; you will suffer. I'm begging you. Let me help you save your life, at least. It's not too late."

She tried to prepare Adelhaid for what she had to do during the next contraction. "I'm going to wash the herbs off my hands and soak them in oil so I can pull the baby out, if you'll let me." Adelhaid pressed her lips together. Then she nodded without saying a word. Barbara sighed in relief.

"Good." Madlen stood in front of the bed. "Barbara, keep massaging her belly. When a contraction comes, rub even harder."

"But I . . . ," she said feebly.

"Do what I tell you." Even Madlen was surprised as she heard herself bark out orders so authoritatively. Without another word, Barbara set the candle down and began to massage Adelhaid's belly. Madlen washed up again and smeared the oil all over her hands up to her wrists.

"Barbara, when I tell you, start pressing down harder so that you can help her body expel the baby. Understand?"

"Yes." Barbara seemed fully focused as she used her hands to massage Adelhaid's stomach. Madlen prepared to reach into her womb. It wasn't long before the contractions started up again. On Madlen's signal, Barbara started to push on Adelhaid's belly with firm downward strokes. Adelhaid bit on her pillow but couldn't suppress her cries of agony. Madlen expected that the bedchamber's guards would soon burst into the room to check on their mistress, but it took only four more contractions before Madlen was able to grab the limp foot of the stillborn baby and pull. Barbara gasped in relief as Adelhaid lay still, completely spent.

"She is losing too much blood. I need more linens." Barbara ran over to one of the chests and came back with a whole stack of fresh clean linens. She wrapped the dead baby up in one, while Madlen did her best to stop the bleeding.

"Is it a boy or a girl?" Adelhaid whispered.

"It's a boy, my lady," Barbara answered.

"I want to hold him."

Barbara looked up at Madlen, startled. The baby was underdeveloped, his body blue and discolored. It was a terrible sight.

"Imagine him," Madlen replied, "pink and wonderful. His eyes are closed and he's sleeping peacefully in the bosom of the Lord. Don't bother him, but keep this lovely picture in your mind, to remind you forever of your son." Madlen expected Adelhaid to disagree violently and insist on holding the child at least once. But to her surprise, she didn't.

"He's wonderful, is that what you said?"

"That's right. He's the most beautiful baby I've ever seen."

"Then I will remember my son just like that forever."

"You are a very wise woman." Hopefully, wise enough to report that bastard, Matthias Trauenstein, and demand justice for what he'd done.

Adelhaid's body relaxed a little more with each passing moment. The blood seemed to stem at the thought of her beautiful baby boy. The bleeding slowly subsided enough so that Madlen had time to prepare a special brew that would strengthen and heal the body. Soon, she stood up, totally exhausted. "She's sleeping now. Let her rest as long as she wants to. She will need time to get her strength back, but her life is no longer in danger."

"I thank you from the bottom of my heart. The Trauensteins will never forget what you did today, and I won't, either."

Madlen smiled as she washed her hands. It was just like Clara always said. In these moments, gratitude knew no bounds. Madlen was curious to see if this would last longer than a blink of an eye.

"Make sure she gets enough to drink. Her body's been weakened by the fever and blood loss."

"I'll make sure."

"Good." Madlen turned to go home.

"Wait," Barbara said, pointing at the stillborn child, still wrapped in towels. "What should I do with it?"

"Bring it to the sheriff and report what happened. Maybe you can save your mistress's life before he kills her." With that, she left for home. It was already pitch-black outside. The rain hadn't stopped. She placed her shawl higher on her shoulders and stepped into the night.

Chapter Four

After Madlen arrived back home, she told Jerg and Kilian what had transpired, not failing to mention that Matthias Trauenstein, Adelhaid's own husband, had caused the miscarriage. Jerg was speechless; he shook his head in disbelief. Kilian, however, cursed the nobleman. It did Madlen good to hear her brother speak against such a monster. Madlen knew very few people who willingly got involved in such matters. Kilian, however, didn't mince words, regardless of the consequences. He didn't have especially high expectations for his life. One day, he would take over his father's woodshop. Day in, day out, he would build tables, benches, cabinets, and chairs. Occasionally, he would fashion a decorative stair railing for one of the noblemen's houses. Every day would be the same as the next.

Madlen knew that Kilian would have been all too happy to take up another profession. He had always been interested in the stories of traveling tradesmen who passed through Heidelberg. When there wasn't enough work in the woodshop, Kilian would go to the nearby tavern and take care of the guests' horses. He would often come home with interesting stories about journeys to distant lands, his eyes aglow. He seemed especially intrigued by colorful tales of the Far East, like no other place in the world. Some years ago, one of the merchants gave Kilian a new leather book with fine blank parchment paper in thanks for nursing his favorite horse back to health. Madlen's brother treated that book like a priceless treasure. Once, he had shown his sister his painstakingly neat drawings of oriental markets and foreign cities, which Kilian had created solely from the merchants' descriptions. He didn't know if they were accurate, but whenever time allowed, he'd pick up a piece of charcoal and draw in his notebook, hoping that one of these days, he'd travel to those foreign lands.

Madlen knew how much her brother was tormented by their humble, cramped living quarters. She also knew that Kilian worked in the shop for his father's sake and bore the brunt of many tasks his father should have done. She loved Kilian with all her heart and admired him for his uncompromising integrity. She prayed with all her might that he would free himself of carpentry work and stale cottage air to take his rightful place in the world. Although she was scared about what would become of her and her father if he left, her fear that Kilian would waste his life was even greater.

"A man like that should be hung from his balls," Kilian said, finally ending his rant about Matthias.

Madlen shrugged. "I'm afraid that won't happen, not now, not ever. Even if he beats Adelhaid to death, one of his guards would swear up and down that she fell down the stairs when the master was out of the house." Kilian hugged Madlen for a moment, unashamed to express his affection for his only sister.

"You must be dead tired. Are you hungry? Father and I already ate."

"No, thank you." Madlen freed herself from her brother's embrace and gave him a big smile. "I just want to lie down."

"Hey, little girl." He lifted her chin with his finger. "You can be proud of what you accomplished today. I'm certainly proud, and I'm sure that Clara would be, too."

She stroked him tenderly on his cheek and threw a glance over at her father. He didn't look up once, cleaning the dirt from under his fingernails.

"Thank you." With that, she took off her cloak and laid it on the chest before crawling into bed. She was still agitated by what had happened to the little Trauenstein baby, but fatigue's iron grip fell over her. She wasn't even aware of the hushed conversation between Kilian and Jerg. Only when her brother and father arose the next morning did Madlen open her eyes. She woke up refreshed, having slept more soundly than she'd slept in days. Surprisingly, what had happened at Adelhaid's home brought an important piece of her back to life. She quickly prepared oatmeal and put the bowls on the table.

"You look much better today," Kilian remarked.

"I feel better." She smiled.

"What will you do now? I mean, now that Clara's dead. You didn't earn any money last night." Jerg slurped down his porridge and looked at his daughter expectantly.

She bit her lip. She hadn't thought about getting paid. "I'll go to the Trauensteins and get my fee," she assured him quickly. Her father nodded.

"Well, the women are used to going to Clara. Yesterday was an exception, but you're no midwife."

"I could try to find a job as a seamstress. You know how skilled I am."

"With whom?"

Madlen thought about it. "Maybe Bernhard, the cloth merchant."

"Why would he need a seamstress? He sells the cloth by the bolt."

Madlen flushed. She had to think of something. Her father would never allow her to sit around and not contribute any money to the household.

"Don't worry about it." He waved her off.

Madlen looked up in surprise.

"In a week, Heinfried will be here to take you back with him anyway."

"Thank you, Father." Madlen stood, her head hung low.

"You don't need to thank him," Kilian said contemptuously. "He's getting so much money for this marriage that he can get by very well without a single coin from you ever again."

Jerg threw his son a reproachful look, which Kilian met steadily. Madlen couldn't say which of them had more hate and anger in their eyes.

"I would like to see your mistress." Madlen straightened out her dress at the door of the Trauensteins' estate.

"She is indisposed at the moment," the guard growled back.

"I know she is, that's why I'm here," Madlen shot back, which wasn't exactly the whole truth. "I helped her in her hour of need. Surely, she'll be glad to receive me."

"Wait here." He went to slam the door in her face, but paused and asked, "What's your name?"

"Madlen."

He closed the door and Madlen waited. When he opened it again, he waved her in. "She's resting in her bedchamber."

"I know the way." She lifted her skirt and climbed the stairs, knocking lightly on Adelhaid's door and waiting until she heard her voice.

"Greetings," she said, stepping in.

"Madlen." Adelhaid pointed to the edge of the bed. "Please sit down."

"How are you?" She immediately felt Adelhaid's forehead.

"Better."

"I'm very happy to hear that."

"I have you to thank for saving my life."

Madlen cleared her throat. "How did your husband take the news of your baby's death?" She would have preferred to use stronger words to describe the wicked man but decided to phrase her question more delicately.

"Well, he was quite dismayed, but we have not given up hope that God will bless us with a child."

Madlen was stunned as a grateful smile played on Adelhaid's lips. Didn't she realize that God had already given them a child, and that Matthias had killed it? An inner voice warned her to be careful, but she couldn't hold back. "Your husband's violent beatings took the child!"

Adelhaid stopped her with a swift wave of her hand. "I was unlucky. I fell. There's nothing more to say."

Madlen lowered her shoulders in resignation. She should have known.

"Of course," she said, forcing a smile as she stood. "I just came to check on you. I'm relieved that you feel better." She didn't dare ask for money.

"And I thank you for everything," Adelhaid replied gratefully. She pointed at the chest. "Open that up and bring me the little blue velvet purse."

Madlen walked to the chest and looked inside. She came back to the bed with the purse and gave it to Adelhaid. "I didn't have any time to pay you before you left. Take this." She withdrew a small pouch. "Thank you again for everything."

Madlen curtsied politely, weighing the pouch in her hand. "This is too much."

"No, I insist."

Madlen nodded. "I must take my leave now. I wish you a speedy recovery."

"Madlen, tell me before you go: Can I count on you, if I happen to be in the family way once again? I'm sure you are just as good as Clara."

"Of course." Madlen curtsied again and walked out of the room.

As she left the house, she inhaled deeply. She simply couldn't understand Adelhaid. She had been beaten and raped until her baby died. And now she claimed that she wanted to get pregnant again by her abusive husband. Madlen clutched the little pouch full of money. In any case, her father would be proud of her. She went to the nearest street corner before daring to look inside the pouch. Her eyes widened in delight. This was more money than she'd earned working for Clara in six months. Her heart beat faster. Perhaps Jerg would think twice about selling her off to the old man if she could bring pouches full of money home on a regular basis. She shook her head. The idea was ridiculous. Few had as much money as this noblewoman, and Madlen was still just a young apprentice birth assistant. Only the truly desperate would hire her. Her morale deteriorated as she made her way home. In a week, Heinfried would take her away. There was no escaping her fate.

When she arrived home, Kilian was alone in the woodshop. "Where's Father?" Madlen asked after she greeted her brother.

"In town. You must have passed him on the way."

"But I didn't see him at all."

Kilian shrugged. "Then you must have missed each other."

"Look at this, Kilian." Madlen held the little money pouch underneath his nose. Her brother took it and weighed it in his hand before he opened it. He whistled appreciatively. "Well, would you look at that. Our little girl."

"It's from Adelhaid. I told her it was too much, but she insisted."

Kilian pulled the pouch's cord tight. "No wonder."

"What do you mean?"

"Don't you understand? She is buying your silence."

Madlen stared at the pouch. "Do you really think that?"

"Of course." Kilian noticed the disgusted expression on his sister's face. "Now don't get any crazy ideas about returning the money. If she wants to give it to you, that's her business. You would not have turned him in anyway."

"I won't take it." She pushed it at her brother, but he took her by the shoulders and looked her in the eye.

"And whatever you do with it, little sister"—he took a step back and lifted his finger—"don't make the silly mistake of giving it all to Father."

"You mean, I shouldn't tell him?"

"Oh sure, and he'll want it all. But don't give him more than twenty-five pfennigs."

"Why not?"

"Madlen, listen to me. The spice merchant is going to put you in a beautiful house where you will want for nothing. But this money"—he pressed the pouch into her hand—"will buy you some freedom. None of his employees will keep your secrets out of kindness. If you don't want your husband finding something out, then I advise you to hide your money and use it wisely."

Madlen shook her head. "I never would have thought of that."

"You have to think like this now if you want a real future." Kilian urged, "Give me the money again."

She handed it to him, and he pulled out some coins and laid them on the wooden table. "Show this to Father later this evening; he'll be more than pleased with the amount"—he closed the pouch back up again—"and put the rest away so no one can find it. Understand?"

She nodded. "Thank you, Kilian."

"Oh, my darling sister. Who will take care of you when I'm no longer by your side?"

Over the next two days, Madlen prepared everything for her upcoming journey, gathering a few personal belongings and tidying the cottage. More importantly, she had to ensure that Clara received a decent burial. There would be no Mass with a priest like she would have wanted, but at least she could be buried in the cemetery within the city walls, and not outside them, in unconsecrated ground.

Madlen took everything out of Clara's little house she thought she might be able to use. She took the mortar and pestle as well as a few of the jars in which Clara kept her herbs. Madlen was certain that Clara would have wanted her to have them. Although she could very well have started without any of these things in her new home, she didn't want to leave these precious items behind. These were the only mementos that she had left of Clara. Madlen could almost smell her dear friend in the jars and mortar, and it gave her a great sense of comfort. She had just sorted out some utensils when someone knocked on the door. Madlen answered and was shocked to see the two constables from the evening Clara died. Luckily, they were unaccompanied by the man who had gruffly grabbed Madlen's arm, which caused her to drop the torch onto Clara's dress.

"The sheriff wants to speak with you," one said, coming right to the point.

Madlen thought about that evening when Clara died. Fear crept up her spine. "Why?" she asked, her voice shaking.

"He'll tell you once we bring you in. Put on your cloak; let's go."

Madlen wanted to protest, but she was too overcome by fear. "I have to tell my brother and my father," she answered quickly, pointing in that direction. "They're over there in the woodshop."

The older constable gave his colleague a sign to go on ahead. As the younger constable disappeared, Madlen screwed up all her courage. "Can you please tell me what's going on?" Her heart pounded at the thought of Clara's jars of herbs, now in her possession.

"It's regarding the noblewoman, Adelhaid Trauenstein." He said nothing more and Madlen sighed in relief. So Adelhaid had turned in that bastard of a husband. She smiled. "In that case"—she grabbed her cloak—"it's my pleasure to accompany you."

The constable looked a bit puzzled as Madlen stepped around him, elated. Suddenly, his colleague came back from the workshop with Jerg and Kilian in tow.

"What's going on?" Kilian called out. "Why do you need to go with them?"

"It's all right," Madlen called back. "It's about Adelhaid." She waved good-bye as she walked away, flanked by the two constables. Finally, justice would be served.

Chapter Five

"So would you like to make a statement, miss?" The sheriff scrutinized Madlen, now sitting on a chair in front of his desk. She calmly returned his fixed gaze, though she was surprised that he had addressed her so politely. High-ranking people like the sheriff usually didn't address commoners this way. Madlen was happy that the sheriff seemed to appreciate her willingness to testify.

She straightened her spine and sat as tall as she could. "Yes, my lord, I do."

"All right then. Begin."

She nodded obediently and began with what had happened when Barbara showed up unexpectedly at her house that day, begging for help. As she moved on to the Trauensteins' estate, the sheriff stopped her. "How did the maid know that you were able to help women with their problems?"

Madlen hesitated. The sheriff's voice was tinged with suspicion. Still, she had no desire to deceive him, even though he no longer seemed very sympathetic toward her. His skin looked addled from too much wine. His face was flushed, and his cheeks and nose were especially discolored. His eyes were dull with a tinge of yellow. It took all her willpower not to advise him that if he wanted to live a long and healthy life, he had to give up wine, at least for a while, so that his body could recover.

"You don't want to answer me?" he said, ripping her from her thoughts.

"Oh, forgive me, lord. What was the question again?"

"How did the maid know that you had these abilities?"

"Yes, of course. Well, I worked alongside Clara, the midwife, for many years. Barbara is the same age as my brother, Kilian. We've known each other for a long time."

"So, would you refer to her as a confidant?"

The question surprised her. Barbara a confidant? She shook her head. "No, my lord. I know who she is and where she works. That's all."

"And she came directly to you because her mistress wasn't well."

At this point, Madlen decided not to go into detail. "Yes, she came to me."

"Then what happened?"

"We went to the Trauenstein home together," Madlen continued. The sheriff listened carefully. She told him that when she found Adelhaid Trauenstein, she was suffering from a high fever and bleeding profusely.

"So you claim that she started bleeding before your arrival?"

"Yes, of course. That's the reason Barbara came to me."

The sheriff raised his eyebrows.

"Why do you ask?" Madlen was starting to feel very uncomfortable. Slowly, it began to dawn on her that she wasn't brought in as a witness, but as a suspect.

"Tell me more."

She hesitated. "No," she said. "I want to know why you're asking me if Adelhaid Trauenstein was bleeding before my arrival."

"Can't you imagine why?" The sheriff raised his voice, looking skeptical.

Madlen's heart began to race, but she did her best to keep calm. "No, I can't," she said defiantly.

"Well, I just wanted to hear your declaration, but if you insist." He pointed to a parchment on his desk. "The town scribe recorded this statement. It says that the bleeding and subsequent miscarriage experienced by the noblewoman Adelhaid Trauenstein occurred after you treated her with an herbal concoction."

Madlen turned deathly pale. "What?" She looked down at the document on his desk. What kind of nonsense was this? She couldn't read what was written there. Her body went ice-cold as wild thoughts raced through her head. "So, that's why I'm here?" She was so scared that she could barely whisper.

"This is an extremely serious matter." The sheriff shot her an icy glare.

Madlen bowed her head. "That's why I'm here?" she repeated.

"Well, since you apparently insist on hearing the words straight out of my mouth: you are accused of killing the unborn child of the Trauenstein family with the administration of toxic herbs."

All the color drained from her face. "That's not true," she said softly.

"Oh no?" The sheriff stood and paced the room. "Then why did the maid confirm it?"

"Barbara?"

"Correct. What do you have to say about that?"

Madlen remained silent. Blood rushed loudly in her ears; only the sheriff's deep voice dampened the noise. Her breathing was fast and shallow. She put her hand on her bosom; she couldn't seem to get enough oxygen into her lungs.

"Don't pretend to be an innocent little weakling," the sheriff roared. "We both know that you're not."

Madlen gasped, swallowed, tried to breathe, her pulse racing.

"Stop with this play acting!" He grabbed her by the shoulders and shook her. Madlen stared at him, aghast, unable to free herself from his grip. "Now, come on, just admit it." He shook her again and stared into her eyes angrily. Then he let go and pushed her back into the chair. It was a moment before Madlen could gather her thoughts. His chilling accusation echoed through her head. She was being charged for the death of the Trauensteins' child. She shut her eyes and took several deep breaths to gather strength, just as Clara had shown her.

"I did not trigger her bleeding," she whispered, raising her head. The sheriff sat down again, now calm and collected. Had he pretended to be enraged simply to elicit a confession from her?

"Why are the Trauensteins accusing you of this?" He sneered.

"So that there's no need to confess what really happened."

"And what would that be, girl?"

It occurred to Madlen that he was now addressing her like the commoner she was, abandoning any pretense of respect.

"I came to the Trauensteins' home," Madlen continued, determined to make her statement. "Adelhaid Trauenstein was in her bedchamber. She had a high fever and was bleeding profusely, which had started the night before. I asked the maid for some herbs, to make it easier for her to bear the pain of her contractions."

"So you admit, you did use herbs?"

"Medicinal herbs, found in any household."

"And which ones did you use, if I may ask?"

"Arnica, sage, chamomile, oil, and honey."

The sheriff rubbed his chin. "Isn't sage used to expel the baby from the womb?"

"No," Madlen declared, though sage often created this exact effect. But if she'd omitted it from her list, it would have seemed more suspicious. "Sage has a calming effect when applied externally and mixed with oil. I rubbed her body with it to relax her muscles."

"I understand." It was clear such details made the sheriff uncomfortable. "What happened next?"

Ellin Carsta

Madlen regained her confidence. At least she now had his ear. Her challenge now was to convince him of her innocence.

"As I already told you, the maid came to me because Adelhaid had started bleeding the night before. It was a stroke of luck that the poor woman hadn't already bled to death when I arrived."

The sheriff was silent, waiting for her to continue. His eyes seemed cloudy. She wondered whether he was even listening or just impatient to guzzle down his next bottle of wine.

"I tried to listen for the baby's heartbeat, but the child was already dead—hence the bleeding. Her womb was trying to expel the baby."

Madlen could see the sheriff's obvious discomfort with her description of this gruesome event.

"And what do you believe was the reason for this, miss?"

Madlen noted with satisfaction that his respect had returned. She hesitated, not knowing whether she should say what was on her mind. "I asked Adelhaid what happened. She told me that she'd fallen down the stairs."

"Hmm." He rubbed his chin again. "I would like to believe what you've said. There's only one thing that doesn't seem to make sense."

"Yes?"

"Why would the maid report you?"

Madlen shook her head. "Believe me, I have no idea."

"Hmm," he said softly and fell silent for a while. "Could it be that the maid, this Barbara, had something to do with the mistress falling down the stairs? And now she's trying to make you responsible for the miscarriage?"

"No," said Madlen evenly. "I can't imagine that."

"It's to your credit that you didn't immediately seize the excuse." He rubbed his chin again, which now looked raw and red.

"May I ask you a question, my lord?"

"Of course."

"Did Barbara come to you with the dead child and accuse me?"

"No, no," he blurted out. "The maid was caught trying to bury the dead baby in the forest. Someone saw her and turned her over to the constables, at which point she said you were responsible."

Everything started to make sense. Matthias probably came home and forced Barbara to bury the child. When she was caught, she sought only to avoid punishment by her master.

"If you're looking for the true culprit, you needn't look any further than the Trauenstein house." Madlen fixed the sheriff with a steady gaze.

"What are you trying to say?"

"If you really want to find the perpetrator of the crime, I recommend that you go to the Trauensteins' house and speak with Adelhaid yourself. Look at her injuries. You will see straightaway that her injuries have nothing to do with the administration of herbal concoctions."

The sheriff's face turned beet red. From anger or shame, Madlen couldn't say. "I can't very well examine the noblewoman myself," he grumbled.

She forced a smile. "No, I didn't mean that. Adelhaid's injuries are obvious to all; her poor face, her whole body is black and blue. These wounds were not caused by one or more severe falls. They were . . ." She hesitated briefly. "Brought on by something else. When you see her, you'll know at a glance that I speak the truth."

The sheriff looked at her for a moment, then made a decision. "You stay here. I'll assign a guard to the door."

"Of course, I won't go anywhere," she promised.

"Good." He stomped out and barked orders at a guard before disappearing around a corner.

As she went to the window, she felt the guard's eyes staring at her. She could see the sheriff hurrying down the street toward the marketplace. It would take him only a few minutes to reach the Trauensteins' estate. Madlen smiled. In her silent prayer, she thanked God for the idea of sending the sheriff to see Adelhaid. She could tell by the look on his face that he at least wanted to believe her. Certainly, the sight of

Adelhaid would suffice to confirm her story. Again, she turned quietly to God to ask Him to help her through whatever might happen in the next few hours. So far, she'd avoided accusing Matthias of raping and beating his own wife, but surely it would be obvious that the death of the child was due to her husband's abuse. With a sigh, she turned away from the window, paced the room for a while, and finally settled in the chair. The guard didn't let her out of his sight for a moment.

It took longer than she'd expected and Madlen dozed off. When she heard the pounding of feet on the wooden stairs, she awoke instantly, standing as the sheriff entered the room.

"Did you see her?"

He nodded. "You can go for now, miss. I will appoint a constable to accompany you safely home."

"Thank you." She nodded obediently and considered whether to ask him about Matthias but lost her nerve. She was simply glad to have survived the whole ordeal in one piece. For a sheriff to take a commoner's word over that of a rich nobleman's was more than she could expect, especially since the sheriff's job and salary depended on those same wealthy citizens. "Please, one more thing."

"Yes?"

"You said that I could go for now?"

"That's correct. I'm sorry, but it's not over yet, my child."

"Why not?"

"Adelhaid's husband, Matthias Trauenstein, insists on filing charges against you. He grieves deeply for his dead child."

It took every bit of will she had not to spit on the ground. "He insists on filing charges?" she echoed.

"Yes. Some of his fellow noblemen have heard about the death of the child. He thinks that they might get the wrong idea if there's no guilty party."

"If someone is to blame for the death of this child, then . . ." She broke off.

"Yes?" The sheriff threw her a challenging look.

"Then, at least it's not me," she finished.

"For your sake, I will try to persuade Matthias Trauenstein to drop the charges. I will send word as soon as something happens."

"Thank you, sir," she said politely and curtsied daintily. Then she lifted her head and looked him directly in the eyes. "I do not give thanks lightly, sir. I hadn't dared hope that I would meet a man of such honor in the office of the law."

"I take my duties quite seriously."

"I know that now." She nodded. "I wish you well, my dear sheriff." With that, she left the room.

Chapter Six

Two days later, Madlen received a message saying that Matthias Trauenstein had refused to drop the charges. Anger and despair changed to fear and hopelessness. She had heard of such legal processes, and the outcome was always the same. The accused was always convicted, especially if it was a commoner's word against a nobleman's. Kilian thought that Madlen needed a lawyer. Madlen was torn. This unbelievable injustice made it almost impossible for her to think clearly. How dare this bastard do this to her? In the meantime, she'd heard some rumors floating around the city about him. She knew now why this cowardly dog Matthias wanted to hang this on her. In a few weeks, Matthias hoped that he would be elected to city council. It was common knowledge that this nobleman was moody, temperamental, and often completely out of control. Many people proclaimed that Matthias was behind Adelhaid's miscarriages. The city council would never allow anyone in their ranks with such a tainted reputation. Matthias needed a scapegoat. And Madlen, who hadn't done anything but save his wife's life, had entered the picture just in time. Still, she couldn't figure out how he'd persuaded Adelhaid to lie for him.

Madlen's thoughts churned. She decided to use the money she'd received from Adelhaid to hire a lawyer, but Andreas von Balge wasn't even a real attorney, not yet anyway. Though he studied law at Heidelberg University, founded just last year, he was far from done. But Madlen couldn't afford anybody else, and even if she could, it was doubtful that an experienced attorney would accept the case. Andreas von Balge, who'd moved from Bremen to Heidelberg to study with the famous Marsilius of Inghen, a professor at Heidelberg University known for his brilliance, seemed quite happy to help a young woman in whose innocence he firmly believed. At least that's what he told Madlen. He was Kilian's friend. Madlen didn't yet know whether the young legal advocate could actually help her, but he was her only hope. Upon his appointment, he immediately explained that the ongoing war between the Swabian League and the Bavarian dukes was to her advantage because her case could only go before the sheriff and six appointed members of the council. Andreas had already spoken with the sheriff, who told him that if it were up to him, the case would never go to trial. The sheriff had believed Madlen. Now the only thing left was to convince the council members that she didn't have anything to do with the child's death. The proceedings would start in two days. In exactly three days, Heinfried, her future husband, would arrive in Heidelberg. Jerg was exceedingly uneasy. He warned Madlen that her advocate better not draw out the trial longer than necessary. If Heinfried heard about the accusation, he would withdraw his offer to marry her. Jerg had already mentally allotted the money Heinfried would pay him for Madlen's hand in marriage. For Jerg, it meant security for many months.

"I'm not terribly worried about Matthias Trauenstein's lies," Andreas von Balge explained, as he took a sip of the beer that Madlen had placed on the table in front of him. Jerg went to the workshop during their conversations, but Kilian remained.

"But he's not the only one accusing Madlen," Kilian said.

"Exactly. Matthias wants to make Madlen look guilty."

A cold chill went up Madlen's spine.

"I'm more concerned," he continued, "about this maid, Barbara. It will be difficult to get her to admit that she lied because she's frightened. She has much at stake."

"But isn't that obvious to the sheriff?" Madlen asked.

Andreas shook his head. "That's hard to say. Even though the sheriff may see through the lies, there are still six other men that must be convinced, too."

"Do you already know who these six men are?" Kilian asked, taking a sip from his own beer mug.

"Unfortunately not. We'll only know who they are when the trial starts. The names are kept secret so neither side can have undue influence."

"I seriously doubt that Matthias won't find a way to learn their names. He has many powerful friends."

Andreas nodded at Kilian. "I agree with you on that, but that doesn't mean he'll succeed in convincing them of Madlen's guilt before the trial." He thought about it for a second. "You know many young men in the city, don't you?"

"Yes, of course. Why?"

"Go to the tavern this evening," Andreas suggested. "Listen carefully. The trial has attracted much attention. Everyone will be talking."

"And everybody knows that Madlen's my sister."

"Exactly. Talk to the young men, the boys, the guards, or groomsmen that serve the noblemen. Believe me. This will be talked about in the council members' households. And then you spread rumors."

"What kind of rumors?" Madlen tilted her head.

"Kilian can simply throw a name around and claim that he heard that he's one of the six chosen to sit at the trial. This will loosen the tongues of those who have actually heard a thing or two in their masters' houses."

"We definitely won't be able to ascertain all six of them, though," Kilian insisted.

"We don't have to. We only need two."

"What are you planning?" Madlen rubbed the goose bumps on her arms.

"We need to learn as much as possible about them. For example, maybe one of the members has a daughter the same age as Madlen. I'll comment on Madlen's character and attempt to highlight similarities between her and the young women they know and love. They will realize that the speech could be about their own daughters and be more sympathetic toward Madlen. Do you understand?"

Kilian nodded slowly. "And you believe this would influence their decision?"

"Yes." The advocate seemed quite confident. "Madlen is innocent. We just have to convince them that this Matthias Trauenstein has no scruples so we can defeat him without a long, drawn-out fight." He emptied his mug, satisfied. Madlen fervently hoped that he was right as he said his good-byes.

A few hours later, Kilian pocketed a few coins and made his way into the city, determined to find out as much as possible to help his sister. The advocate's plan of action seemed quite clever, but Kilian doubted it would be so easy to win the case. Matthias Trauenstein was known throughout the city for his angry outbursts and brutality. It was common knowledge that he punished his servants with a whip. Why would he spare his own wife the same fate? But would his battered servant testify about his treatment, or would the noblewoman, his own wife, who was beaten so badly that she lost his child? If not, Heidelberg citizens would be more likely to believe Matthias Trauenstein's allegations. After all, it was widely believed that Matthias wanted a legitimate heir even more than Adelhaid. These thoughts plagued Kilian the entire way to the Red Oxen tavern, where carpenters, plumbers, and other craftsmen as well as merchants met to drink their troubles away.

Kilian felt the looks when he walked into the tavern, and all conversation ceased. He was relieved when he saw Berthold, an apprentice plumber, who immediately raised his arm. "Kilian! Come sit with us over here."

The other guests apparently took this as a sign to continue their conversations. Kilian walked over and sat down at the only open spot on the bench. "Greetings, everyone." Some looked skeptical but eventually loosened up and included him in their conversations. Soon the forthcoming trial came up. "Don't get me started," Kilian complained. "Whatever anybody claims, my Madlen wouldn't hurt a fly, and certainly not a baby. But let's not talk about it."

"I hear she has a lawyer?" Berthold remarked.

"Yes, and we hope this will all be over soon. From what I know, all the members of the council have to agree. I heard that Remigius from Hollen is one of them, so I'm not worried. Madlen helped his wife with the birth of his baby daughter last year. There were complications. But thanks to Madlen and Clara, they were able to bring a healthy child into the world."

"Remigius from Hollen? How do you know?" asked one of the younger men, a servant whose name Kilian didn't know. He worked for Bernhard, the cloth merchant who was under consideration for the council.

Kilian shrugged. "I have it on good authority. Of course, the names of the jurymen aren't supposed to be common knowledge. But gossip travels fast in our quaint little city of Heidelberg." He laughed throatily, as his drinking companions nodded. He beckoned the waiter. "A round of beer for me and all my friends. And keep our mugs full."

The men at the table happily took note of his generosity, and when the beer came, they raised their mugs with Kilian.

"To my sister!"

"To Madlen, to your sister!" they all toasted together before gulping down their brew.

It was difficult for Kilian to wait for the trial to come up again, but he had to be patient. If he pushed the subject, he could fail in his quest altogether.

"And we were all warned to keep everything to ourselves before the trial," complained Bernhard's servant as he took another sip of beer.

"What's your name?" asked Kilian.

"Sebold" was his terse reply.

Kilian's heart beat faster. Was it time to advance his agenda? "And you work for Bernhard Stickling?" he said casually. "Isn't he one of the jurymen?" He carefully measured the reaction of his drinking companions.

Sebold shrugged. "You didn't hear it from me."

Kilian breathed easier. "As far as I know, there are more than six names being discussed. The final choice still hasn't been made."

"Perhaps," Sebold said. "I don't know for sure. But it seems to me that everything's already been decided."

"Maybe our masters just want to brag about the possibility," interjected Thomas, a servant to an architect who'd been commissioned to design a new church, surpassing St. Peter's Church in size and splendor. Whether it would actually happen, no one could say; the ongoing city wars and other lingering disputes were stymieing progress.

"I didn't know that your master would be one of the jurymen," Kilian said to Thomas as he deftly continued to make assertions intended to loosen even more lips. "So now it's not six but ten names in the running for the honor of being on the jury. Hopefully, there won't be any shoving or quarreling when the trial starts."

The men laughed and chatted about their masters' shortcomings. Someone mentioned another juryman's name, and Kilian smiled to himself with satisfaction. Now he knew the identities of three of the jurymen. That was more than he'd dared to hope for. After ordering and sharing two more large pitchers of beer, he excused himself and made his way back home. He had accomplished his task. First thing in the morning, he would go see Andreas von Balge. He felt good when he arrived home, his father and sister already asleep. He undressed and crawled under his bedcovers quietly. A warm feeling filled his body. *I can help Madlen,* he thought, and fell asleep, a happy man.

Chapter Seven

Madlen put on her good dress as she readied herself for the trial. Yesterday, Kilian told her he had discovered the names of some of the jury members. He'd gone directly to Andreas to fill him in about the men who would ultimately decide Madlen's fate. In the afternoon, Kilian returned home and immediately went to the woodshop to do at least some work for his father that day. Madlen heard Jerg roaring about how he couldn't tolerate him wandering all around town instead of helping him in the woodshop. When the two came home that evening, Madlen put dinner on the table and tried to appease her father by telling him that Kilian had just been trying to help her. Jerg told her to spare him all the drivel. No matter what happened at the trial, he said, life went on and he had to earn money, which he couldn't do without the help of his son. She should handle this alone; after all, she was the one who went to Adelhaid and brought their dead child into the world.

Venomously, Kilian spit out that their father had been all too happy to take the money Madlen received for this service. Without warning, Jerg gave his son a resounding slap in the face, and Kilian tumbled to the ground. Horrified, Madlen rushed to her brother's side to make sure he wasn't seriously injured. His eyes glowed red with unmitigated hatred, and she wondered whether one of them would end up killing the other after Heinfried took her away. Afterward, she ate in silence and Jerg consoled himself with a tankard of beer before insisting that the siblings go to bed so as not to bother him anymore. Kilian never had the opportunity to give his sister all the details about his work with Andreas von Balge.

Now that morning had come, she focused on making herself presentable to make a good impression at trial. Jerg had already forced her brother into the woodshop. Madlen's hope of having Kilian by her side during the trial scattered like dust blowing in the wind. With a sigh, she pulled her long dark-brown hair into a braid, straightened her dress, and finally made her way to town.

Her feet seemed to find the way all by themselves. Madlen couldn't say how she reached the town hall on the market square. The trial would take place in this venerable building, where noblemen could make life-or-death decisions about the accused. She swallowed hard as guards standing to the left and right of the entrance opened the door for her. Blood roared through her ears as she climbed the stairs. For a moment, she had to gather herself so as not to lose consciousness.

How much she would have liked to simply turn around and walk away, passing by the guards standing on the city wall until she reached the outskirts of the city. She'd walk over the long wooden bridge that reached the other side of the Neckar River. Madlen had never crossed that bridge, although she often wished she could. One of the traveling merchants had told Kilian that it took a grown man over two hundred steps to cross the Neckar River. Two hundred steps! His eyes shining, Kilian had reported after his conversation with the merchant that it took just two hundred steps over the wooden planks to reach the opposite shoreline. Only two hundred steps to where the boats were docked and ultimately to freedom. These were steps that she would probably never make.

Still, the thought of crossing the bridge both frightened and excited her. She'd never stepped a foot outside of Heidelberg, spending her whole life in the confines of the city walls, mostly limiting herself to her father's cottage and Clara's little hut on the path leading to the castle. When she was little, she had imagined that the castle was enthroned on the cliff above them for their protection. She still had that feeling as she gazed at the brown stone walls. In the summer, the stones warmed her. In the cool evenings, Madlen leaned against them after a hard day's work and daydreamed for a minute or two. Then she would climb a couple of feet higher until she stood on a small ledge leading to a cave hidden by bushes. There, she could see all the way over to the other side of the Neckar River. There were also hills and rocks there, offering no protection, maybe even preventing people from ever escaping from the valley. Sometimes, Madlen even imagined the world came to an end on the other side of the rocks. But she knew better. From the merchants' descriptions, the forests and valleys behind the hills were some of the most picturesque landscapes found anywhere.

Sometimes Madlen dreamed of just running away. She would jump down from the ledge, cross the market square to the bridge, and just keep moving, continuing past the boats, then up onto the rocky paths. When she reached the top of the hill, she wouldn't even turn around. She'd continue to go out where everything was quiet, where no market-place pulsed with life, a place wholly unlike the town hall looming in front of her right now. It was almost like her skin was on fire as everyone gawked, trying to determine whether the accusations were true. Did she really stir up a batch of poison and murder an innocent unborn child? Faces loomed in front of her, appearing and disappearing from her field of vision. She was startled when one of the guards cleared his throat; she gazed at him nervously.

"You'll need to go upstairs now," he explained. "The doors to the courtroom are open."

"Thank you," Madlen croaked; her voice almost failed altogether. She gathered up her skirts and climbed the stairs as the guards' looks burned into her back. *Was this the baby murderer?*

Madlen heard some voices and turned around when she reached the end of the hall. Constables struggled to hold back the people trying to secure the best seats. Madlen's throat was dry as she entered the courtroom, and she was relieved to catch sight of Andreas von Balge, who immediately strode toward her.

"You're here. I must say, you look perfect. Conservatively attired. Exactly right."

Madlen's head spun. She just nodded and let him lead her to her seat.

"I'm here beside you. I won't let anything happen," he reassured her. Unfortunately, his words fell on deaf ears. It seemed to him that Madlen wasn't able to hear a word he said. "Is everything all right? You look pale."

Madlen stared at him. Pale? What was he thinking? That this was going to be a breeze for her?

"I know what you're thinking," he continued. "Don't worry. I'm not taking this lightly," he said so softly that only Madlen could hear it. He leaned in closer. "It's important that you smile and radiate certainty that an acquittal is imminent. Appear to be surprised over what you've been accused of, although you already know. Believe me. Those who win their cases have to convince the sheriff and the jury of their innocence. And above all"—he raised his index finger—"the winner is the one the jury wants to see win. Nobody wants to see someone trembling with fear." He looked at her urgently. "Smile." He touched her lips.

Madlen tried, but it was impossible. The advocate pinched her arm.

"Ow!" she said indignantly.

"Smile right now, or I'm going to leave the courtroom."

She opened her eyes wide. Very slowly, she raised the corners of her mouth, at first hesitantly, then a little more, until she beamed brightly at Andreas von Balge.

"Very good," he said, then turned to the front door as more and more people poured in. Matthias Trauenstein was not among them. Andreas turned and put his mouth close to Madlen's ear. "Listen to me. Can you see the table facing us?"

She nodded as she continued to smile.

"Soon, Lord Trauenstein will take his place there. And there in the front"—he pointed with his chin—"the sheriff and the jury will sit together at a long table. It's important to listen to them. You should take careful note and nod repeatedly when they ask you something as a sign that you are listening closely. However, when Matthias says something, shake your head almost imperceptibly, as if every single word he says is a lie."

She stopped smiling briefly. "As if every single word he says is a lie," she noted, then again tried on a cheerful demeanor.

"Very good. That was very good."

Madlen sighed. This man drove her crazy.

"Once Matthias starts to testify, make sure you gaze out over to the spectators in the courtroom as you listen in disbelief to the lies of your accusers. You need to connect with the people in the room. Do you understand that?"

"Yes, I understand."

"Good." He poked her lightly. "There he is."

Immediately, she turned toward the door, where Matthias Trauenstein appeared. Her accuser gave her a withering look. "Raise your head and smile at him," the advocate ordered. She obeyed his request and noted that her genuine smile seemed to unsettle the nobleman. Matthias quickly looked away, avoiding Madlen. She had just won her first small victory.

"Did you see that?" von Balge asked conspiratorially. "You scared him. He didn't know where to look."

Madlen gave her advocate an amused grin. "You're right. It will be my pleasure to smile through the entire trial if need be."

"Not the entire trial." Andreas von Balge raised his hand defensively. "Never smile when it comes to Adelhaid's suffering. This could be interpreted as arrogance or even a sign of derision. Instead, you must radiate genuine concern."

"That won't be hard to do."

"Very good," he replied crisply.

More and more people pushed into the courtroom.

"It won't be long before the sheriff and members of the jury enter the courtroom. We'll stand up to show our homage to them."

"All right," Madlen answered softly. "Were you able to use the information that my brother brought you and find out something about the members of the jury?"

"Yes, indeed," he said with a broad grin. "Especially one of them."

"Who?"

"Does the name Ewald Oberdinger mean anything to you?"

Madlen wrinkled her forehead. "No, although I've heard his name once or twice."

"What about the name Agnes Oberdinger?"

"I'm not sure."

"Four years ago, Agnes had a baby. It was a tough birth."

"Agnes. Of course. Now I remember."

"Well, Agnes thinks very highly of your abilities."

A warm feeling flooded through Madlen. "I remember it well. The baby hadn't rotated."

"And you saved her."

"No, Clara did."

"The midwife that passed away recently?"

Madlen suddenly got a lump in her throat. "That's right. That was Clara."

Suddenly, the back door opened and the sheriff entered the courtroom, followed by six men. Their demeanor was serious as they went to their seats.

Andreas signaled Madlen to stand and look at the men with a respectful and open demeanor. He nodded deferentially as the men reached their seats.

"You may sit," said the sheriff loud and clear. Chairs squeaked here, scratched there. Finally, it was quiet in the room. The sheriff waited a moment, letting his gaze fall upon all present.

"Good citizens of Heidelberg," he began with a loud voice. "We are here today to decide the guilt or innocence of this young woman, daughter of Jerg, the carpenter."

Madlen happily noticed that he said "guilt" softly but said "innocence" loud and clear. He was on her side, of that she was quite sure.

"First, I would like to say," he went on, "that both sides have declared their acceptance of the judgment of the court, which under my chairmanship, includes six members of the council." The sheriff looked at Matthias Trauenstein first, who nodded, and at Andreas von Balge, who followed suit.

"Let's do everything in our power to ensure justice is served in alignment with the views of our Heavenly Father, our Creator." He inhaled deeply and turned to the defendant. "Madlen. You are accused by Matthias Trauenstein of poisoning his unborn child before removing it from its mother's womb. What do you say?"

Andreas von Balge signaled Madlen to speak for herself. She rose slowly. Immediately, the sheriff made a movement with his hand.

"Thank you for your respect, but please, keep your seat." He smiled politely, and Madlen sat down again. "Thank you."

She cleared her throat. "I have not committed the crime of which I am accused."

The sheriff waited for her to continue, but she only looked on in anticipation of his next question.

"Do you want me to tell you what really happened?"

The sheriff nodded, but Andreas von Balge held up his hand.

"First, I would ask the accuser to present his testimony."

"Why?" Matthias Trauenstein replied. "Is this common?"

Von Balge smiled. "No, unless the high court—in this case, the sheriff and the members of the jury—demands it." He looked questioningly at the sheriff, who looked right and left to verify that the jury members were in agreement.

"We do not call on the defendant," the sheriff said. "Please, Matthias Trauenstein, report what happened to the best of your abilities."

This turn of events didn't seem to sit well with Lord Trauenstein. He shot the advocate a furious look. "If it so pleases the court, this is what took place: The defendant was asked by our maid to check on my wife, who was indisposed, as often happens during pregnancy. The defendant came to our house and mixed a brew with her toxic herbs. A short time later, my wife started to bleed heavily and almost passed out from pain. Finally"—he stretched out his arm and pointed at Madlen—"*she* snatched the still-living body of our baby from my wife's womb and suffocated him until he was no longer moving." He lowered his arm and closed his eyes for a moment.

The courtroom burst into whispered excitement at the nobleman's horrific description. He looked up and was shocked to see that she shook her head with a knowing smile. The advocate, however, scribbled some notes.

Andreas stepped in front of the table. He held up the piece of parchment.

"First of all, everybody in this room feels for your loss. You have our sincerest condolences."

Matthias nodded quickly.

"Did your wife have any health problems before the miscarriage?"

"No."

"No?" The advocate lifted his eyebrows in surprise.

"No." Matthias repeated.

"If that's the case, can you please tell me who Hyronimus Auerbach is?"

Matthias looked surprised.

"You don't know? Well, in that case, let us bring him up to refresh your—"

"He's a doctor," Matthias admitted.

"Can you repeat that, please?"

It was obvious the nobleman was seething. "He's a doctor," he repeated.

"The man is a doctor." He looked at the full courtroom. "And now, please tell me, why was this man at your house?"

"He's a friend."

"Really?"

"Yes, of course."

"So, you're saying that this man never treated your wife."

"Yes. That's correct."

"So far as has been reported to me, he visited your home quite frequently, your friend the doctor."

"Yes. My friends come by often."

Thoughtfully, Andreas placed his finger on his lips. "Would it be fair to call this man, this physician, a very good friend?"

Matthias smiled arrogantly. "Yes. In fact, he's my best friend." He looked into the crowd to make sure his words did not miss their mark.

"Oh, that's so wonderful," gushed the advocate. "I treasure such warm friendships." He peered at Matthias. "What are the names of Hyronimus Auerbach's daughters?"

"What?"

"His daughters. The daughters of your good—excuse me—your very best friend. What are their names, and how old are they?"

Matthias Trauenstein's face turned red. "I . . . I . . ." He snorted. "I haven't seen them in a long time. I'm not very good at remembering names."

"Not even one of his three daughters?" He waited. "No? What a shame. Then at least tell me how old they are. Are they pretty?"

Matthias balled up his hand into a fist. "They're not girls anymore; they're grown women. And yes, all three are very pretty."

Andreas von Balge shot him an icy smile. "Shall I fetch the good doctor?"

"As far as I know, he's not in town," Matthias said, slightly more confident.

"You are correct." The advocate paused thoughtfully and turned to the audience. "He is, in fact, with his offspring on a pilgrimage. His two sons, to be exact."

"That proves nothing!" Matthias Trauenstein jumped up and knocked over his chair.

"Please, my lord," the sheriff snapped. "You wanted this trial. Kindly take your place."

The nobleman hesitated, then picked up the chair and sat back down. Andreas shot him a dangerous smile. "Oh, yes," he continued. "It proves to the court that you are an unrepentant liar, my lord. Therefore, any intelligent person must question every single word that comes out of your mouth." His smile grew broader. "Frankly, I'm quite curious as to what else might come up upon closer inspection." With that, he turned and went back to the defendant's table, Matthias's angry gaze aimed at his back.

Chapter Eight

By noon, Andreas von Balge had disproved every single word of Matthias Trauenstein's allegations. Madlen was very satisfied with his work as she accompanied him to lunch at the inn across the street from the town hall for the scheduled two-hour break. Exhausted, she let herself fall onto the bench while Andreas ordered. "We'll need your strength when we go back to the courtroom."

"But I—" Madlen began to protest.

"Don't worry. This meal's on me. You've already paid me well."

"Thank you."

"This afternoon will be more difficult once the maid makes her statement. I hope that she says exactly what Matthias Trauenstein tried to make the court swallow earlier. No one will believe a word of it."

The host came to the table with two tankards of beer and a platter of ham, bread, and lard. "Here, my good people. On the house."

"Why?" Madlen asked. She was puzzled.

The man's beer belly hung low as he stood with his legs apart. "I was in the courtroom and came back here shortly before you arrived." He raised his index finger in warning. "In my opinion, this nobleman's allegations against you are evil, my child. Trauenstein should be careful he doesn't take an evening walk around the dark streets of Heidelberg, or he'll be the one in need of a doctor. Now, enjoy your meal." He turned and went into an adjoining room.

Andreas held up his tankard, pressed it to his lips, and took a nice, long slug. "In the blink of an eye, you'll be back in your cottage, leading a carefree life."

Madlen tried to smile. The advocate was probably right, but though he was confident, she still had her doubts. It was almost too easy. She ate a bit of ham and bread silently and only took a tiny sip of beer before the advocate chugged down the rest of her brew.

"Thank you, sir," Andreas called out as they took their leave.

The host opened the door. "My pleasure, my lord. Now go show this nobleman that he can't shove us around anytime he wants. I hope they hang him."

"Why do you say that?" Andreas von Balge asked, although he already knew the answer.

"He beat his wife so badly that she lost the child. We all know that."

Some of the other tavern customers nodded approvingly.

"But," the advocate pointed out, "first things first: we've got to acquit our Madlen here of any and all charges."

"Good luck, girl," called out one patron. "All the good people of Heidelberg are praying for you!"

"Nail this bastard!" said one after another.

Andreas thanked them with a nod and a wave of his hand, then left the tavern with his client. At that moment, he knew exactly why he never wanted to be anything other than a full-fledged lawyer. They walked confidently back over to the courtroom.

Madlen felt something had changed as she entered the room. Before she'd felt suspicious and judgmental glances from the guards; now the same men opened the doors, gesturing amiably and nodding sympathetically.

It wasn't long before the room overflowed with so many spectators that the guards had to refuse entrance to any more. Usually, when court proceedings started in the morning and still hadn't reached a verdict by lunch, the average Heidelberger had better things to do than continue to follow the case. Usually, the man on the street would hear enough gossip to anticipate the decision of the court. But Madlen's case was different. Not too long ago, it seemed as if this was just a case of improper administration of powerful herbal remedies. But now it seemed clear that a rich nobleman was purposefully tormenting a young woman by accusing her of something that he was guilty of. In the last few decades, there had been minor revolts against feudal lords and other nobles. Commoners were fed up with the rich and powerful. Until today, Madlen hadn't received any special attention in Heidelberg, but for many Heidelbergers, now the allegations against her reflected what angered them most about their daily lives. Simple, honest folks were fed up with arbitrary injustice. Madlen looked over at the spectator stands and saw a young woman raise her fist. Madlen nodded confidently as others made it clear that they stood behind her. Their support reassured her, and yet she still had a sinking feeling about Barbara's testimony, though she surely knew that Adelhaid Trauenstein would have died if Madlen hadn't helped her. And even though she had never wanted to do anything but help people, she secretly wondered whether she would be so willing to do so in the future. The terror of the last few days had shaken her so badly that she'd been unable to eat or sleep properly, and her already slight frame became even thinner and more frail looking. It would take some time before she regained the confidence to help others again. Madlen winced when Andreas grabbed her arm. He pointed to the young woman now being led into the courtroom by a guard. "Is this the witness?"

Madlen nodded. "Yes, that's Barbara."

"She won't look at you," Andreas whispered to Madlen. "Try to get her to meet your eyes."

"I'll try." Madlen lifted her chin, but the maid kept staring directly at the floor, refusing to look up. It wasn't long before the sheriff and the jury solemnly reentered the courtroom and once again took their places.

"The court wishes to continue." The sheriff looked around the room. "I don't see Matthias Trauenstein; he's supposed to lead the prosecution." He shook his head.

A murmur went through the courtroom as the people looked around. Suddenly, the door opened again, and a gasping Matthias Trauenstein entered. "Please forgive me!" He rested his hands on his knees to get his breath back.

"What happened to you?" the sheriff asked.

"It's my wife, Adelhaid," he blurted out. "She's not well."

"But she's due to testify this afternoon, immediately after the maid," the sheriff said indignantly. "Are you trying to tell us that she won't be able to make her statement?"

Matthias Trauenstein stood up straight again. "Adelhaid told me herself that she wanted to appear. I beg of you: Would it be possible for her to come tomorrow? I'm afraid she doesn't have the strength today."

The sheriff traded looks with the jurymen. Andreas von Balge followed their gestures. "They all agree," he whispered.

"We have nothing against her testifying tomorrow morning," the sheriff announced. "Today we'll hear the maid's testimony and, first thing in the morning, your wife's. But one thing is quite certain, Matthias Trauenstein, your wife must absolutely appear here tomorrow."

Matthias acknowledged him with a bow. "It's of the utmost importance that she does so. Believe me." He took his place.

"Good. Good." The sheriff cleared his throat. "Now to you, maid. Your name is Barbara, correct?"

"That's correct, sir," she squeaked, looking up for only a split second.

"And from what house do you come?"

"My father is Hugo, the barrel maker's servant, my lord."

The sheriff nodded. "Now please tell us in your own words what led to the death of the Trauenstein infant."

Barbara's face turned red. Quickly, she glanced at Matthias Trauenstein, who threateningly raised his eyebrow. "My mistress didn't feel very well," she finally began. "She was only a few weeks away from delivery, and her usual midwife was no longer available."

"She passed away. Everyone in this courtroom knows this," the sheriff corrected.

"Yes, my lord." She lifted her head. "I knew that Madlen had learned many things from Clara . . ." She hesitated and looked again at her master.

"Stop that," warned the sheriff. "Look at us over here."

"Yes, my lord." She straightened her chair so that she could follow the sheriff's orders and look only at the jury.

"Continue."

"Like I said, Clara was dead, and I thought Madlen would be able to help my mistress. So I went to her." She paused for a moment.

"Maid, at this rate, we'll be sitting here till dawn. Must I ask you to continue after every single sentence?" the sheriff said indignantly.

"Forgive me. Madlen and I ran to the Trauensteins'. When we arrived, Madlen told me to fetch some herbs."

"Which herbs?"

Barbara counted off on her fingers. "Arnica, sage, artemisia, oil, and honey. I went to look immediately. We had everything except for artemisia."

"So far as I know, none of these herbs are poison?" the sheriff asked.

"No, my lord."

Matthias Trauenstein started to clear his throat loudly. Barbara pressed her lips together. Her shoulders trembled. "But Madlen had her own herbs," she continued, so quietly that it was little more than a whisper.

"What did you say?" Andreas von Balge addressed the witness.

"It's not your turn," the sheriff scolded. "Let the witness make her statement before you examine her. You are well aware of procedure."

"Forgive me. But there was never any talk . . ." Andreas broke off. "I will question the witness afterward, as is our right."

"So, maid, you said that the defendant herself brought herbs with her. What kind exactly?"

Barbara looked at Madlen for a half second, then focused back on the ground. "As far as I could tell, it was foxglove."

A murmur went through the courtroom. Even the uneducated knew that this plant would put any sufferer out of his or her misery.

"Foxglove?" The sheriff raised his eyebrows high. "Are you quite sure of that? Look at me when you answer."

Barbara looked up. "Yes, my lord, I'm sure." She pressed her lips together until they turned white.

"What happened next?"

"Madlen prepared a paste and rubbed it deep into my mistress's belly."

Again, the courtroom erupted; some coughed in embarrassment for the maid, and others whispered to their neighbors.

"Quiet!" the sheriff thundered. He turned again to Barbara. "And then?"

"My mistress got sick, her stomach cramped, and she suffered terribly."

"That happened only after the defendant applied the herbal ointment?"

"Yes, my lord. She started bleeding, and Madlen said that she had to get the baby out before it died."

Up to this point, Madlen had listened to Barbara's testimony dispassionately. But now Madlen put her hands in front of her mouth in astonishment. "Why are you saying this?" she gasped. Her heart beat so wildly in her chest that she felt she might pass out at any moment.

"Please no questions yet," the sheriff warned. She sat there, ashen, her eyes torn open in shock.

Barbara swallowed hard. "A little while later, she pulled the baby out."

"And did it live?"

"Yes, but not long. It was simply too small."

The advocate peeked inconspicuously at the jury and the court-room spectators. Many of their faces were pale as the gruesome images took shape in their minds. Her words horrified everyone. Von Balge fervently hoped that the sheriff's examination would be completed as soon as possible so that he could start his examination and quickly disprove the maid's testimony.

"What did the defendant do then?"

"She stayed and tried to comfort my mistress, but eventually she left us to deal with the dead infant ourselves."

"And what did you do?"

"My mistress was ashamed to have lost yet another baby. She knew there was no way to bury the infant in consecrated ground. So, I walked to the forest to bury him. It was there that I was arrested."

"When did your master become aware of these events?"

"When I was released from your custody." She nodded at the sheriff. "I went directly home. Matthias Trauenstein sat on my mistress's bed as they mourned their unbearable loss together."

The courtroom was dead silent. The sheriff traded looks with the jury and exhaled audibly. "Now the court asks the advocate to begin his examination. I warn you to tell the truth."

"You scared this girl to death," Matthias Trauenstein commented indignantly.

"She's scared all right," Andreas von Balge immediately countered, "but that has nothing to do with the sheriff."

"What are you trying to say?"

"You know exactly what I'm saying," the advocate replied quietly but firmly. "Whether you want to admit it or not, even the most simple-minded in this courtroom knows exactly what you've done."

"Oh, and what would that be?"

"Gentlemen! Let us restrict our line of questioning to one that will move the case forward. Master von Balge, conduct your examination."

"Thank you." Andreas took several deep breaths as he kept his gaze fixed on Matthias Trauenstein. He walked around the table until he stood a short distance away from Barbara.

"Would you prefer to leap up and run out of the courtroom right now?"

"What kind of a question is that?" Matthias snorted.

"Keep your peace." The sheriff's face turned an angry shade of crimson.

"Thank you." Von Balge nodded. "I'm so sorry, maid, but it's best that I'm completely frank with you from the onset: I don't believe a word you've said." He waved his hands and swept his arms toward the courtroom spectators. "And I can assure you, most of these fine citizens don't, either." He took a couple of steps and tapped his finger pensively against his lips.

Barbara could no longer hide her shivering shoulders, as she lowered her head and stared at the floor. Madlen could tell that her eyes were closed.

"Look at me, please." Von Balge waited until she obeyed his command. "Do you find it difficult to make this statement here today?"

"Who wouldn't find it difficult?" Trauenstein answered. The sheriff shot him a stern glance.

"The one point on which we agree," von Balge taunted.

The spectators chuckled lightly.

"When you ran to Madlen's house to pick her up, how long did that take?"

"I don't know exactly."

"Well, did she come with you willingly, or did she have concerns?"

Barbara looked over at Matthias Trauenstein uncertainly.

"Please keep your eyes on me," von Balge demanded. "What did Madlen say when you asked her to help your mistress?"

"She hesitated at first."

"My client hesitated. I see. What do you believe was the reason for that?"

"She said that she didn't know whether she could help. She hadn't worked in the field of midwifery as long as Clara."

"Aha. She had doubts. But you were able to persuade her. How?"

"I don't remember."

"You don't remember? Did you not tell my client that your mistress would die if she didn't help her?"

Barbara remained mute.

"Answer the question!" Andreas clapped his hands together and the maid winced; she looked at him in shock.

"Yes!"

"Yes, you said your mistress would die?"

Barbara pressed her lips together and whispered, "Yes, that's what I said."

Matthias Trauenstein hit the palm of his hand on the table. "He's intimidating the witness by yelling at her like this."

"The only one that's yelling here is you," von Balge said condescendingly.

Trauenstein sprang up. "You lousy son of a whore. I'll . . ."

The sheriff stood up from his chair. "Sit back down now immediately. The scene you've made here is unworthy of a Heidelberg nobleman."

It was obvious how much Matthias seethed with anger as he clenched his jaw. "Forgive me, good sir. I forgot my manners. The death of my child and the frail state of my wife's health have taken a toll on me."

"I accept your apology, Matthias Trauenstein," von Balge said, nodding politely then turning to the sheriff and the jury. "Thank you for your intervention, my lord, although I can assure you that there are not enough words in the entire world that could possibly offend me, coming from a man like this."

The spectators laughed openly, and even two members of the jury couldn't help but smile. Matthias Trauenstein's face turned a dark shade of crimson.

"But let's get back to the point, shall we? Maid, you told my client that your mistress would die without her help."

"Yes, my lord."

"And why is that?"

Barbara's lips began to twitch. "She was weak, very weak."

"But a person wouldn't normally be in danger of dying simply from weakness. Something else must have happened."

"She wasn't doing well. I don't know any more than that." She glanced quickly over to her master.

Von Balge sighed. "I understand. You must be paralyzed by fear." He looked over at Trauenstein, letting his gaze linger on him calmly; Matthias looked away.

"Moving forward. You managed to persuade my client. Please tell me exactly what she did then."

"She came with me."

"No, I mean, exactly. Did she put on her shoes, or did she already have them on?"

"She didn't have her shoes on. She put them on, then her cloak."

"And you both went directly to the Trauenstein residence?"

"Yes, like I said."

"Interesting. And did you both stay together until you entered the Trauensteins' home?"

"That's correct."

"You both climbed upstairs and went directly to Adelhaid's bedchamber?"

"Yes, my lord."

"And there, the defendant examined your mistress then sent you to fetch herbs?"

"Yes, my lord."

"How long did that take?"

"Just a few moments. We had everything in the kitchen."

Andreas tapped again on his lips. "Then explain something to me: When did my client have the opportunity to obtain the foxglove?"

Barbara's eyes opened wide. She looked over at Matthias Trauenstein.

"He can't help you. Please answer the question."

"I . . . I don't know, my lord."

Von Balge moved closer. "I urge you to consider the serious consequences of your next answer before responding. Are you absolutely sure that you saw the foxglove plant, or is it possible that you were mistaken?"

"Perhaps I was mistaken." She exhaled a long, low sigh.

Matthias Trauenstein hissed audibly.

Andreas walked even closer to Barbara's table. "Since we've come this far, isn't it time to indulge the members of the court with a bit more truth?" He turned around and took a few steps. "Isn't it true that your mistress was bleeding profusely and sent you to my client to beg for help to save her life?"

Barbara nodded silently.

"I have no choice but to insist that you say the words aloud."

"Yes. She'd been bleeding."

"Since when?"

"The entire night before. She'd lost a large amount of blood."

"And why was that?"

Barbara shook her head. "I don't know." Terrified, she looked at Matthias Trauenstein, whose face reflected sheer hatred.

"You do know."

"Please," the maid begged. "Please don't make me say it."

Andreas looked at the sheriff then at the jury members. "We will spare you from saying these words at this time. But believe me, sooner or later you will need to make this statement."

Barbara sobbed loudly.

"So, my client saw the condition your mistress was in and pulled out the child? Is that correct?"

"Yes, my lord."

"And by doing so, she was at least able to save your mistress's life?"

Barbara nodded.

"The child. Was it still alive when it came into this world?"

The maid shook her head. "No, its whole body was blue. It had died in the womb hours before."

The advocate looked at the courtroom spectators then at the sheriff and jury. He looked at Madlen. Although she knew that the verdict would be to her benefit, she looked at Andreas solemnly. Barbara's fear was almost palpable. He could see compassion tinged with regret for the woman in his client's eyes.

"I know how hard it must have been for you to tell the truth here." He looked over at Trauenstein and swept his arm out. "I believe, without exception, that I can speak for everyone in the courtroom when I say that you and your mistress have our deepest sympathy. I expect that in regard to the charges against my client, no further testimony will be required." He looked at the sheriff. "Or does it please the court to continue to question and embarrass the witness?"

"That will not be necessary," the sheriff replied.

"All right. I move to exonerate my client immediately of all charges."

Shouts of agreement rang through the courtroom. A woman barked at Matthias Trauenstein, saying that he should be ashamed of himself and that he should disappear from Heidelberg altogether.

"But my wife hasn't even taken the witness stand yet."

The Secret Healer

"Spare us further testimony, Trauenstein. We'll be coming after you soon to explain how your wife's injuries ultimately led to the death of your unborn child." The sheriff snorted angrily. "The jury and I will retreat for our final judgment on the matter," he announced. He rose to follow the jury. "This won't take long."

It wasn't an exaggeration. Only a short moment later, they went to their chairs and sat behind the sheriff. "The defendant is acquitted of all charges. The city clerk will make a record of the verdict."

Some spectators cheered, congratulating Madlen and shaking her hand before they left the courtroom. Although she should have been relieved, all feelings of liberation escaped her. She thanked Andreas then looked regretfully at Barbara, who still sat sobbing on the witness chair. Matthias Trauenstein was the first to leave; he'd basically bolted out of the courtroom. Madlen looked at Barbara again. She felt sorry for the young woman, and a feeling of bitterness boiled in her soul. Whatever her master would inflict on her now, Madlen wouldn't be able to help her. Barbara would suffer greatly, of that Madlen was quite sure.

Chapter Nine

She cried all the way home. Her head felt clouded, incapable of even one clear thought. The last few days had been so tense and frightening as the trial loomed. Although everything had gone in her favor, she had no idea how to move on. Her heart still pounded wildly at the thought of what could have been. Her good-bye to Andreas von Balge was short and sweet; victory was written all over his face. She, however, felt miserable and just wanted to go home.

And yet, tomorrow it would no longer be home. Heinfried would arrive at noon, pay her father, and take her away. Just like that. She'd never thought about how much Heidelberg, her birthplace, meant to her. The Neckar seemed to be the boundary between Heidelberg and the rest of the world. Her hometown, which once felt suffocating and provincial, now became a place she never wanted to leave. Up until now, she had thought very little about what kind of man Heinfried would be. She certainly didn't have it easy living with her father, but they always scraped by. Now, the idea of being dragged away from her home and brought to a foreign place she probably would not be able to stand made her blood run cold, not to mention the dreaded thought of having Heinfried touch her. Her brother had only embraced her a handful of times when she needed comfort. Thanks to Clara, however, she'd come to know true affection. It was normal for them to greet and bid farewell to each other with a warm hug and sometimes even a stroke on the cheek, like a mother's touch. The thought that a complete stranger, her future husband, would touch her whenever he wanted made her break out into a cold sweat.

"You're here!"

Kilian startled Madlen, waiting outside their cottage for her. She hadn't noticed him there because she'd been looking at the ground her entire way home.

"And?"

"I was acquitted of all charges."

"Thank God." He grabbed her, and Madlen enjoyed the hug like never before. They remained in this thankful embrace for several minutes, finally stilling her wildly beating heart.

Kilian pulled away. "Let's go inside. Irma's cooked something so that you could rest when you got home."

"Irma? Why is she cooking for us?"

Kilian looked at the ground and pushed away some dirt with the sole of his shoe.

"You and Irma?" Madlen blurted. "I would never have thought."

"Not exactly." Kilian looked at his sister. "She's got a good heart and, of course, would be a good wife. But I just don't want her, and I can't seem to make that clear to her."

Madlen noticed that her brother had a bad conscience. "Have you somehow given her reason to believe you feel something for her?"

He bowed his head and looked at the ground again. "Well, you know, I helped Hans when his ox died suddenly. He needed lumber for the new stall. My good friends Fridel and Herrmann got in touch with me to let me know about Hans's situation and Irma and Agathe did, too. I suppose we became friendly. And two days later, when I brought new chairs to the potter, I happened to run into Irma again."

He raised his hands defensively. "We only talked, I swear. And I didn't think anything about it. But she started showing up, wanting to do me a favor here and there. And now she's preparing supper because you were in court."

"You need to tell her." Madlen stroked her brother's arm.

"But I never once made her a promise. I didn't even kiss her." He wrinkled his forehead angrily.

Madlen just smiled, and immediately his gaze softened. "Yes, all right, I'll tell her," he sulked.

"Good." She hooked her arm in his. "But I'll still eat her supper." Madlen grinned impishly and together they went into the house. "Is Father still in the woodshop?"

"No." Kilian closed the door behind him. "He's sitting in some tavern, drinking whatever money you'll bring." He spit the words out bitterly.

"Yes." She sighed as she sank into a chair. "Tomorrow's almost here."

Kilian walked over to the cast-iron pot quickly, trying to conceal how much the thought of her leaving hurt him. "We'll eat first, and then you tell me what happened in court." He turned to his sister. "I would have loved to be there with you, but you know how Father is."

"Don't worry. I'm just glad that it's all over." She stood up and went over to him. "Come on. Let me get my fill of soup." She picked up the ladle. Suddenly, she became aware that this could be the last time she would be able to share a meal with her brother.

Kilian noticed. "What's the matter?"

"Oh, it's nothing." She wiped away her tears quickly. "I'm just relieved that the trial is over." She scooped up some soup, filled a bowl, and handed it to Kilian, who took it to the table and sat down. Then Madlen joined him.

"Yet another reason that I have to tell Irma the truth," Kilian said after tasting the soup. "Her cooking isn't even remotely as good as yours."

Madlen smiled. "Sweet brother," she said with a giggle. At that instant, there was a knock on the door. Kilian stood and answered it.

"Is your sister here?"

"Who are you?"

"I'm a servant for Adelhaid Trauenstein. She sent me."

"What does she want? Hasn't your mistress done enough to my sister?"

Madlen didn't move a muscle. Still, the man could see her from the doorway.

"That's exactly what this is about. My mistress had no idea what her husband had done until he told her she must testify in court." He looked past Kilian over to Madlen. "She would like to apologize to you."

"Tell your mistress it makes no difference to us." Kilian took a step forward to obstruct the man's view of his sister.

"Please, understand. My mistress has no peace. She's been crying for hours because of the injustice that was brought upon your sister. She wants to make good."

"And how does she plan to do that?" Kilian snorted angrily. "My sister could have been sentenced and punished harshly because of these lies. And she only wanted to help."

"My mistress will do everything in her power to make up for the injustice."

"How?"

"She begs your sister to come to her so that she can personally apologize and give your sister enough money to henceforth live a care-free life."

"I don't want her money," Madlen shouted, jumping up from her chair. She came to the door and wriggled her way in next to her brother. "If your mistress continues to let herself be beaten, that's her business. But when she allows others to suffer, there will never be enough money in the world to free her soul. You tell her that."

The man pressed his lips together. "You're correct. I think this is one of the reasons she asked you to come; she's truly sorry. She doesn't have the strength to leave the house at the moment. Still, she wants to press charges against her husband. I sincerely hope that it will come to that. He beats her, sometimes even breaks her bones. And not just her. He violates the maids and bludgeons almost everyone who gets in his way. Someone must do something." He breathed in deeply. "But without you, I'm afraid my mistress won't have the strength to fight. Your spirit is an inspiration to her." He took a step back. "But I understand your position. Please excuse me if I have bothered you. Even if you cannot forgive, you should know that Adelhaid Trauenstein will not close her eyes at night, without regretting what happened to you. And she will continue to do as long as she lives." He looked at Kilian. "That won't be long at any rate. I'm one of the few who are loyal to her, but I cannot protect her from her husband if no one stops him. Forgive me for my intrusion, but I had to try to save the life of this good-hearted woman." With that, he turned on his heels and walked away.

Kilian pushed Madlen gently back into the cottage and shut the door. Lost in thought, she took her seat.

"Have I done the right thing?"

She expected to hear him spit out an angry remark about Adelhaid, but he remained quiet for a while before replying, "I really don't know. You know how much I despise bastards like Matthias Trauenstein. He rapes the maids and beats everybody under his service black and blue. He didn't even stop at his own wife, though she carried his child in her womb."

"Do you really think that she knew nothing about the trial?"

"I can well imagine it. After all, she never leaves the house. If he told the servants not to mention it, nobody would have said a peep."

"But wasn't she supposed to appear at trial?"

"With her charming husband pressuring her to lie? I wouldn't be surprised if she refused and he immediately gave her another good thrashing." Kilian shoved his soup bowl away. "I'm not hungry."

"What should I do? Go to her?"

"Her trusted servant wouldn't have come here if he feared that Matthias would be at home in the near future. You could have gone with him to at least see Adelhaid and listen to what she has to say. You could even convince her to go to the sheriff. In any case"—he paused briefly—"she wants to give you money to mitigate the injustice. This is your last chance. You gave everything you had to pay your advocate. It would only be right for her to compensate you for this."

"It would allow me to be more independent from Heinfried's every whim," Madlen said, thinking aloud.

"Absolutely."

Madlen stood up. "Will you accompany me?"

Kilian arose. "I would never let you go there alone again."

On the way to the Trauenstein estate, they barely spoke, holding each other's hands tightly the whole time. Only when she climbed the steps and knocked did Kilian let go. Their recent visitor opened the door, looking surprised. "Come in," he said. "What a relief to see you."

Madlen and Kilian entered together. Inside, everything was calm. Even the kitchen was completely silent. Except for the guard, it seemed there was no one home.

"Please wait here. I'll go upstairs and inform her that you're both here."

Madlen nodded. An eerie feeling crept over her whole body. Was it because this house reminded her of what had just been done to her? She didn't know. It wasn't long before the guard came out of Adelhaid's bedchamber and approached the hall landing. "You can come up now. But please, only you. That is her wish."

Madlen looked at Kilian with hesitation.

"It's all right," her brother replied. "I'll wait here."

"One moment." The guard went into the bedchamber again. Apparently, Adelhaid Trauenstein had called to him from her bed. When he emerged, he came back downstairs. "My mistress wants me to give this to you." He approached Kilian and gave him some coins as Madlen climbed upstairs. "Your wait will seem shorter if you buy a beer for yourself in the pub across the street."

Madlen turned to her brother. "Go ahead. I'll come over as soon as I'm done."

"All right." Kilian put the coins in his pocket, opened the door, and left the house. As he did so, he realized that the guard latched the door shut behind him. He paused for a moment, wondering why he would be so overly cautious. Then he pushed the thought away and went to the tavern, where he ran into his friend, Hans, joining him and two other men his age at their table.

Madlen took a deep breath before entering Adelhaid's bedchamber. It was as dark as the last time she was there; she could barely see a thing. "It's me, Madlen," she said tentatively, approaching the bed quietly. Adelhaid didn't say a word; she seemed to be waiting until Madlen came into her line of vision. Or was she sleeping? "Adelhaid, can you hear me? Are you awake?" She tiptoed closer to the bed when suddenly the door behind her slammed shut. Madlen's heart skipped a beat. The weak light from the open door had at least lit the room somewhat; now Madlen saw nothing but black. She gasped with fear. "Adelhaid?"

She heard a rustling, and even though she couldn't see, she felt someone approach her. "Who's there?" Suddenly, somebody grabbed her shoulders. She felt their breath close to her face.

"Well, well, who do we have here?"

Madlen gasped. Even though she'd never spoken to him directly, she recognized the voice of Matthias Trauenstein immediately. She closed her eyes. A trap! She would almost certainly pay for her mistake with her life. Her whole body began to tremble.

"Look who's scared now, you little whore." He gripped her tighter. "Aren't you sorry for making a fool out of me in court?" Madlen suppressed a scream as he grabbed her even tighter. What was the point? It was the guard who had lured her into the trap.

Matthias let go of her shoulder and grabbed her hair. The shawl that covered it fell to the ground. Madlen thought she heard someone whimper from the corner. "Adelhaid, are you here? Say something!" Madlen begged.

"Of course she's here." He threw her like a sack of potatoes onto the bed, hurling her with so much force that she landed on her stomach and bumped her head into something hard. She screamed loudly.

"Go ahead and scream, you little whore. That's what I like."

Again, Madlen heard somebody whimper, this time a little louder. "Please, Adelhaid, help me," she pleaded. "If you're in the room, please help." Madlen couldn't hold back her tears. Soon, he'd be throwing himself on her to rape her.

"You want to see my wife?" she heard him say. He seemed to be standing a little farther away now. A small flame glimmered as a candle was lit. Madlen sat up. Slowly, she recognized a silhouette. Matthias Trauenstein stood motionless, staring at her. In spite of the weak light, she could see the insane twinkle in his eyes. She broke into a cold sweat. There must be something else lying on the bed. She was sitting on something hard and immovable. Madlen raised her hands to her face. She screamed when she realized that they were both red with blood. From the corner near the door, she again heard somebody whimper and slowly realized what was going on. Shakily, she looked at the bed where she sat. Madlen yelped, jumped up, and landed on all fours on the ground. Matthias Trauenstein laughed scornfully, louder and louder.

"What's the rush? Didn't you long to see my wife? Well, she's lying there, as you can see."

Madlen gasped again; breathing seemed all but impossible. Her whole body knotted up like a rope, as Matthias laughed louder and louder until he finally grabbed her by the hair again and stood her up. He held her head and forced her to look at the bed.

"Yes, go ahead and look. Isn't my wife wonderful? Don't be scared of all the blood." He held Madlen even tighter and clutched her head so she couldn't look away. "This is all your fault. She didn't have to die, but you and your oh-so-clever advocate forced me to do this. Now who am I supposed to sleep next to at night?" His mouth was right next to her ear. "Unfortunately for you, you'll be locked away until you swing from the gallows." He pushed her forward, and Madlen landed again on Adelhaid's corpse.

"Barbara, you know what you have to do."

Madlen dimly recognized Barbara, who staggered over to the door and opened it. A faint glow of light fell into the room. Madlen couldn't see what Barbara was doing. She couldn't think clearly. She looked to the side and saw Adelhaid's face. Blood flowed over the white linen pillow. Her eyes were still open, and Madlen had the feeling that Adelhaid was staring at her reproachfully.

"Do you know what's going to happen now?" Matthias laughed, but it wasn't the full, deep laugh he'd had before. It sounded high and light, as if he'd lost his mind. "Barbara has informed the guard. Now he'll go to the street and scream as loud as he can that you've killed my wife."

"Nobody will believe you." Madlen became sick to her stomach.

"Oh, of course they will. There's the knife with which you stabbed my wife over and over. I advise you to surrender yourself to the sheriff."

"Why would I do that?" Madlen asked weakly.

"You still don't understand?" Again he laughed. "I would have thought you were smarter than this. But what can you expect from a little whore like yourself? You've stabbed my beloved wife to death with a knife because she wanted to tell the truth that it was you that poisoned her and killed our child."

"Nobody will believe that. Not after what happened in the courtroom today."

"Oh, but I think they will. Our lovely Barbara will swear that she got money from you to lie in court." He tapped his head. "I figured it all out."

"You'll never get away with it. When the sheriff arrives, he'll believe me, not you. And where would I have gotten enough money to pay Barbara? No, nobody will believe you." Madlen looked desperately for a way out. There had to be a way to convince him that his scheme would fail.

"You were able to pay that expensive advocate."

"From the money that Adelhaid gave me in thanks for saving her life," she sobbed.

"Or that you stole after you poisoned her and killed our son."

Madlen realized that he had indeed considered everything. Every little detail. She looked down. Her dress and hands were tainted through and through with Adelhaid's blood. She had to flee. She acted as if she wanted to get up, then she raised her arms and shoved Matthias away with such a powerful push that he staggered backward in surprise. She stumbled to the door, where she almost ran into Barbara. The frightened woman pressed herself against the wall and cleared the way for Madlen's escape.

She ran to the stairwell. The guard was nowhere to be seen. She ran as fast as she could down the steps.

"Stop, you whore!" she heard Matthias yell from above.

She jumped down the last few steps, ran over to the front door, and raced out. Outside, people were already gathering thanks to the guard's racket. Some screamed in terror as they saw Madlen's blood-soaked dress. She ran like a hunted animal as she sped away from the house and Matthias Trauenstein's cries. Nobody made a move to stand in her way, when suddenly someone grabbed her hand. She saw Kilian's face pop up in front of her as he pulled her away with him. No one ran after the siblings. The good citizens of Heidelberg were too stunned to comprehend what they saw.

They both ran from the marketplace until they reached Ingrim Street and turned into a small alley. At first, they thought they heard footsteps, but they seemed to be alone.

"You've got to hide," Kilian gasped.

"But I don't know, I can't . . . ," Madlen protested.

Her brother dragged her farther. "We don't have time to argue. Come on!"

Madlen could not have said how long they ran. "Let's go to our old cave. Nobody will find you there. I'll run back and pretend that I lost you and am trying to find you, too. Maybe I'll learn what's going on at the same time. You stay there until I come back. Do you understand?"

Madlen didn't react, unable to comprehend. He grabbed her by the shoulders and shook her. "Madlen! Come now! Keep yourself hidden. Do you hear me?"

She nodded and followed his instructions. He hurriedly turned around and ran back to the marketplace, calling loudly for his sister in the neighboring streets.

Madlen crept deep into the cave, until she couldn't go any farther. She crouched, leaning against the wall, then moved her legs to her chest. Her whole body shivered, unable to absorb what had happened in the last few hours. Only her sticky bloodstained hands and the smell of blood on her dress convinced her that this wasn't a bad dream.

Chapter Ten

It was ice-cold in the cave. After a while, she cried herself to sleep. Outside was as dark as it was in the cave. Not even one small ray of light. When she woke, Madlen's whole body trembled. She sat up and blew into her freezing-cold hands, then rubbed her arms. She'd only stayed overnight in the cave one time before. She'd been seven or eight years old and hiding from her father because of some trivial thing she'd supposedly done. He had been drunk that day and had beaten her with a willow branch. Kilian hadn't been around to protect her. Madlen didn't dare go home before Kilian's return. So she'd huddled on the ground and finally fallen asleep. Just like now. Except now she was holed up here for a much worse reason. Slowly, her thoughts cleared and she pondered the day's events. All the terrible things that had happened in the last few hours came rushing back. The horror of being tricked, Adelhaid's death, the blood, the realization that Matthias Trauenstein had planned everything to the smallest detail.

"Madlen? Are you here?"

It wasn't her brother's voice, so Madlen pressed her body even closer to the wall. She hardly dared to breathe.

"Madlen?" the voice repeated. "It's me, Andreas. Are you in here? Kilian sent me."

Madlen's heart was in her throat; blood rushed in her ears. What should she do? Was this yet another trap? Had the advocate been spying on the siblings and waiting until Kilian went away? But why? What were his intentions? Madlen sighed. Either way, he would find her in the cave; she might as well reveal herself. "I'm here," she said, her voice trembling.

She heard footsteps as Andreas moved farther in. "Thank God. I thought I might have gotten the wrong location." Madlen could still only hear him.

"Where are you?" he asked in a tone of concern.

"What do you want?"

"What do you think?" He groaned from the stress of crawling on all fours. "I want to help you." He got so close that Madlen could feel his breath when he spoke.

"I'm right here." She reached out her hand and touched his arm.

"You can't even see your hand in front of your face. Good thing. From outside, nobody would ever guess there was a cave here at all." He sat down to make himself a bit more comfortable. "How are you?"

"What do you think? I fell into Matthias Trauenstein's trap, and I'll probably end up swinging from the gallows."

"I wish I could say something reassuring, but it doesn't look good for you. Over two dozen witnesses saw you flee in your blood-smeared dress."

"Should I tell you what really happened?"

"Your brother pieced together what happened from talking with some of the other witnesses and has already filled me in."

"Where is Kilian?"

"He's probably already back at your cottage, where guards are stationed, waiting for you to come home. They'll be waiting a long time."

"But where should I go?" A bit of hope germinated in her breast. "Are you here to show me the way out? Do you have something that can be used against Matthias Trauenstein? Did Barbara confess? Or the guard?"

Von Balge sighed. "I am so very sorry. Things look bad for you. After your brother notified me, I went directly to the sheriff." He shifted. "Nobody is ready to believe our side of the story. The maid testified that you paid her off. And the guard swears up and down that you and your brother showed up uninvited at the Trauensteins', longing to talk to his mistress. When you arrived, your brother went to the tavern to leave you and Adelhaid alone to sort things out. A short time later, the guard heard screaming. When he stormed in from the hall, the guard swears he saw you repeatedly stab Adelhaid with the knife. She was already dead, so he was unable to help his mistress."

Madlen felt sick. For a moment, she thought she might throw up, but she was able to suppress it. Lucky, since this cave would undoubtedly be her home for some time.

"But they're lying, they're all lying," she cried.

"I know." He would have loved to take her into his arms but forced himself to maintain a professional demeanor.

"The guard told the sheriff that he was trying to wrest the knife from your hands when his master came home. As he stormed by to save his wife, you tried to escape. Matthias Trauenstein held you tightly as the guard ran outside to call for help. You finally succeeded in freeing yourself from Trauenstein's grasp and fled. You know the rest."

"He really thought of everything," Madlen said flatly.

"There's very little we can do about that."

"But the guard came to my house! It was he who wanted me to come to Adelhaid. Kilian can swear to it."

"He's your brother and wants to save your skin. Nobody will believe him."

She suppressed a sob. "And Barbara?"

"She confirmed exactly what the guard and Matthias said."

"Then all is lost."

"I would love to be able to disagree with you. But you're right."

"But doesn't anybody wonder, even the sheriff, why on earth I would want to kill Adelhaid?"

"Barbara lied, and Adelhaid wanted to make clear that it was you that killed her child? It doesn't make any difference. The sheriff told me it would do no good to discuss it further. In his and Heidelberg's eyes, you're guilty of the death of Adelhaid Trauenstein."

"They'll hang me."

"That would be the most merciful punishment you could hope for."

Madlen sobbed.

"As much as I might wish that I could defend you, there is nothing I can do. Matthias Trauenstein planned everything out. You have only one choice now: run for your life!"

"But where should I go?"

"Somewhere where nobody knows you."

"The only people who know me are in Heidelberg."

"Then it should be easy." Andreas seemed confident now. "We'll smuggle you out of Heidelberg, and you'll need to get as far away as you can."

"But the city walls. The guards will be expecting me."

"Well, of course. Nobody said you should march out of the city in your bloodstained dress."

"But—"

"I've spoken to your brother. We've got a plan. But you'll need to hide out here for a little while longer. The constables are keeping an eye on Kilian. They're hoping that he'll get careless and lead them to you."

"He isn't in custody?" Her voice trembled.

"No, he's safe at the cottage. He asked me to bring you this." Andreas held out a bag, but Madlen couldn't see it. "There's enough food and drink to last you a few days."

"Thanks." She felt his sleeve brush against her arm and grabbed it. "Why are you doing this?"

Andreas pondered for a moment. "It's just my nature. I've always wanted to help people. This is why I'm here in Heidelberg studying with the great thinkers and professors of our time. Gone are the days where anyone can just take what he wants. There are laws now. And I want to defend and protect innocent citizens to the fullest extent of my knowledge of the law." He paused. "And if all my knowledge of the law can't help someone, I'll do whatever else I can. It's simple."

"You're a good person."

Von Balge laughed throatily. "There are some in my hometown of Bremen who would certainly contradict that statement."

"Do you have many enemies there?"

"I wouldn't call them enemies. More like jealous and miserable fellows who were born rich and couldn't compete with someone who worked hard to get what he wanted." He laughed again, this time cheerlessly. "I left many bad memories behind."

"Was it worth it?"

"To leave it all?" He thought it over again briefly. "To be able to study here and one day be called *syndicus, corpus iuris civilis*—a real attorney? Then to be able to return to Bremen and flaunt it under everybody's nose? Oh yes, it's worth it. It will all pay off in the end."

They talked for a while longer. The advocate was able to give Madlen a feeling of security, although she never forgot the severity of the situation she was in, hiding in a dark cave wearing a bloodstained dress. But Andreas's views, his wishes and dreams and the confidence with which he bore them, finally calmed her. As he left, she had to pull herself together so as not to show how much she feared being alone; she could not beg him to stay. As he crawled out of the cave on all fours, dawn announced a new day.

Outside, daylight came then turned into night without a soul discovering Madlen. She nibbled on the remaining crusts of bread that Andreas von Balge had brought her the night before. She wasn't hungry, but she wanted to keep up her strength. She didn't know what Kilian and her advocate had dreamed up to free her from her desperate situation. Were they able to think up anything at all? And when would this happen? Tonight, tomorrow, or next week? She didn't know. She didn't know anything more since she'd been tricked by Matthias Trauenstein. Life as she knew it two days ago was a thing of the past. Clara had always said that everything happens for a reason. Was that really true? And what sense did it make if she'd been blamed for a murder she didn't commit? What about all her effort to convince Heidelberg of her innocence? Had all that been blown away like dust in the wind?

She had to think of Kilian. The cottage was only a stone's throw away from this cave. She longed for him so much that she could hardly breathe. Should she dare come out of these confines and quietly sneak out in the hopes that the constables had grown weary of waiting? Carefully, she crawled toward the mouth of the cave, choked with fear. It had already gotten so dark that you couldn't see your hand in front of your face. She knew this area very well, a lot better than the town's constables, who spent most of their time standing guard in the marketplace to keep thieves at bay. Of course, they'd notice immediately if somebody stood close to the cottage. She crawled forward until the cold night air hit her. Madlen shivered but breathed deeply. The fresh air did her good. Yes, she would sneak to her cottage to see Kilian and tell him that she was doing all right. Just as she was about to take her chances and crawl all the way out of the cave, a thought held her back. Her father. He'd be there also, very close. Did he understand what had happened? Today was the day that Heinfried was supposed to come to Heidelberg and take her with him. How would her father react when he found out that Heinfried would no longer go through with their business deal? Above all: What would her father do when he laid eyes on Madlen? He'd gotten a deposit from Heinfried. Of course, Heinfried would either demand to be paid back or demand that Madlen herself be delivered to him. Her heart beat quicker. She'd certainly been gullible in her short life, but she wasn't stupid. Madlen could only imagine her father's reaction, and there wouldn't be much that Kilian could do about it. Her father would drag her to the sheriff himself, maybe even enjoy the sight of her hanging after all the aggravation she had caused him.

Carefully, she pushed herself back a bit into the cave. Yet, she didn't like the idea of not seeing Kilian. Her heart sank deeper and deeper every second. As she inhaled deeply, she recognized a smell. She stuck her head outside the cave for a moment. She had always loved snow, as it brought a beautiful stillness over the land and left her feeling peaceful and calm. Snowflakes fell onto her nose, her cheeks, and her forehead. It was the first snow of the year. She wondered for a brief yet horrible moment whether this would be the last time in her life that she would see, feel, and taste the snow. A layer of snowflakes covered her lips, and she licked them off, careful not to miss any. She blinked into the darkness. Far away, she saw the faint glow of a tallow lamp, clearly lighting the way for someone. She immediately slid all the way back into the cave, turned around, and crawled on all fours into the corner. She huddled there for a long while. With a sigh, she rolled over and listened for anyone approaching the cave. She hoped that it was Kilian holding the tallow lamp, sneaking over to the cave to visit her under the cover of darkness. She listened intently as her limbs trembled, but there wasn't anything out there but silence.

When the new day broke, Madlen took a drink and crawled to the mouth of the cave. It was still very early, and the snow had laid a white blanket over the land. She was tempted to take some snow from outside of the cave, but decided against it. It was too dangerous. Someone might notice. She craned her neck but couldn't see anybody. Although she wore only her dress and cloak, it wasn't cold inside the cave. Yet here the harsh wind stung her face and she shivered violently. She took a deep breath once again and crawled back inside. Where was Kilian? Was it possible that her brother had forgotten her? She shook her head angrily. What nonsense. He would never do that.

The hours dragged on endlessly. Every now and then, she poked her head out of the cave to see if someone had come for her. But there were no tracks. Some distance away, she could see a few figures, but nobody approached the massive stone face in which Madlen hid. She remained sitting until it got too cold. Then she crawled back and crouched down. This time, she didn't fall asleep. Her heart beat restlessly, and every noise frightened her. A faint glow illuminated the cave; it seemed to be very weak as she listened. Was there something at the mouth of the cave? She sat up soundlessly. There! Someone was there. She held her breath and held her hand in front of her mouth; it was the crunching sound of footsteps in the snow.

"Madlen, it's me, Andreas," she heard him whisper.

"Thank God!" She sighed in relief.

"Shh. Be quiet and come to me. Do you still have something to eat?"

"A little."

"Good. Bring it with you."

Madlen picked up the linen bag and crawled toward the mouth of the cave. She could clearly see his outline and was relieved to finally see another person so close to her.

"We don't have much time," he said. "Kilian's prepared everything. You must do exactly as I tell you."

She nodded eagerly.

"Good. And take this." He handed her a little pouch that Madlen recognized immediately. "You're going to need it for your escape."

"But that's the money I paid you for defending me in court. It's yours."

"You need it more than I do now. Hide it. Who knows? Maybe one of these days, you can return it to me. I won't miss a coin or two."

Without thinking, she bent over and pulled him close to her. "I don't know how I can ever thank you."

Andreas von Balge cleared his throat. "Just do what I tell you," he replied quickly. "You'll be out of Heidelberg before you know it."

"Thank you." Tears welled up in her eyes.

He nodded, then briefed her on his plan. By the time she finally crawled all the way out of the cave, crippling fear had given way to fierce determination.

Andreas von Balge led the horse by its reins as it pulled the cart. Kilian walked on the right to ensure that the stacked goods did not slide out. They tried hard to seem nonchalant as they strolled over the bridge. A good half dozen guards stood at the watchtower, enduring the winter cold. Kilian saw one guard nudge his colleague and scrutinize them closely. "Hey, you down there. What do you have in your cart?"

"Just some goods that I need to deliver. Nothing special."

"Wait a minute!" He signaled the two other guards. "We want to take a look."

"There's nothing here, I assure you . . ." Kilian fell quiet.

"Stop, I said!" Immediately, two guards stormed down, while the other tower guards started to gather, too. The horse balked as the men came running. Kilian threw Andreas von Balge a frantic look.

"Who are you?" asked a guard. Eight guards surrounded Andreas, Kilian, the horse, and the cart.

"What kind of question is that?" Andreas shot back. "Since when is it illegal to cross the Neckar River?"

"I'll ask you one more time, who are you?" The guard bared his teeth.

"What is your problem?" Andreas replied snidely. Kilian threw him a furtive glance, one the guards didn't catch.

"Say, you're not the advocate who defended that child murderer, are you?"

"She didn't kill a child or anyone else. But I don't expect you to believe that."

The guard ignored him and glared at Kilian. "And you, I've seen you before. Aren't you her brother?"

Kilian shrugged.

"What are you two bringing to the other side of the Neckar?" The guard raised his eyebrows.

"Watch out!" Five craftsmen struggled to carry a heavy wooden beam on their shoulders across the narrow bridge. "We need to bring this beam to the boats over at the pier," said the man in front. "Step to the side so we may pass."

The guards huddled together, giving the carpenters a wider berth. As soon as they had passed, the guards surrounded Kilian and Andreas again.

"What do you have in your cart?"

"Goods," Kilian answered tersely.

"Just goods?" He seemed skeptical. "An advocate and the brother of an escaped murder suspect are bringing goods over the Neckar. You expect us to believe this?"

"Believe what you want to. Now let us through," von Balge demanded gruffly.

"You're not going anywhere," the guard decided. "Clean out the cart. I want to see what's inside."

"You have no right to do this," Andreas protested.

"The sheriff decides what's right in Heidelberg, and it's our duty to enforce the laws on his behalf." He pushed past Andreas, who stood protectively in front of the cart. "Now let me through before I break both your legs."

Two men pushed Kilian and Andreas back, while the other guards began to dump baskets, blankets, and boxes out onto the bridge. When they managed to empty about half of the cart, a guard called out, "Here's something!" He hurriedly lifted another box, and a young woman, her head covered in a simple muslin veil, jumped out. She could only take a few steps before the guards grabbed her. Her blood-smeared dress made the guards' ringleader smile broadly. "Well, well, what have we here?"

The young woman kept her head down.

"Well, if it isn't the little murderer." He glanced at her dirty face. "Take all three to the sheriff. There will be a nice reward in it for us."

The horse was taken away, but the cart still stood near the bridge as the carpenters returned from unloading the wooden beams. There were only four now, but no one noticed. Everyone was too busy celebrating the alleged killer's capture.

Chapter Eleven

Madlen was relieved, but it wasn't yet time to rest. She had to get as far away from Heidelberg as possible before the guards realized they'd been tricked. Madlen chuckled at the thought of the sheriff's anger when he realized that Irma had been turned over to him instead of her. Poor Irma. She hated having to put on that bloodstained dress. But she'd done Kilian one huge favor. Madlen had pulled on her brother's hose, shirt, and jacket and topped it all off with an old hat. She carried the huge wooden beam with some of Kilian's friends. As her brother had said, nobody would give the carpenters a second look while he and Andreas von Balge staged their distraction and Irma was found hidden under boxes. If the circumstances hadn't been so dead serious, Madlen would have found it easier to laugh.

But now that she was outside of Heidelberg and completely alone, she didn't feel like laughing at all. At the beginning of her journey, on the path that took her north over the hills toward Heppenheim, she'd walked so quickly that she hardly had time to think; the only thing that mattered was escaping unnoticed. But now, half a day later, she felt empty and frightened to be somewhere so unfamiliar. She would have turned around if she wasn't sure she would end up dead. But what would life be like for her now? Everything was new and uncertain. She didn't know. Kilian had advised her to join a group of traveling merchants as soon as possible. She was easy prey as a woman traveling alone. She trudged on, her oversized shoes making it difficult to move forward. Again and again, they'd slide off and she'd lose her balance and fall.

She stayed close to the edge of the forest, where she'd be able to hide easily if she happened upon a horde of unruly men. But she didn't see a soul all day. Although it was still afternoon, it had started to get dark. She decided to look around for a safe place to sleep for the night. Faster than expected, she found shelter under several trees that must have blown over during a fierce storm. She gathered branches and tried to build up another wall for added protection. But it didn't amount to much, so she simply sat as close as possible to the tree trunk. She drew up her legs to her chest then threw her arms around them, longing to be in the warm cottage with Kilian, even with her mercurial father. It was better than being alone in this godforsaken wilderness, without any prospects. She thought about whether she should take Kilian's advice to find her father's sister in Worms, though it was a good deal away from here. Still, it would probably save her life. The sheriff wouldn't look as far away as the Rhine. She had almost no memory of her aunt. She'd only seen the woman once, more than ten years ago. Madlen remembered that Agathe's eyes looked like her father's. Other than that, the two seemed to have nothing in common. Whenever the topic of his sister came up, Jerg had nothing but bad things to say. Madlen had no idea why the two had had a falling out. And maybe that wasn't even the case. Maybe they just didn't get along. Each one lived their lives the way they wanted, and they didn't want anyone to get in the way. Reinhard, Agathe's husband, had been dead for years. How he died, Madlen didn't know. She had to admit she'd never been that interested in any of her relatives until now. She'd make a decision where to go first thing tomorrow morning. Perhaps the opportunity to join a group of traveling merchants would present itself. Where she would end up, only the good Lord knew.

Early in the morning, a crackling noise startled her; her clothing was frozen as stiff as her limbs and Madlen had trouble getting back on her feet. She wouldn't survive another night in this freezing weather. Although she'd fallen asleep early in the evening, she felt exhausted and powerless. She jumped up and tried to get blood rushing back into her frozen legs. But every time she tried, a sharp pain shot through her body. Bravely, she continued to hop until she felt the tips of her toes tingle. Her stomach growled so loudly that she winced. She looked around in fright. If someone was nearby, they might hear her. But nothing stirred. She was here by herself, reassuring on the one hand, but on the other, very sad. She'd lost everything, although she'd committed no crime. Kilian had told her that she should stop near the edge of the Odenwald. This would lead her toward Heppenheim, and from there she could go to the Rhine. She trusted her brother, but she doubted whether he knew the right way. So far, she hadn't seen any people or cottages, though she should have reached the next village yesterday. Maybe she was lost? She decided to continue her way along the edge of the forest. At some point, she was bound to encounter another person.

She walked till almost noon, when she finally spied a small village in the distance. Her whole body tingled at the prospect of speaking to another person. Her violent shivering seemed to be getting worse. Hadn't she felt the sun on her skin just a few weeks ago? Winter had stolen over the land with a vengeance. Soon, at least, she would be delivered from the cold; she would be able to pay for a stay at an inn or even in a barn. Feeling slightly queasy, she walked along the frozen path.

A woman came out her front door to empty a bucket. Madlen felt her gaze. She gathered all her courage. "Forgive me, please. Is there a tavern here?"

The woman scrutinized Madlen. With her baggy clothing and big shoes, she must have made a really strange impression.

"It doesn't look as though you can afford a tavern, and the host isn't exactly famous for being charitable."

Madlen shrugged. She didn't know how to respond.

"Do you want to eat or do you also need accommodations?"

"Both."

"For how long?"

"Just a day. I don't want to sleep outside tonight. Tomorrow, I have to go on." The thought of spending another night in the cold made Madlen shudder.

"If you'd like, you can stay in my cottage," the woman offered, after she'd scrutinized Madlen for a little while. "For a coin, I'll feed you, give you a place to sleep, and send you off with breakfast in the morning. But only porridge."

"Do you live here alone?"

"Yes, if you must know. But don't think I couldn't fight should one of your friends try to steal from me." The woman raised her eyebrows, suspicious.

"Oh, no, of course not. I only want to make sure there's enough room." Madlen nodded at the woman's cottage, even smaller than her own cramped house.

"It'll do. Well, what now? Do you want to stay here or not?"

"Indeed, I would."

"But you'll pay me immediately so you don't disappear early in the morning."

Madlen agreed. "I'll pay you once we're inside the cottage."

"They call me Hedwig. And you?"

"Ma . . ." Madlen coughed. "Maria. My name is Maria."

"Come on in, Maria. You'll freeze to death out here."

She followed the old lady inside. Though the exterior of the cottage didn't seem particularly inviting, Madlen changed her mind when she entered. There were two beds, a table with two chairs, some shelves, a fireplace, and a small chest.

"So, nobody lives with you?" Madlen pointed at the beds.

"No." Hedwig shuffled toward the hearth and put on the cast-iron pot. "Someone lived here for a long while, but he's gone now. It's better that way."

Madlen could hear a tinge of regret in Hedwig's voice, even though she appeared matter-of-fact. "I'm sorry."

"You shouldn't be. I was wrong about him. That's just the way it is. As a widow, sometimes you believe things that are too good to be true." She laid a log onto the fire and stirred the soup; its wonderful smell permeated every corner of the little cottage. Hedwig turned to Madlen. "Why are you wearing men's clothes?"

Madlen knew enough to keep her mouth shut; she just shrugged.

"You don't have to tell me. It's none of my business." When Hedwig turned to devote her attention to the soup, Madlen pulled open the money pouch around her neck and took out one of the coins. She immediately stuffed the little sack back under her clothes.

"Here. Your money."

Hedwig accepted it. "If you want, you can take off your wet things and hang them up. You can find something else over there in the chest to change into."

"That's very kind of you, my lady. Thank you."

"Just call me Hedwig."

"Thank you, Hedwig." Madlen smiled. She went over to the chest and took out a piece of clothing. "Can I wear this?"

"Go ahead." Hedwig waved her hand as if swatting away an insect. "And then spread your wet things over there." She pointed at two shelves with a thin rope stretched between them. "They'll dry soon."

Madlen took off her wet clothes and swiftly pulled on the dry ones. She didn't feel comfortable exposing herself to a stranger.

"Where are you going?"

"I don't know exactly. In the direction of the Rhine."

"Why the Rhine?"

"I have relatives there. But here"—Madlen swallowed hard—"I have no one."

"Why not? Is your husband dead?"

"Not my husband," Madlen corrected. "My father. I lived with him until a couple of days ago," she lied, feeling guilty. In reality, she wanted to wring her father's neck.

"So where do you come from?"

"Speyer," Madlen spit out quickly; it was the first city that came to mind.

"A truly noble city," Hedwig said appreciatively. "But then you've been on the road for days. Did you sleep outside the whole time?"

"No, just one night. Other than that, I always had shelter."

Madlen's blood spiked from hot to cold. This Hedwig asked many questions. Madlen had to be careful with her answers. After all, it was still possible that the sheriff had sent men after her. Revealing too much, even to an old lady, could be her undoing. But it was as if Hedwig could read her mind.

"Oh, forgive my questions. I just don't have visitors often."

For a moment, Madlen felt sorry for the old woman. She seemed lonely. But Madlen still had to keep up her guard. "I know how you feel," she said sympathetically. "I was often alone even when my father was still alive. I enjoy chatting with you, my lady."

"Hedwig," she corrected.

"Hedwig. Right."

Hedwig seemed happy. A smile scurried across her face as she filled a bowl with soup and put it on the table. "Here. This will do you good. Enjoy."

The two women talked for several hours. Hedwig told Madlen that she had been a farmer's wife, living just a short distance away until her husband was killed by someone in a dispute. After that, the feudal lord refused her the right to continue cultivating the land. They took away her farmhouse as well as all her fields. She had to sell her oxen and her cow just to survive for a little while.

Finally, she found a job with a butcher's wife, helping her in the house and also assisting the butcher. As she explained to Madlen, she seemed to have done all right with this work, and sometimes she was even rewarded with a pot of lard to take home.

Madlen hung onto Hedwig's every word. What a woman! After her husband's death, she didn't compromise her dignity and sell herself in a brothel, as Madlen had so often seen in these cases. She refused to become despondent over the obvious injustice meted out to her by the feudal lord. Rather, she'd looked to the future and made the best of a terrible situation. Her stories gave Madlen hope. She wanted to do the same thing. She pumped Hedwig for advice without hinting at the real truth behind her own situation. She admitted only that she was focused on being a healer. Hedwig seemed skeptical. The profession wasn't considered proper for a woman. She advised Madlen to find some other way to make a living if her relatives on the Rhine could not support her.

"Don't rely on a man. Even though he may be the best match for you in the entire world, believe me, at some point you'll regret it."

"My father wanted me to marry shortly before he died. I would have been taken care of then."

"For a little while, yes. Thank God that you chose another path. Now you will learn to take care of yourself. There is no greater gift."

"So you wouldn't consent to another marriage?"

Hedwig looked down. "If someone came along who was blind enough to take me as I am, I would probably agree. But give up my work? Never. I wouldn't share my money either, even if he beat me."

Madlen gazed at her. "I wish I was as strong-willed."

"You can be, believe me. The Lord has given that to you. Just ask him; he'll show you what you're capable of if you want it bad enough."

"I should ask God?" Madlen looked at the old woman in amazement. She never would have thought that this simple woman had such steadfast faith.

Hedwig laughed and shook her head. "But of course. With the Lord on your side, you are always stronger than your opponents." She stood up from the table. "Now lie down and rest. If you leave early tomorrow morning, you'll reach the Rhine before nightfall. And Maria?"

"Yes." Madlen looked expectantly at Hedwig.

"Do it right now. Lie back and say a silent prayer to God. He will wake you up early in the morning, and you will feel the power he graced you with overnight."

Madlen didn't quite know what to think, but she gratefully accepted the invitation to grab the blanket and lie down in a warm bed. She briefly touched her chest to make sure that the money pouch was still around her neck. It gave her a sense of security to hold onto the little pouch. She thought about the right psalm to recite. Which prayer would please God and help her on her journey? She didn't know. Words, phrases, and songs passed through her mind, though none seemed to fit. She pondered long and hard, and without realizing it, she prayed silently. Then she prayed some more. She laid all her fears and worries in God's hands until she finally fell asleep.

In the morning when she awoke, she felt rested, strong, and yes, fearless. How was this possible? Had God really heard her prayers and sent help to her as she slept? Or was it Hedwig's firm conviction that led her to believe that this was God's merciful assistance? She couldn't tell. But she knew that she would never forget this feeling and was deeply grateful for Hedwig's advice. Yes, she did believe that God gave her courage and strength. God was on her side; she felt it with every fiber of her body. She couldn't feel any happier than she felt right now.

Chapter Twelve

She arrived in the vibrant city of Worms in the late afternoon. The guards standing watch over the gate didn't stop her. Without any goods, she made no impression on them since she didn't seem to have business in the city. She was glad she took Hedwig's advice to slip one of the old lady's worn-out dresses over her men's clothing before departing. Now she seemed a lot bigger than she actually was. Anyone she ran into would deny having seen a young, boyishly thin woman, as the sheriff probably described her. And the extra layer of clothes also had another advantage: the cold had less effect as she marched on. The opportunity to spend the night at Hedwig's had proven to be very helpful to Madlen. But as good of a soul as Hedwig might be, she didn't hesitate to take an extra coin for the old raggedy dress she'd given up. But that didn't make any difference to Madlen; she was more thankful for the advice, which kept her at least as warm as the dress's extra fabric.

She admired the hustle and bustle of the Worms harbor. There were dozens of young men carrying boxes on their shoulders, walking quickly here and there, ships sailing in to unload their wares and pick up new crates at the harbor. Others unloaded large merchant vessels, surefootedly carrying freight over narrow planks. There was movement everywhere. Madlen was impressed as she stared openmouthed at all the activity.

"Out of the way." A young man carried two big crates and could barely see a thing as he almost ran over Madlen.

"Don't just stand there; get to the side if you need to stand there and gawk," he said as he passed her and approached a small boat, already overloaded and low in the water. "These are the last two," she heard the man say to another man. "If you take more, the boat will sink before you sail her out of the harbor."

The other man grumbled something unintelligible. Madlen watched as he pressed some coins into the younger man's hands. He took the money, tipped his cap, and nimbly walked over the plank to shore, his work apparently done. His gaze fell on Madlen.

"Are you waiting for someone to fetch you?" He approached her with a wide grin.

She gathered all her courage, cleared her throat, and willed her voice to obey her. "Do you know a woman named Agathe?"

He stood still for a moment and scratched his head. "Agathe? I know somebody named Agathe. What's the answer worth to you, girl?"

Madlen turned on her heels and stepped away. He followed and finally caught up to her. "Where are you going in such a hurry? Don't get upset."

Madlen did not slow her pace.

"Now wait a second, sweetheart. Tell me, which Agathe do you mean?"

Madlen stopped and cocked her head to the side.

"I don't want any money," he assured her.

"She probably lives close to the harbor." Madlen thought harder about what she actually knew about her aunt. "She's a widow and works as a seamstress, as far as I know."

"Seamstress?" He scratched his head.

"Her husband's name was Reinhard," Madlen said. It was the last bit of information that she had.

"Agathe." His eyes started to twinkle. "Yes, I know her. If you want, I can bring you to her."

Madlen couldn't quite put aside her suspicions. "You can just tell me where I can find her."

He grimaced playfully. "Well, I deserve that. I'll bring you to her anyway." He took off and Madlen followed. He walked very slowly so she could catch up to him.

"What's your name by the way?"

"Maria," Madlen answered quickly, the same name she'd given Hedwig. It seemed wise to keep up the pretense for now.

"My name is Kuntz." He searched Madlen's eyes, but she looked straight ahead. "And what do you want from Agathe, Maria?"

Madlen didn't answer.

"You're as mute as the fish I catch." He sulked.

They went farther along the harbor. The houses were built a lot closer to the wharf than they were in Heidelberg. There were also quite a few huts that didn't appear to house any people at all.

"What are these structures?"

Kuntz followed Madlen's view. "Just as I thought. You're not from here."

"The huts," Madlen repeated.

"They're not only in Worms. I believe that most of the harbors along the Rhine have them. They temporarily store goods."

"Why doesn't everybody just pick up the wares that were intended for them?"

Kuntz looked up suddenly. "How can anybody know so little about trade?" He laughed but stopped when he saw Madlen bow her head in embarrassment. "Forgive me. I didn't mean to be rude." He spread out his arms. "I can hardly believe that you've never seen this before. I'm so used to all the hustle and bustle. I know there are harbors where even bigger ships sail, ones that travel over the ocean, carrying cargo we could only dream of here." As Kuntz's eyes lit up, Madlen almost chuckled.

"One of these days, believe me, I'll be on one of them, traveling afar. I'll see with my own eyes the sights the sailors talk about in their stories. There, on the sea, where there are fish as big as a church and people who dance and laugh all day long, where beautiful girls ensnare men and there are exotic goods wherever you turn."

Madlen smiled. "Can we continue on our way?"

Kuntz nodded.

"You want to sail? My bro . . ." She cleared her throat. "My cousin, my uncle's son, wants to go to sea, too."

"Oh really? What country does he want to travel to?"

"I don't know exactly, and believe me, neither does he."

Kuntz laughed. "Same with me. I know that many don't believe me. But one of these days, I'll take off." He stepped closer to Madlen. "Every penny that I earn, I save so that I can buy my passage."

"How much does something like that cost?" Madlen asked, looking wide-eyed at Kuntz. Perhaps she could earn enough money to fulfill her brother's dreams.

Kuntz waved her off. "A fortune, I can tell you that. But I'll do it anyway." He stopped again.

"I hope you do."

"Thank you." He lifted his arm and pointed. "We're here."

"Where?"

"At Agathe's, of course."

"Really?" Madlen looked over at the house, amazed. She never expected her aunt to be so well off.

"And you're sure that this is the right Agathe?"

"Yes, why do you ask? What's wrong?"

"Oh, nothing. So, you don't know another Agathe, another widow whose husband was named Reinhard?"

Kuntz shook his head. "No, and I know just about everybody in this town."

"All right." Madlen turned again to the house. It was built of stone; it must have cost a fortune. But maybe only a fortune in her eyes. There were a lot of houses like this here. Did these people simply have more money than those in Heidelberg?

"Thank you, Kuntz. I can manage the rest myself."

"Why don't you knock on the door first to see whether this is the right Agathe?"

She'd had the same thought. But even if Kuntz was wrong, she didn't want to spend any more time with him. He was too nosy.

"No, thank you anyway."

"That's your decision. I just wanted to help." He didn't budge.

"Why are you waiting?"

"I just want to stand here. Everybody in Worms has a right to stand where he wants."

"I will only knock if you leave."

"As if I am that interested," he said, with a dismissive wave of his hand. "I only wanted to help you. But I have better things to do." He turned away.

"Thank you, once more, for your help. It was very kind."

He nodded, grimaced, and took a couple of steps.

"Oh, Kuntz?"

He turned around to face Madlen again. "Yes?"

"I really do hope you fulfill your dreams! Tell the big fish I said hello."

A smile crept across his face. "I'll do it, and when I do, I'll throw my cap in greeting to the sea."

She laughed and watched him for a moment to see how quickly he disappeared amid the throngs of people. Then she turned to the house and took a deep breath. She went up to the door, her legs wobbly as she hesitated a moment. She screwed up her courage and knocked. A woman yelled out that she'd be right there. The door opened just a crack. Madlen could barely make out the woman's face, but she was far too young to be her aunt.

"Agathe?" she asked carefully.

The woman looked confused.

"I'm not Agathe," she finally said. "Who are you?"

"My name is . . ." Madlen hesitated. If she used her real name at the wrong house, her carefully disguised tracks would be uncovered. On the other hand, she had to say a name her aunt would recognize.

"Is it possible for Agathe to come to the door?"

"What do you want with her?"

"Jerg sent me."

"Jerg?"

"That's correct."

The woman scrutinized Madlen again. "Wait here please." A little while later, she opened the door wide enough for Madlen to see another woman in the house.

"You say that my brother . . ." She took a step forward. "Madlen?"

"Maria," she corrected hurriedly, hoping that she would have the opportunity to explain later.

It was clear that Agathe didn't understand why her niece had introduced herself as Maria. But she stepped forward and embraced Madlen warmly. "Whatever the reason, I'm so happy to see you." Her heart skipped a beat as she pushed Madlen away from her a bit. "Or did something happen to your father?"

Madlen shook her head. The look of sincere concern in her aunt's eyes touched her. "No, he's fine."

"Then come in; you're always welcome in my home." She pulled Madlen by the hand into the hall.

"Roswitha, warm up some spiced wine and bring it to us." She put her arm around Madlen's shoulder. "Let's find some peace and quiet so you can tell me what brings you here."

Madlen was surprised that Agathe hugged her over and over again. She was obviously overjoyed to see her, although she didn't know why. She leaned close to Agathe, so that neither Roswitha nor anyone else in the house could hear what she had to say. "I'm in trouble. I'm sorry to bother you so."

Agathe looked deep into her eyes as they entered a dining room that apparently doubled as a sewing room. "Whatever it is, I'll help you as much as I can. Sit down and tell me everything." She looked at Madlen. "Or do you want to take a bath first? You might be more comfortable if you got out of these filthy clothes."

Madlen hesitated. She hadn't counted on so much warmth and friendliness. For a moment, she was so overwhelmed that she didn't know how to behave.

"Don't worry. I'll get you something to wear."

"That would be nice," she said hesitantly.

"I'll take care of it." Agathe left the room in a hurry. When she returned, she told Madlen that she would bring her to the indoor bathroom and then go look for a dress. Madlen was too astounded to object. A bathroom! She followed her aunt silently upstairs and watched a male servant fill up a big tub with buckets of warm water. It was a while before it was full enough and the servant left the room. She hesitantly began to undress, when her aunt came into the room and carefully laid out towels and clothes for her. Madlen didn't dare tell her that this was the first bath she'd ever taken. She entered the tub carefully and sank up to her shoulders in the warm water. It was wonderfully invigorating for her tired limbs. Agathe came in again with scented soap and washed her hair; Madlen thought that she must be having a wonderful dream, though it was still the middle of the day. She'd never seen or heard of anything like this. It was as if she had entered a totally different world.

She emerged from the tub when her skin became wrinkled. Madlen laughed at the sight of her fingers. "I hope that goes away."

"Don't give it a thought; after you've emptied a bottle of spiced wine, your fingers will look like they usually do."

Madlen smiled. Her hands—in fact, her entire body—had never been this clean, even after scrubbing with soapy brushes before treating a pregnant woman. Everything here at Agathe's seemed so foreign. If she had told her relative the real reason for her sudden appearance, she might have forfeited all of this in a blink of an eye. Agathe had received her with a cordiality that she could barely comprehend. She wanted to tell her the truth, even if Agathe decided to throw her back out onto the street.

She told her every detail of what had taken place in Heidelberg, taking small sips of spiced wine and letting it slip down her throat. She started from the terrible moment when Clara burned to death to a few days later when Barbara stood at her door begging for help. She also didn't exclude the prearranged marriage to Heinfried. Agathe didn't speak; she nodded every now and again and from time to time asked a question to make sure she understood her niece exactly. Finally, Madlen ended up telling her about how Andreas, Kilian, and Irma had distracted the guards at the Neckar River bridge so she could escape from Heidelberg.

"Does Jerg know that you're here?"

Madlen gulped. She shook her head slowly.

"And Kilian? Do you think that he'll tell your father?"

"No. Jerg lost a large sum of money because my marriage to Heinfried came to naught. He would probably want to see me hanging from the gallows himself. Kilian knows that. He would never say anything."

"Then you have nothing to fear." Agathe leaned toward Madlen and took her arm.

"Does this mean that I can stay for the time being?"

"As long as you want. From the bottom of my heart, I am so happy that you're here. I'll tell Roswitha that you're the daughter of a close friend. Though I trust her, the fewer people that know the truth, the better."

Madlen nodded.

"Let's continue to call you Maria. And where do we want to say you're from?"

"Speyer?" Madlen suggested. "That's what I told Hedwig."

"Speyer," Agathe repeated. "Yes. Maria from Speyer, welcome to your new home."

Chapter Thirteen

As the days went by, Madlen felt as though she'd never lived anywhere else. She'd never felt so happy and secure. During her first two days, her aunt showed her every corner of Worms; she familiarized Madlen with the peculiarities of the Jewish Quarter and introduced her to her business colleagues. Madlen knew that Agathe had worked many years as a seamstress and she asked many questions about her sewing skills. Agathe did not live on what she'd inherited after Reinhard's death. She'd built up her dressmaking business and made a small fortune. Her aunt was famous in Worms and beloved by all; everyone seemed to have a friendly word for her. Madlen was taken in with similar heartfelt warmth as Agathe introduced her as the daughter of a friend. She often mentioned that she herself had always wanted a daughter. Madlen didn't dare ask why Agathe and Reinhard had never had children. She had no desire to open up old and probably still tender wounds. When Madlen told her aunt on the first night how she had helped Clara with her midwifery work, Madlen thought that she noticed a bit of sadness in Agathe's eyes. Now that she was being introduced as the daughter Agathe never had, Madlen realized how much her aunt's unfulfilled dreams of having her own brood must have hurt.

"Will you show me how to sew dresses?" The women strolled side by side along the open stalls of the marketplace.

"You want to learn how to sew?"

"The women who wear your dresses seem so happy. It's a wonderful profession."

"Well, being a healer, from what you've told me, seems to be much more important."

Madlen waved her hand dismissively. "Oh, what do I really know about healing?"

Agathe hooked her arm in Madlen's, swinging her wicker basket in the other. "Certainly, nobody would have asked for your help if you didn't know what you were doing."

"I couldn't save that baby," Madlen said sadly.

"Even the best healer in the world can't bring the dead back to life." Agathe sighed. "But you were successful in saving the mother's life." She raised her hand when she realized that Madlen was going to object. "Even though it ended badly because that coward murdered her, you should still be proud that you helped her."

"Thank you. It does me good to hear you say that." Madlen stopped. "I've often wondered why all this happened to me. Please believe me, I only ever wanted to help."

Agathe looked at her sympathetically. "I would advise you not to ask yourself such questions. You'll never really find an answer."

"But it's so hard. Sometimes I feel so persecuted, and I don't know why."

"There's much that we don't understand, but in the end it will all make sense."

Madlen couldn't quite accept her explanation, but she was thankful that her aunt tried to encourage her.

"Let's go." Agathe pulled Madlen along as they strolled past the marketplace stalls. "We'll go home, and I will teach you how to make a fine dress."

Madlen smiled. She wondered whether Agathe had a painful experience sometime in her past. She had a feeling that something terrible had happened besides Agathe's husband dying much too early. Still, she didn't dare ask for fear of offending her or, even worse, making her dwell on a tragic event. But Madlen hoped that one of these days she would know what it was that made Agathe the thoughtful, loving woman she was today.

It had taken her two days to sew together the two pieces of linen that would make up her first dress. Madlen sewed every single seam with pride. Of course, she wasn't as good as Agathe, but she would be one of these days.

"You should be very proud of yourself," her aunt said in praise. "I'm sure that your customer will be very satisfied."

"My customer?"

"Indeed. The dress has already been sold to a fine noblewoman. She chose the fabric weeks ago. And look what a fine job you did with the beadwork. A genuinely wonderful garment."

"Thank you." Overjoyed, Madlen hugged her aunt. "I'll sew the seams on the next dress even straighter."

"That's right. Never be content with what you've already done. Always seek improvement with every stitch."

"I can promise you that I will."

Agathe smiled, but suddenly a coughing fit shook her body. Madlen patted her on the back. "Are you all right?" She looked on with concern.

"I'm all right," her aunt uttered, though somewhat distressed. "It happens every now and again." Agathe laid her hand on her chest. "Especially in the evening. My chest feels so heavy sometimes I can barely breathe."

"How long has this been going on?"

"For quite a while. I don't know exactly when it started."

"Has it gotten worse?"

"Sometimes it's worse and sometimes it's better. But don't worry. I'm not really that sick."

Madlen felt her aunt's forehead, a worried look on her face. "You're burning up, Agathe. You should lie down."

"Thank you, but I have too much to do right now. These dresses won't finish themselves."

"Will you allow me to put my ear on your chest?"

"I don't see why, but yes." Agathe spread out her arms and Madlen came closer, wrapping one arm around Agathe's waist and putting her ear on her chest to listen. She stayed that way for a while, until Madlen sat back up again.

"Agathe, you need to lie down. I hear a strange sound when you breathe."

Her aunt turned pale. "And what does that mean?"

"Something in your body is preventing you from breathing freely. We have to try and resolve it. How long did you say you've had this cough?"

"I think it started shortly before the harvest. It didn't happen often at first, but now it's more frequent."

"I believe that you have some sort of infection."

Agathe went weak at the knees. "Can something be done about it?"

"Yes, but we must take action right away. I'll sew the dresses if you lie down. And Roswitha can take care of the herbs with my instructions."

"I'll send for her. What should she bring?"

"Above all, we'll need frankincense."

"Frankincense? We use that in church at High Mass."

"There must be a way to get ahold of it. It will take care of the cough. And then we'll need coltsfoot, a medicinal plant. Its flowers are yellow, and the leaves look like a horse's hoof."

"I've never heard of it."

"You can find it near streams or brooks. It blooms in the spring."

"But in winter you won't be able to find it, right?" Agathe started coughing again.

Madlen made a decision. "I'm sending Roswitha to bring back some frankincense. I'll take care of the coltsfoot myself. All you need to do is lie down. The cold winter air will only make your cough worse. Pull your blankets up to your neck to keep your chest warm."

"All right." Madlen accompanied Agathe upstairs to her bedchamber. "Tell me the truth. Am I going to die?"

Madlen looked at her seriously. It was hard to give an honest answer. "This is a very serious illness, even though it might not feel like it at the moment. Once the rattling sound starts in the chest, it usually gets worse very quickly." She pressed her lips together. "But I know my medicinal herbs better than most people. I won't let anything happen to you."

"Thank you, my dear." Agathe hugged Madlen tightly, then climbed upstairs. Was it because she now knew that the beast lurked in her breast that she took her time, or had climbing those stairs always caused her trouble? As she reached the upper hallway, she gasped and stopped to take a painful breath. Agathe tried to remain calm, but each step she took felt more difficult than the last. She heard Madlen inform Roswitha about the situation and ordered her not to return to the house without the frankincense.

By the time Agathe reached her bed, her heart was pounding against her chest. She'd lost all her strength from one moment to the next. She let herself sink down onto the bed, feeling too weak to even lift her legs so she could lie on the mattress completely. She heard the front door close downstairs.

Now that the house was quiet, she could hear for herself the rattling sound that arose from her chest with each breath. Why had she never noticed that before? Up to now, her cough only bothered her occasionally. But a woman like Agathe rarely heeded a little cough. The thought of her health deteriorating terrified her. Would she die? She wasn't an old woman yet, but at the age of forty, she wasn't young anymore, either. Had she spent enough years on this earth to put her life in God's hands? Was her life really nearing its end? Agathe refused to believe this, but even now, a coughing fit started, this time accompanied by some sort of smelly discharge. She hastily put a handkerchief over her mouth. Agathe braced her upper body so she could at least get a little air. As the cramp in her chest eased off a bit, she sank down powerlessly. She could almost feel death's bony hand reach out and touch her.

Madlen trotted along the harbor up to the meadow that ran along the Rhine within the city walls. She gazed at the thin layer of frost that shrouded the grass, weeds, and other vegetation. In her mind's eye, she could see Agathe's face, which had become more dear and familiar to her each and every day. But the image was juxtaposed with her memory of Clara, who had also treated her with love and kindness. Suddenly, the image of Clara's dress catching fire flashed into her mind. Madlen shook her head to rid herself of those images. Now this terrible thing with Agathe. Though she couldn't help Clara, she could do everything in her power to save her dear aunt's life.

This wasn't the first time that she had heard the cough now racking Agathe's body. In Heidelberg, people said that the traveling merchants brought these diseases overland from their travels up and down the river. This was the reason some townsfolk kept their distance. But they only kept their distance from the merchants—people still happily bought their wares, Madlen noted with scorn. She was convinced that these wares contaminated and spread disease, affecting people, food, and drink alike. In Agathe's case, she wasn't surprised her aunt got a nasty cough considering the variety of people and goods she was exposed to on a daily basis. She lived right on the harbor, where so many foreign ships moored. Everyone there knew her, and often she bought goods directly from the ships as they unloaded their freight. She also sold her clothes all over town and sometimes beyond, for instance whenever she got an order from a traveling merchant who wanted a dress for his wife. Yes, Agathe was exposed to many contagions. It made it all the more important now to do everything she could to help Agathe fight the infection spreading through her body.

Madlen swept her eyes over the ground, bending down from time to time to determine whether she'd found something she could use. She knew almost all the plants and their medicinal uses. Most of them didn't help with coughs; however, they were useful for other ailments. Madlen took everything she thought she might be able to use and put it in her basket. Suddenly her heart beat faster. Just a few steps away, she saw a hint of yellow under the frost. She quickened her pace, knelt down, breathed a sigh of relief, and immediately harvested all the coltsfoot she could find. This herb would make Agathe healthy again; Madlen prayed to God that it wasn't too late.

"Hurry! She's getting worse." Roswitha rushed over to Madlen as she entered the house. "Tell me what to do."

"Put some water on with some milk. We're going to prepare a brew from herbs and oil and rub it on her chest. She must be kept warm, but we'll need to wrap ice around her legs, so she won't get too hot."

Roswitha nodded quickly. "I'll get everything together. You'll prepare the herbs?"

"Yes."

Both women went their separate ways. Roswitha went to the bedchamber carrying towels; Madlen went into the kitchen to prepare the herbs. Roswitha found her, and Madlen showed her how to prepare the brew that Agathe would have to drink immediately, as much of it as possible. It wasn't long before the women entered the sick woman's bedchamber. Agathe lay calmly on her bed, her face ashen.

"Right before you came, she had another violent coughing fit," Roswitha whispered.

Madlen nodded. "Agathe, can you sit up a little so that you can drink?" She held out her cup of herbal brew.

"That's so nice of you both. Thank you." Agathe tried to smile. It was plain to see the coughing spasms had worn her out. With a push, she sat up in bed. Madlen perched next to her and handed her the brew. "It's hot, so drink it in very small sips. It'll cure your cough." Agathe took the drink and immediately began to sip it.

Roswitha left the room briefly then returned with a bowl; it was filled with burning frankincense. She put the vessel next to Agathe's bed and fanned the incense lightly with her hand.

Madlen waited until Agathe emptied the cup and handed it immediately to Roswitha so she could fill it up again with the herbal brew.

"More?" Agathe asked as she sighed.

"Yes, much more," Madlen confirmed. "We need to loosen the cough and get the sickness out of your body." She pulled out a cloth smeared with an herbal paste. "I'll put this on your chest. Breathe deeply, in and out, until you're dizzy. I'll sit here and watch your body. When you get too hot, we'll lay some cold wraps around your calves. It won't be pleasant, but it will help you get better."

Agathe smiled, but worry was written all over her face.

"I know what I'm doing, and I'm going to help you." Madlen touched Agathe's hand. She couldn't say where she found the courage of her conviction but felt it was the truth.

Madlen nursed Agathe late into the night. Even when she wanted to use the outhouse, Madlen insisted that Agathe use a bucket so she wouldn't have to leave the protective warmth of the room. Roswitha went numerous times to conjure up some fresh brew and to fill up and light the small bowl of frankincense. When it got very late, Madlen noticed that Roswitha seemed about to drop dead from fatigue; she was able to finally persuade her to go to bed. Madlen remained by Agathe's side, constantly monitoring her care and wondering why she herself didn't feel the least bit tired. Instead, she wrapped Agathe's chest again with renewed energy, made sure that her body was warm enough, and supported Agathe when she was overwhelmed by a coughing fit or needed to drink more herbal brew, even though it made her throw up. She'd already vomited twice, and Madlen noticed with satisfaction that the vomit as well as the bile had a pungent odor, typical of infection.

"Your body is ridding itself of toxins," Madlen said as she helped Agathe sit up again in bed. "That's a good sign."

"How long do we have to keep on doing this?" Agathe said, glassy-eyed.

"I'm going to make another herbal compress for your chest, and then you should try to sleep. Tomorrow morning, we'll see if you feel better. But you'll need to stay in bed for a couple of days." She expected her aunt to protest, but she didn't. Whether she was simply too weak to protest, Madlen didn't know for sure. She was pleased to hear Agathe breathing steadily again, though she was still wheezing. Still, it was too much to ask for an immediate improvement. Diseases took time to come into the body; they needed time to leave it, too. That's what Clara had always said. In the end, everything was in God's hands. The herbs would help if it was God's will. Madlen was confident. Agathe's body had responded well to the treatments so far.

As her aunt slept peacefully, Madlen had the feeling that everything would be all right. Madlen touched Agathe's body again and again to make sure the fever didn't get too high. She stayed on guard till morning. Finally, Roswitha came and announced that Madlen should sleep for a couple of hours and that she would watch over Agathe. Should things start to take a turn for the worse, Roswitha promised that she would get Madlen right away. And even though she thought she didn't need rest, she fell asleep as soon as her head hit the pillow. Again and again, she woke and listened nervously for noise coming out of Agathe's bedchamber. Anything to indicate that Madlen was needed. But everything remained quiet. Even though she wasn't completely relaxed, at least she got a little sleep. Three hours later, she awoke to a gentle touch on her arm.

"Maria? Can you come?"

"What is it? Is she worse?" She opened her eyes, her heart beating in her throat.

"I don't know. She's complaining about terrible pains."

"I'm coming." Madlen sprang up and followed Roswitha to Agathe's bedchamber. She hurried to her aunt's bed and laid her hand on Agathe's forehead. "How are you?"

Agathe grimaced in pain. "It's my chest. It feels as though someone's pulling a rope around it tighter and tighter."

Madlen lifted her blankets and removed the compress. She carefully wiped off the leftover herbs that had stuck on her skin with a cloth. "Do you feel a little better?"

"Yes, a little."

"That's good." Madlen turned around. "Roswitha, can you please take a wet towel outside until it's nice and cold?"

"Of course." She hurried out.

Madlen turned to Agathe again. "I want to be honest with you. Your chest infection is very serious. But it does seem to be waning. When Roswitha brings back the cloth, we'll lay it on your face so you can inhale the cold deeply. This will cause everything to open up. Then we'll continue with the warm compresses again. It'll be uncomfortable at first, but that's a good thing."

"I trust you." Agathe refused to listen to the voice of doubt that yelled at her from deep inside. This young woman, her niece, had grown so close to her heart. And she knew Madlen felt the same way and would do everything in her power to help her. Roswitha returned to the room with the cold cloth.

"Put it over your face." Madlen covered Agathe's chest with blankets again.

"Just lay it on?"

Madlen nodded. "Give it to me. I'll show you." She took the cloth and slid it over Agathe's face. "Open your mouth and breathe as deep as you possibly can."

Immediately, her aunt did what Madlen told her to do. She took four deep breaths, until a violent coughing spasm erupted. She vomited bile and mucus; she could hardly settle down. Madlen held her close and laid her down softly when the spasm was over. Agathe lay still with her eyes closed. At first, her breathing was short and shallow, but then it became steadier. Finally, Madlen noticed that she'd fallen asleep.

"Make some more brew for her," she asked Roswitha. "We're going in the right direction."

Had she turned around, the doubt written on Roswitha's face wouldn't have escaped her. But Madlen just watched Agathe, breathing deeper and more evenly. Carefully, Madlen laid her head on Agathe's chest. Was she deceiving herself, or did the wheezing noise already sound fainter than it did yesterday? Satisfied, she sat up again and looked at Agathe. "Just have a little patience. I'll make you well again. I promise."

This went on for five more days, as Madlen and Roswitha cared for Agathe without pause. For three of those days, Agathe seemed to be doing much worse. Roswitha begged her to let her send for a doctor. But Agathe forbid it. She trusted Madlen and didn't want the girl to think otherwise. Madlen said several times that she wouldn't be offended if Agathe did send for a doctor. But Aunt Agathe was firm in her resolve. On the morning of the fifth day, something had changed overnight significantly. Upon awakening, Agathe felt much better. She looked at Roswitha, who had replaced Madlen in the early hours of the morning and fallen asleep in the chair next to Agathe's bed. Agathe chuckled, sat up, and laid her hand flat upon her chest. She inhaled and exhaled deeply several times and tried to determine whether this liberating feeling was just temporary or a long-lasting improvement. When Madlen entered the bedchamber, she was surprised to see Agathe sitting up all by herself. Agathe put a finger to her lips to show that Roswitha had fallen asleep. Madlen smiled and touched her on the shoulders gently. "Roswitha, go to bed and lie down a little. I'm awake now and I'll stay here." Roswitha sleepily consented and padded out of the bedchamber, without even looking at Agathe, who gazed at her with amusement.

"You both must be totally exhausted." Agathe stretched out her hand to Madlen, who took it and finally sat on the edge of her aunt's bed.

"You look much better. How do you feel?"

"Better than I've felt in a long time." Agathe took Madlen's hand and pulled it onto her chest. "Feel. It's much easier for me to breathe."

Madlen let her hand lie still for a moment, then bent over and pressed her ear to the same spot. She listened. Her aunt inhaled and exhaled evenly. The rattle was gone. She pushed herself up with a jerk.

"Agathe!" Overjoyed, she hugged her aunt. "I really think we've done it."

"I feel it, too!" Agathe replied. "Oh, my Madlen, I thank you so much. If you hadn't come here, I would never have made it."

Madlen looked at her aunt pensively. "You know, Clara always said that everything happens for a reason. Maybe I had to flee Heidelberg so that I could come here and help you."

"You haven't just helped me," Agathe stated. "You've saved my life. I'll never ever be able to repay you."

Madlen hugged her aunt again. "Oh, Agathe, you've already repaid me many times over."

Chapter Fourteen

Agathe stayed in bed for two more days, able to use the chamber pot by herself and continue working on a dress she'd started before she became ill. Madlen kept her company. The women were chatting when Roswitha came back from the market and stormed into Agathe's bedchamber.

"You're not the only one!" she said, completely out of breath.

Agathe put down the dress. Both she and Madlen seemed puzzled as they gazed at Roswitha.

"What do you mean?"

"I was at the market. All of Worms is abuzz. There's a very severe cough going around." She pressed her lips together. "Several people have already died."

"What?" Agathe's eyes opened wide in surprise.

"Yes, people don't know what to do. They're keeping their distance from each other for fear of infection. Even physicians don't have a remedy for it. I heard many say that it's a punishment from God."

"Sit down, please," Madlen said as she stood and offered Roswitha her chair. "Take a deep breath and tell us again—this time calmly."

Roswitha gratefully settled down with a loud sigh. Madlen sat down on the edge of Agathe's bed. They looked at Roswitha tensely; she took a moment before continuing. "I didn't tell anybody that you also had a cough," the maid quickly assured them. "But from what I heard, it always starts with a cough, then they bring up phlegm, and finally their chests constrict more and more, until they suffocate and die."

"But I'm not dead. It doesn't have to be that way."

"When so many are infected, it's not just a cough," said Madlen thoughtfully. "Agathe, you said that you noticed your cough sometime shortly after harvest?"

"Yes."

Madlen studied her. "It was probably just a slight cough, which is fairly common. But what you suffered over the last several days must have been new."

"Can't you help these people? You were able to do it with my mistress here."

Madlen was about to speak when Agathe held up her hand. "Maria is not a physician. How do you think a doctor would react when a young woman familiar only with the use of medicinal herbs is able to heal those he cannot?"

Roswitha lowered her head. "But won't people die if the doctor refuses to use the herbal remedies?"

"Roswitha's right. I have to do something."

Agathe raised her eyebrows as she gazed at Madlen. "Many years before you were born, I had a dear friend. She also practiced the art of herbal medicine and helped many with their female problems."

Madlen gulped. She knew where Agathe was going with this.

"One day," Agathe went on, "someone begged my friend for help. She did everything she could to save the woman, but in the end, she couldn't. They blamed my friend for her death. If she hadn't fled, she would have been hanged."

Roswitha put her hands up to her mouth in horror. "That's terrible. Whatever happened to her?"

Agathe kept her eyes on Madlen as she answered Roswitha's question. "She had to be clever; now she leads a totally different life. As far as most know, she's probably dead."

Madlen nodded, almost imperceptibly. She understood her aunt's warning; she could not make the same mistake twice. "Agathe's right. It wouldn't be smart to get mixed up in this. And I likely wouldn't be able to help anyway. It was God's will that my herbs were able to cure Agathe."

Her aunt seemed relieved. "So that settles it. We'll pray for the sick and let the doctor help them."

"We can't do anything at all?" Roswitha kneaded her hands. "There are so many I know who are ill."

"Let's allow the doctor to do his job. I'm sure it will be fine," Agathe said, trying to calm the maid.

Tears welled up in Roswitha's eyes. "Sander is sick. I talked with Mechthild, his sister. She doesn't think he can be helped."

Madlen searched the maid's face. "You love this Sander?"

Roswitha nodded and covered her mouth and nose with a handkerchief as she tried to suppress her sobs.

Madlen looked at Agathe earnestly. "What if I don't go myself, just prepare brew and compresses for Roswitha to take care of this Sander herself?"

Roswitha looked up and threw her mistress a desperate look.

"Do it," she said tersely. "But you"—she pointed at Roswitha—"you must swear by all that's holy that you'll never say a word about who prepared the remedies. Swear it!"

"I swear it, mistress. Never will one word cross my lips."

"Then you two better hurry along. If you're going to help Sander, you must do so quickly."

Madlen and Roswitha immediately sprang into action. In the kitchen, there was only a bit of herbs and frankincense left. Madlen scratched it all together, prepared the brew and the paste, and immediately smeared it onto the compress.

"You have to find more frankincense; I'll go replenish the herbs." Madlen noticed Roswitha's eyes, now red from crying. She took a step toward the maid and gave her a short, reassuring hug. "Don't worry. You have to trust that everything will be fine."

Roswitha nodded but didn't say a word. She was too scared that the man she loved and wanted to marry would be lost to this treacherous cough. She thanked Madlen, gathered everything she needed, and left the house. Madlen placed a cloak over her shoulders, picked up a knife and a basket, and left shortly after. She would need some time to collect enough coltsfoot. She looked up at the sky. Thick snowflakes fell soundlessly to the ground. Only a few people were at work around the harbor; everything seemed quiet and peaceful. She pulled the hood of her cloak over her head. Since so much snow had fallen in recent days, she'd have to sweep the entire meadow to find any vegetation at all. She sighed. *Even rain would have been better. Snow covers everything.* She pushed the thought aside, tightened the laces of her hood under her chin, and trudged resolutely through the wintry weather.

It took Madlen several hours to gather enough herbs, scavenging every piece of recognizable vegetation for its medicinal properties. She was overjoyed when, near the base of the city wall, next to a small stream fed by the Rhine, she found a large patch of coltsfoot. She carefully snipped each plant into her basket and kept searching until it got too dark and she decided to go home. She sincerely hoped that this new bunch of herbs would suffice to heal Sander. Otherwise, she would need to find a spice merchant, and she still wanted to keep a low profile.

When she arrived back at Agathe's home, she didn't see Roswitha anywhere. Upon entering her bedchamber, Madlen saw that her aunt had dozed off while sewing. She snuck out and immediately went to work in the kitchen. As soon as she finished, Roswitha came through the front door.

"How's Sander?"

Roswitha's cheeks glowed red from the cold winter air. "He's not doing very well. Mechthild is with him now; she's making sure he keeps the compress on. He could hardly keep any of the herbal brew down. He vomited over and over again."

"Remember how it was with Agathe. It's a good sign that his body is fighting the infection."

Roswitha had tears in her eyes. "I'm so afraid he will die."

Madlen pointed at the compress, now filled with the herbal paste she had finely crushed with her mortar and pestle. "It's ready. You should take it back to him now."

All of a sudden, Roswitha stepped toward Madlen and grabbed her hand. "I know that my mistress would not approve, and I am asking much of you, but could you come with me? To assess his condition?"

Madlen stepped back with a start. "But I'm not a doctor. I will only see the same thing as you, believe me."

Roswitha sobbed. "It doesn't matter whether you're a physician or not. One look into the eyes of a patient is enough for you to know whether you can help him or not." She paused. "You can tell whether it's already too late."

Madlen held Roswitha close as she wept. "Don't worry. Your Sander is going to get well. You must believe." The maid's whole body trembled.

"Agathe's sleeping. I'll go with you and see what I can do for Sander."

"Thank you!" Roswitha hugged Madlen's neck and kissed her on the cheek. "I'll never forget you for this."

"Let's go. We don't have much time."

***

Darkness fell swiftly as the two women sped through the streets of Worms with their baskets. After a couple of short knocks, a young woman opened the door. When she recognized Roswitha's face, she let them both in.

"This is Maria," Roswitha said, and the woman nodded politely. "She can help Sander."

"I will try," Madlen clarified. She was uncomfortable giving Roswitha any false hope. Silently, Mechthild led them into a dark room, where Sander lay on a narrow bed. The pungent smell of incense and herbs permeated Madlen's nostrils as she entered.

"My name is Maria. Will you allow me to press my ear against your chest?"

The patient seemed too weak to answer, his body racked by violent coughing spasms. Maria approached and listened intently. But this was different than it had been with Agathe. "His heart is beating too fast and he's burning with fever. Roswitha, soak some clean cloths with water and lay them outside. We'll need to wrap them around his legs, otherwise the inside of his body will cook." Sander twitched uncontrollably, and with each spasm he arched his back. "We have to calm him down." She remembered how she would mesmerize laboring mothers to relax. "We'll need a candle," Madlen said.

Mechthild threw Roswitha a short, anguished look, but Roswitha nodded and went out. When she came back, she held a flickering candelabra.

"Prepare the compress," Madlen ordered, and the women left the room.

She closed her eyes and tried to calm her breathing, radiating confidence and tranquility. Sander needed that more than anything else.

"Sander," she began, her voice full and sonorous. "Open your eyes and look at the candle."

He didn't react, his body continuing its uncontrollable spasms of coughing.

"Sander." Her voice sounded even deeper now. "Open your eyes. Open them."

His eyelids flickered as he tried to obey.

"Very good. Look at the flame. The candle will calm you." Slowly, she swayed the candle back and forth. It took a moment, but she noticed that his eyes followed the flame. "Very good," she repeated. "Look at the flame, Sander. The candlelight will give you peace and quiet." His gaze followed the candle as she moved it from right to left. Madlen thought back to that very first birth. She had recited psalms then, and those same words were the first to occur to her.

"Hail Mary, full of grace, the Lord is with thee," she said, her voice sonorous as she moved the candle. His eyes kept following the light, his body relaxing little by little. "Blessed are you among women and blessed be the fruit of thy womb, Jesus." She realized how inappropriate these words were for a sick man but pushed the thought aside and continued. She was satisfied to note that Sander became quieter as she spoke the words of the Holy Scriptures. She couldn't remember everything she'd said, but Sander lay still, his eyes following the candle. He was stable.

Roswitha entered the room and paused when she took in the scene. Madlen continued to speak in a calming tone. "Now we'll be wrapping your legs; the cold compresses will do you good and soothe your body. You'll enjoy the coolness and feel better." Roswitha understood that these words were directed at Sander, but were also instructions for her. She pushed aside the blanket, uncovered his legs, and started wrapping them.

"This will do you good, Sander. Keep looking into the flame. Holy Mary, mother of God, pray for us sinners, now and at the hour of our death. May Almighty God have mercy on us. He forgives us our trespasses and leads us to eternal life. The Almighty and Merciful Lord pardons us and forgives our sins."

Roswitha carefully lowered Sander's legs and covered him again.

"Close your eyes and sleep a little, Sander. Close your eyes."

He let his eyelids slowly close; his head fell to the side.

"Very good." Madlen got up from the edge of the bed and gestured to Roswitha to leave the room with her. She took the candle. Quietly, she shut the door behind them and blew out the flame, placing the candle on a narrow shelf. The women walked down the hall to an adjacent room, where Mechthild stood before a small stove, stirring the contents of a cast-iron pot. She turned to look at them.

"He's sleeping now, which is good," Madlen explained. "The coughing spasms have slowed, but they could start again as soon as he wakes."

"How did you do that?" Roswitha said, gazing at Madlen.

"What do you mean?" Madlen felt uncomfortable. She knew that she'd made an unusual impression by holding the candle like a priest and reciting psalms.

"When I left the room, he could not lay still for even a second, and when I came back, he'd changed completely."

Madlen thought through the best way to explain what she'd done. "I had to calm him down," she said, somewhat helplessly. "That was the only idea that occurred to me." She wondered whether the woman would throw her out. "What would you have done?"

Roswitha's and Mechthild's perplexed faces told her that this emergency explanation had done the trick. "I'm just glad that it worked. Now we need to reduce the fever and let his body discharge the sickness. Is the fresh brew ready?"

"Yes." Mechthild turned back to the kettle and fanned the steam rising out of it. "Shall I serve up the next batch now, or wait?"

"We should let him sleep for a while," Madlen decided. "I'll tell you exactly what to look for. Then I'll go."

***

Less than an hour later, as Madlen walked back to Agathe's house, a thought crossed her mind. She'd seen the frightened look on Roswitha's face when she entered the room to wrap Sander's legs with the cold compresses and saw Madlen chanting. What did she think of her now? That she'd cured him with some kind of secret magic? This line of thinking could be dangerous for Madlen. She was annoyed with herself for going against Agathe's advice. Hadn't she sworn to never again help someone and put herself in harm's way? How could she be so stupid? Hadn't she learned a thing from the destruction of her former life? Her heart beat in her throat when she opened the door to Agathe's house.

"Maria, Roswitha? Is that you down there?"

"I'm here," she shouted upstairs. "I'm coming right up." She barely had enough strength to drag herself up the stairs, but she had to tell her aunt the truth. Hopefully, she would not be too cross. She entered hesitantly. Agathe sat in bed, working on a dress draped over her legs. She looked up and stretched out her hand as Madlen entered.

"There you are. Where were you for so long?"

Madlen cleared her throat. "I was with Roswitha at Sander's house." Madlen waited for a scolding, but Agathe only smiled sweetly.

"That's what I thought. How is he?"

"You're not angry?"

"Come, sit next to me." Agathe tapped on the bed and waited until Madlen sat down next to her. "Why should I be angry at you? It's simply your nature to help others. Naturally, I would like you to listen to me and be more cautious, but I understand."

"I thank you so much." Madlen was relieved, although the look on Roswitha's face popped back into focus. "But it would have been better if I had listened to you."

Agathe looked at her seriously. "What happened?"

Madlen described the whole scene to Agathe as accurately as possible. "I discovered this method quite accidentally when I attended my first birth," Madlen said.

"And do you use it often?"

Madlen shrugged. "Only when I think it might help."

"You didn't try it on me when I lay devastated by coughing spasms."

Madlen smiled. "You were calm and responding well to the treatments."

"I understand."

Madlen hesitated. "Do you think that I should explain what I was doing more clearly to Roswitha?"

"Only if she asks. If I were in your place, I would treat it as a normal part of the process."

"It is for me."

Agathe smiled. "For you, yes. But you wouldn't have told me about it if the look on Roswitha's face didn't alarm you."

"Yes, that's true."

Agathe grabbed Madlen's hand. "Don't worry about it too much. When Sander is cured, it will be clear to Roswitha that you were the only one who could have saved her sweetheart's life. Nothing more and nothing less."

"I hope so." Madlen sighed. "Well, let's not talk about it anymore. How are you?"

"I'm wonderful. I haven't had this much strength in many weeks."

"I'm so glad." Madlen bent over and laid her ear on Agathe's breast. She heard only calm, even breathing, nothing that caused concern.

"And what is the healer's prognosis?" Agathe asked, as Madlen stood.

"I'm really quite satisfied," Madlen said, looking at her seriously. "Maybe tomorrow I'll allow you to get out of bed."

Roswitha didn't come home that night nor by noon the next day. Though Madlen was very worried, she hesitated to return to Sander's house. On the other hand, she feared that Roswitha might herself be at the mercy of the infection.

"Since Roswitha isn't here, I'll need to go to the market myself," Agathe said. "Will you accompany me?"

"Do you really want to go out again so soon? I can go alone."

"No, my darling. I'm completely healthy again; I feel fine. It's time to go back to work and I need some new goods."

"Fine, I will go with you."

An hour later, as they went past the market stalls, Madlen's mind drifted elsewhere. She thought about Roswitha and how she only had Mechthild's help to fight for the life of her beloved. Did this shy young woman know enough? Could she make the necessary assessments for a successful treatment? Madlen made a decision.

"Agathe, would you be too upset if . . ."

"If you went to Sander's house? Of course not."

There was much that Madlen wanted to say, but she settled on just one thank-you. She gave her aunt a quick peck on the cheek and ran off to Sander's house.

She knocked and waited. Nothing. She knocked again, at first just once, then again and again. Finally, she turned the doorknob and walked in.

"Roswitha? Mechthild?"

She heard Sander coughing in the adjoining room. She quickly walked over to the room and stepped in. She saw Roswitha, her eyes filled with tears, as she held Sander, newly racked with coughing spasms. "I'll take him!" She grabbed Sander under his arms and pulled him upright with a jolt. Again and again, she jostled him up and down. "Get some water," she ordered Roswitha. She trembled all over, uncertain whether to leave Sander's side. "Come on!" Madlen snapped, and immediately Roswitha ran out. A moment later, she was back.

"When I lift him up again, you need to pour water down his throat." Madlen strained to pick Sander up and signaled to Roswitha. She put the cup to his lips; some of the water ran down Sander's throat, the rest ran down the corners of his mouth. "Again!" Madlen ordered and Roswitha obeyed. They both kept trying until the cup was empty, then Roswitha went out and filled it back up again. When she returned, Sander looked a lot better lying down again on the bed. Although he still coughed, he sounded like he was getting air again on his own. Trembling violently, Roswitha looked at Madlen and sobbed. "I thought he died."

"He wasn't far from it. What happened?"

"I fell asleep," Roswitha said tearfully.

"Where is Mechthild?"

"She had to go to work."

"Why didn't you send her to me? I would have come."

Roswitha burst into tears. "I wanted to, but Mechthild said that there wasn't anything more you could do. And I didn't want to leave him alone."

"I'm so sorry, Roswitha. I should have come sooner. But I thought . . ." She stopped in midsentence. She had to remain level-headed.

"How much frankincense is left?"

"It's all gone." Roswitha sobbed again. Madlen laid her hand on Sander's chest. His whole body shook from within. If she wanted to do something for him, she had to do it fast. She pulled her hand back, approached Roswitha, and held her shoulders.

"You have to go and pick up more frankincense. Do you still have enough of the herbs that I gathered?"

"Yes, but I couldn't prepare a fresh compress because I had to stay by his side. Is he going to die because of me?"

"Just go pick up some frankincense; run as fast as you can. I'll take care of everything else."

Roswitha hesitated, glancing at Sander. Madlen guessed what she was thinking. "He'll live if you come back quickly. Today is not the day that we let anybody die."

Roswitha nodded, turned on her heels, and fled the house. She didn't even put on her cloak.

Chapter Fifteen

It was four full days before Madlen left Sander's house next. In that time, she thought more than once that death would win the day. Sander's coughing spasms were far worse than Agathe's had been. Madlen learned a lot about how the illness ran its course. She wasn't certain whether the cough wasn't only one symptom of a broader illness people had contracted. By chance, she found that the herb vervain helped the body drain and drew out fluid, an excess of which prevented the patient from breathing. Every time he sat on the bucket, Sander's body seemed to release more and more of the sickness tormenting his body. As he coughed up phlegm, the rattling in his chest lessened until it was barely audible. After her last examination, Madlen could finally tell Roswitha that he was out of danger. Still, he had to stay in bed for at least two more days, for his body to recover completely.

She returned to Agathe's house exhausted but happy. Roswitha had gone back and forth to keep her current on Sander's condition.

"Agathe? I'm home."

Aunt Agathe walked out of the kitchen into the hall. "Thank the Lord!" She went to Madlen and hugged her warmly for several minutes. She pulled away when she heard a knock on the door.

"Wait here." Agathe went to open it. "My God, Otilia, what's happened?" She let the sobbing visitor in, tears streaming down the woman's face.

"Is she here?" Otilia looked past Agathe.

"What?"

"Is that the healer?"

"Please, whom do you speak of?" Agathe tried to keep her voice even as her heart beat nervously against her chest. How did Otilia know that Madlen might be the healer?

Otilia shoved past Agathe and went directly to Madlen. As soon as she reached her, she fell to her knees and grabbed Madlen's hand. "Please, Maria, if that's your name, please help me. It's my daughter. She has the cough. You have to help her." She stayed on her knees and twisted toward Agathe. "Please, Agathe, I'm begging you. We've known each other for so long. You know that my Reni is a good girl. She's never hurt anybody. And now she's sick, so sick." She turned again to Madlen. "Please, help me. I'll give you everything that I have."

Madlen was embarrassed to see this strange woman kneel in front of her. What should she do?

"Please, Otilia. Get up." Agathe helped the visitor stand. Only with another nudge did she let go of Madlen's hands. "Come, Otilia. Please sit down and tell us what's happening."

"Please," she pleaded again. "There's no time. She's going to die, Agathe. My Reni is going to die."

Agathe struggled to keep her composure. "How did you hear that we could help you?"

"Mechthild. She said that her brother also had the cough. And now he's healed." She pointed at Madlen. "She healed him."

Madlen didn't know what to say, staring at her aunt helplessly.

"She's not a healer, Otilia. She . . ." She was at a loss for words.

"Please, Agathe," Otilia begged. "What have I done to you? Why would you let my Reni die?"

Agathe made up her mind. "Does anybody know about this?"

"No, only me." Otilia looked beseechingly between the two women. "Now I understand. You're afraid. You're afraid because the doctor can't help but she can." Otilia pointed at Madlen again. "You're afraid of the consequences if somebody accuses her of miracle healing."

"There's no such thing as miracle healing," Madlen clarified. "It's the herbs, just the herbs, nothing more."

"Then will you help her?" Otilia's voice sounded hopeful. "I promise you, I swear that I'll tell no one. I'd rather die. I beg you. Please help my Reni. She's all that I have."

A quick glance between Agathe and Madlen was enough. "I'll go fetch my herbs," Madlen said. "I need frankincense, though. Send your maid to Mechthild's brother. Roswitha will be there. She can bring the rest of the herbs; they should help."

Otilia nodded. "I thank you so much!"

"I don't know whether I can save your daughter," Madlen said, trying to prepare her for the worst. "But I'll do everything I can."

Otilia's eyes welled up with tears again. Agathe went to her chest and took out her cloak. "I'll come with you. Two sets of helping hands are better than one."

Neither Madlen nor Agathe could say how the news spread through all of Worms. But wherever a cough occurred, cries were raised on high for the healer. Although no one knew where she came from, who she was, or where she lived, someone knew someone else who could contact the mysterious woman. Madlen never got more than a few hours of sleep, and Agathe tried to throw them off track with false addresses. Madlen couldn't save all the sick people, there were just too many. And she had to be careful not to reveal her identity; she didn't want to risk being discovered. Agathe had heard rumors that a physician paid two men to discover the healer's identity. So far, Agathe could rely on the secrecy

142

of those Madlen had saved. For her own protection, Madlen began to wear a mask when she visited the sick. Not only did it keep her from getting infected—though she seemed to be immune—no one could see her face, thus protecting her from being recognized. Agathe even kept away completely, continuing to lead her life as normally as possible. She convinced Madlen, despite her heavy work schedule, to accompany her to the market or to customers to give the impression that she was nothing more than the daughter of Agathe's good friend, who helped her produce fine dresses. But she didn't delude herself. The rumors that there was a woman who could cure the cough that had plagued many towns and killed hundreds of people spread far beyond the borders of Worms. Time and again, people came with their patients in ox-drawn carts, seeking the healer, their last and only hope. The never-ending city wars and accompanying unrest kept the local governments from having enough time to take care of the problem. As soon as the Rhine alliance became victorious, independence would cause Worms, just like other Rhine cities, to finally answer to the king and gain freedom for the realm. There would be a city tour. Certainly, the top city leaders wouldn't risk Worms's reputation and endanger commercial transactions with rumors of an alleged healer. One way or another, powerful men would want to ensure that Madlen was snuffed out.

She also worried about something she had learned accidentally two days before. It was only a rumor, but her experience proved there was usually some truth to them. Disturbed by the idea of miraculous cures, the Church sat up and took note of the healer. In recent years, the Church had given up more and more power to the princes. It was said that Pope Urban VI had become increasingly upset about the Church's dwindling power. The city wars only fortified the political power of kings and princes, angering him even more. The local bishops knew all too well that the Church had begun to lose its lambs. So the Pope carefully calculated a plan to endorse the establishment of more universities. At least this way, he could have a voice demonstrating his benevolence as well as emphasizing the deeper meaning of the Church's religious tenets. Since the cough was quickly becoming an epidemic, it could very well be the spark that ignited a wildfire. However, the Church seemed bent on manipulating these events for its own purposes.

Agathe noticed men who asked too many questions had been surfacing in Worms lately. Initially, she figured that these minions acted on behalf of the doctor, but they acted so conspicuously that everyone seemed to know to remain silent. Worms's doctor had lost significant prestige. The prevailing opinion was that he didn't know his trade. As such, citizens stubbornly insisted on finding out more about the healer, who had saved the lives of so many people. The physician, in contrast, bled his patients, then sat back and watched them die. But now a new threat loomed over Madlen, one significantly more alarming than the quack's spies. Apparently, there was a man in town hired by the Church to scope out the possible existence of a healer. Agathe tried to learn more, but no one seemed to have more information about this man's identity. The only thing that Agathe could find out was that he was a high-ranking citizen and a confidant of the archbishop of Trier.

"It's too dangerous," Agathe warned. She sat down with the completely exhausted Madlen, who listlessly shoved some bread and cold roast beef into her mouth.

Madlen took a sip of spiced wine to wash down her meal. "You're right. I can't fight this anymore. It's simply too much."

"Everyone in town is talking about you, and who knows who else. It's only a matter of time before someone discovers you. The people only protect you because they still expect you to help them. What if you cure them and then these same people need money? What would keep them from turning you in?"

"Do you really think that someone could do that to me?" Madlen shook her head helplessly. "And I'm careful. I only come when they themselves have purchased the exact herbs we'll need from the spice merchant. And nobody knows exactly when I'm coming. I never promise anyone anything."

"Except for Mechthild and Otilia. They know who you are."

"I saved Mechthild's brother and Otilia's daughter. You don't really think they'd tell anybody?"

Agathe shrugged. "Life has taught me that most people are capable of anything given the right circumstances. Maybe they'll be thankful until the day they die, maybe not. No one can say for sure."

"So what should I do?"

Agathe scrutinized her niece. In the last few weeks, she'd gotten very little sleep, sometimes none over a period of two or three days. She was pale and had dark circles under her eyes. It was obvious that she would soon collapse from exhaustion. "From today forward, you will not treat anyone else," Agathe said firmly.

"What?"

"You heard me. I'll spread a rumor that a young woman fled on a ship leaving Worms in the middle of the night."

"And you think people will believe that?"

"People always believe what seems to be the most likely story. A young woman sneaks onto a ship in the middle of the night. She didn't want to be found, but somebody saw her. From that moment on, the secret healer will never be heard from again. Not even her patients will hear from her again."

"But if I don't treat them, many will not make it," Madlen protested.

"Then they will die." Agathe nodded. "There will never be a right time for you to stop. You said it yourself: there are too many, and there are more every day. No matter how much you try, you can't save them all. But if you don't stop, they will find you. There are many people trying to track you down; each passing day increases your risk."

Madlen stuck a piece of meat in her mouth and chewed. She saw the faces of the people she had helped. If she stopped, many would not escape the disease with their lives.

"It's the only way," Agathe stated emphatically.

"You're right," Madlen finally said. "I don't want to run away from here to escape punishment." She lowered her eyes. "Although I haven't done anything wrong. It's our leaders who are in the wrong."

"Of course," Agathe agreed. "But they have the power, not us." She put her hand on Madlen's. "When you've finished eating, go right to sleep. Early tomorrow morning, you'll wake after a good night's rest, and your only task will be to help me sew. Can we agree?"

It hit Madlen hard, but she knew it was the right thing to do. "Yes, Agathe. I promise. It means a death sentence for some, and their glassy eyes will haunt me for a long time, but I feel relieved. I can sleep. Sleep and take care of everyday things. As terrible as it sounds, I'm glad this burden has been taken off my shoulders."

"Don't forget about all the people you've already helped. Enough for an entire lifetime."

Madlen turned her cup in her hands. "Have you ever wished for a different life?"

"What do you mean?"

"Something other than being a seamstress?"

Agathe smirked. "Once, yes. At that time, I was helping Reinhard with his fishing."

"You fished?"

"Sometimes. More often, it was simply a matter of carrying boxes, selling at the market, mending nets, and scrubbing boats." She smiled at the memory. "Reinhard was a good man, but when he died I sold everything and started a new life. I switched to the seamstresses' guild; there were too few in Worms. With the proceeds from the boat and fishing equipment, I bought cloth and sewed my first dress. At first, I had only two dresses for sale at market, but eventually word spread." She opened her arms wide. "Once I'd built up a base of clients, I had enough to afford this house." She didn't mention the rich patron who had given her enough money for a license. She had done a lot more for it than just sewing clothes. But she was embarrassed today by what she had done to achieve her dream of being a seamstress. When Gerald, as he was called, had died a year earlier, he'd willed her a considerable fortune so that she could live a carefree life.

"I thought you inherited this house from Reinhard after his death."

Agathe smiled, and Madlen could see a bit of pride sparkle in her eyes. "No, my darling, I earned this house. Actually, I live very well as a dressmaker. Now to get back to your question: yes, there were times in the distant past when I wished I led a different life, and I got my wish; it's the life I lead today."

Madlen nodded. Her aunt had pulled herself up on her own, and doing what she loved. Could there be a better existence? "Have you ever thought about marrying again?"

Agathe shook her head. "Sometimes, when I was alone, the thought did occur to me that it might be nice to have a man by my side again."

"But you haven't found anyone?"

"Well, let's just say I haven't found one that I liked well enough. You know, a woman is considered helpless without a man. At least, that's what people say. Well, I was able to take care of myself and live the way I wanted. Why should I give all that up just to be with a man?" She shook her head again. "No, it's not for me." She searched Madlen's eyes. "But you wouldn't have asked me this if there weren't something else that you longed for. What is it? Can you tell me?"

Madlen hesitated and let out a loud sigh. "I know it will never happen."

"Why not?"

"Because I'm a woman. I'm only a maiden, but I would love nothing better than to learn to read and write." She stopped.

"And then?"

Madlen looked deep into Agathe's eyes and grabbed her hand. "I have no greater wish than to study medicine at the university. To listen to the words of the wisest men in the world. I would like to learn about all different kinds of illnesses, and how to heal them. Properly. Not only because I'm familiar with herbs and have observed the sick. No. I would like to be among the brightest scholars so I could ask them questions and learn how to lay my hands on a sick body and make it healthy." Madlen's heart beat so hard that she thought it would jump out of her chest. She pulled her hand back. "But I'm just being silly, aren't I?"

"Oh, no. You are not." Agathe looked at Madlen in a different light. "I know many women who understand their husband's craft better than their husband does. But nobody has ever done it. Unfortunately, it's impossible for you to go to a university. At the mere uttering of this desire, most people would think you've lost your mind."

"I know," Madlen said softly.

"But I do think it's possible for you to learn how to read and write."

"Really?" Madlen said, eyes wide with excitement.

"I know a man, a young monk, to be exact. We speak quite often when I collect donations for the Church. He's a truly open-minded man. It's hard to imagine that he dedicated his life to God. His name is Brother Simon. We've often talked about the fact that there can be no greater happiness than for a person to learn to read and write."

"And do you think he could teach me? Me?"

"Well, Brother is not very religious in the traditional sense. He accepts donations to benefit the community instead of investing the money in outdated religious rituals."

It occurred to Madlen that she'd only spent a few coins of her money when she traveled here; in fact, it had barely been touched. She could use it to learn how to read and write.

"I see what you're thinking. I'll take care of the donation."

"But as I already told you," Madlen replied, "the advocate gave me back the money that I'd paid him. I could also—"

Agathe held up her hand to silence her. "You'll be glad to have something to fall back on one day. Just let me handle this. I'll speak with Brother Simon, and we'll come to an agreement. If this is your fondest wish, I want to ensure that you learn how to read and write. And the sooner the better."

Madlen jumped up and hugged her aunt so tightly that she almost fell off her chair. "You're smothering me," she croaked with a grin.

"Thank you so much. For everything!" Madlen kissed her aunt on the cheek.

"You are the daughter that I always wanted." She waved her off. "And soon, my daughter will read and write."

Chapter Sixteen

"Brother Simon, may I introduce you to my foster daughter, the woman we talked about."

Madlen bowed politely.

"A woman with a great thirst for wisdom, or so I've heard. I'm so happy to meet you."

"It's so kind that you've agreed to help me." Madlen nodded in deference to the man in the simple brown robe. He was handsome, so very different than she had imagined a man in the service of God would be. In Heidelberg, the men who had dedicated their lives to the Lord were mostly weak old men. Brother Simon, not much older than Madlen herself, had nothing in common with them.

"Well, your foster mother can be very convincing, as you know." He smiled at Agathe. "It would be my pleasure to teach you. Do you have any experience with reading or writing?"

"Unfortunately, no."

"Then we'll start the same way I learned. I only ask you to be patient with yourself and don't give up. The Lord helps those who believe in him and in themselves."

"I'll be very industrious and learn as much as I can, that I promise you."

Brother Simon led his visitors into a room lined with bookshelves that reached the ceiling. "As you can both see, we have more books than any one person could read in a lifetime. How often would you like to have your lessons?"

"As often as possible." Madlen glanced at Agathe briefly. "Of course, I have to tend to my duties as a dressmaker. But I can make myself available in the evenings."

"I will come to your house every other day. I would prefer to teach there, where it is quieter. If we discover that every other day is too much, we can adjust."

"That would be wonderful." Madlen nodded excitedly. She looked for reassurance from Agathe, who smiled almost imperceptibly.

"Good. Then we're agreed."

"Brother Simon!" Madlen turned as a man's deep voice called out from the door. "There you are. And I see you have visitors. I hope I'm not interrupting anything?"

The man's gaze moved from Madlen to Agathe and finally back to the young monk. He took another step into the room. "Allow me to introduce myself. My name is Johannes Goldmann." He bowed graciously.

"Goldmann?" Agathe said. "I think I know your parents. Isn't Elsbeth your mother?"

"Yes, and my father is Peter."

"Ah, the council member. Yes, I know them both well. Your mother often buys dresses from me. My name is Agathe, and this is my foster daughter, Maria."

Madlen curtsied quickly. The man was a good two heads taller than her and towered over Brother Simon. His hair was the color of spring wheat the likes of which she'd never seen before. He had a powerful build, with wide shoulders. She would have pegged him for a craftsman, not the son of merchants. He was older than Madlen, but not quite thirty.

"This is, indeed, a rare pleasure." Johannes couldn't take his deep-blue eyes off of her.

Brother Simon cleared his throat. "What can I do for you, Johannes?"

"Ah, yes, what did I want?" Johannes kept looking at Madlen; embarrassed, she smiled and looked at the ground.

"Johannes?" Brother Simon persisted.

"The priest," he spit out. "I'm looking for the priest. Have you seen him?"

"He'll be in the church, readying everything for Mass. Go on."

"Thank you." Johannes smiled at Madlen. "It was a special joy to meet you. Do you come here often?"

She shook her head. Agathe finally broke the silence. "Johannes, please send my heartfelt greetings to your parents." She stepped behind Madlen and laid her hands on her shoulders. "Maria is also a seamstress, by the way. Perhaps we'll see you again when your dear mother comes to purchase another dress from us."

"I will deliver your greetings." Johannes bowed. "If I remember correctly, she spoke only yesterday about ordering a new dress." He grinned broadly, and Madlen couldn't suppress a chuckle.

"Well, we would be delighted to welcome you, too, when your mother comes to make her fabric selection."

"Thank you kindly." He bowed once again and touched his hand to his forehead as if wearing a hat. "I wish you a wonderful day. Ladies, Brother Simon." And with that, he left.

Madlen was elated, her cheeks red with excitement as they returned to Agathe's house. They strode arm in arm, chatting cheerfully yet making sure no one else could hear what they said. "I'm so excited that I will finally learn to read and write. I would have never thought it possible. Have you ever seen so many books? What are they about? Do you think that there will also be medical books?"

"It seems you can barely think straight from happiness. It's wonderful to see."

Madlen squeezed Agathe's arm. "I'm so thankful to you."

"Are you happy because of the books, or for some other reason?"

"What do you mean?" Madlen wondered.

"As if you didn't know. I thought that Johannes's eyes would pop out of his head when he saw you."

"Yes, I noticed that," Madlen admitted with embarrassment.

"How could you have not? The poor man forgot what he was there for."

Madlen giggled.

"His father is a powerful man in this town. He sits on the council, and he's the spokesman for the merchants. Still, don't expect too much. I may be well-known, but the Goldmanns are in the upper class; we are far beneath their social standing."

Madlen waved it off. "That doesn't matter to me. Right now, the most important thing is my lessons."

"That's as it should be, although Johannes is a very handsome, educated young man. If I remember correctly, his mother told me that he's a lawyer."

"The last lawyer I knew, Andreas von Balge, was also a very nice man, but the circumstances under which I made his acquaintance still give me chills."

"I can very well understand that. But you needn't stop living your life."

"I won't." Madlen held up her head as she continued to walk arm in arm with her aunt. "I'll learn to read and write. How many literate women do you know?"

Agathe shrugged. "None, as far as I know."

"You see. This will open up all sorts of opportunities. And even if I never become a doctor, I will learn everything I can from their books, written by the best and wisest people on earth. I will become so smart, Agathe."

"You already are."

"You know what I mean. I'll know more than anyone you or I know."

"The question is, what will you do with all this knowledge?"

"I'll cure every disease known to man." The words sprang out of her mouth, and she recognized her error.

Agathe stopped abruptly. "I thought you understood that's not possible for you."

Madlen stammered, "Yes, of course." She looked around and whispered, "I'm not going to be a healer anymore. I promise you."

"But you just said something completely different." Agathe refused to budge.

"I only meant that I'll know how to cure people. Nothing more." She pulled on Agathe's arm. "Come now, and forget what I said. I'm going to keep my promise."

"Good! And don't you ever forget that."

"No, I won't forget." Madlen assured her, but neither she nor Agathe actually believed it.

"He's already been here?" Agathe looked at Madlen in surprise. "But he must have come here directly after meeting us."

"I don't know." Roswitha shrugged. "He only told me to tell you that Elsbeth Goldmann and her son will be here tomorrow for a new dress."

Agathe laughed. "Now we're earning our daily bread because of your charm." She patted Madlen's cheek lightly.

"But Brother Simon is also coming tomorrow," she argued. "I won't even have time to greet Johannes and his mother."

"Then this young man will be disappointed." Agathe handed her cloak to Roswitha, who carried it away. "On the other hand, the fine fellow seems persistent. I don't believe this will stop him from arranging another meeting."

"His mother will soon have more clothes than she could ever wear," Madlen gushed. She played with a strand of her hair. "I almost hope that he and Brother Simon are not here at the same time."

"Our little girl has taken quite a shine to someone," Agathe teased.

"Perhaps," she replied, then kissed her aunt's cheek and ran upstairs to her bedchamber.

"It won't be long until mealtime," Agathe called after her, as the overjoyed Madlen spread out her arms, fell onto her bed, and gazed at the ceiling. *Reading, writing, and Johannes.* She wondered what would become of it all.

Even though she didn't want to admit it, she took more time the next day to fix her hair. She also wore a brand-new dress, which she'd received from Agathe just yesterday evening, to her great surprise. She picked up her needle and thread and continued to work on a dress before putting it away just seconds later to pick up some new thread or sip her drink.

"Well now, why so restless?" Agathe couldn't suppress her smile.

"It won't be long before Brother Simon gets here." She pressed her lips together. "Then I won't be able to see Johannes and his mother."

"You'll see them some other time," her aunt replied serenely, without looking up.

"But . . ."

"But what?" Agathe let the dress fall onto her lap. "Didn't you tell me just yesterday that you longed for nothing more than to learn how to read and write? If that's true, you shouldn't place so much importance on the appearance of a man. I don't want to say that only one or the other is possible, but if you are so easily distracted from achieving your fondest wish, then maybe it wasn't so important to you after all."

Madlen pressed her lips together. "I'm sorry. You're right. I got carried away."

"It's perfectly acceptable for you to make plans to see Johannes. He likes you. But don't think that you can have everything at the same time." She wagged her finger at Madlen. "Believe me, that will not happen."

"I hope you're not angry with me."

"Of course not. Why would I be?"

"I disappointed you."

"You haven't," Agathe clarified. "You are the one who must choose what's really important. But," she said, holding up her finger again, "you really have to decide. Otherwise, the money I gave Simon will go to waste."

"I want to learn how to read and write. That's what I've always wanted."

"Then focus, and do not let yourself be swayed."

"I assure you I won't, Aunt Agathe. I'm so grateful."

A knock at the door made Madlen turn her head. She heard Roswitha open the door. Holding her breath, she listened vigilantly; it was two voices, a man and a woman.

Agathe got up from her chair. "Come. The Goldmanns are here. Let's greet them together." She gestured to Madlen, and they went into the hall.

"Elsbeth, how wonderful to see you." Agathe held out her hands.

"Agathe, my darling. The pleasure is all mine."

Madlen snuck a look at Johannes as the women greeted each other. He was tall, even taller than her own brother, Kilian. One look at Elsbeth was enough to know that he looked much like his mother.

"And this must be your Maria?" Elsbeth nodded and smiled at Madlen, curtsying as she lowered her head.

"I've heard so much about you, child," she said, glancing at her son; his attention was focused on Madlen.

"Let's go to the fabric room. I recently acquired a gorgeous Byzantine silk, which would complement your lovely eyes just perfectly," gushed Agathe.

Before Madlen could follow them, Johannes took her by the arm. "Must you join the fabric selection?"

"Why shouldn't I?" Madlen's eyes sparkled in amusement.

"Well, you could keep me company and tell me a little about yourself. Where do you come from? You have never visited Worms before, as far as I know. I'm certain that I would not have forgotten you."

"How often do you come with your mother to select fabrics?"

He grinned. "Never."

"Then how did you know that I would be here?"

"Hmm, a clever defense for which I have no argument."

"A legal expert that cannot argue his case? Isn't that unusual?"

"So, you've been asking about me?"

Madlen felt as if she'd been caught red-handed. "No, my aunt mentioned it."

"Your aunt?"

Madlen's face went beet red. "Well, she really isn't my aunt," she explained quickly. "But she was such good friends with my mother for such a long time that my mother often referred to her as my aunt."

"Oh, I also refer to my father's best friend as my uncle Max."

"Then you know just what I mean."

They gazed at each other without saying a word.

"Can I offer you something, kind sir? A spiced wine, perhaps?"

"I thought you'd never ask." He raised his right eyebrow.

Madlen giggled. "I've never seen that before."

"What?"

She pointed at him. "Someone able to lift just one eyebrow."

"Does it amuse you?" He lifted his eyebrow again, making Madlen burst into gales of laughter. Then someone knocked on the door.

Madlen turned around. "Please wait." She went to the door and opened it. "Brother Simon, come in."

"Greetings to you, Maria." His gaze fell upon Johannes, clearly astonished to see him. "And to you, too, Johannes."

Madlen considered both men. Then she turned to Johannes. "Please forgive me, but I must take my leave with Brother Simon."

"May I ask the purpose of your visit?" Johannes scrutinized Simon.

"I'm teaching Maria the meaning of the Holy Scriptures." He held up a book.

Johannes frowned. "What a shame. May I be so bold as to accept your offer of spiced wine some other time?"

"I would be absolutely delighted." Madlen smiled warmly.

"Would tomorrow be acceptable?" He lifted his right eyebrow again.

"That would be perfect."

"The same time? Or will there be another lesson in the Holy Scriptures?"

"No, not tomorrow."

"Good. Now, I will help my mother choose her dress fabric." He grimaced and went toward the room that Elsbeth and Agathe had disappeared into.

"Shall we?" Madlen pointed to the dining room, where they both took their places at a large wooden table.

"I hope that you're not upset that I took some liberties with the truth," Simon began. "Not everyone would understand why a young woman would want to learn to read and write."

"It suits me just fine," Madlen confessed.

"Good." Brother Simon took out a piece of parchment paper and slid a pen and inkpot over to Madlen. "Let's begin." He opened up the Bible. "Do you see these letters? Try to write them on the parchment." Madlen's hand shook a little. Then she picked up the pen.

Chapter Seventeen

In the next few weeks, Johannes was at Agathe's house so often that Roswitha had to plan meals to include one more person. Madlen and Johannes spent practically every free minute together. Sometimes it even bothered Madlen when she had to break away for another lesson with Brother Simon. But she was curious, absorbing everything he showed her. Soon she was able to read complete sentences. Writing, however, was significantly harder. Agathe watched with joy as Madlen blossomed, even as she noted her anguish when the news of more fatalities spread. But since her solemn promise to her aunt, Madlen didn't even visit any of the stricken, let alone heal them. Secretly, she missed it. But being an accomplished dressmaker, learning to read and write, and spending time with Johannes pleased Madlen so much that she could successfully chase away those gloomy thoughts. One night, as she lay alone in her bedchamber, unable to sleep, she teared up when she thought of her beloved brother, Kilian. Her longing to see him seemed overpowering. What wouldn't she give to spend just a single moment with him again?

"Can you ever imagine moving away from here?" Johannes asked, holding Madlen's hand in his as they sat on a boulder near the Rhine.

The snow had melted weeks ago, and sun rays beamed down, announcing the coming spring.

"Out of Worms?" Madlen gazed at the harbor. "No, not really."

"And if I must go?"

"Must you?"

Johannes shrugged. "It's possible."

A shiver ran down Madlen's spine; she didn't know what to say.

"Maria. Would you come with me?"

She shrugged. "I can't."

He laid a finger on his lips. "Would you consider coming with me as my wife?"

She looked up, her eyes wide open in surprise. "Do you mean it?"

"Yes, I want to marry you."

She pressed her lips together as she thought it over feverishly. "What do your parents say? We're not in the same social class. And what about Agathe?"

"Don't worry about my parents or Agathe. Do you want to marry me?" Johannes searched her face.

"Yes," she whispered.

Overjoyed, he pulled her close, kissed her, wrapped his arms around her, and squeezed her tight for several minutes. Again and again, his lips sought hers, until neither one of them could breathe.

"You've made me the happiest man in the world."

They sat there for a long time. Only when it got dark did Johannes bring Madlen home. They said good-bye with a long kiss at the front door. Madlen finally broke away from his embrace and went inside. As she closed the door, she giggled when she heard Johannes emit a cry of jubilation.

"What's so funny?" Agathe said as she stepped out of the sewing room.

"Agathe." Madlen hugged her aunt's neck. "I'm so very happy."

"I'm glad. Can you tell me why?"

"Johannes wants to marry me." Madlen was almost a little scared what her aunt's reaction would be. But after a split second, she shouted joyously.

"Really?" She hugged Madlen and hopped up and down with her. "I'm so thrilled for you. He is a wonderful man. I'll give you a dowry. Maybe not as much as a person of his standing might expect, but enough." The women embraced again happily.

"Thank you so much." Madlen gave her aunt a peck on each cheek. They shared the news with Roswitha when she came out of the kitchen.

"You deserve to be happy," Roswitha said as she stroked Madlen's hair. "And if my Sander doesn't ask me soon, I'll sort him out good and proper."

That evening, the women drank so much spiced wine that they suffered terrible headaches the next day. But even that wasn't enough to diminish their joy. They imagined the wedding celebration, along with the proper dress and the food that would be served. Only for a second did the thought occur to her that Johannes didn't even know her real name. Would this be her downfall? She didn't want to think about it. She wanted to enjoy the lovely moment.

"But we'll miss you so much here," Agathe said with a smile.

"Why?" Madlen seemed puzzled.

"Well, you'll be living in your new husband's house."

"I never even thought about that." Madlen's expression became serious. "But I don't want to leave."

"That's part of married life."

Madlen seemed pensive. "But I can still keep on sewing dresses, right?"

"Of course. You're a very talented seamstress."

"Then I'll spend my days here and go back to Johannes in the evening."

"I don't think it's that easy," Roswitha warned. "Who's going to run the household when you're always here?"

"A maid?" Madlen suggested stubbornly.

"We shouldn't worry about this. The most important thing is that you have a man you love. You do love him, right?"

Madlen's face turned red. "More than I can say."

The wedding took place just two weeks later. It wasn't too lavish, just a nice gathering at the Goldmanns' house, focusing on the young pair instead of fostering business contacts, as was often customary in these social circles. Johannes needed a few days to persuade his parents to give him their blessing to marry a woman below his family's social standing. When they agreed, Madlen was overjoyed. Her only regret was having to lie to everyone about her past. She had talked about this for a long time with Agathe, and they both came up with a detailed, though false, history of Madlen's life that they would strictly adhere to.

Johannes agreed, per Madlen's request, to get a foothold as a lawyer in Worms. So far, it had been difficult because of the ongoing city wars. People had little reason to have their legal affairs clarified when the decision could become invalid under the next leader. So Johannes contented himself by assisting his father with business negotiations; he was also quite happy to spend time with his new wife.

When Madlen first stepped into Johannes's bedchamber on her wedding night, she was very nervous and insecure. Shouldn't this be one of the happiest moments of her life? Finally, she could be as close to Johannes as she had secretly wanted over the past few weeks. But when the time came, she would have liked nothing better than to rip open the door and run away.

He put his finger under her chin and kissed her tenderly. Madlen stood frozen, unable to return his kiss or lay down in her new husband's arms.

"What is it?" He looked at her in wonder. "Did I do something wrong?"

She shook her head; no longer able to suppress her shivering.

"Are you cold?"

She shook her head again.

"Have you lost the power of speech?" He wrinkled his brow. Finally, he broke out into a large smile.

"I don't know . . ." She paused.

"Do you love me?"

"Of course, I do."

"Good. Then everything will take care of itself."

To her surprise, he walked over to a chair next to a window. He took off his shoes, then his hose, and finally his doublet and shirt until he stood completely naked. Madlen hardly knew where to look. Without hesitation, he walked over to the bed. Only when he slid under the covers did she look at him again.

"We're married, but that doesn't mean that I'm going to force you to do anything. If you want to stay where you are, you can. If you want to stay dressed or lie next to me here, you can do that, too. Do whatever feels comfortable."

"Are you angry with me?" She was on the verge of tears.

"Why would I be angry?" He tapped on the other side of their marital bed. "Though it would be easier to talk if you sat here. I promise I won't try to get nearer to you unless you say so."

She sat on the bed shyly.

"That's better." He smiled. "I've never met a woman like you. Heaven forbid that I would ever do anything to hurt you. I love you, and you say you love me, too."

"I love you with all my heart," she whispered.

"Do you remember the day on the river when I asked you to marry me?"

"Yes."

"We sat there for a very long time. You leaned on me, and I held you in my arms."

"I remember."

"Would it be better if you leaned on me, and I simply held you? Nothing more."

Madlen took off her shoes and slid closer to Johannes until he put his arms around her.

"That's nice." Madlen sighed.

"I think so, too."

They were quiet for a while as Madlen stroked his arm tenderly. "Can I get under the blanket? I'm cold."

Without a word, Johannes lifted the blanket. His nakedness made a shiver go up and down her spine. She moved closer to him, and he put his arms around her again. Madlen's skin tingled. She felt her heart beat faster. She wanted to slide her hand down his naked body. She felt his breath on her ear, and she tilted her head to the side to kiss his neck. His body tensed and he cuddled up closer. Madlen turned until he loosened his embrace and their lips met. They kissed each other tenderly, and Madlen began to explore his body with her fingertips. He let it happen, then stroked her dress, gently massaging her breasts. Suddenly, Madlen jumped out of bed and stripped off her clothes. She took great pleasure in seeing how much her nakedness excited her husband. He slid down lower and lifted up the blankets. Madlen accepted the invitation, pressing her body tightly against her husband's. Their hands slid over each other, and Madlen enjoyed it in a way that she would have never thought possible. Johannes slid down deeper, then kissed her breasts, letting his hand glide down to her crotch. She did the same, felt his stiff member, and her desire became so intense that she drew his pelvis closer to her. He lay over her, breathing heavily. Slowly, his manhood inched inside her as Madlen groaned. She lifted her pelvis, forcing him to push himself in even further. His slow, deliberate thrusts grew faster. Johannes took possession of her and she embraced him, pulling him in even deeper. After several strong thrusts, she felt him release himself inside her. He dropped his head on her breasts for a moment; then he lifted his head to gaze into her face.

"I love you," he breathed and kissed her on the mouth. Then he rolled underneath her, took her in his arms, and held her tight.

Everything around Madlen spun so much that it made her dizzy. She had only one desire: for this moment to never end.

Chapter Eighteen

"You're what?" Madlen said, her eyes wide. "But Roswitha!"

The maid looked at her with tears in her eyes. "I know." She sobbed violently. "We're not married. It was a weak moment."

"And what does Sander have to say about it?"

"That's the problem. He doesn't want to hear about it."

"What's that supposed to mean? It's his child, too."

Roswitha howled. "He says I'm not the right woman for him."

"And he realizes this now that you're pregnant? What a pig." Madlen snorted with rage.

"He never intended to marry you? Or not now, under the circumstances?" Agathe asked.

She howled again and shook her head, not saying another word.

Madlen put her hand protectively over her stomach. She'd been married to Johannes for a little over three months now. A few weeks ago, she felt a change in her body for the first time. Her menstrual cycle had stopped, and she woke up every morning feeling sick to her stomach. Sometimes it was difficult to reach the large washbowl before she threw up on the floor. Initially, she'd been too shy to tell Johannes, which was just as well because she wanted to be sure. Still, he had observed her as she remained sitting on the edge of the bed, too dizzy to stand, and he saw her stomach gradually softening. When she finally shared the joyful news, he was so thrilled that he hugged her almost too tightly, whirling her around.

It was with a heavy heart that she now learned of Roswitha's desperate condition. She'd been blessed with such luck since she'd been forced to leave Heidelberg, though she still missed her brother. But what hadn't she gained in Worms? Aunt Agathe was one of the kindest people she'd ever met. She knew now that the resentment her father harbored for Agathe was his alone. Then there was the opportunity to save so many lives, to learn so much. And now she could read, though writing was still hard for her. Finally, she had found love and happiness with Johannes, for whom she carried a child. Could there be anybody in the world who led a fuller life? It seemed unfair that so much had been given to her as Roswitha sat sobbing because she had trusted the wrong man.

"What do you want to do now?" Madlen stroked Roswitha's head lovingly, sinking into the chair in front of her.

"I don't know." She sobbed. "No one will want me now. I'll have to raise this baby by myself and die alone."

"You shouldn't say things like that," Agathe cautioned. "I always wanted children, and the Lord saw fit not to give me any."

"I want children, too, once I have a husband," Roswitha said with tears in her eyes. "But I don't have one, just this bastard in my womb from a man who would have died if Maria and I hadn't helped him."

"It's a shame," Agathe agreed, sparing Roswitha a scolding for giving herself to a man before marriage. It wouldn't change anything now. "But it's useless to cry over it." She laid her hand on Roswitha's arm. "You can continue to work here. Neither one of you will go hungry. And one of these days, you'll meet a man who won't mind that you made a mistake."

"We all know that won't happen. I've been used and discarded. And that's how everyone in Worms will see it."

"But if you go away, we won't be able to help you," Madlen argued, baffled that Roswitha would seek salvation outside the city.

Roswitha continued to sob. "I can't have this baby!"

"You have no other choice," Agathe sighed.

Roswitha looked up. "That's not true." She looked at Madlen for a long time. "You know how to do it, don't you?"

A shiver ran up and down Madlen's spine. "No."

"But it's my only hope," Roswitha pleaded.

"I don't know how." Madlen looked at the floor.

"You know." Roswitha's face went dark. "I asked you how you knew to calm Sander with a candle. You said that you had seen it done at a birth. I knew even then that it wasn't the whole truth. You know about woman problems. I never revealed to anyone who the secret healer was, even when everyone in town searched desperately. You can help me get this bastard out of my womb. Do it!"

Madlen's face turned red as she looked at Agathe helplessly.

"How dare you!" Agathe sprang out of her chair. "This is how you thank Maria for saving Sander, because you said that he was the love of your life? You should be ashamed of yourself."

Roswitha howled. "Please, forgive me! I'm so sorry. I'm desperate. Please!"

Madlen's cheeks got red; her heart beat quicker. Roswitha had threatened her. She had felt safe in this house, but now her throat closed up just thinking about being found out. She stared at Agathe.

"Maria and I are on your side. I forgive you because I can under-stand your desperation. But you'll regret it if you ever threaten either one of us again. Whether you have a baby or not, I will throw you out of the house and leave you lying in the dirt. I'll make up a nice story, accusing you of theft, or even worse. Do you hear me?" Agathe's eyes sparked with anger.

"I'm so sorry," Roswitha murmured.

"As you should be." Agathe lifted her head. "Look me in the eyes. I want to see that you know how serious I am." Agathe was enraged.

Roswitha didn't dare look at her mistress. "I'm so sorry."

Agathe regained her composure and scrutinized Madlen. Her niece pressed her lips tightly together. It was clear to see that Roswitha's words had scared her.

"I'm too upset to continue with you right now," she said harshly. "Go in the kitchen and see about your duties."

The maid got up, her legs shaking. "Please, please, forgive me."

"Go! I don't want to see you right now."

Roswitha lowered her head, sobbing as she ran out.

"I'm scared," Madlen said, when Roswitha was out of hearing range. "What if she tells somebody?"

"She won't." Agathe nodded in the direction of the door. "The only ones who know your secret are Sander; Mechthild; her mistress, Otilia; her daughter, Reni; and Roswitha. I've known Otilia for many years now. She and her daughter wouldn't say anything. As far as the others, I can handle them if need be, but I'm sure that won't be necessary. Roswitha was looking for a way out. Sometimes people say things that they don't mean in desperate times."

"I hope so. What if Johannes finds out?"

"You will have to lie, and very convincingly," Agathe stated simply. "If the rumor comes up and he or another member of his family says something to you, laugh. What nonsense! You're a seamstress. That's all."

Madlen's heartbeat calmed down, yet her fear lingered. The idea of losing everything made her shudder.

Agathe read her mind. "Nothing will change, believe me." She patted her niece's hand. "Having said that . . ."

"What?"

"If it were really possible for you to gather herbs that would purge Roswitha's womb, it would fix many things."

Madlen froze.

"Even though no one admits it, our Roswitha is not the first and won't be the last woman who goes against God's plan and gives herself to a man before marriage. Roswitha could find someone else to give her something. But she might be in better hands with you."

Madlen admired Agathe for continuing to look out for her maid. Would she herself have mustered such magnanimity on a day like today?

"I think I can help her."

Agathe nodded. "Good." She winked. "But we won't say anything just yet. She needs to calm down a bit and think about what she's done."

The rest of the day, Roswitha scurried through the house as quiet as a mouse, minding her duties; she didn't say a word to either Agathe or Madlen, who tended to their dressmaking as usual. In the afternoon, Brother Simon came by for a lesson, but she was hardly in a condition to focus on her studies.

"You seem distracted," Brother Simon pronounced. "Is there something the matter?"

"It's nothing really." Madlen put her hand on her stomach. Brother Simon's face brightened.

"Is that what I think it is? Are you expecting?"

Madlen smiled. "It's still very early on. Please pray that the Lord sends us a healthy child."

The monk nodded. "That is the greatest gift the Lord could ever give. Blessed be thy womb."

"Thank you."

"Would you prefer to end our lesson for today? I believe it's proving to be of little value for you."

"Yes, I think we had better leave it."

He stood. "Of course. I'll be back as usual in two days, but it won't be too long before there will be nothing else I can teach you."

"I can't believe that, but I'm thrilled that I've made so much progress."

Brother Simon pushed his chair under the table. "Until next time, take good care of yourself."

Madlen smiled and showed him out before entering the sewing room where Agathe worked. "Brother Simon's gone."

"So. Did you learn much?"

"Not really. My mind was elsewhere. Roswitha's words kept going through my mind. Brother Simon thinks I'm distracted because I'm expecting."

"So, you told him?"

"He guessed."

"Would it calm you to speak to Roswitha again?"

"Yes, please."

Agathe loudly summoned Roswitha. She must have been crying for hours. Her eyes were red and her eyelids swollen. She came to the table shaking. Agathe indicated with a nod for her to sit.

"Did you think about everything?"

Roswitha nodded but didn't dare look at either woman. "I deeply regret it." She put her trembling hands on the table and kneaded them nervously.

"We still want to help you," Agathe continued in a soothing tone. She was tempted to lecture the maid once more, but decided to let it go.

"Really?" Roswitha looked up.

"Yes." Madlen took a deep breath. "Although we forgive you, don't you dare do anything like that again!"

Agathe looked over at her niece in surprise. She would have never thought her capable of such ferocity. Still, it was good for Madlen to have her say.

"Of course not." Roswitha shook her head.

"Good. Now we must take care of this difficulty."

The maid looked up, hopeful.

"If you are sure, I can give you something that will purge your womb."

"Really?" Roswitha's eyes opened wide. She looked between Madlen and Agathe.

"Yes, but it will be painful, very painful. And sometimes women bleed profusely, but their unborn children continue to grow in their wombs."

"Then what?"

"We can try the herbs first. Should that be unsuccessful, there is another way." Madlen took another deep breath. "We can remove it, but it's not going to be pleasant. You need to be prepared."

"Nothing can be worse than this bastard in my belly, which I am doomed to hate."

Madlen bit her lip to keep from speaking. The hatred with which Roswitha spoke of her unborn child made her stomach twist.

"It must be done as quickly as possible. The spice merchants arrive tomorrow. We'll go to the market and buy the herbs together. If all goes well, it will take between three and five days for the womb to expel the baby."

"Thank you." Roswitha lowered her head. "I know that I don't deserve your help."

"In the future, think about what you're getting yourself into," Agathe warned. "We'll help you this time, but I will not tolerate this in my house again."

"You must know." Madlen held her chin. It was difficult to say. "Even if everything goes well, some women are unable to have children in the future."

"What?" Roswitha's eyes widened in shock.

"It doesn't happen often, but it can happen."

The maid chewed on her fingernails. "But I want children. One day."

"You have to make a decision and live with the consequences." Agathe gave her a serious look.

Roswitha gulped. "I want to do it." She bit her lower lip. "Maria, will I know afterward whether I can have children?"

"If we use only herbs, there's no danger. However"—she hesitated—"if we turn to more extreme measures, anything's possible. But yes, I'll know after."

"And you'll tell me right away?"

"Yes, I promise you."

It took four days to prepare everything. Madlen searched a whole day for decaying wheat, which forms an ergot fungus. This fungus combined with arnica and a large amount of rosemary and sage would cause cramping and bleeding that would lead to a miscarriage. After Madlen had mixed everything together, she prepared a warm brew for Roswitha, which she drank in one big gulp.

"What happens now?" She looked at Madlen nervously.

"Carry on as you normally do. Walk as much as possible. In a few hours, I'll prepare some more brew. But nothing will happen today or tomorrow, other than slight discomfort. As soon as you feel your stomach cramping, sit in a warm bath. That will intensify the contractions. At that point, you shouldn't leave the house. I'll stay with you and see it through."

Roswitha's entire body shivered as she held her hand out to Madlen. "I'm afraid."

"I know, but nothing will happen to you. I'll look after you."

Roswitha broke out into tears. Madlen took her in her arms until she calmed down again. "Come on. We're going for a walk. Tell me something about yourself."

***

Over the next few hours, the women walked up and down the stairs, moving throughout the house, carrying out their ordinary duties. Madlen tried to distract Roswitha as best as she could. Agathe sat quietly in her sewing room. She didn't want to be a part of what was happening. Even though she was the one who suggested the procedure, it was still repugnant to her: a God-given life would meet its end through no fault of its own.

Roswitha drank four large cups of brew all day into the evening. The disgusting herbal concoction made her feel sick. She couldn't feel any changes yet, only dread of what was to come. After returning home late that night, Madlen slept restlessly, as Johannes snored next to her. She had lied to him and said that Agathe had more dress orders than ever before. She would need to go back to work early in the morning. Johannes reminded her not to wear herself out in her delicate condition. Besides, it was no longer necessary for her to work. Her husband earned more than enough, but Madlen insisted on continuing, and Johannes didn't want to force her to stop. When their first child was born, she would have to abandon her sewing anyway. He could bide his time until then.

The next morning, Madlen left early to go to her aunt's house. Roswitha was already in the kitchen; Agathe was still sleeping.

"How are you?" Madlen asked as soon as she entered.

"Unchanged."

"I told you it would take several days."

"I can hardly wait"—she pointed at her stomach—"for this to be out of my body."

"You have to be patient. Is the water hot?"

"Yes."

"Good. Then I'll prepare another cup right away."

"It tastes disgusting."

"Yes, but this is surely the lesser of two evils: a disgusting taste versus having a baby out of wedlock."

"Yes, please excuse me. I don't feel well."

"But you don't have pain yet, right?"

"No. It's more like a heart-pounding fear of the unknown."

Madlen stirred up the ingredients. "It's ready."

"Thank you."

"Remember to move as much as possible."

"I will."

"I'm going to the sewing room. Come get me as soon as you feel something."

Roswitha nodded. "Thank you so much."

"All right." Madlen had a bad feeling as she left the kitchen. She'd watched Clara administer herbs for a miscarriage more than once, but as soon as Clara gave them the herbs, the women got dizzy and went off to their own devices. They only came back if there were difficulties. But Madlen was restless while waiting for Roswitha to lose the baby. She continued to work on a beautiful dark-blue dress, which she hoped her mother-in-law would like. Johannes had placed the order, but he said yesterday that there wasn't any hurry now that Agathe and Madlen had more work than usual. She hadn't responded, not wanting to compound one lie with another.

Madlen had already been working for several hours when Agathe entered the sewing room. "Good morning. How long have you been here?"

"Quite a while," Madlen said as she put down her sewing. "You look pale. Didn't you sleep well?"

"No. I was thinking the whole time about Roswitha. She may have a big mouth, but she didn't deserve this. Please, do everything to keep her healthy."

It did not escape Madlen's attention that her aunt spoke of Roswitha's health. It was still difficult for Agathe to accept what they had done.

The women spent the whole day together, with no change in Roswitha's condition. They all strove to avoid the topic as much as possible. Everything remained calm. At the end of the day, Madlen embraced both Agathe and Roswitha as she said her farewells and promised to be back early the next morning. On the way back to her marital home, she said a silent prayer that the Lord wouldn't let anything happen that night.

When she opened her eyes the next morning, her first thought was Roswitha. Today was the third day of treatment. From Madlen's previous experience, something would occur today or, at the latest, tomorrow. When she worked with Clara, they had only performed a handful of these procedures to terminate an unwanted pregnancy. She sincerely hoped that the herbs would suffice and that it wouldn't be necessary to force the baby from the body. Johannes rolled over and embraced her.

"Good morning. Do you have to get up already?"

She kissed him tenderly. "You know that Agathe's counting on me. It will only be two or three more days; soon, we'll have everything done." She freed herself from his arms and sat on the edge of the bed. First thing in the morning, she usually needed a little time for the dizziness to subside.

"Come here," her husband whispered.

She stood. "You can get that out of your head," she teased. "I have to get dressed. Sleep a little bit more and dream about me."

"And if that's not enough?"

"It's going to have to be." She laughed, walked to the chair over which she'd draped her dress, and put it on.

"Two days. Whether the dress orders are fulfilled or not, I won't let you out of bed."

"Is that a threat?"

"A promise."

"Good! I'll hold you to that promise." She grazed his lips with a light kiss. "I have to go now."

He growled, turned over, and fell back asleep.

Chapter Nineteen

Yet another day went by, and nothing happened with Roswitha. Everyone's nerves were stretched to the breaking point. As dusk came and it was time for Madlen to go back to her husband, she felt nervous. She feared that the contractions would start that night when she wouldn't be there.

"I think I will go tell Johannes that you don't feel well," she said to Agathe. "I'll say that I would be more comfortable staying here with you for the night."

"I'm relieved, though I didn't want to suggest it."

Madlen grabbed her cloak. "I'll hurry and be right back."

"Thank you," Roswitha whispered, looking pale.

"It's going to be all right," Madlen said as she went to the door. Roswitha followed her and closed the door tightly behind her.

When Madlen arrived home, she learned that Johannes had accompanied his father on a business trip, so the only ones at home were Elsbeth and the servants. She explained to her mother-in-law as quickly as she could that Agathe was feeling poorly and she wanted to spend the night with her.

"I hope it isn't this terrible cough?" Elsbeth asked anxiously.

"No, of course not." Madlen leaned closer to her mother-in-law. "It's women's problems. You know she's at the age now."

Elsbeth nodded knowingly. "I understand. I'll just tell the men that Agathe ate something that didn't agree with her. Can I do anything?"

"No, but thank you for asking." Madlen hugged her, turned on her heels, and hurried back to her aunt's house. She thought about how frustrating it was to wait for the contractions to finally start. It must be so much worse for Roswitha. Madlen put her hand on her stomach. In the last few days, she had thought only about the miscarriage. She didn't want to think too hard about her hand in destroying another life. For her, there was nothing more important than protecting the unborn child in her womb. Would Roswitha regret this one day? After this, she might not be able to have another child. Would she be able to accept that? Madlen was still fretting when she reached Agathe's house. The door was locked from inside. She knocked and called out. "I'm back! Open up!"

An instant later, Agathe opened the door. Madlen saw the panic in her aunt's eyes.

"She's lying down upstairs," Agathe explained. "She's not doing well."

"Did the contractions start?"

Agathe shook her head. "No, but she's crying. Shortly after you left, she told me how afraid she was that the herbs wouldn't work. I tried to calm her, but she wants you to get it out another way."

"That's much too dangerous. More than a few women have died that way."

"Try to speak to her."

"All right." Madlen hung up her cloak and went upstairs. Roswitha lay in her little bedchamber, directly off of Agathe's room. "I'm back," she said softly as she entered.

She heard Roswitha sobbing. "It's simply not working. I beg you to get it out."

Madlen walked over and sat on the edge of her bed. "I already told you that it can take up to five days." She stroked Roswitha's hair tenderly. "Tomorrow is the fourth."

"What if nothing happens?"

"It will happen."

"And when it doesn't?"

Madlen sighed. "We're going to wait two more days. If nothing happens, then I'll get it out."

Roswitha nodded. "I don't think there's another way."

"We'll see. Go to sleep now. Let your womb do the work."

Madlen barely slept a wink as she lay there listening to every little sound. She missed having Johannes by her side, his breath, his smell, even the sounds of his light snoring. In the early hours of the morning, she got up to check on Roswitha. She snuck up to her bed and listened to the maid's breathing. It calmed her to hear Roswitha sleeping so soundly. Whatever worries Madlen had were unfounded. She crept back to her own room and lay down again. She couldn't sleep but wanted to rest a little before night turned into day.

"Good morning." Roswitha came into the kitchen the next morning, as Madlen prepared the brew.

"Good morning," Madlen replied and passed her a cup. Roswitha obediently began to empty it.

"I'm hungry," the maid noted. "Is that a good or bad sign?"

Madlen shrugged. "I don't know. It won't hurt in any case. No matter what happens in the next few hours or days, you'll need all the strength you can muster. So let's eat." She smiled. "I'm hungry, too."

They waited for Agathe and all ate breakfast together. Roswitha had a hearty appetite, and everyone's mood had lightened. After breakfast, they all went back to work. Roswitha cleaned up and stopped by the sewing room to speak to Madlen and Agathe.

"I have to pick up some things from the market," she announced.

"I don't think that's a very good idea," Madlen retorted as she laid a dress on her lap. "You know the contractions could start at any time."

Roswitha shrugged calmly. "I feel good. I don't believe the herbs are working for me. And we need some things from the market."

"Then I'll come with you."

"All right, if that's what you want."

Agathe nodded at both women. "I'd also prefer that you go together."

Madlen got up and went over to the door where Roswitha stood. "We won't be gone long."

They both took their cloaks and were already in the hall when someone knocked loudly on the door. "I'll get it." Madlen was extremely surprised to see Sander. He took off his cap and bowed quickly. "Maria, how nice to see you," he stammered. "I want, um, ah . . . is Roswitha here?"

"How dare you?" Madlen looked at him angrily.

"So you know?" He kneaded his hat with his hands. "Please, I need to see her."

The door opened wider, and Roswitha stepped up next to Madlen. "What do you want, Sander?"

"I, well, can I speak to you?"

"What is there to speak about?"

He threw a look at Madlen. "Can we be alone? I have something to tell you."

"Maria has my trust, and she knows what's happening. I want her to stay here."

"Well, all right, if that's what you want." He stepped from one leg to another. "I wanted to say that I'm sorry. I don't know why I said those things. I was a coward." He looked Roswitha directly in the eyes. "I've thought it over. I was wrong. I wanted to ask if you would still marry me."

Roswitha was speechless as she stood there, frozen in place.

"I can understand it if you decide to send me away, but I . . . I want this, I really do. I mean, especially now because of . . ."

Roswitha stared at him. Sander wanted to marry her. Everything was going to be all right. She could keep the baby. Suddenly, a strange feeling came over her. It wasn't just excitement. This was something else. Her stomach began to cramp, a stabbing pain so fierce that it forced her to her knees. With a cry, she grabbed her stomach. Frightened, Madlen saw the blood creeping to the edge of Roswitha's dress. The contractions had started.

Roswitha screamed in agony as Madlen and Agathe held her on the bed.

"Make it stop!" The maid cringed in pain.

"You have to be strong. The contractions will get weaker. Then you can rest until a new one begins. We're here for you."

Roswitha dug her fingers into the blankets and arched her back. "I can't stand it. It's tearing me to pieces. I'm going to die!"

"You won't die."

"But my baby . . . Please, save my baby. I don't want to lose it."

Madlen looked at Agathe anxiously.

"It's too late for that," Agathe said in a quiet tone that frightened even Madlen.

Roswitha gasped as the contraction faded. She sank back down onto the pillows, her strength almost gone. She cried then grabbed Madlen's hand. "Isn't there anything you can do?"

Madlen shook her head sadly. "No. There's nothing we can do now."

"This is my fault. All my fault. Sander will never forgive me." She sobbed so violently that her whole body shook.

"If he really loves you, he'll marry you despite this. And if it's God's will, he will send you many more children, and you will forget what happened here today."

"But I've killed our child. When he finds out . . ."

"He will never find out!" Agathe hissed angrily. "Only the three of us know about this. You will say nothing, not to Sander or anybody else. Do you hear me?"

Roswitha nodded. Then she felt another cramp. The next contraction was under way. All of a sudden, Agathe grabbed her and pulled her up by her shoulders. "Swear to God and on your own life that you will never tell anyone what happened here. Swear it!"

"I swear it!" Roswitha yelled with all her might; Agathe broke her grip.

Roswitha continued to scream in pain. Madlen laid her hand on the maid's stomach. The contractions were strong. It was almost time.

"I'm going to pull the baby out now," Madlen announced. "Agathe, help me. Sit behind Roswitha and hold her tightly." Madlen pushed the blankets aside and pushed up Roswitha's petticoat. "Put up your legs like so." She put them in the right position. "All right. We're going to wait on a contraction, and then you push as hard as you can. I'll pull it out."

Roswitha didn't see that Madlen had a special hook that she'd laid next to the bed. Her pain was too strong to feel what Madlen was doing. When Madlen gave her a sign, she pushed as hard as she could when the next contraction came. Madlen did what she had to do, then she tended to the bleeding. When it was all over, Roswitha collapsed in exhaustion. She wasn't in any condition to cry or speak.

Agathe stood and let Roswitha down gently onto the pillow as Madlen put the bloody towel and its contents into a bucket. Roswitha's petticoats were still pushed up so that Madlen could see whether she was still losing blood. She was relieved to see the thin trickle grind to a halt. Everything had gone well.

"You can still have children," Madlen said, though she couldn't be sure.

The maid didn't react at all.

Madlen cleaned up everything as well as she could. She replaced the cloths under Roswitha until there was no more blood. She washed her hands and helped the maid change her undergarments. Finally, she covered her up. Roswitha was totally exhausted.

"Sleep a little. Sander will be downstairs. I'll tell him that you had a miscarriage."

"Yes." Roswitha touched Madlen's arm. "I won't say anything, I swear. This is all my fault. I know that you only wanted to help me."

Madlen was relieved, especially since Roswitha had pleaded with her to save her child. Madlen had felt frightened and desperate at the same time. A life had been wiped out; a child had died. No matter how many mistakes she'd made in her life, this was definitely the biggest. In the future, she would stay away from people who needed her help. No more herbs, no more healing. She would sew and be happy with her husband and child. Nothing more.

"Were you serious when you said that I could have more children?"

"Yes, everything's all right." She knew that she could be lying, but she wanted to make things easier for Roswitha. "And I must tell you something else."

"What?"

"The baby . . . it wasn't like it should have been. You would have lost it anyway. The herbs accelerated the process but had nothing to do with it."

"Really?" Roswitha's face lit up. "Do you mean that I didn't do anything?"

"No, you didn't. It might have been already dead for days, maybe weeks. Neither you nor I had anything to do with it." She smiled. "It was good that you drank the herbs. Otherwise, your body would have been poisoned by it."

Roswitha broke out again in tears, this time tears of joy. "I thank you."

Madlen bent over so that she could hug her. "But you need to sleep now. Agathe and I will speak to Sander. And if he doesn't want to marry you now, you can be happy that he's gone."

Roswitha smiled and shut her eyes. Madlen went over to Agathe, and they spoke quietly. The women left the room together.

"That was very clever of you," Agathe whispered as the women closed the door behind them. "You and I are the only two people who know the truth. It's better this way."

Madlen took a deep breath. "Let's go talk to Sander."

"I hope he's smart enough to only ask about his future wife's health. He may have survived that cough, but he won't survive my wrath." Agathe stomped off, and Madlen couldn't resist a smile.

Sander was waiting for them downstairs. He'd been pacing up and down the hall, his concern for Roswitha written all over his face.

"Sander," Agathe began. "I'm so sorry. Roswitha lost the baby."

"How is she?"

"She is fine," Madlen said. "We were able to stop the bleeding."

"Why did she lose the baby?" He gulped. "Was it the sheer shock of seeing me?"

Madlen held up her hand to quiet him. "That didn't have anything to do with it. It was neither you nor her. The child just wasn't healthy, so her body rejected it."

"So what will you do now that you don't have to marry her?" Agathe's anger was evident as she raised her eyebrows.

"Can I see her?"

"Yes. She's asleep now, but she'll be happy to see you when she wakes up."

"Thank you." He looked at Agathe. "If she still wants me, I would like to marry her," he said. "And I'll treat her well."

"I would highly advise you to do so," Agathe said, her tone softening. "Not everyone gets a second chance to make things right. Think about that."

"I thank you both." He looked from one woman to the other. His gaze remained on Madlen. "I can't even imagine what would have happened if it weren't for you, Maria. First, you saved my life, now you saved Roswitha's. How can we ever repay you?"

Madlen smiled. "It's all right. Go. Your future wife needs you now."

He nodded then strode hurriedly upstairs, taking two steps at a time. Madlen heard him say Roswitha's name softly as he entered her room. Then he closed the door. She looked at Agathe, and they fell into each other's arms in relief. They could put this all behind them now.

Chapter Twenty

"I need to speak to you." Johannes gave Madlen a serious look when he came home and gave her a quick kiss on the forehead.

"What happened?"

He led her into the dining room of the Goldmann house, a room that could seat twenty people and was sometimes used for city council meetings. "Sit down."

"You're scaring me. What is it?"

"Have you ever heard about the secret healer?"

Madlen opened her eyes wide and turned red. Her heart beat wildly, and she was barely able to say a word. "What?" she croaked.

"I need to tell you something, and I hope you won't be mad at me."

Madlen just stared at him. What would happen now?

"I returned to Worms to be with my family." He held her hand. "Before that, I lived in Trier and worked as a Church lawyer. Do you know what that is?"

Madlen nodded; she couldn't bear to wait any longer to hear what Johannes knew about her secret.

"Rumors started some months ago about a woman with healing powers. She could expel diseases from the sick with the use of special herbs, but it also required the souls of innocent children. She had powers that only the devil himself could have given her."

"I don't understand."

"I couldn't tell you about it before. I'm sorry that I lied to you, but I swore an oath. The archbishop himself requested that I find out everything I could about this woman. By the time I arrived back in Worms, she'd disappeared, as if swallowed up by the earth. However, I just got a message from someone who says he knows this woman. He'll be here in two days."

Madlen's thoughts raced around in her head. *What was her husband trying to say? Did he know her secret or not?*

"The archbishop demands results. He wants this woman to be charged with her crimes, and he wants me to take over the case. As soon as I meet this man, I have to travel back to Trier and stay there for a long time. I know that you don't want to leave, but I have no choice. I've made a commitment to the archbishop. I have to hand this secret healer over. I can't resign from my service until then."

Madlen was unable to respond. She closed her eyes. Her own husband would be the one to arrest her and bring her to the gallows? He had lied to her like she had to him. But she'd never expected this. But who was this man who claimed to know her identity? Maybe just somebody hoping for the bounty. But what if it wasn't?

"Maria, please say something. I know you're mad, but I had no other choice."

She cleared her throat. "And this secret healer, do you have any idea who it could be?" Her heart beat loudly.

He shook his head slowly. "There are many who have been treated by her, but all refused to identify her. When I tried to bring up the subject, I was met with silence. They didn't want to hear that they had, in fact, made a pact with the devil."

"What makes you think they made a pact with the devil?" Madlen felt dizzy.

"I talked with a doctor. He said that there is no medicine that will cure this cough. And for those unfortunate enough to catch this terrible disease, the only possible help is bloodletting and prayer. God alone decides who lives and who dies. Everything lies in the hands of the Almighty."

"But if this woman healed somebody . . ."

"It is only because she's in league with the devil. When they are in the delirious throes of this disease, they promise everything and make a pact to give the devil the souls of their own children."

Madlen had never heard Johannes talk like this. Although she knew the devil existed, she never had anything to do with him. She only knew the medicinal properties of herbs. Now her own husband seemed foreign to her, and she knew that she could never trust him with her secret. She saw his eyes ablaze with the fire of religious fervor. He would take her to the gallows himself if he ever found her out, of this she was quite sure. A thought came her way. "You said earlier that there was someone who knew this woman. From where? Did she heal him?"

"No, he doesn't live in Worms, but he's heard the stories from a traveling barber."

"What does he say she did?"

"She swayed a candle to summon the devil."

Madlen opened her eyes wide. How could someone know about that? A dark foreboding gripped her heart.

"And where did the barber hear about this?"

"Someone told him. A woman whose brother was healed. She didn't see it herself. But that's what happened. And that's what this woman did when she tore babies from their mothers' wombs and took them with her. The husband of a pregnant woman who died came here to find out who was responsible. Together we'll find this secret healer and bring her to the gallows. Unlike most, he knows what she looks like; usually she wears a mask."

Madlen tried to calm her shaking hands. "And this man whose wife died. What's his name?"

"Why do you want to know?"

She shrugged.

"You don't know him," Johannes continued. "His name is Matthias Trauenstein, a highly respected citizen of Heidelberg. Let the people of the Neckar River have what they want. Justice is just as important to them as it is to us here on the Rhine."

Everything started to spin around Madlen. She felt sick and her stomach started to cramp. Her face contorted as she held her stomach.

"What is it?" Johannes looked at her worriedly.

"My stomach hurts," she moaned.

"I'll get the doctor!" He immediately jumped up and ran out of the room. Madlen steadied herself, breathing deeply. Elsbeth hurried in. "My God, Maria, what's the matter? Johannes said you were in pain. Is it the baby?"

"I don't know." Madlen groaned. "I feel sick." She'd hardly squeezed the words out when she felt bile rise in her throat. She desperately looked around for something but threw up right on the floor.

"Don't worry," Elsbeth called out anxiously. "You have to lie down." She turned to the door. "Helene!" she called so loudly that it made Madlen wince. "Helene, come help us, quickly." It wasn't long before the young woman stood in the doorframe.

"We have to lay her down," Elsbeth explained. "Johannes has already run to get the doctor." She turned again to Madlen. "Don't worry. Everything's going to be all right. You need to lie down. Do you think we'll be able to go upstairs together?"

Madlen nodded then pressed her lips together as she tried to get up. It was if the ground was collapsing underfoot. The whole room seemed to sway. Helene and Elsbeth supported her as she walked. She would have stumbled several times going upstairs if not for the women's firm grip on her.

"Well, all right. We did it." They led Madlen into her room and let her sink down onto the mattress. Her heart was beating far too quickly. Madlen knew that she must calm down. This was pure poison for the child. But the fear was so great that Madlen wasn't able to calm her breathing.

"You are burning up, my child," Elsbeth said as she lay her hand across Madlen's forehead, then touched her face tenderly. "What happened?"

Madlen was unable to answer. The tears ran down her face. Her whole world had collapsed. What should she do now? How could she explain it to Johannes?

"Please don't cry, my darling. The doctor's coming soon. And everything's going to be all right with the baby, of that I'm sure. Don't worry." Elsbeth tried her best to soothe Madlen. She sent Helene into the kitchen and told her to bring some spiced wine. She was noticeably relieved when she heard Johannes's voice, and a few moments later, he and the doctor entered the married couple's bedchamber together.

Johannes hurried into the room and bent over Madlen. "The doctor is here. Everything's going to be all right now."

The doctor approached the bed. "Maria, your husband brought me here. Describe exactly what kind of pain you have." Elsbeth and Johannes went to the other side of the bed, and the doctor sat next to her. He felt her forehead and her cheeks.

"Your husband told me you're expecting. Sometimes a woman in your condition can experience brief bouts of weakness." As he spoke, he held out a sharp instrument used for bloodletting. Madlen's eyes flashed in terror.

"I'm doing better," she lied. "It's just a moment of weakness, like you said. Thank you. I don't need any help now."

"Well, I'll be the judge of that." He held up the sharp medical instrument with a look of satisfaction on his face. Madlen panicked.

"Johannes, I'm better now." She looked at her husband urgently. "I simply want to rest."

"We'll start with a bloodletting then observe whether your body cools down and relaxes a bit." The doctor acted as if he hadn't heard a word Madlen had said.

"No!" Madlen pulled her blankets higher.

"But oh, why so scared of a little bloodletting?" The doctor laughed.

"Johannes. Tell him to go!" she screeched.

"But Maria, he just wants to help you."

"Now, now." The doctor tried to pull the blankets away, so he could grab Madlen's arm. She screamed in desperation.

"Stop it!" Johannes went around to the other side of the bed.

"What are you thinking? Didn't you just come begging for my help?"

"My wife says she's feeling better. She knows what she wants."

"Her bodily fluids must be brought back into line so they don't poison the baby. A bloodletting is the only way to accomplish this."

"Such nonsense!" Madlen screamed. "Get away from me and my child, or you will live to regret it!"

"But Maria," Elsbeth exclaimed indignantly, "he just wants to help. You're in such an awful state."

"I'm better now," Madlen replied as calmly as possible. "And I want nothing more than to sleep and get my strength back. I will not allow you to stab me with that thing."

"Many people are afraid of this treatment," the doctor said jovially. "Believe me, after the first time, you won't be afraid."

"Tell him that he needs to go!" Madlen looked straight at Johannes.

"It would be better if you could go now." Johannes pulled out a small pouch of money. "Please take this as my thanks for your efforts. If we should need you again, I will make sure to bring you back."

"And the bloodletting?"

"Not today."

The doctor shook his head in frustration, got off the bed, and took the money. "Your decision is not wise." He tucked the pouch into his vest and began to collect his medical instruments. When he was done, he gave Madlen a serious look. "I hope for everyone's sake that this doesn't damage your child."

She nodded but didn't reply.

He said his good-byes to Johannes and Elsbeth, who apologized profusely for her daughter-in-law's stubbornness and went to see him out.

"What in the world was that? The man is an experienced doctor who's helped many people. You should have taken his help."

"Isn't that the same doctor who claims the cough can only be cured by bloodletting and prayers?"

"What do you mean? Why are you so angry with me? Is it because I didn't tell you about my contract with the archbishop?"

Madlen knew she shouldn't say anything. She was scared and desperate. But Johannes was right. She was angry. Angry at him, angry at this quack doctor, angry at everybody that she'd helped who had betrayed her.

"Maria." Johannes sat on the bed. "This isn't like you. Please talk to me."

"I just want to rest." She needed a way to escape this situation. "Please leave me alone."

"But I just . . ."

"Please, Johannes." She placed her hand over his mouth. "I don't think it's too much to ask to let me sleep now. I don't feel well, and I need some peace and quiet."

"Forgive me." He stood up immediately. He'd never seen his wife like this; the look she gave him made him uneasy. Did he see hate in her eyes?

Madlen turned onto her side so that she didn't have to look at Johannes's face. She heard him blow out the candles and leave the room.

She pulled the blankets over her mouth so that he couldn't hear her sobbing.

Chapter Twenty-One

"You have to leave right now." Agathe paced up and down the room.

Madlen had come early in the morning to tell her aunt what had happened. She sat, her face ashen, her shoulders drooping, nervously kneading her hands. "But where can I go?"

"I don't know, but you can't stay here. As soon as this Matthias shows up in Worms, Johannes will realize who the secret healer is. And even if everybody in Worms tries to protect you, you are still wanted for murder in Heidelberg. Matthias Trauenstein would have every right to drag you back there."

Madlen shook even more violently. "I want to die."

Agathe stopped cold. "Don't say that." She went to her niece and held her by the shoulders. "Don't ever say that again. Do you hear me?"

Madlen nodded numbly.

"I know a fisherman. My husband and I often helped him back in the old days. Hugo owes me. I'll go to him right away. He'll take you down the Rhine."

"And then?"

Agathe put her hands on her face and rubbed her eyes. A devastating headache pounded against her temples. "I really don't know," she said desperately. She dropped her hands back onto her lap. "But we have to keep our wits about us and be smart. Otherwise, your life and your child's won't be worth a pfennig."

Madlen laid her hand on her stomach. "I'm so scared, Agathe. I don't know what to think anymore. I don't want to run away from Johannes, or from you." She cried. "I've never tried to hurt anybody." Her shoulders shook.

Agathe went over, stood next to her, and stroked her tenderly. "I know. But we can't change it. Nobody will believe you." She patted Madlen lightly on the back. "Believe me, I'm so very sad that you have to go. But there's no other way. If we don't prepare everything now and Matthias Trauenstein comes to town earlier than expected, it will be too late."

Madlen nodded. "What should I do?"

"You can't go back to the Goldmanns' house; you have to leave Worms today."

"You mean without seeing Johannes for the last time?" Madlen could barely breathe.

"You must. Go to your old room and gather everything that can help you. I'll give you all the money that I have. You'll need it to start a new life from scratch."

"But where should I go?"

"Try traveling downriver to the north." Agathe thought about it feverishly. "I know a merchant in Emmerich, who often buys clothes from me. The city is independent and part of the Hanseatic League. You could go to the merchant . . ." She looked down on the weeping Madlen. "Are you listening to me at all?"

Madlen sobbed so violently that she was hardly able to speak. "I'll be running my whole life. I'll never belong anywhere, and I'll always be alone. And what will become of my child? I can't do it, Agathe."

"What are you saying?"

"I know that you mean well. But I'm not going to run again. What kind of a life would that be?" She looked at her aunt in despair. "No. I'm going to stay put. If they hang me, then they hang me. That will be the end of it."

"Madlen, pull yourself together. Think about your child."

"I don't have the strength. I felt so safe here with you. You were like a mother to me."

"Then let me protect you now, like a mother would." Agathe sat down in the other chair and held Madlen's hands in hers. They stayed this way for a moment, without speaking. Agathe looked at her pregnant niece. It was true. She loved her as if she were her own daughter. The more she thought about it, the clearer everything became. "What if I went with you?"

Madlen looked up. "What?"

"If I accompanied you, perhaps it would be even less suspicious. In the eyes of the people, you would be a woman who simply left her husband and disappeared from the city. There could be all kinds of reasons if you were accompanied by your foster mother. People would just assume that it was a dispute between man and wife."

"Actually, that's not even wrong."

"And if I were you, I would leave quickly so that Johannes doesn't have time to ask any questions."

"And Roswitha?"

"She'll be marrying Sander soon. I'll ask Otilia if she can take Roswitha into her household until then. She would not refuse me this favor."

Madlen liked the idea better the more she thought about it.

"And your work? You love making dresses. You said it yourself. You don't have to give that up for me."

"And I won't. One can purchase fabric anywhere. It will be difficult to start anew, but I did it before, and I can do it again. And now there are two of us. You can help me with sewing, and I can help you with the new baby. We'll be there for each other. Just like a real mother and daughter. What do you say?"

Madlen smiled brightly. "You'd do that for me?"

Agathe squeezed her hand. "Pack your things, but don't bring too much. I will take care of the boat and speak to Otilia."

"Thank you." Madlen looked at her aunt tearfully.

"We can do this. You, me, and the little person growing inside you." She smiled bravely.

"Only one more thing," Madlen asked. "What about Johannes?"

Agathe shook her head slowly. "As much as it pains me to say this, you can't see him again."

"Not even to say good-bye to him? I promise not to say anything."

"You can't promise that. Believe me, this is how it must be. He loves you. He won't let you go. Besides, it will be easier for him if he doesn't see you again."

"Why is that?"

"He'll think that you simply left him without remorse. He'll hate you for it. And it will make it easier for him to get over you."

"He'll hate me," Madlen repeated softly.

"Yes, but it's better than seeing you hanging from the gallows."

The thought frightened Madlen. "You think he would despise me for what I've done?"

"Yes, because he wouldn't understand it. And it's his duty to surrender you to the archbishop. The woman he loves, the mother of his child, led to the gallows by his hand. Do you really think that he could live with that more easily than you leaving without a word?"

Madlen pondered her aunt's words as they echoed through her head. She was right. Running away and leaving Johannes in the dark was kinder, even though he wouldn't realize it at first. "I'll pack up our things together. You take care of the boat and Otilia. We don't have any time to lose."

***

The sun warmed their backs as the boat slowly sailed north on the Rhine. Madlen stood on the railing, looking back until Worms disappeared from sight. Then she stepped onto one of the crates sitting next to the railing as the landscape slid past her. She knew she didn't have any other choice.

She was impressed with how quickly Agathe had resolved all outstanding issues and returned to the house. She even took time to collect money from those who had not yet paid for their dresses. Though her livelihood was taken care of some time ago, now Madlen was worried about the immediate future. Agathe had given up everything for her. Once again, she asked herself what she'd done to deserve such kindness. "We've forgotten to cancel the lesson with Brother Simon," she said suddenly.

"That's right. I knew there was something else. Well, all right. He'll figure it out when he comes knocking on our front door."

"I have two books he gave me."

"Don't be too glum. He was paid well, and soon you would have no longer needed him. It's going to have to do for now. Don't fret."

Agathe seemed to know all the right things to say to console Madlen. She was both happy and relieved to have her by her side. Without her, she might have thrown herself into the Rhine in despair.

"What are you thinking about?" Agathe asked as she squatted on the crates next to her.

"This and that. I wonder what kind of life awaits us."

"We'll have the life we choose to create." Madlen knew that her aunt would never show her how hard it was to leave all that she had built in Worms.

"I hope you won't regret taking this step." Madlen laid her hand on the railing and tilted her head.

"I won't regret it," Agathe stated confidently. "I don't believe in regret. I make decisions, and then I live with the consequences. If I questioned everything I did, I wouldn't be able to move forward."

"You're so brave. I often think of all the things that could go wrong. I'd like to be more like you."

"Like me?" Agathe laughed. "Believe me, you don't want to do that. I've made so many mistakes. But we all make mistakes. Some more than others. And yet, we always have the opportunity to do better next time."

"It always seems like you have an answer for everything."

"There are no difficulties that can't be resolved." Agathe smiled mysteriously. "I believe that God gives us challenges to overcome. It's his way of letting us grow."

"So do you think that God is just testing me?"

"It's possible."

"But why?"

"Only He knows why. We are too unenlightened to understand everything, but we can rely on the fact that all will be well in the end."

"How do you know? That it will end well?"

"I just know. Believe me. One day, you will understand all of this."

It took five days to reach Emmerich; they docked at dusk.

Madlen was completely exhausted. With each day, the oppressive feeling of confinement weighed on her more and more. She paced up and down the boat to get a little bit of exercise. When they finally arrived, she could hardly wait to get off.

Agathe's initial plan was to stay with one of her steady customers, but she eventually rejected that idea. She wasn't sure whom she could trust. So they decided to stay at a tavern before finding a decent place to live. As they walked ashore on the narrow plank, they paused and looked around. Emmerich looked quite different than Worms or even Heidelberg, both of which were surrounded by hills. Here, everything was flat. Houses were densely packed into straight rows. Madlen liked it immediately; the harmonious construction was simple and exuded a certain calm.

"Hugo, do you know of an inn suitable for two women?" Agathe asked the captain, who moored his boat, then accompanied them ashore.

"Try the Golden Rooster. I stayed there myself a couple of times when I had business here. There's a woman in charge. Fronicka kept the tavern after her Ewald passed on. And believe me, she has everything under control there. A man who didn't mind his manners could get a certain body part sliced off." The skipper laughed throatily. Agathe didn't actually want to know exactly what he meant by that remark.

"And where is the Golden Rooster?"

"Go straight ahead to the marketplace. You can't miss it."

Agathe paid him. "Here, as agreed. I thank you for everything. And you know that . . ." She held up her finger to warn him.

"If somebody asks me, I will say that I brought you to Rotterdam. From there, you wanted to go to Bruges."

"Exactly. Thank you."

"My pleasure. I'm indebted to Reinhard and you far beyond this little boat ride."

"We were friends, just like we are now. We're even now."

He tipped his cap. "I hope that you'll find happiness. May God protect you."

"Have a safe trip home."

The women waved good-bye, as the boat slowly pulled away from the dock and he set sail. It wasn't long before he'd disappeared from sight.

"Then off we go to the Golden Rooster." Agathe picked up their baggage.

Madlen did the same and gazed at the houses as she tried to keep up with Agathe. "I like this city," she said. "It looks totally different than ours."

"Do you mean Heidelberg or Worms?"

"Actually both. The land is so flat here. There are no hills."

"You're right. It didn't occur to me. All right now, let's go. Hopefully, they'll have a room for us there. I just want to lie down on a bed and not see or hear anything more for today."

They found the Golden Rooster immediately. Fronicka, the landlady, eyed the two of them before assigning them to a room on the top floor. "But the charge is the same."

"I'll pay you for one night in advance. We'll do so every day." Agathe gave her some coins.

"How long do you plan to stay here?"

"We don't know yet."

"Neither one of you are from here. I can hear it in your speech."

Agathe looked at the landlady evenly. "You have a fine ear," she replied.

A little while later, they moved up to their room, furnished with three simple beds, a table with two chairs, and a chest. Madlen put her sack on the third bed, when there was a knock. A maid brought fresh water for washing up and quietly left.

"What do we do now?" Madlen sat on a chair.

Agathe chose a bed and lay down. "Rest," she said, stretching out her tired limbs.

"But it's not evening yet," Madlen argued.

"You're pregnant and I'm old. Let's go to sleep. Tomorrow is another day; we can get started on our new life then. But I want to rest now."

Madlen sighed. She hadn't found the trip as strenuous. To lie down in the middle of the day and sleep seemed strange. She wanted to go out and see Emmerich. "Do you have anything against me going out alone?"

Agathe opened one eye. "Of course, I do. For the love of God, let me rest a little. If you go out running around in a city that you don't know, I'll be so worried that I won't be able to sleep a wink. Please, can't you just simply lie down?"

Madlen was moved by Agathe's concern. Her aunt had sacrificed so much to make sure she was safe; shouldn't she be able to indulge her aunt's simple request? "You're right. Let's sleep. It will do me and my child good."

"Thank you." Agathe turned her head to the side and fell asleep almost instantly. The tension they'd felt since they departed Worms subsided a little. Agathe was completely worn out; she was unable to stay conscious for one moment longer.

Chapter Twenty-Two

Johannes was a nervous wreck. Two days earlier, Maria had disappeared from the face of the earth, as had Agathe. He searched all over Worms, but any clues to his wife's whereabouts led nowhere. Was it possible that the women had fallen victim to a crime? He ran through the streets, asking everyone he met if they'd seen his wife. The answer was always the same. Consumed by panic and despair, he ran like mad, calling their names again and again. He went to the harbor, and for the umpteenth time went to Agathe's house and knocked on the front door. Nobody opened the door, and there were no signs of activity inside. A boy no older than ten walked by. He looked at Johannes. "They're gone," he said simply.

Johannes turned to him. "What did you say?"

"You can stop knocking," he explained. "The women left on a boat. Nobody's home."

"You saw which boat they got onto?"

"Yes, I did." The little boy put his hands on his hips.

"What did the women look like?"

The youngster cocked his head to the side. "One of them is a seamstress. Her name is Agathe, and she owns this house. And the other one was younger." He scratched his head. "She had long dark hair. And she had"—he tapped his finger right on his upper lip—"a spot right here."

"A mole," Johannes murmured as a cold chill ran up and down his spine. Thoughts raced feverishly through his brain. "Can you say whether they were somehow forced? Was somebody with them? Did you see any signs of violence?"

The youngster shook his head. "Nope. The skipper helped them board, and they took sail."

"When was that?"

"Just two days ago," the boy said.

Johannes shook his head in disbelief; he was completely confused. The boy turned and started to walk away.

"Do you know which skipper it was?"

The boy thought it over for a moment. "Yes, but he's not back yet."

"Tell me his name."

Johannes walked over to him and put a coin in the little boy's filthy hand; he smiled, greatly satisfied. "His name is Hugo. He used to be a fisherman, but now he transports merchandise."

"Hugo. And you know for sure that he's not back yet?"

"I was just at the pier. His boat wasn't there. Can I go now?"

"One moment," Johannes said and took another coin out of his pocket. "I'm giving this to you so that you'll keep your eyes open. As soon as Hugo comes back, you let me know."

The boy wrinkled his forehead.

"I'll give you another coin."

"Two."

"Fair enough, two. But you have to be very vigilant."

"I promise." The youngster solemnly put a hand to his chest.

"Good. Then we have a deal."

The boy gave him a broad grin. "I'll run to your house right away. You can count on me, my lord." With that, he disappeared around the corner.

Johannes sat limply on the front stairs of Agathe's house. Maria was gone. He couldn't believe it. She had left him because of a little disagreement. Or was she afraid to come home because something happened with the baby? The last time they saw each other, she had some pain but rejected medical treatment from the doctor. Everybody knew that bloodletting helped bring the bodily fluids back in balance. Why had Maria reacted so squeamishly? And when the doctor had gone, she had given him a look of such contempt, the likes of which he'd never before seen from his wife. What had happened? His stomach hurt. He needed to speak with his mother as soon as possible. Elsbeth had to tell him every word of what Maria said when he went to fetch the doctor. When he reached home a few moments later, he was completely out of breath. One of the guards opened the door and let him in.

"Is my mother here?"

"Yes, she is with your father in his office."

"Johannes!" Elsbeth entered the hall. "You're here. I need to speak with you."

"I have to speak with you, too. Come on." They both went into the adjacent dining room, and Johannes closed the door behind him. "What happened when I went to fetch the doctor?"

"Excuse me? What are you talking about?"

"The evening when Maria suffered her bout of weakness. You were alone with her. What happened when I was gone?"

Elsbeth looked quite confused. "Nothing," she answered.

"But something must have happened."

"Wait a minute. Let me think about it." Elsbeth closed her eyes. "You said that Maria wasn't doing well and asked me to take care of her while you fetched the doctor."

"Correct. And what happened after that?"

"I went to her. Maria's whole body was trembling. She was terribly pale, the poor thing. I believe I told her that it would be better for her to lie down." Elsbeth looked over at the chair that Madlen would sit at during meals. "Then she stood up and vomited. I called for Helene, and we brought her upstairs to your bedchamber. You know the rest."

"No. There must be something else. Did she say anything? Were things going poorly for the baby? Can you remember anything else?"

"Johannes, what is this? You're frightening me. I promise you, there was nothing else. As soon as she lay down, you came in with the doctor."

"Did you two have a fight? Did you say something that you now regret, insult her somehow? Please, Mother."

"As I've already told you," Elsbeth said loudly, "there wasn't the slightest disagreement between us. Never. I loved her from the first moment I met her. You know that."

Johannes covered his face with his hands. "I just don't understand it."

"What is it, Johannes? What's happened?" His mother looked at him pleadingly.

He took a deep breath. "She's gone, Mother. Maria left me."

Elsbeth looked at him in disbelief. She wanted to say something but couldn't find the words. She opened her mouth and then shut it again.

"I ran into a little boy. Maria and Agathe left Worms two days ago on a boat. She's gone, Mother. Simply gone." He rubbed his eyes.

"That can't be," Elsbeth insisted. "I simply don't believe it. The little boy must have been mistaken. Or he deceived you. Maria would never leave you. She loves you, Johannes. I know it."

"Yes, that's what I thought," he replied bitterly. "But she must have fooled us."

They both sat there for a few minutes, trying to comprehend what had happened.

"You have to look for her," Elsbeth said finally.

"As soon as the skipper comes back, the boy will let me know. I'll find her and confront her."

"I'll go with you," Elsbeth said immediately. She put her hand on her son's arm. "I'm sure there's a reasonable explanation for this. Perhaps someone got sick. I thought you said that Agathe was a good friend of her mother's? That's it." Elsbeth raised her index finger confidently. "Her mother. She's ill, and the two women went to help her."

"And Maria didn't have time to let me know?" He raised his eyebrows. "You really don't believe that, do you, Mother?"

"It's the only explanation. They were in a hurry, a big hurry. She had no other choice. Or"—she held up her finger again—"she came to tell you, but you weren't here. She couldn't wait because the boat wanted to set sail. In a couple of days, she'll be back and tell you all about it. Yes, you'll see."

He sighed. "The boy told me that both women quietly boarded the boat and left Worms. Neither of them appeared to be rushed. No. She didn't think it was necessary to let me know. No woman that loves her husband would do that."

"But your child?"

Her remark cut him like a knife. His mother was right. Maria was carrying his child. How dare she snatch their unborn child away from its father! "I'll wait until the skipper returns to Worms. And then I'll find them, even if I have to beat it out of him. I'll find her, Mother."

She quickly grabbed his arm. "Don't become bitter. You don't know the truth."

He smiled joylessly. "It will be difficult for me to do that." He turned to go.

"Oh, Johannes. Earlier, this Heidelberger you were expecting came here. I told him that you were away on an urgent matter. He'll come back tomorrow."

Johannes sighed. He hadn't thought about Matthias Trauenstein at all. It didn't suit him to fulfill his duty and meet this man right now when his thoughts were on his Maria's disappearance. But he knew that he had no other choice. "Did he say when he'd be back?"

"Tomorrow around noon. I offered him accommodations here at the house, but he rented a room in the tavern instead." Elsbeth was clearly displeased. She wouldn't approve of her own husband staying in a tavern on business trips instead of accepting the hospitality of his business partners. Beyond any doubt, Peter Goldmann was a proper and magnificent husband, with a spotless reputation. But Elsbeth did not delude herself: when Peter was gone for several weeks, she'd rather not know what he did to make his time more pleasurable.

"Under the circumstances, it's better not to have him in the house right now," Johannes confessed. "But I do need to speak with him. I am obliged by the archbishop."

"Agreed." Elsbeth pressed her lips together. Though she was only too happy to contribute some words of comfort to her son, she still couldn't believe her daughter-in-law had deceived them.

"I'll be in my bedchamber, thinking all this over in peace and quiet."

"Supper is almost ready. Helene has prepared a lovely—"

"Thanks, Mother, but I'm not hungry. I need to lie down."

"All right. I'll let you know if something comes up." She smiled at her son as he returned to his room. The sadness in his eyes pained her.

When Johannes opened his eyes, it was morning again. He felt miserable; he'd gotten virtually no sleep, racking his brain for what prompted his wife to take this step. But he couldn't think of a thing that could have led her to turn her back on him and Worms.

He swung his legs sluggishly out of bed and sat for a moment on the edge of the mattress. He turned, as though he might find Maria lying next to him. The sight of the unused pillows made his blood boil. He stood up with a jolt, got dressed, dipped his hands in the washstand basin, and splashed cool water onto his face. But that didn't help clear his head. His whole body hurt, and he would have preferred to fall right back into bed. He rubbed his eyes as he left his bedchamber and entered the hall. He heard muffled sounds coming from the kitchen.

Slowly, he descended the stairs, pushed his hands through his hair, and went into the kitchen. "Good morning, Helene. Are my parents home?"

"Your mother went to the market with Tilda, and your father's working in his office. Can I serve you your breakfast?"

Johannes still wasn't hungry but decided to eat anyway. He couldn't think without something in his stomach. On one hand, he had to speak with the Heidelberger. On the other hand, he was burning with anticipation. The little boy would probably come to the house today.

"Yes, but not much. Just a slice of bread and ham."

Helene nodded and immediately set out to perform her duties. Johannes sat on the small kitchen bench and began to eat as soon as Helene served him. She gave him some spiced wine to wash it all down with. The wine smelled terrible to Johannes. "Just give me some water and take this away." The maid was somewhat puzzled but did what her young master asked.

Johannes ate and brooded quietly. When he was finished, he stood, said good-bye, and went to his father's office. As he approached, there was a knock at the front door and the guard opened it. Elsbeth came in carrying a basket on one arm, with Tilda following close behind.

"Oh, Johannes, you're here. You look terrible."

"And a good morning to you, too, Mother."

"Go upstairs quickly, put on some decent clothes, and comb your hair. I just ran into this Heidelberger, and he asked whether it was possible for you to receive him as soon as possible. It would have been rude to put him off. He'll be here any minute."

Johannes nodded, let go of the office doorknob, and went upstairs to his room. Just as he finished grooming himself, he heard the visitor arrive. Johannes looked down from above as a tall, dark-haired man entered the house. He was rich, you could see that at a glance. Johannes was used to sizing up people as quickly as possible. He thought of

Maria, the one he'd failed to size up accurately, and it left a bitter taste in his mouth.

"Oh, there he is now," Elsbeth said, pointing up at him.

Johannes forced himself to smile as if he was actually looking forward to meeting with the Heidelberger. He walked down the steps calmly and stretched his right hand out to the man. "Johannes Goldmann. Welcome."

"Matthias Trauenstein. Thank you for your kindness in receiving me so early in the day."

"Please." Johannes pointed over to the dining room door. "Let's go in there so we can speak in private."

"Helene, please serve our guest." Elsbeth clapped her hands.

Matthias Trauenstein bowed compliantly, and he and Johannes went into the dining room. "Please. Sit down."

"Thank you." Matthias took a seat. "I must say, your home is quite impressive."

"My mother," Johannes explained. "She had a hand in the decoration of the entire house. You won't find a room that wasn't decorated exactly to her taste."

Matthias Trauenstein sighed. "I know very well what you mean. My wife, Adelhaid, was equal to your mother in every way." He put on a sorrowful expression. "But as you already know, she's gone."

Johannes was surprised how quickly the Heidelberger got straight to the point.

Helene knocked, then set a tray carefully on the table. The visitor stared at her backside. It almost looked as if it was everything the Heidelberger could do to keep his hands off her. There was something in the eyes of this stranger that Johannes loathed. "Thank you, Helene. I'll serve our guest myself."

The maid nodded, curtsied, and left the room.

"A pretty young thing, I must say." Matthias grinned lasciviously. When he noticed the disapproving glare on his host's face, he changed his demeanor instantly. "It's hard for a widower," Matthias tried to explain. "Since my wife passed on, or rather, was murdered, my world hasn't been the same."

"Tell me, please, how it all came about. I only know bits and pieces."

Matthias Trauenstein adopted the saddest facial expression he could conjure up. Then he began to tell the story of how a young woman named Madlen tore his unborn child from his wife's womb and afterward stabbed his helpless wife with a knife until she finally bled to death. He embellished the story with a sordid tale of devil's herbs and witch's spells.

"Now you understand why I must catch this woman," he concluded.

"Yes, I understand. But how do you know that it's the same woman who healed so many residents of Worms of the deadly cough?" Johannes raised his hands. "Though that she was in league with the devil is not in question."

"The candle," Matthias explained. "My wife told me shortly before she died. This is how the wench was able to summon the devil."

"I understand." Johannes was starting to have his doubts about whether events had taken place exactly as Matthias Trauenstein described them. Would a woman who had just had her baby ripped out of her womb and been repeatedly stabbed with a knife really be well enough to report something as incidental as the swaying of a candle? On the other hand, Johannes had to investigate every clue.

"Well, then. Describe the woman to me. If she's here in Worms, I'll make sure to find and interrogate her."

"She's here." Matthias balled up his hand into a fist. "She must be here. She was seen, and she's the same woman, of that I'm sure."

Johannes waited until his visitor got a grip on himself.

"At first, the woman seems inconspicuous, but once you've seen her, you'll never forget her." Johannes almost expected that Trauenstein would describe a wench with red glowing eyes, a crooked nose, and thin, bony fingers.

"She's slight, almost like a boy. Her hair is dark brown and long, very long." He pointed to his own waist. "Her eyes are bluer than I've ever seen in any human before."

Trauenstein's description started making Johannes nervous.

"Her most striking feature, however, is a mole right above her upper lip." He tapped right above his own mouth a few times. "Tell me, have you ever seen this woman in Worms?"

Chapter Twenty-Three

When she tried to smile, Madlen found that it was easier than she'd imagined. Or at least not as hard as she'd thought. She had barely slept a wink last night. She'd been thinking about Johannes so much and what he must think of her. Would she ever see him again? She had asked her aunt yesterday evening, shortly after they came back from the outhouse. "I hope not, if you want to live" was her harsh response. Madlen had waived any further questions, curled up under her covers, and turned to her side. When she heard Agathe breathing evenly, she lay on her back and stared off into the darkness.

After barely sleeping, she dozed off briefly in the morning, plagued by violent nightmares; she felt powerless and weak. She had a blinding headache, and she felt nauseated the whole night. She plodded heavily downstairs behind Agathe to the tavern's dining area. It was empty except for them. The landlady quickly brought them two bowls of porridge then left again. They were alone, sitting opposite each other at a long table.

"You look awful," Agathe said when she got a glimpse of the poor girl.

"I feel as awful as I look, too," Madlen replied sullenly.

Agathe reached across the table and put her hand on Madlen's. "It will get better, believe me. I can very well understand your despair, but you have to make an effort to look ahead." Agathe glanced right then left to make sure no one overheard them. But neither Fronicka nor anyone else was around. The women were by themselves. "Think about your child," Agathe urged.

As tears welled up in Madlen's eyes, she breathed deeply to keep the tears from running down her cheeks. "That's what I'm doing." She hesitated before continuing. "But I wonder whether it wouldn't have been better to stay and surrender to my fate." She gulped hard. "I can't keep running. Someday, they will find me, arrest me, and convict me—whether it's for what happened in Heidelberg or for curing people in Worms—and then my child will be all alone in this world, without a mother." She couldn't hold back her tears any longer. "I know how it is to grow up without a mother." She lowered her head, her voice a low whisper now. "If they hang me now, then my child dies with me, escaping the agony of loneliness."

Agathe put down her spoon and went around the table to sit on the bench next to Madlen. She hugged her niece tenderly and patted her head protectively. "Come on, cry it out now. It's going to be all right."

Madlen released a flood of tears. Everything felt so wrong and unjust. She was angry and scared, at her wit's end. She didn't know whether to scream or curl up and hide away forever in a dark cave. She held onto her aunt and sobbed bitterly.

Madlen didn't know how long she'd been sitting there before she let go of Agathe's embrace. Agathe stroked her cheeks tenderly, wiping away her tears. "Better?"

Madlen nodded silently, although she didn't really feel any better at all.

"Go to the room and wash your face. Then when you come back down, we'll go to the market together to see what Emmerich has to offer. We can see whether the ladies here value a properly made dress."

Madlen nodded. "Thank you." She arose from the bench shakily and adjusted her skirt before walking over to the staircase that led to the top floor.

Agathe gazed at her niece with concern. Madlen had to pull herself together, or she wouldn't remain anonymous for long. Her aunt fervently hoped that she'd have the necessary courage to keep on fighting.

About an hour later, the women strolled through Emmerich; it was a splendid and diverse city, something that Agathe hadn't expected. The marketplace stalls were jammed together; there seemed to be an abundance of weavers and brewers. Ladies strolled around, showing off their expensive outfits; well-dressed men made their business deals. The hustle and bustle reminded Agathe of the buzzing and whirring of beehives in old Haubold, near the harbor of the same name. Agathe had always kept her distance to prevent herself from being stung by the bees. Her memory of Haubold and Worms made her smile. But she quickly shoved those thoughts aside in case loss and sadness took hold. She looked around again. They didn't know much about this city near the border of the Netherlands, and the little she knew was from Ruppert, a merchant. From his descriptions, she'd imagined Emmerich to be much smaller and less colorful.

Now she and Madlen strolled around the market, continuing to inspect one stall after another. But her niece was hardly aware of anything. Agathe stopped suddenly. Madlen turned to her aunt. "What's the matter?"

"Sweetheart, that's enough." Agathe looked at her sternly. "You have not spent one second thinking about anything other than your worries. You must stop now," she hissed.

"But I . . ." Madlen couldn't spit out another word.

"No. Enough is enough. If you've given up," Agathe whispered as quietly as possible, "then we should just go back so you can turn yourself in."

"Are you angry at me?"

"Yes, I am. You're not the only one who left everything behind. I did, too. I don't want everything we've done so far to be in vain." She pulled her niece away from the stalls and all the people running around. "I'm going to tell you this once: I don't know whether it's safe here or not. But we had to go somewhere, and this is a good location for business. I willingly left everything behind to help you. But if you want only pity, then I'm the wrong person for this job, and you should return to Worms. I will stand faithfully by your side until your trial is done and you are executed. I promise. But you must decide here and now. Will you at least try to live, or do you want to give up? This indecisive back and forth, this yes and no, ends right now."

Madlen was terrified as she looked into Agathe's fiercely determined eyes. Her heart beat wildly. Wasn't she right about this? She'd left everything behind to help her. She'd given up everything when she left her old life behind. And for what? For a desperate young woman sunk into the depths of self-pity.

"I'm so sorry," she finally said softly.

"What do you say? I expect an answer from you with a loud, determined voice."

"I'm sorry." Madlen held up her head to give her voice more power. "I've only been thinking of how unfairly I've been treated. But that's over now." She lifted her chin proudly. "Please, help me. I want to live, here, with you and my child. Can I rely on you?"

The corner of Agathe's mouth twitched. "Yes, you can." She quickly leaned forward and gave her niece a kiss on the forehead. "I'm very proud of you, my little girl."

***

Madlen didn't allow any more gloomy thoughts to enter her mind. As soon as Johannes came into her mind, she just pushed him aside and focused on the tasks at hand. "There are so many cloth merchants here."

"Cloth merchants, yes, but not very many dresses for sale," Agathe noticed. "I'll find out where Ruppert lives. He always buys dresses from me."

Madlen remembered. "We only have two dresses ready, and one of them was made for Elsbeth. That's not many. Shouldn't we select some fabric right away so we can start making more?"

Agathe shrugged. "I don't want to assume the worst. First, we should try to sell the dresses we already have. If we can't find a buyer, then we can save money to pay for some fabric."

"Why do you think that nobody here will buy our dresses?"

Agathe made an expansive hand movement. "Look at the ladies. The dresses that we currently produce are far too simple for their fancy tastes."

"Can we alter the dresses we have now?"

"Yes, we can do that. Before we sew new ones, we should buy some pearls and make the dresses very ornate. We should come up with a completely original but lovely design. The ladies here have their own seamstresses. If the dresses we offer aren't any different, they'll have no reason to buy from us."

"And then?" Madlen looked at her helplessly. "How will we survive if we can't sell our dresses?"

"We'll just have to see. Let's try it first."

"All right." Madlen didn't want to dwell on this uncertainty. Previously, she had no doubt that the dresses they produced would be highly prized everywhere. She quickly tried to distract herself from these thoughts. "This Ruppert fellow you mentioned, have you known him for a long time?"

Agathe thought it over. "It's been about six years. He is always traveling on business from his home base in Emmerich to Bruges, and then from Trier and Worms to Strasbourg, until he makes his return journey. I don't believe he's home very much."

"So he's probably not here in Emmerich right now?"

"Who knows? We'll ask and hope for the best. And if he's not here, we can try to sell off our dresses anyway." She laid her arm on Madlen's shoulder. "Believe me, little girl, it will all work out."

All of a sudden, something rolled around in Madlen's abdomen. She put a hand on her belly, a startled look on her face.

"What?" Agathe looked worriedly at Madlen's face.

"A movement," she said. She waited for a minute, but there was nothing further. Her pregnancy was at the end of the third month, so it wasn't uncommon to feel movement at this point. However, the stress of the last few days could be dangerous to the health of the unborn child.

Agathe looked at her niece, still worried. "And? Is it better now?"

Madlen nodded. "It just lasted for a moment." She made an effort to smile.

"Should we go back to the tavern so that you can lie down for a moment?"

"That won't be necessary." Madlen looked around until she noticed a small boulder just beyond the marketplace stalls. "Let's go sit over there for a bit of rest. Then we can get going again."

She was bent over slightly when she sat down on the boulder, relieved to rest her legs for a bit. Agathe stood next to her, stroking her back gently as Madlen struggled to calm her breathing. She knew that Madlen was making a fierce effort to be tough thanks to her strong words from earlier.

"How's that now?"

"It's getting better. Thank you." Madlen tried to smile. "You know, that's completely normal. The earlier stages of the pregnancy can be rough. In two or three more weeks, things will be much easier."

"It almost seems as though you've already had three children," Agathe joked.

"I've been around so many women during this special time that it does feel almost as though I've experienced it myself."

"It must be a wonderful feeling." Agathe sighed.

"What do you mean? To be pregnant?"

"Yes, and to help pregnant women. So many would be forever thankful to you."

Madlen smiled. "Some, of course." Her facial expression changed. "And if it weren't for those other negative experiences, I couldn't think of a more fulfilling way to live . . ." She shrugged. "Oh well, in the future, these pregnant women can deal with the real midwives— thanking and cursing them at the same time. I'll have nothing more to do with it."

"Do you regret it?"

Madlen stroked her growing little belly pensively as she thought about her reply. "I don't regret it, but I miss it. Everything would be different if I were a man. My greatest wish would have been to be a doctor, a wise one. Or to at least have become a real midwife, yes. But of course, that's no longer possible. I have no desire to be hunted down like an animal again."

Agathe stroked her niece's back tenderly. "Who knows where the road will lead us. If I've learned anything in my old age, it is that every-thing is possible."

"Right now, I hope that God's will doesn't lead me too far from here. I don't want to be forced to move again." She let her eyes scan the marketplace. "I like Emmerich, though I had never heard of it until a few days ago. The people seem different here. They seem so . . ." She looked for the right words. "Carefree," she finally said.

"It's nice to hear you say that. I thought the same thing. I believe it's because we're so close to the Netherlands."

"Why is that? Are the Netherlanders like this?"

"I haven't met so many of them yet," Agathe said. "I think two in my whole life." She held up two fingers. "But they both were . . ." She paused with a telling smile. "Yes, they were both carefree."

"Agathe, I would love to hear the stories you have to tell about them."

"Yes!" Her aunt laughed gleefully. "I can imagine you would. But my lips are sealed."

Madlen laughed with her and stood. "Now, let's get going again. Thank you for letting me rest."

"Anytime. We're in no hurry."

They went from stand to stand. Agathe stopped at a weaver's stand. "Good man," she said to the merchant.

"What can I do for you fine ladies today?" He flashed a toothless, yet charming smile.

Agathe held up her hand. "Thank you, but we don't need anything right now. That doesn't mean, however, that we won't be needing something in the future."

"I knew immediately that you had a sense for the finest woolens and woven goods."

"Right now, we're looking for a dress merchant. Is there one here at the market?"

"You look like a clever women who knows how to help herself. Why would you want to buy a finished dress when you are so well served with fine fabric and yarns?"

Agathe cocked her head to the side. "You mean no one sells dresses here?"

"No one at this market, as far as I know."

"All the better. Tell me, what does a person have to do to be able to sell goods from his own stall?"

"What do you have to sell?"

"Dresses," she answered succinctly.

"Ah, now I understand. Simply have your husbands pay the fee to the head of the marketplace."

"Where does one find this head of the marketplace?"

The weaver looked around. "He's in and out throughout the day, checking to make sure everything's just so." He craned his neck. "I can't see him anywhere right now. Look for a man in an oversized coat."

"A coat? In this warm weather?"

The weaver just shrugged. "He probably thinks that it makes him look more important. Along with his hat." He used both hands to pantomime a wide brim.

"We'll keep an eye out. Thanks, and we hope you have a successful business day."

"If you need woolens, don't go to those other cutthroats, just come to me. You won't regret it."

"We'll keep that in mind." She waved good-bye. "See you soon."

They strolled back and forth through the market at least five times before Madlen nudged her aunt and pointed to a man.

"You're right. He fits the description exactly. Come on."

The women walked directly to him. At first, he didn't even seem to notice them, as he busied himself by inspecting the stalls.

"Excuse me." Agathe stopped directly in front of him, forcing him to stop in his tracks.

"Yes?"

"Are you the head of the marketplace?"

"Yes, I am, my good lady. How can I help you?"

"Well, my daughter and I are new to this city. We've come a long way to conduct business here. Emmerich is known far and wide for its magnificent opportunities for trade, as you well know," Agathe said smoothly.

He nodded graciously. "I do, my good woman."

"We would like to operate a booth at your market. What would that cost us?"

"Two guilders a day."

"What?" Agathe was astounded. "So much?"

"But of course. That's the standard price."

"And for a little booth?"

"That is for a small booth. If you wanted something bigger, it would cost you all of four guilders daily."

"God Almighty. We would need to sell a great deal of goods to just break even."

Her comment didn't seem to faze him. "When you've had some time to think about it, come back to me. Now, I must attend to my work."

"Wait a moment, please." Agathe shot Madlen a quick look to ensure that she was in agreement. "We'd like to have a stall for tomorrow."

"Then send your husband here early tomorrow so we can do the necessary paperwork. You can start offering your goods when the market opens."

"My husband?" Agathe repeated, a puzzled look on her face. "We're operating the stand ourselves." She pointed at Madlen and then at herself.

The man wrinkled his nose. "What? Two women alone? Well, you can save your money. Only men are allowed to do business here."

"What are you saying?" Agathe pointed at the stands. "More than half of the stands are staffed by women."

"True," the man explained. "However, these women work the stalls on behalf of their husbands. Women can't conduct proper business by themselves; everyone knows that. Emmerich is a member of the Hanseatic League." Pride was evident in his voice. "Here we adhere closely to their laws, and they are quite clear. Women cannot conduct business, and neither you two nor I can change it." He touched his finger to the rim of his hat. "Have a pleasant day." Agathe and Madlen stood there dumbfounded.

"Did I understand this correctly? We can't do business here because we're women?" Madlen looked at Agathe in disbelief.

"That's exactly what it means," Agathe explained.

"What will we do now?"

"Find Ruppert," Agathe said succinctly. "Come on. If we don't have a husband, then we just need to find someone who can masquerade as one."

Chapter Twenty-Four

Johannes was completely beside himself. He tried to usher the Heidelberger out of his home as quickly as possible. With warm, soothing words, he reassured him that he would do everything in his power to locate the secret healer while indicating that he'd heard that this woman had already left Worms many months ago. Still, Matthias wouldn't let it go. He reminded Johannes of the duties that had been conferred upon him by the archbishop. Johannes knew that he had to be careful to at least give the appearance that he wanted to find the woman. Of course, he wasn't lying when he said that he didn't know her whereabouts. But what would happen if Trauenstein shared his detailed description with others? Wouldn't everybody in Worms inevitably recognize Johannes's wife? How in the world would Johannes explain to the archbishop that he had married the woman who was in league with the devil? No, that was out of the question. And not just because of him: his mother, his father, the prestige the Goldmanns had built up over so many decades. Everything was at stake now, and all thanks to Johannes's careless decision to marry a woman with magical powers. How had he fallen in love with her so quickly? Had she used Lucifer's power to capture his heart and soul? It had to be. Johannes had never felt like this about any other woman. Yes, now it made sense.

He paced up and down the main hall of the Goldmanns' home, impatiently waiting for the moment when the little boy would inform him of the skipper's return. He waited for hours, but nothing happened. Johannes decided to get out and try to find out as much as possible by himself. He would track down the maid who had lived in Agathe's home. His mother had heard that Roswitha, as the maid was called, had been taken into the household of Otilia, an acquaintance of hers. He would make his way there first. She would certainly know more. The idea that his wife wasn't even a seamstress left a bitter taste in his mouth. Was that a lie, too, like everything else? Johannes had only reported fragments of his conversation with Matthias Trauenstein to his mother. He hadn't mentioned the fact that he recognized his own wife as the sorceress; the shame of having fallen under her spell was too great. And worse, she was now carrying his child in her womb. Had he played into the hands of the devil by haplessly helping to bring the spawn of Lucifer to life? He crossed the hall hurriedly and left the house. Otilia's house wasn't far from his own. He tried to settle down as he walked down the streets. He had to be clever. When he finally arrived in front of the house, he collected himself and knocked on the door. A guard greeted him.

"Your mistress has a maid in her employ; her name is Roswitha. I would like to speak with her, please."

"With the maid?" The guard seemed surprised. What would such a refined man want with a simple maid?

"Yes."

"Please come in and wait here." The guard opened the door then disappeared into an adjoining room. A short time later, Otilia entered the hallway. "Johannes? I haven't seen you in a long time. I hope your parents are doing well?"

Johannes bowed politely. "Thank you. Yes, they are fine." Johannes thought about where he'd met this woman before. She seemed to recognize him. "You don't remember me? Reni is my daughter. You played together often as children."

"Oh, of course." Johannes hit the palm of his hand on his forehead. "Reni."

"What can I do for you?"

"Actually, I didn't want to bother you. I wanted to speak to Roswitha."

"And what do you want with her, if I may ask?" Otilia smiled.

"Please forgive me if I seem rude. I would rather speak to her directly."

"Actually, it does seem rather rude," Otilia replied arrogantly. "You must understand that it's my duty to protect my servants. Roswitha is very busy, and she's a very shy young woman. She would be uncomfortable speaking to you alone. I'm sorry." She pointed to the door.

"I don't understand." Johannes looked at the guard, who proceeded to guide him toward the door. "You're throwing me out?"

"You're throwing me out?"

Otilia laughed. "Of course not. With your fine upbringing, I trust you'll have the decency to leave the premises on your own accord." She smiled kindly.

"I'm running an investigation," Johannes said angrily. "Roswitha is a witness, and I demand to speak with her immediately."

"A witness? For what?"

"I can't tell you."

"And under whose authority are you conducting an investigation?"

"I'm not at liberty to disclose that."

"Then I'm sorry. Come back with constables, whoever they may be, and let them take Roswitha. But not without giving her mistress a proper reason. You, of all people"—she tapped his chest—"should know the law."

"Your behavior is outrageous," Johannes said with disgust. "Or do you have something to hide? Is that it?"

"Oh, my dear Master Goldmann, this has gone too far. I have much to do, and you are wasting my time. I'm taking care of my servants, and that's all. You must go."

The guard came threateningly close to Johannes. "You should leave now."

"Until recently, the maid served Agathe, the seamstress." The guard tugged on Johannes's arm and marched him over to the door.

"Her loss was my gain," Otilia replied with a smile. "Have a pleasant day, Johannes Goldmann." With these words, another guard appeared, a giant of a man. He opened the door, grabbed Johannes by the arm, and threw him out. Johannes almost tumbled down the steps but caught himself at the last moment. Stunned, he stood before the closed door. Nothing like this had ever happened to him before.

"She did what?" Elsbeth looked at him, her mouth wide open in shock.

"You understood me, Mother. Otilia threw me out onto her front steps."

"But something must have happened. Why would Otilia do such a thing?"

"She had no reason."

Elsbeth sat pensively on her chair. "That is quite odd. I've always known Otilia as an honest, friendly noblewoman. What would she have against you so suddenly?" Elsbeth rubbed her chin thoughtfully; then she looked at Johannes. "What do you want from this maid, this Roswitha?"

"She was Agathe's servant."

"And?"

Johannes could feel blood surging through his head. Should he tell his mother the truth? "I hoped that she would have information about Maria's disappearance."

Elsbeth looked at him sympathetically. "Oh, Johannes. I understand how hard this must be for you, but I've come to the conclusion that your wife has left you and doesn't intend to return. You need to get your marriage annulled."

Johannes had already considered this option himself, particularly in light of the fact that he'd become an instrument of the devil. Still, he preferred not to tell Elsbeth. His mother was a strong woman, but the truth would devastate her more than she would ever admit.

"I just want to know why she left," he replied.

"I know, but you must prepare for the possibility that you might never get an answer."

Johannes thought it over. "You know Roswitha, right?"

"I've seen her a couple of times, yes. Why?"

"I have to talk to her."

"Johannes. Otilia is her mistress. If she's forbidden it, you could get into trouble."

"Not if it's for an investigation." The words popped out of his mouth.

Elsbeth looked at him intensely. "What do you mean by that, Johannes?"

He immediately regretted saying it. "I just thought that somehow if I . . ." He didn't know what to say.

"Johannes, I want to know this instant what this is really about. And don't you dare lie to me." Elsbeth glared at him angrily.

He knew immediately that it was no use. He could never get a lie past his mother. He moved his chair and sat down opposite Elsbeth. He took a deep breath and told her everything that had happened as accurately as possible, especially the description that Matthias Trauenstein had given him of the sorceress. Elsbeth was shocked, listening with her hand in front of her mouth.

"Now you know why I must find her. She's in league with the devil, Mother; she fooled us all."

Elsbeth gaped. "I simply don't believe it." She looked her son directly in the eye, feeling completely drained. "And you have no doubt that this is the same woman?"

Johannes shook his head slowly. "There are too many similarities. Especially the mole." He tapped his finger on the place just above his upper lip. "Or have you seen another woman who fits this description so closely?"

Elsbeth pressed her lip together. "No, you're right. He's described her to the last detail."

"I told her myself that the Heidelberger was coming to Worms to give me the description of the woman who killed his wife. That's why she ran away."

"My God, Johannes, I can't imagine how you must feel right now. What will you do?"

"I must find the secret healer and bring her before court to stand trial. She will face charges of murder and infanticide. It's my job to ensure that justice is served."

Elsbeth shook her head. "Do you mean that you want to see her hang?"

"If that is the decision of the court," he said coldly.

His mother didn't respond. What would this mean for Johannes and their family? Would it mean the loss of all that they had worked so hard for all these years?

"I need your help to get ahold of this Roswitha," Johannes said.

"What can I do?" Elsbeth replied numbly.

"What is the name of her new husband?"

"Sander?"

"Exactly. Sander." The name seemed vaguely familiar. "Sander," he repeated pensively. "The very same Sander who was saved from the cough?"

"Could be."

"I need two guards who can keep their mouths shut."

"What are you planning?"

"The craftsmen will be done with their work soon; they'll be eager to drink a pint at the pub." Johannes looked at her. "Let's see whether this Roswitha won't come to me herself." He smiled, baring his teeth in a way that gave Elsbeth goose bumps.

"Where am I?" Sander blinked when the guards pulled the linen sack off of his head.

Johannes stood with his legs apart in front of the bound man. He scrutinized Sander as the man tugged violently on the ropes cutting deeply into his wrists.

"I wouldn't do that," Johannes advised, observing the wounds. "Although I'm not a doctor, I imagine it's painful when the ropes cut deeper into your flesh."

Sander tried again to free himself. "Let me go!" he growled. "What do you want with me?"

Johannes dragged a chair from the corner of the room and set it at a safe distance in front of Sander. Johannes studied him. "You're an extraordinarily lucky man," he began finally.

"Me? How's that?"

"Well, you were cured of that terrible cough." Johannes watched Sander's expression change. Though still angry, the reason for his detainment slowly dawned on him.

"I had a cough, yes. But not the one that so many have died from," he lied.

"Is that so? I heard something else entirely."

"From whom?"

"I'm asking the questions."

Sander lowered his head, and Johannes waited. Sander finally looked up. "Do you want something else or can I go now?"

"Your cough," Johannes reminded him.

"I already told you, it wasn't so bad. Why is this so important?"

"I decide what's important," Johannes growled.

Sander sighed. "What do you really want?"

"Who healed you?" Johannes demanded.

"Nobody. The cough came and then it went. That's all."

Johannes shook his head with pity. "Oh, Sander. We both know that's not the truth. But I see that we're not getting anywhere here." He stood up and neatly parked his chair back in the corner. Then he waved to the guards, who went through the wooden door together.

"Where are you going?" Sander looked at them in a panic.

"Us? It's time to eat. I'm hungry." Johannes opened the door.

"And what about me?" Sander roared.

"You appear to need a little time to think. Let's hope it's not too cold for you down here, so far underground."

"You can't do this to me. I haven't done anything wrong."

"Yes, but we're going to do it anyway." Johannes laughed as he locked the door from the outside. When they locked an even heavier door at the top of the stairs, Sander's yells couldn't be heard at all.

"Did you do what I asked you to do?" Johannes asked Elsbeth when he came home.

"Yes." His mother nodded. "But I wasn't comfortable with it at all." She touched Johannes's arm. "Is Sander all right? You didn't do anything to him, did you?"

"Mother." Johannes took her hands in his. "You know me better than that. I only do what I have to do in order to get answers. I've not forgotten my humanity."

She sighed in relief. "You don't realize how much better that makes me feel. I was afraid . . ." She bit her lip.

"Don't worry. I'm only scaring him." He balled up his hand into a fist. "This Roswitha will talk, and I'll learn what I need from her in order to find Maria."

"And what then?" Elsbeth's voice trembled.

"I'll try her, then convict her. That's my job."

"But Johannes." Elsbeth was horrified. "She's your wife. You married her; don't you at least want to give her the opportunity to explain?"

"What? Why she ripped an innocent child from its womb and murdered Adelhaid Trauenstein in cold blood? Or the magical healing that she did in the name of the devil?"

Elsbeth was stunned. She had never seen her son so angry before. His grief had transformed into coldhearted hatred. Elsbeth wondered whether it had been a mistake to assist her son with his plans. She wanted to say something, but the front door squeaked open. A moment later, a guard knocked on her door and entered with her permission.

"Excuse me, my lady. A maid who calls herself Roswitha is at the front door. She would like to speak with you."

"She actually wants to see me," Johannes answered. "Send her in."

The guard nodded. Johannes turned to Elsbeth. "You shouldn't be here. I thank you for your help; I'll do the rest on my own." Her son's voice sounded harsh.

"I'm staying," Elsbeth replied firmly, as she straightened her skirt and sat to await the visitor. Johannes wanted to argue, but there was a knock, and the guard let Roswitha enter. She curtsied and looked at the Goldmanns shyly. It was obvious that she'd been crying.

"I was told that Sander would be here." She stared at the floor.

"Really?" Johannes folded his arms in front of his chest. "Well, I think that there must be a misunderstanding. Did you tell her this, Mother?"

Elsbeth fell silent. She looked at her son expectantly.

"Well," he continued, "Sander is not here, but I know where he can be found."

"Where?" Roswitha's body began to tremble.

"I will gladly tell you, once I have some answers."

Roswitha nervously chewed her lower lip. "What do you want me to do?" Her trembling became even more violent.

"Sit down," Johannes ordered, moving a chair away from the table. The maid obeyed without looking up.

"I only have one question," Johannes stated.

"Is Sander all right?" She lifted her head to look at Johannes through tearful eyes.

"We can go into that in a moment," he replied dismissively. Johannes started to pace the room. Horrified, Elsbeth followed his movements. It was if he were a completely different person.

"We haven't seen each other in a long time, Roswitha."

The maid didn't answer.

"That last time was in Agathe's home."

She nodded mutely.

"Your Sander had the cough and was healed. How did that happen?" he said, suddenly changing his tune.

Roswitha winced as if someone had dealt her a blow. "He just had a light cough." Her voice wasn't more than a whisper.

"Just a light cough. Really? I heard otherwise."

"It was just a light cough," she reiterated, although she didn't dare meet his gaze.

"If you say so." Johannes's eyes fell on Elsbeth, who was tense and pale. He would have preferred that she wasn't in the room for this.

Johannes knew that Elsbeth would be quite displeased with the way he forced Roswitha to talk.

"Are you happy with your new husband?"

"Yes, my lord."

"You're lucky that you found a new job. Or did Agathe take care of that?"

Roswitha looked up, gazing first at Johannes then at Elsbeth. It was obvious that she hadn't expected this question.

"Well, don't you want to answer?" Johannes asked.

"Yes, it was Agathe who arranged it," Roswitha admitted.

"How nice of her," Johannes replied sarcastically. "And Otilia just so happened to have an open position?"

"She was looking for a maid, yes, at least until Agathe comes back."

"Wait a minute." Johannes lifted his eyebrows. "Agathe's coming back?"

"Yes, my lord."

"And do you know when?"

"No, my lord."

"But you are sure that she's coming back?"

"Yes, my lord."

"And how you can be so sure?"

"She told me. As soon as . . ." She chewed on her lower lip, looking for the right words. "As soon as she's taken care of business, she will come back with your wife."

Johannes laughed. "How nice to hear that from the mouth of a maid." He banged his fist on the table. Elsbeth and Roswitha yelped.

"I've had enough. Where did they go? Tell me right now!"

Roswitha's eyes were wide with terror. "I . . . I . . . please."

"Please what?" Johannes put his hands on the table and moved his face right up to hers.

"I, really, I really don't know. I swear to you. I don't know," the maid stammered.

She gulped as she tried to look past him to Elsbeth, but he wouldn't let her.

"You seem to have less concern for Sander than I thought."

Roswitha broke down in tears. "Please, Sander hasn't done anything."

"He let the secret healer fix him, and we both know who that is, don't we?"

Roswitha felt her whole body pulsate. "You know?" she asked in disbelief.

"Yes, I know everything. So you can stop lying." He banged on the table again, then folded his hands behind his back and paced the room. "What I don't know is where my faithful wife went. You will tell me, if you value Sander's life at all."

"But you're not . . . Sander has nothing to do with this."

"It's up to you. I'm going to find Maria, with or without your help. Tomorrow, I leave Worms." Johannes felt Elsbeth's eyes sticking to him like glue. He'd just made the decision, but he was confident that it was the right one. He lifted his head. "No one, except me, knows where Sander is. Think about that. If I leave tomorrow and you haven't told me where I can find these women, Sander will stay where he is and rot. No one will find him. It's your decision. Tell me where they went, and I'll set Sander free. If not, I'll present you with his decomposed remains when I return in a few months."

Terrified, Roswitha blurted out, "A skipper named Hugo took them. He sailed with them on the Rhine."

"Where did they go exactly?"

"I heard Maria and Agathe talk about a merchant who buys her dresses whenever he moors in Worms."

"And where does this merchant live?"

"I don't know exactly."

Johannes took a deep, exasperated breath as the maid struggled to remember.

"I know it's a city close to the Netherlands. I just can't recall the name." Tears welled up in her eyes. Suddenly, she lit up. "Emmerich! That's it. The place is called Emmerich." Her heart beat wildly in her chest. Whether it was due to relief or because she'd betrayed her mistress, she couldn't say.

"Emmerich, you say?"

"Yes, my lord. I'm sure of it. That's all I know, I swear." She looked at him expectantly. "Can I get Sander back now?"

Johannes hired a skipper the very next morning to take him north on the Rhine, although he would not reveal his exact destination until they arrived. The pouch filled with money was all the skipper needed to sail out.

"I have to pick up some goods first. It'll only take an hour."

"I'll be waiting here." Johannes took back the money pouch.

"Hey, wait a minute. You need to pay me."

"I'll pay you half as soon as we make sail and the other when we arrive."

The skipper mumbled something, but he left it at that. Some people were simply distrustful these days.

Chapter Twenty-Five

They had to ask half the population of Emmerich before they found out where Ruppert lived. Agathe fervently hoped he was home. She knocked, and a toothless woman opened the door; she was a good twenty years older than Agathe.

"What do you want?"

"We'd like to speak with Ruppert. He lives here, yes?"

"So what if he does? What do you want with him?"

"Tell him that Agathe from Worms is here."

"From Worms? You've traveled a long way. Has he done something wrong?"

"No, he hasn't. Can't you let us speak to him?"

The old lady looked sullen as she finally let both the women enter. "Ruppert!" she bellowed upstairs. "Ruppert, you good-for-nothing, come on down. You have a visitor."

There were signs of life upstairs. "Who is it, Mother?"

"A woman named Agathe from Worms," the old hag yelled back. "Come down here right now; otherwise, I'm going to throw them both out again."

Agathe and Madlen traded looks until Ruppert came downstairs. He stopped at the next to last step, gazing at his visitors with confusion. "Agathe, is that really you?"

"It wasn't easy to find you, Ruppert. This is my foster daughter, Maria." Agathe hesitated briefly before saying her niece's name. She wondered whether it was wiser to give her a completely different name. But there was no turning back now.

"Greetings to you both!" He walked over to the women. "To what do I owe the honor? What are you doing in Emmerich?"

"So many questions," Agathe said, trying to distract him with her charm. "Do you have a moment?" She looked around. The house was dark and small and smelled musty. "Why don't we take a little walk?"

"As you wish." He followed as the women stepped outside. "Mother, I'm going out again."

They left the house together and walked a bit before Agathe continued, "You live with your mother?"

"When I'm here, yes. It doesn't make sense to have my own place since I'm away so often. And I can take care of her when I'm home. You've seen her. She's gotten old and needs help."

Agathe had a completely different impression of the old lady. She was bossy and irritable and didn't seem helpless in any way. But she nodded. "Old age is not easy. It's good to have a son who can take care of you."

Ruppert smiled. "Now tell me, what are you doing so far away from Worms?"

"Haven't you always raved about Emmerich?" Agathe let out a forced laugh.

"No, seriously." Ruppert looked at her pointedly.

"We want to operate a booth to sell our dresses, but the head of the market will not admit us unless a man takes part in the business contracts."

"Yes, that's the way it is here." Ruppert realized that she still hadn't answered his question. The women had something to hide, and he would be much happier if he knew what it was.

"Can you help us?" Agathe asked.

Ruppert scratched his head. "You need me to get permission so you two can do business here?" He thought it over. "What's in it for me?"

Agathe had worried that the merchant wasn't the friendly man she had done business with for so many years. She had to offer him something. "As long as we do business under your name, we'll give you ten pfennigs for every dress we sell."

"Twenty pfennigs," he countered.

"What's the use of selling dresses if we don't make a profit?"

"You want me to believe that you don't make more than twenty pfennigs' profit on every dress you sell?" He laughed throatily. "Agathe, how stupid do you think I am?"

"Ten pfennigs," she insisted.

He stopped, and Agathe and Madlen followed suit. Ruppert scrutinized the women. Then his expression changed. "Ten pfennigs and a small kindness from time to time." He smiled crookedly and let his gaze rest on Madlen.

Agathe laughed scornfully. "You've completely lost your mind." She grabbed Madlen's hand and pulled her away with her. After a few steps, Ruppert caught up with them.

"Wait, wait, can't a man make a little joke?"

Agathe stopped again. "How many jokers do you think I've met in my life?" She approached Ruppert until her face was inches from his. Suddenly, he felt a sharp point where the braiding held his jacket together. "Sir, this is a knife whose blade I make sure to sharpen every single day. You were too distracted by your vulgar thoughts to notice that I was wearing it, or how quickly I pulled it out. I was wrong about you, Ruppert. I mistook you for an honest businessman, but I know the look in your eyes. You weren't joking. We'll take our leave now." The knife tip bored deeper into his flesh. "If you are ever in Worms again, spare yourself a trip to my house. I want nothing to do with you ever again. Do you understand?"

Ruppert had broken out into a cold sweat. He felt a trickle of blood make its way down his stomach, where the tip of the knife had broken his skin. He nodded.

"Good." Agathe drew her knife back. "Now be on your way." He scurried off, and she linked arms with Madlen. "People can really fool you sometimes."

They walked a while silently until they reached the booths. Madlen was the first to dare speak. "Did something bad happen to you?"

"You need to accurately assess the men you meet. A woman must be able to defend herself; otherwise, all is lost."

Madlen stopped and looked her aunt right in the eyes. "I'm right, aren't I?"

Agathe dodged her niece's intense look and peered over her at the booths. "We have to try to find someone else to help us now."

"Will you tell me?"

Agathe paused, then shook her head. "We have too much to do. If we can't find anyone to help us today, we won't be able to sell anything tomorrow."

Madlen understood that pushing the issue was futile. She swallowed down the feeling of terror and followed her gaze. "And if we can't sell here, can we give something else a try? Maybe Fronicka can help us?"

"That's not a bad idea. Come on, we'll go and ask her." They left the stands and walked back to the Golden Rooster, where they'd already spent five nights. When they entered, they asked after Fronicka, but the maid said that she was out shopping. The women sat in the tavern with spiced wine. Soon, the craftsmen would return after work, and then it would be anything but harmless there for the two women. Agathe knew how to save her skin, but she was worried about Madlen, who was even more vulnerable in her current condition. Agathe was relieved when the landlady returned to the tavern.

"Fronicka," Agathe said immediately. "Can we speak to you?"

"Of course." Fronicka handed her shopping basket to the maid, who disappeared instantly into the adjoining room. The landlady came to their table, and Agathe pointed at a chair. "We would like to ask you a question."

Her interest piqued, Fronicka took a seat. "What can I do for you?"

"We're seamstresses, and we have a few dresses to sell. It's different here than back home; women may only do business on behalf of a man."

"That's correct," Fronicka confirmed. "I have the tavern here only because it belonged to my husband when he was alive. I also paid a large sum to the city leaders not to take it away from me when my Ewald died."

"I understand." Agathe pressed her lips together. "Is there any way to sell dresses here without a middleman?"

"You don't want to pay?" Fronicka affirmed.

"Above all, we don't want to be dependent on a man," Madlen explained.

"I like you," Fronicka said, amused. "What kind of dresses do you have?"

"A more simplistic style than the women here wear," Agathe admitted. "We'll be adding some pearl work soon."

"There could be a way," Fronicka thought out loud. "Initially, you wouldn't sell many; this type of business takes some time to develop."

"How?" Madlen said, perking up.

"You must understand that the real business deals are not made at the market in Emmerich. At first glance, there seems to be a wide selection of goods, but if you look closely, they offer the same old stuff, made the same old ways. People buy these things, but what the people really want is something unique."

"Unique?"

"Exactly. And you can only get those things if you know the right people." She pointed at the door. "Take my ham, for instance. My ham is famous far beyond Emmerich's boundaries. I would never tell anyone where I get it. Nobody knows but me, and of course, I won't tell anybody." She smiled. "Or my honey, with which I sweeten my recipes. Everyone knows that it's the best honey, but where does it come from?"

"You have a secret ham recipe and special honey?" Agathe was amazed. She had never heard of such a thing. In Worms, everyone knew where to get what product at what price. Such secrecy wouldn't have occurred to anybody.

"But of course! Emmerich is home to people from all regions. And we are very proud members of the Hanseatic League. Emmerich may not be big, but it is important in commercial trade. If we find something only we can offer, we make sure to keep it under lock and key."

"And how will this help us?"

Fronicka smiled again. "Let me see one of your dresses," she said.

"They're upstairs in our room. Shall I go get one?" Madlen offered.

"Oh heavens, no!" Fronicka stood. "We certainly won't bring these special goods down here where anybody could see them. Come on. Let's go to your room."

The women climbed the stairs, and Agathe unlocked the door. She carefully spread the two dresses out over the beds. Fronicka gazed at them, rubbing her chin as she pondered. "And you say that you're planning to change them?"

"Yes, of course. What do you think?"

"They have to be different than anything the women here have seen."

"I know," Madlen said suddenly, picking up a dress. "I noticed that the ladies wear almost all their jewels around their necks. What if we sew the jewels directly onto the dresses?"

Agathe looked at Madlen; she was speechless. She had never heard such creative ideas from her. She was just about to speak when Fronicka beat her to it.

"That's it! Why didn't I think of that?" She looked excitedly from Madlen to Agathe, inviting their opinions.

"But where could we get those kind of jewels?" Agathe argued. "Something like that is expensive. The ladies would have to pay a fortune for every dress."

"They'll gladly pay you a fortune, believe me," Fronicka assured her. "But you're right, these types of fine jewels are hard to find."

"How about necklaces and cording attached so that they drape like jewels?" Madlen said daringly.

"Exactly!" Fronicka held up her finger. "I know a woman who creates almost all the gold jewelry for her husband. He's very famous, far beyond the borders of Emmerich, but in reality, it is his wife who makes the goods. Anyway, he's so drunk most of the time he can't even walk straight." She laughed. "I'll speak with her to see if she'd be willing to create simple gold chains for you."

"Oh, Fronicka, that would be wonderful. When can you meet with her?"

"Now." Fronicka wasn't the kind of woman who wasted time. "I'll go to her right away, and you should accompany me so she can begin fashioning your order as quickly as possible. I'll prepare a way to sell these unique dresses to a very wealthy lady." She looked at the dress's cut. "But you'll need to let out some fabric from around the middle. The woman is rich and eats accordingly."

Agathe laughed. "About how big is she?"

Fronicka blew some air out of her cheeks and lifted her arms to indicate that the woman was at least twice her size. "I think about so.

And think what she'll say when you present her with a dress that fits her like a glove, sight unseen? You won't be able to sew fast enough to keep up with her orders."

"We'll share some of our profits with you for your help," Agathe announced.

Fronicka waved her off. "That won't be necessary."

"Not necessary? You don't need money?"

"You know, I fought my way through life for a long time by myself. And it gives me such pleasure to help women like yourselves. Our goldsmith is a drunkard and a lazy bastard; the most wonderful pieces of jewelry come out of his workshop because his wife is quite skilled at the craft. The wine I offer here is sent from a large vintner in wonderful oak barrels and is popular because his wife has quite a refined palate. The baker here can't even haul sacks of flour, and yet we have the best bread because his wife and daughter work themselves to death. Wives and daughters create fine goods that merchants come from far and wide to purchase. And yet it's always the man who gets credit. I see it over and over again." She looked at Agathe, then at Madlen. "And here you stand, two women who work and want to find happiness. Who could help you better than a woman who all too often had to get what she wanted all by herself?" She smiled. "No, I don't want your money. I want you to succeed."

Agathe and Madlen were speechless. The people here in Emmerich were different. Madlen wanted to begin her new life more than ever.

Chapter Twenty-Six

Johannes took the time to write a long letter to the archbishop, informing him that he was in the process of tracking down the secret healer. He didn't reveal her identity but announced that it wouldn't take much longer until he'd be able to bring this woman as his prisoner to Trier.

He gave the letter to Elsbeth to send. His mother promised to send it, even though she hated the thought that there would be no turning back once the message was delivered. Afterward, Johannes packed up some things, tied up the bundle, and said good-bye to his parents. He went to the harbor, where the skipper was waiting for him.

"I'm bringing another passenger. He'll help me with loading and unloading."

Johannes scrutinized the young man and nodded his approval. They unmoored the boat and pushed off the dock into the deep waters of the Rhine, sailing quickly downstream. Johannes had not informed the Heidelberger of his journey. Though Trauenstein had wormed his way into becoming an official investigator for the archbishop, Johannes's own trials and tribulations weighed far heavier on him than the threat of this Heidelberg nobleman accusing him of misconduct.

Thoughts swirled through his mind as Worms shrank into the distance. A few days ago, his wife had seen the same view. Was she sorry that she had to leave him? He wondered whether everything had been a lie or whether Maria had really loved him, even just a little. Or had she used every opportunity to manipulate him, to cover up the devil's evil activities by being at the side of a respected citizen? He shook his head. No matter what she felt or didn't feel for him, it was his duty to catch her and denounce her as a handmaiden of the devil. Terrible images loomed in his mind's eye; he saw his pregnant wife with a rope around her neck. He felt his heart beating violently. Could he bear the sight of that?

"Are you all right?"

Johannes flinched when the young man approached him from the side.

"Oh forgive me, I didn't want to frighten you. I thought the rocking of the boat might be bothering you."

"No, that's not it. I was just . . . oh, it's not important."

"Let me know if you need anything. I promised to lend the skipper a hand so that he would take me with him."

"Where are you going?"

"To Rotterdam. And from there, I'll be taking a ship over the big sea."

"I've never understood that." Johannes shook his head.

"What do you mean?"

"The longing to go to foreign lands. I could hear it in your voice."

"Was it really that obvious?" The young man grinned. "But yes, you're right, my lord. I've wished for this my whole life."

"Then I hope that you find what you're looking for."

"I thank you, my lord."

"What's your name?"

"Andreas."

"Well, Andreas, we'll be spending some time together over the next few days. You can call me Johannes."

"Thank you, Johannes. And you? Where are you going?"

"To Emmerich."

"I've never heard of it."

"It's usually a four-day sail. However, I've made an agreement with the skipper to keep sailing well into the night. We should be there in three days or less."

"Are you in such a hurry?"

"Oh, yes." Johannes looked pensively over the water.

"May I ask why?"

Johannes thought about it briefly. "I must ensure that justice is served," he said.

"Justice in whose name?"

"In the name of the archbishop."

Andreas whistled through his teeth. "I hope you succeed."

Johannes, who had been clutching the railing so tightly that his knuckles were white, loosened his grip. "I will. You can bet on it."

Over the course of the next two days, Johannes studied the landscape bordering the Rhine, sometimes with such intensity that he didn't see it at all. The young man, Andreas, was a pleasant traveling companion. They talked for long stretches about this and that, though Johannes took care not to reveal too much. Andreas told Johannes that he hadn't been in Worms for long before he had the great fortune of running into the skipper, who agreed to take him in exchange for a few pennies and his help in loading and unloading. Emmerich wasn't far from the border of the Netherlands. Andreas would not have to go much farther to reach his destination. Johannes listened carefully as he spoke of other countries and cultures. Something seemed vaguely familiar about this Andreas. He couldn't say why. Probably because the men had understood each other so well from the beginning. Their social standings were worlds apart, yet Johannes had a feeling that Andreas would become an asset to him.

"You should lie down and rest a little. We'll be arriving in Emmerich early tomorrow morning," reported the skipper, who used all his might to keep the boat in the middle of the river's strongest current.

"Good. You've kept your promise," Johannes said. "You've truly earned the bonus."

The skipper acknowledged this with a smile. Johannes rolled up in his blanket and closed his eyes. When his wife's image appeared to him, he opened his eyes again. He didn't want to think about her now. When he dreamed of her, try as he might, he couldn't conjure up thoughts of revenge or condemnation. Rather, he saw her smiling in front of him—beautiful, charming, and seductive. No, he didn't want to see her.

"Tomorrow, you'll be close to fulfilling your duty," Andreas said suddenly in the dark of the night.

"I know," Johannes said a little bit irritably. "That's why I'm going to sleep."

"Good night."

"Good night," Johannes replied and pulled his blanket a little bit higher, although he could still feel the warmth of the sunny day. Thoughts swirled around his head again, but he stopped trying to suppress them. She was still alive and well. Soon, other gruesome pictures of his wife burned in his brain. He wanted to enjoy them.

They arrived in Emmerich before dawn, as promised. The harbor was quiet. The boats floated calmly, and nobody seemed to be awake. Johannes paid the skipper the promised fee.

"It was my pleasure," the skipper said as he gratefully held the money in the palm of his hand. "If there's nothing else I can do, I'll go to lie down now." He pointed to a back corner, where he'd rested only briefly in the last few days in order to sail as much as possible.

"Sleep well." Johannes gestured to Andreas. "Let's get off the boat and let this man have some peace and quiet."

The skipper touched his finger to the brim of his cap. "I wish you good luck." He waited until both men walked over the plank and had their feet on the ground. Then he slid the plank back into the boat. It was securely moored, and the skipper soon fell fast asleep.

"Where are you going now?" Johannes asked Andreas.

"I want to take a look around. If I like it here, I'll stay a few days. And you?"

Johannes paused then yawned. "It's too early to ask myself that question." He scratched his chin. "If you want, we can look for a guest house."

Andreas seemed to think it over.

"It's on me," Johannes added quickly, guessing that his companion's pockets were light.

"All right, I'll go with you."

They strolled through alleyways and streets. So far, there seemed to be no signs of life; the whole town was sleeping soundly. Johannes had always liked this time of day, even as a child, looking around a town that normally pulsed with life. He often snuck out of the house in the wee hours. The early morning air was so special—like the arrival of the first snow. He imagined how it was here in Emmerich when people went to work or took care of their business affairs or simply stood on the street, chatting with neighbors, discussing this and that.

The men jumped out of the way when, suddenly, a woman flung open a door and poured out a bucket of water onto the street. She laughed when she saw their startled faces. "Oh, I'm sorry. I didn't see you there."

"Hopefully, you were emptying out some old water and not the chamber pot," Johannes replied, unable to suppress a smile.

"Don't worry, it was just water. And I missed you."

"But not by much."

"We've just arrived here. It seems that the whole of Emmerich is still sleeping." He looked up at the sign: "The Golden Rooster."

"And you'll find no shelter at this hour." She shook her head. "But at least it's not cold. You can thank your lucky stars that it's not winter." She gave them a broad smile. "Well, then, welcome to Emmerich." With that, she went back inside and shut the door.

Johannes and Andreas continued walking but weren't able to find an inn that was open. They lay in a small meadow underneath a massive oak tree and slept until the rest of the city woke up. Suddenly, Johannes awoke with a start.

"What is it?" Andreas asked anxiously.

Johannes looked around. "Strange. It almost seemed like someone was watching us."

Andreas didn't mention that he'd had the exact same feeling. "Who would be watching us?" he asked. He kept his attention on the surrounding environment. If there really was someone, he wanted to recognize their face.

Although they both wanted to stay alert, they both fell sound asleep until awakened by the noise of Emmerich's hustle and bustle. Johannes sat up with a great deal of effort. The people didn't notice them at all, although they must have made a peculiar sight, sprawled in the grass with no place to stay. Johannes touched his companion and shook him a little. "Andreas, it's time."

Immediately, he stirred. "Where do you want to go now?"

"I have to ask around a bit." Johannes wondered whether it was smart to ask Andreas to accompany him. "Do you want to come with me?"

"My pleasure," he said. "I'll be staying here for at least one more day."

"All right." They left the meadow and went toward the market. As if by magic, dozens of booths had appeared to offer their wares where it had been empty hours before.

Johannes strode forward, searching people's faces, while Andreas followed behind. It was impossible to walk side by side in this crowd. When he could, Johannes stopped and waited for Andreas to catch up to him. "This place is packed. I don't think I can go any farther."

"If you tell me what you're looking for, I might be able to help you," Andreas offered.

"It's a long story," Johannes sighed. "For better or for worse, this is something I have to do by myself. What do you say we meet for a beer later this evening?" Johannes asked evasively.

"I'm in no hurry," Andreas replied. "Where?"

"At the tavern we were at earlier—the Golden Rooster."

"All right. I'll be there," Andreas agreed.

"Then good luck with whatever plans you have for today," Johannes said in parting. "We'll see each other later." With that, he disappeared into the crowd.

Andreas walked through the throngs. He still had the feeling that he was being followed. But though he craned his neck as much as he could, he didn't see anyone. He shook his head.

Johannes stood in front of a spice merchant's stand. "My good man?"

"Yes. What can I do for you?"

"I'm looking for a woman."

"Who isn't, my good fellow, who isn't?" The spice merchant laughed throatily.

Johannes rolled his eyes, but he needed information from this man. "She has long, dark hair, down to here." He pointed to his waist. "Blue eyes and"—he touched right above his lip—"a mole right here. She's strikingly beautiful. Have you seen her? Maybe she wanted to buy herbs from you. There could have been another woman with her, a little older."

The spice merchant thought it over. "Hmm. I don't think I've seen anyone like her. Strikingly beautiful, did you say? No, nobody like that here today."

"It wouldn't have to be today. It could have been a few days ago."

The man shook his head. Many people come by here. I don't notice every person's face. But I would probably recognize someone like that. No, so far I haven't seen her, that's for sure."

"I thank you for your time. Have a good day."

Johannes asked around at a few other stalls, but the answer was always the same. He strolled through the entire market, stopping by every spice or herb merchant. Then he went around the market and asked all the cloth merchants and weavers. But no one had seen the women. Finally, Johannes conjured up a new plan. "My good woman," he said to the cloth merchant. "Tell me, do you know Emmerich?"

"I would like to think that I know the area. Why?"

"How many inns and taverns would accommodate two women?"

"Two women without a man?"

"Correct."

"The White Stallion or perhaps the Golden Rooster. There are lots of taverns that will accommodate strangers as long as they have money; it doesn't matter to the hosts whether they are men or women. And there are two widows right at the harbor that will accommodate anyone."

Johannes nodded. "Where exactly do these widows live?"

"Right on the harbor. The house is a little bit crooked, and the door is painted quite colorfully. No one knows why. But you can't miss it."

Johannes struggled to find his way back to the harbor. Soon after he arrived, he looked around and found the house with the colorfully painted door. It was a little lopsided, as though the tides had tried to pull it out to sea. Resolutely, Johannes walked up to the house and knocked on the door. It creaked open, and a servant looked at Johannes expectantly.

"Is this the house where the widows live?"

"Who are you, and what do you want?"

"Just some information."

Again, the servant waited. Johannes described the women and asked the servant whether he might have seen them or if they'd ever stayed there.

"What do you want with them?"

"Just answer my question."

The servant grimaced, scrutinized Johannes, then went to close the door.

"Wait." Johannes held up a money pouch and counted out three coins. "Here. For you. Are the women here?"

The servant accepted the money. "No, they're not."

"Give me back my money right now, you cutthroat bastard."

The servant put the money in his pocket. "I answered your question. Have a nice day." He slammed the door in Johannes's face.

The lawyer foamed with rage as he beat against the door several times to no avail. He had no other choice but to give up and amble away. The man had tricked him. It made no sense to stay around here any longer. At least, he believed the women definitely weren't here. The man certainly would have let himself be paid well to bring them to Johannes.

Next, Johannes went to the White Stallion, but the answer was the same. It started to dawn on him that Roswitha had probably led him astray. But he disregarded that notion. She knew that Johannes would return to Worms and inevitably confront her. Johannes doubted that a simple maid would lie to him knowing the consequences; she wouldn't want to leave everything behind and start somewhere new.

No, her answer had been truthful. The question was whether Maria and Agathe had decided not to go to Emmerich after all. Johannes's stomach lurched at the thought. He wondered how the women were able to make a living. He'd asked the spice merchants and the cloth merchants. Either Maria was using herbs to heal people, or she and Agathe were sewing dresses, like they'd done in Worms. He couldn't imagine they were able to support themselves any other way.

He sat down sullenly on a bench in the White Stallion and ordered a beer. Lunchtime was already over; though his stomach growled, he had no appetite. Johannes listened in to conversations at neighboring tables, but there was no mention of a woman that fit Maria's description. Everyone seemed to be much more interested in talking shop and chatting about the new, magnificent church that would be built soon. Nothing else seemed to be of interest. He paid, got up, and went toward the door.

As he walked through the threshold, he froze. Was that a shadow that had immediately disappeared around the side of the house? Johannes waited a moment then surged around the corner to catch whoever it was. But nobody was there. He felt silly. Who would be interested in following him? He shook his head and made his way to the tavern where he'd been with Andreas this morning. The Golden Rooster wasn't far. The women were probably staying there. After all, they had to be somewhere.

Chapter Twenty-Seven

"How do you like it?" Madlen held up a dress so high that she disappeared behind it. Then she lowered it to see her aunt's expression.

"Can you put it on again? I'm concerned that the chain might be pulling the collar down. It's not sitting right."

"All right." Madlen stripped her own dress off and pulled the new one on.

Agathe stood, then went over to her niece. She gathered up some fabric from the back, taking up any extra. "It sits on you like a sack," she noted. "So we can hardly tell how the chain lies. We don't have any other choice but to try. You're getting very scrawny, child. Even scrawnier than usual."

"I know," Madlen said, somewhat frustrated as she slipped out of the dress again. "I try to eat for the child's sake. But when I see food, I want to throw up."

"What is it?" Agathe held Madlen by the shoulders, trying to meet her eye. "The tension has subsided somewhat lately."

"I miss Johannes," Madlen admitted as she bowed her head in shame. "Sometimes I can hardly breathe, I miss him so much."

"If you were to go back, then you really wouldn't be able to breathe. Now, you have to force yourself to eat. I don't have to tell you that it's not good if your baby isn't getting the nutrition it needs."

"I'll try to do better. I promise."

"That's good. Come on and get dressed. We need to speak with Fronicka and go visit this customer. Perhaps we'll sell our first dress today."

"That would be wonderful." Madlen slipped her own dress on and quickly tied up its laces. "Well, I'm ready. Let's finally do some business again." She smiled, but Agathe could see that it was halfhearted. She didn't say anything. "That's right. We need to look ahead. Come on. Let's go sell a dress."

They went downstairs to see Fronicka and found her at the stove tasting the soup the cook had prepared.

"Fronicka, do you have a moment? The dress is ready."

The landlady laid her spoon aside. "I have some things to do, but they can wait. Where's the dress?"

"Upstairs in our room."

"Good. I'll need just another moment, then I'll come up and get you."

"Take your time. We're not in a hurry."

Agathe and Madlen went upstairs; the tavern door opened.

"Greetings, my lady."

Fronicka recognized the man she'd seen early in the morning. She nodded. "Well, you've passed the time a little."

The stranger smiled. "So, you remember me."

"Of course. I never forget a face. Would you like something to drink?"

"Not now. I'm meeting a young friend later. At the moment, I just need some information."

"I'd be happy to help you if I can." She cocked her head to the side.

"I'm looking for a woman with long hair and blue eyes. She has a mole right above her lip and is probably traveling with another, somewhat older woman. Have you seen them?"

Fronicka furrowed her brow and shook her head. "No, I haven't. And like I told you, I never forget a face."

He shrugged. "Thank you." He seemed pensive.

"What did you want from them? Perhaps somebody else can help you?"

"No, I don't think so. But thank you for your trouble." He went over to the door. "I'll see you when I come back later."

Fronicka waited a moment, keeping an eye on the door. Then she hurried upstairs to the women's room and knocked. Madlen opened the door right away and was shocked to see the expression on Fronicka's face.

"What's the matter?"

Fronicka closed the door and locked it behind her. "Who are you, and why is a man looking for you?"

Agathe's eyes shot open as she sat on the bed, thoughts racing through her head. "What? Who's looking for us?"

"A man. Tall with very blond hair, wide shoulders."

"Johannes?" Madlen's voice wasn't more than a whisper.

"I don't know his name. What does he want with you?"

"He's my husband," Madlen said softly. She looked at Agathe with tears in her eyes. "What is Johannes doing in Emmerich?"

Her aunt shrugged. "I don't know." She looked at Fronicka. "What did he say?"

"Only that he was looking for you. He described you both exactly. Anyone that's seen you here would recognize you from his description."

"We have to get out of here right away." Agathe looked back and forth between Fronicka and Madlen.

"Run away again? But where to?" Madlen sobbed.

"What's happened that you've had to run away from this man? Did he beat you?"

"No." Madlen sank down on a chair weakly.

"What is it then?" Fronicka's voice got louder.

"We can't tell you without putting you in danger," Agathe answered quietly.

"You've already put me in danger," Fronicka argued. "He'll come back here sooner or later. And he'll know that I lied. So spit it out."

Agathe looked at Madlen, who nodded slowly. She told her why they had to flee Worms but didn't dare breathe a word about what had happened in Heidelberg.

"When people are at a loss, it's always God or the devil," Fronicka said with disgust.

"I swear to you that I'm only familiar with the use of medicinal herbs." Madlen put her hand protectively on her abdomen. "This I swear by all that is holy."

"You don't need to swear to me," Fronicka said, waving her off. "There is no shortage of these kind of stories. People always conjure up a dark side when there is something they don't understand. That's how it's always been and probably always will be. But you're no longer safe here. You have to leave as quickly as possible."

"We have to run away again." All the strength had disappeared from Madlen's voice.

"Yes, you have no other choice."

"But where can we go?"

"To Rotterdam, or maybe even farther."

"But what will happen when Johannes comes back and discovers that you've lied to him? You could get into a great deal of trouble."

"I'm always in trouble. That's how it is when a woman like me refuses to cooperate with men." Fronicka shrugged. "I'm used to it. I have friends here in the city that hold me in high regard. Believe me, I'll be just fine."

"I'm sorry that we dragged you into this." Agathe looked at Fronicka with regret.

"If we stand around much longer, he'll find you," Fronicka warned again. "Quick. Pack your things." She pointed at the dress lying on the bed. "We'll go by Apollonia's place and talk her into buying the dress. You're going to need the money."

The women packed everything up as quickly as possible. They didn't have a lot. They only had to pack up two bolts of fabrics they'd bought to make dresses with. Everything else was already packed. They were too deep in thought to make small talk. Everything seemed to be getting more and more desperate, especially for Madlen. *Johannes. How could he have found us?* Her heart beat violently against her chest when she thought of her husband. As much as she feared the consequences of being discovered, she also had to fight her longing to see him. It might very well be that she would never get the chance again. She loved Johannes with all her heart, regardless of whether she wanted to or not.

"It's not always going to be like this," Agathe tried to assure her. "Johannes will make every effort to find you. But after a while, his ambition will dwindle."

"Are you sure?" Madlen looked up. "What if this is how it goes my whole life?"

"One of these days, something else will come up, and nobody will talk about the secret healer anymore. You have to be patient and be smart."

Madlen nodded, though she was too choked up to respond. She quickly stuffed the rest of her things and pulled on the bundle cord tightly. "I'm ready. Can I help you with anything?"

"No, this is the last little bit. We can head out now."

Fronicka had told them she would wait for them downstairs. Their hearts broken, they descended, making sure that no one else was in the lounge. Fronicka heard the creaking of the stairs and came in from the next room. She took the dress for Apollonia and hung it over her arm.

"Come on. We don't have any time to waste." The three women left the house. Fronicka stopped briefly and looked in all directions. Johannes was nowhere to be seen. She waved at Agathe and Madlen, and they hurried across the market, then down a street and into a small alley. There were frescoes high on the facade of a building. Fronicka stopped and knocked on the door without hesitation. A young man opened it, and his face brightened when he realized it was Fronicka.

"Greetings, Barthel. Is your mistress available?"

He nodded eagerly. "Please, come in. I will inform her immediately that you wish to speak to her, my lady."

After the servant disappeared, it wasn't long before a large woman appeared in the upstairs hallway. "Fronicka, what a pleasant surprise. I wasn't expecting you."

"Apollonia!" Fronicka opened up her arms. "I just couldn't wait to show you something I know you'll love."

The lady of the house gracefully stepped downstairs.

"I'd like to introduce you to two seamstresses that have made a wonderful dress especially for you. I hope you like it."

Immediately, Agathe took a step and bowed. She wasn't used to this. In Worms, she was the one to whom people bent their knee. She asked Fronicka for the dress, then signaled Madlen to grab one side; together they held it up by its sleeves.

"What makes this dress unique is the jewelry sewed right onto it. Do you see?"

Apollonia moved close to the dress, then fingered the gold chain sewn around the collar.

"I've never seen anything like this."

"It's a completely original design."

"And do you think it will fit me?"

"I'm afraid it could be a little too big," Madlen lied. "The dress's cut is unusual in that it is quite narrow around the waist."

"On the other hand, it could drape even more beautifully," Agathe argued, having seen through Madlen's little charade.

The words had the calculated effect. "I'd like to try it on," Apollonia said effusively. "Will you help me, Fronicka?"

"But of course." The landlady took the dress from Agathe and Madlen and followed Apollonia upstairs. Barthel, who'd watched the whole scene quietly, sighed almost inaudibly as he watched Fronicka. Then he said good-bye to Agathe and Madlen and went across the hall to one of the adjoining rooms. A short time later, Apollonia came back out of the room with Fronicka. "I didn't expect it to fit so magnificently," she announced as she stood behind the upstairs railing.

Apollonia turned around to show off the dress, obviously enjoying the amazed looks on their faces.

"Oh, it looks wonderful," Madlen exclaimed sincerely. She was surprised. The dress fit Apollonia like a glove, and the chain draping softly around the collar was an exquisite complement to the entire outfit. Agathe smiled.

The women quickly came to an agreement. Thanks to Fronicka, Agathe and Madlen got their full asking price, without negotiation. Apollonia kept the dress on. After the women left the house, it was clear that all they had to do now was say good-bye.

"I'll take you to the harbor so that you can find a reasonable price from a good skipper."

"We can't possibly thank you enough," Agathe said, touching Fronicka's arm lightly. "Why are there incredible people like you, and also those who want nothing more than to see people hang?" She tried to smile.

"So that balance is not lost." Fronicka also tried to smile, yet the closer the women got to the harbor, the slower they walked.

When they finally reached the harbor, Fronicka stopped, looked over the many boats, then pointed. "Over there. The man's name is Jacques. He's from Bruges. I'll ask him when he's sailing out and whether you can sail with him."

"Thank you." Agathe could barely hide her anxiety. "We'll wait over there." She took Madlen's arm and pulled her away from the hustle and bustle. The women stayed and watched as Fronicka spoke with Jacques. Suddenly, Madlen felt someone touch her shoulder and she winced.

"Well, where do you think you're going, my beloved wife?"

Madlen turned around, and Agathe yelped in terror.

Johannes gave Madlen an ice-cold stare. She was unable to speak. Her heart pounded wildly, and she thought she might faint straight away.

"Please, Johannes," Agathe stammered, but he didn't even look at her. Instead, he held Madlen's shoulders so tightly that her eyes watered. "Did you really think that I wouldn't be able to find you? Did you really believe that?" His brow furrowed, and his mouth twisted contemptuously.

"I . . . I want to explain everything to you. I . . ."

"Spare me your explanations. I know exactly who you are. I fell into your trap. But believe me, I won't make the same mistake again."

"Please, Johannes. I beg of you."

"I loved you," he roared suddenly, and Madlen nearly crumpled. "I loved you so much, and you used me. You're going to burn, you she-devil, and if not that, I will relish the moment when you go to the gallows and I hear your neck break."

At this very moment, a massive cudgel smashed down on the nobleman's head. Johannes lurched and turned around as his knees buckled; he struggled to keep from falling to the ground. "Andreas?"

The man smashed him again and Johannes collapsed. Madlen screeched.

"Shh . . . you want everybody to hear you?"

Madlen couldn't believe her eyes. "Kilian?" She sobbed. "What? How?"

"I'll explain everything later, once we're sure that we're a safe distance away from here." Four brutes stormed up to Kilian and grabbed the women; a violent tumult ensued. Suddenly, a frighteningly familiar face loomed out of nowhere; Madlen's blood froze in her veins.

"Well, now, who do we have here?" Matthias Trauenstein bared his teeth.

"Help! Help!" Agathe shouted. She caught a punch to the face and dropped to the ground like a ton of bricks. Madlen began to scream as Kilian tried desperately to shake off his attackers.

"No!" screamed Madlen desperately.

"Leave her alone," Kilian shouted. On a signal from Matthias Trauenstein, two henchmen held him as the others pummeled him mercilessly. He absorbed the blows until a solid punch to the chin left him lying lifeless on the ground. Madlen screamed in anguish, but Matthias only laughed.

Some people craned their necks to see what was going on. Fronicka looked back worriedly, trying to see what had happened.

"Come on. Get out of here!" Matthias signaled the men to leave Kilian.

Madlen hung powerlessly between the two henchmen, stumbling as they dragged her away. She couldn't see anything through her tears.

"If you make even one more sound, I'll slit their throats." Matthias cocked his head back toward Agathe and Kilian. Madlen choked back a sob. She felt sick and thought she might throw up at any second. The brutes held her under her arms so tightly that her feet barely touched the ground. She heard Fronicka's voice calling as if from far, far away. Madlen lost all strength to fight back. Her final hours here on earth had come to pass, and she knew it. The child in her womb would never see the light of day.

Chapter Twenty-Eight

"This is all your fault!" Johannes held the wet cloth on the huge bump on the back of his head. He glared at Kilian, who was slumped in the chair in front of him looking at the floor, his face pummeled to a black-and-blue pulp. "I would have brought them before the archbishop, but this Trauenstein will kill her."

Agathe wasn't capable of speech as tears streamed down her cheeks.

"I should have known that something in your face was familiar to me," Johannes continued. "Her brother, naturally. The same eyes; I should have seen it." He snorted with rage. "But I did not know that my faithful wife had a brother. Maria never told me."

"Madlen," Kilian clarified. "Her name is Madlen, not Maria. And shit on your archbishop. My sister has never done anything to anyone." He spit out.

Johannes was foaming. "What makes you think a wretch like you can talk to me like that?"

"Stop immediately!" Fronicka shouted. "You two have to behave when you're in my house, otherwise I'll kick you both out onto the street."

Johannes and Kilian mumbled something unintelligible, then fell silent.

"What can we do now?" Agathe asked.

"First, I want to know the whole truth," Johannes demanded.

"What would you like to know?" Kilian looked him right in the eye.

"Agathe is your father's sister?"

"Yes."

"And your mother?"

"She died giving birth to Madlen."

"And your name is Kilian, not Andreas?"

"Yes. I didn't know whether Madlen had ever mentioned my name. So I told you my name was Andreas."

"And how did you find out about me?"

"I followed Matthias Trauenstein from Heidelberg to Worms. He announced to everyone in town that he knew where to find Madlen, the one who killed his wife. He wanted to bring her before the court, in order to restore his reputation in the city."

"Why did his reputation suffer when his wife was murdered?"

"How nice of you to ask, instead of assuming the worst about my sister," Kilian said. He tried his best to contain himself before continuing. "I'll tell you what really happened in Heidelberg."

"Wait, let me get some beer." Fronicka signaled the maid; she came back shortly with mugs and placed one in front of each person. Fronicka dismissed the maid with a nod and picked up her mug. "We'll be able to think better with a little bit of brew."

Kilian began to speak, and little by little, Johannes saw a completely different picture than what had been painted by Matthias Trauenstein. He was able to resolve the many contradictions in the alleged events described by the nobleman. Agathe and Fronicka followed the conversation, nodding silently; they were horrified as Kilian told them what happened when Madlen was first exonerated and stumbled upon Adelhaid Trauenstein's death.

"So you really believe that this Matthias Trauenstein murdered his own wife just so she could never tell her side of the story? And so that he could be selected as a member of the city council?" Johannes was stunned.

Kilian shook his head. "I know it for a fact. The man is not in his right mind and will do anything to achieve his goals."

"And Madlen came to Worms to escape him?" Johannes looked to Agathe.

"You can't imagine how she suffered, as she stood at the door, helpless. I may have broken the law when I took her in and lied for her, but it was the right thing to do. I would do it again." Agathe lifted her head proudly. Kilian looked at her with admiration.

"When Matthias Trauenstein found out that there was a woman in Worms that fit Madlen's description, I knew that she was in grave danger. I followed him and took it upon myself to nose around a little in Worms. I found out that Madlen had married you and could piece the rest together when I heard that you were looking for the skipper that sailed with two women down the Rhine."

"And then you found your way on the same ship and made friends with me?"

"That wasn't planned. I liked you, that's all. Even though I knew that you were after my sister, I wanted to get to know the man she married."

"And with whom she was expecting a baby," Johannes added thoughtfully.

"I only learned that when my sister and I ran into each other at the harbor."

"When you hit me, you mean?"

"After you grabbed my sister," Kilian clarified.

"Don't start up with that again," Agathe demanded.

"Well, Matthias must have followed us." Johannes rubbed his chin.

"We led him directly to her." Kilian took a big slug of beer.

"It's simply unbelievable, what Maria, sorry, what Madlen had to do. She was only trying to help." Fronicka sighed.

"Where do we look for her? Matthias must have hid her somewhere in the city," Kilian suggested.

"She could be anywhere. But you're right. We have to do something." Johannes looked at Fronicka. "He doesn't know the city, but you do. Where do you think he would take her?"

While Fronicka thought it over, Agathe chimed in. "He won't keep her here." She looked at the others. "Think about it. If he wanted to kill her, he would have done so at the harbor. But he didn't. What does that tell us?"

"That he's planning on doing something with her." Fronicka got goose bumps. She didn't want to imagine what this bastard would do.

Agathe continued. "What did Matthias want to achieve from the very beginning with these false allegations?"

"To keep up the pretense of being a respectable citizen," Kilian said.

"You're right." Johannes drained the rest of his mug. "He caught her to bring her back to Heidelberg and put her on trial. If I had brought her to Trier and given her over to the archbishop, he wouldn't have been able to use her to improve his reputation." He hit the palm of his hand against his forehead. "I'm such an idiot. I led him directly to her."

"To an innocent woman," Fronicka clarified.

Johannes knew that it was the truth. He'd fallen in love with a beautiful, honest woman, and she was in love with him. A pure, innocent creature that never harmed anyone. And now, due to his own stupidity, she was in the hands of a maniacal murderer who'd stop at nothing to get his way.

"We need to head out immediately." He looked at his brother-in-law. "He'll take her to Heidelberg the quickest way possible, and we have to do the same. Even though he's got a head start, it will take a minimum of one or two days until Madlen's trial starts. All is not lost.

Will you help me?" Johannes stretched his hand over the table and Kilian grabbed it. They shook.

"We should get some horses and get under way immediately."

"I'll go with you," Agathe said, defensive when she saw the men's reaction. "I'm a very good rider. You'll see."

"There's no time to wait." Johannes stood up. "Fronicka, where do we get horses?"

Less than an hour later, Agathe, her nephew, and Madlen's husband saddled up. Fronicka attempted to find out whether anyone had seen Matthias, but to no avail. They ruled out the harbor. The Rhine's current would make rapid travel impossible, and it wouldn't matter to Matthias whether riding a horse made Madlen suffer in her condition.

"We can't drive the horses like this the whole time," Kilian cried out to Johannes, as he let his horse go at a full gallop.

"What?" Johannes strained to hear.

Kilian gestured to slow down a little. "If we drive them like this for too long, we'll have to change horses quite often," Kilian tried again.

Johannes was reluctant; he wanted to try to catch up with Trauenstein. But Kilian was right. The more often you changed horses, the slower you arrived at your destination. So, he reined in his mount.

"You're right," Johannes said. "I was so deep in thought that I didn't notice how fast we were going."

Agathe sighed with relief; it had taken all her effort not to lose the others. They rode through the night, stopping when they reached a small grove of trees that could protect them a bit. They let their horses graze, and Agathe took off the bundle Fronicka had given her. "When do we ride again?"

"As soon as dawn breaks and we can see the road ahead," Johannes replied. "Let's try to get a little sleep after we get something to eat."

"We need to keep a lookout," Kilian insisted. "I can take the first watch."

"Good. Wake me up when you need a replacement."

They barely spoke as they chewed their bread and dried meat, washing it all down with a little beer; before they left, Fronicka had filled up their leather drinking pouches. Agathe and Johannes lay down, while Kilian sat up and kept watch. In the deep of the night, Kilian struggled to keep his eyes open; he gently shook Johannes's shoulder. "Can you take over now?"

Johannes blinked. "Yes, I'm awake." He blinked again, yawned, and rubbed his eyes. Then he sat up. Kilian rolled up in his cloak and turned onto his side. A few moments later, he fell asleep.

Dawn broke over the small clearing at the edge of the forest. Johannes woke his companions. Although Kilian had only had a few hours of sleep, he was wide-awake. Agathe yawned; she'd fallen into a deep slumber.

They decided to eat a little as they rode and let the horses canter, instead of letting them rest too long and then driving them too hard later. Agathe watched Johannes and Kilian as they talked. The two men understood each other very well. No wonder Madlen loved them both, though in very different ways. She was the link between the two. Johannes and Kilian seemed to understand that they could only free her as a team.

They rode until noon. The sun was high in the sky when the three agreed to water the horses and dismount for a moment to stretch their legs. They had only crossed paths with other people once, with a small group of merchants. Otherwise, the whole area seemed to be deserted. They didn't stay long. Once the horses had turned away from the river and grazed for a while, the three travelers picked up their reins and got back in the saddle again. They would arrive in Mannheim hours later; it was already starting to get dark.

They decided to stay overnight at an inn they saw along the way. Agathe hoped that the landlord might have seen Madlen, Matthias, and his henchmen, but he had not. She thanked him and ordered food for everyone. Then she sat down at the table with the men.

"I wonder whether they went by boat." Agathe looked at Johannes and Kilian.

"That would definitely take longer. The Rhine's current is quite powerful," Kilian stated.

"What if Trauenstein isn't in as much of a hurry as we thought?"

"What do you mean?"

"Well," Agathe explained, "we thought that he wanted to get back to Heidelberg to put Madlen on trial. But what if he wasn't in a hurry?"

"Why would he be taking his time?"

"I don't know. But Matthias must have known that we'd follow him." She turned to Johannes. "You said yourself that he would never manage to get Madlen there before us. He must be planning something else."

"Like what?"

"I don't really know." Agathe let her thoughts wander. Maybe they were searching for witnesses to Madlen's alleged crimes? What else could it be? What was this creep Matthias up to? She shrugged. "I'm probably wrong; he's bringing her to Heidelberg as fast as he can. Maybe they kept riding through the night."

"Maybe," Johannes repeated pensively and looked at Kilian, who returned his look. What Agathe had said made sense. Matthias must know that it didn't matter whether he hurried or not. A quick trial and conviction wouldn't be enough. What did the bastard intend to do?

Chapter Twenty-Nine

Madlen wasn't shaking much anymore, but she could hardly sit still.

Matthias held her prisoner for the whole day on the boat, which he and his henchman had used to travel from Worms to Emmerich. They gagged and blindfolded her and brought her beneath the deck. Not too long after, Matthias Trauenstein had sat down next to her with a big fat grin on his face. He looked at her a long time, scooting closer and sweeping one finger above her breast. She wanted to slide away as she held her breath and closed her eyes, expecting him to beat her at any moment. But he was much more interested in playing on her fears, telling her over and over again the kind of pain she'd have to endure. He didn't lay a hand on her; instead, he stood up suddenly and left. The next day, they waited until it was dark before they got off the boat and switched to horses, leaving Emmerich under the cover of night.

Madlen had overheard the men talking about how the others probably had a good start by now. Now there was no danger of running into them on the way. Matthias walked the horse slowly; there was no reason to rush. He had thought of everything. He would be the one who determined when Madlen arrived in Heidelberg. He could take all the time in the world to instill fear into every cell of her body and break her will. How he regretted not being able to touch her. But that would be a mistake. He had to bring her back to Heidelberg safely, to show that he was a man of noble character. It had taken all his willpower not to take her right there on the boat, especially after seeing how frightened and helpless she was. He'd almost broken down at the sight of her shapely breasts. But he had the Heidelberg council seat on his mind. Now they wouldn't be able to deny him his rightful place on the council. This little slut had caused him enough trouble. He had to break this woman; she had to obey. That's just the way it was. After all, only Adelhaid had ever rebelled against him; her last miscarriage had taken a heavier toll on her than he'd expected. In any case, the dispute between the Swabian League and the Bavarian dukes was going to last a while longer. He could use this time to take Madlen to trial, win and restore his somewhat tainted reputation, and finally get the respect he sought from those old goats on the city council.

He looked down at Madlen scornfully as she cowered on the forest floor. It was a pitiful sight, and Matthias thought again about what a pleasure it would be to have his way with her. She would probably lose the bastard she carried in her womb. Most people probably couldn't tell she was pregnant; he couldn't say how far along she was. But there was something growing in her belly. He could do something to change that. Matthias didn't want to take the risk that the court would have pity on her because of the little bastard inside her. He'd been surprised when he noticed her condition, because he'd thought that she was the kind of woman who would marry before giving herself to a man. Above all, Matthias wondered who the father was. He tried to get an answer, but she wouldn't say a word. He thought about punching her in the abdomen. She'd probably lose the child and the injuries could be hidden under her clothes. But what would happen if somebody examined her in Heidelberg and found bruises? No, then the whole venture would have been in vain.

Madlen's only thought was to protect her child at any price. She'd seen his maniacal look when she refused to name the father of her child. He had stared at her belly, his face distorted with rage; his eyes filled with anger and blind hatred. Madlen had learned what Matthias was capable of when she'd seen Adelhaid's body. But he held himself back with Madlen. Just in case, Madlen kept herself hunched over, so if he suddenly became enraged, she could protect her belly from his kicks and punches. She'd learned from Clara where the baby lay in its mother's womb. If she could shield this area enough, she wouldn't have to worry too much about her child.

Madlen tried not to focus on Matthias's threats. She breathed deeply and evenly, trying her best to relax her shoulders. She thought about the candlelight that she'd used so often to calm her patients. She silently prayed and recited psalms and verses, humming a little song in her mind. She imagined she was far away from this place, safe and secure in Agathe's house. Shortly before she fell asleep and her mind wandered, her fear returned. Did he want to kill her? Madlen doubted it. For some reason, he still needed her. She thought she knew what his plan was. He wanted to take her to Heidelberg, bring her to trial, and get a conviction for the alleged murder of his wife. Escape was impossible. They'd been on the road for a few days so far; they hadn't even stopped once at an inn, preferring to stay in the protective cover of the forest. She didn't know how much longer it would be until they reached Heidelberg.

She wondered how badly Kilian's blow had injured Johannes. He'd surfaced in Emmerich out of the blue and tried to protect her from Johannes, only to be beaten down by Matthias's thugs. Even Agathe had been beaten unconscious. And how were they now? Had they survived those vicious attacks? But they'd only been unconscious when the henchmen dragged Madlen away. At least that's what Madlen believed.

***

They rode three more days, staying close to the forest; hiding themselves whenever people approached in the distance. Matthias wanted to make sure that nobody saw them, especially that Worms woman or the little bitch's brother. It was absolutely necessary that Matthias kept his prisoner intact so he could quietly hand her over to city leaders in Heidelberg. He couldn't be reckless and risk damaging his image as an honest, upstanding citizen—a broken man who wanted nothing more than justice for the murder of his beloved wife.

He imagined in vivid detail how he would ride across the Neckar River bridge and announce to the guards that he'd finally captured the devil's daughter as his prisoner. People would want to check to see whether he'd harmed or violated her right away. He had acquired a certain reputation over the years, which he had to repair by any means necessary. Certainly, the sheriff, miserable cur that he was, would ask her ever so sympathetically if Matthias had harmed her. Now she couldn't say anything about him, if she didn't want to lie. And he knew she wouldn't.

He rubbed his hands together at the thought. Before now, he'd never been able to exert self-control, but he had learned from his past mistakes, although he still refused to admit that he'd gone too far with Adelhaid and made her lose another child. No. The woman had talked back to him and more than deserved the punishment. But that had always been his flaw: once he'd become enraged, nothing could stop him. Whimpering and begging provoked him even more. Adelhaid should have known that after so many years; no, she just had to keep on appealing to him to think about their child. She had provoked him until he'd completely lost control.

Now, however, he was very pleased as they finally reached the bridge over the Neckar; he couldn't have been in a better mood. He reined in his horse and turned around. Madlen rode with one of his henchmen directly behind him. She looked up timidly. "Well, aren't you happy that you're finally back home?" He laughed throatily, baring his teeth.

"Oh, it's a shame that I couldn't take you. A real shame. But I tell you what: when the trial is over and you're waiting in your cell for your execution, I'll pay you a little visit, and we can make up for lost time." He grinned and laughed. "We want you to have a smile on your face when you go meet your maker, right?" He turned around and drove his horse forward, laughing louder and louder until they finally reached the first guard post.

"Halt! Who's there?" the tower guard called down.

"Matthias Trauenstein and companions. Open up."

"The city gates are closed. You're too late."

"Then open them again. And then you can accompany me directly to the sheriff, because I have a prisoner to hand over to him. I'm sure he will commend you for bringing us directly to him."

The guard briefly consulted with his colleagues. Finally, the city gate opened just wide enough to let the little group ride through. Matthias nodded obligingly as he passed.

"Come, guards, accompany us and receive your commendation. This is the woman who killed my wife. The sheriff's been looking for her for a long time."

"The she-devil?" the guard asked, his eyes popping wide open.

"Look at the mole over her upper lip. She's the one, no doubt about it."

The guard came closer, trying to look at Madlen's face, but she looked down. The henchman sitting behind her grabbed her gruffly under the chin and lifted her head.

"It is indeed," the guard said in astonishment. "I will make sure that the sheriff receives you at this late hour." He quickly stepped to the front of the group and proceeded on foot as the others followed on horseback.

***

At first, the sheriff was quite displeased to be awakened in the middle of the night. But when he realized what was happening, he quickly got dressed and let Matthias Trauenstein bring the prisoner before him.

"Thank you for receiving me at this late hour." Matthias bowed submissively.

"Not at all; you've done something incredible." The sheriff nodded. "Can I offer you anything? Wine or something to eat? My cook is a gem, and it would be her pleasure to prepare a meal for such a heroic man."

"I must decline. I wanted to do my duty but am exhausted and want nothing more than to go back to my own home. Could I wait until tomorrow to make my statement? As you can see, the prisoner's physical requirements have been amply met. Although she resisted fiercely, my men and I succeeded in bringing her here unscathed. But watch her carefully. She is not to be trusted. She'll do everything in her power to find a way to escape."

"Nobody has ever escaped from the Heidelberg jail. I'll bring her there myself immediately. She escaped from me once; it won't happen again."

Matthias stood. "What a relief to know that she is in your custody. I know from now on that justice will be served; I'll finally be able to sleep in peace. Good night, Sheriff. I'll come back tomorrow to make my statement."

"All of Heidelberg is indebted to you for your service." He threw a look at Madlen, who had silently followed the conversation. "You have done well in surrendering her to me unscathed. I will make a note, in case she accuses you of some crime to distract the court."

"You are a righteous servant of the people, Sheriff. We may not have always spoken the same language, but I hope you know that the lies you have heard about me have no basis in fact. I'm relieved that you can see my true colors with your own eyes and that I'm only concerned that justice be served." He nodded at the sheriff, then looked at Madlen for the last time. "This time there will be no escape for you. My wife will be avenged and will finally rest in peace." With that, he left the room.

The sheriff scrutinized Madlen as he walked around her. "A noble dress that you're wearing. How did you manage that while all of Heidelberg was looking for you?" His voice was contemptuous. "I must confess that you managed to deceive me. I really believed that you weren't guilty. But you will pay for what you did to poor Adelhaid Trauenstein."

Madlen was tempted to speak, but the sound of his voice told her that it was pointless. She only wanted to go to her cell and rest. She didn't know how long it would be until her trial began, but it wasn't important. She could only imagine what everyone presiding at the trial must already think of her. No. Her fate was sealed. She was almost happy about it. Once and for all, this nightmare would finally come to an end—the escape, the hiding, the eternal fear. It would all be over in a few days. Madlen sighed as the sheriff grabbed her arm and brought her to the jail. Without saying a word, she entered the cell and heard him turn the key in the lock behind her. She went over to the cot, lay down, and rolled onto her side, falling asleep almost instantly. She felt nothing but relief.

Chapter Thirty

The news that Matthias Trauenstein was back in town and that he'd handed over the woman responsible for the death of his wife spread like wildfire. Agathe, Kilian, and Johannes had already been in town for two days and went to Madlen's father, Jerg, to ask him whether anything had been done in regard to Matthias. Jerg said no, appearing rather surprised by Madlen's husband. But neither Madlen's husband nor Agathe's arrival meant much to Jerg. Since Madlen had escaped and the arranged marriage to Heinfried had fallen through, Jerg had barely left the house. He'd spent the money before he'd gotten it and couldn't pay back his debts. "Nobody's helping me," he said sullenly, then went back to his woodshop and simply left Johannes, Kilian, and Agathe standing. The three decided to stay in a tavern. Kilian wanted to pay a visit to Irma.

The next morning, they awoke to the rumor of Madlen's return. Agathe, Kilian, and Johannes sat in the tavern, trying to figure out what to do next.

"The dungeon walls are impenetrable," said Kilian. "The best thing to do is to try to free her when she's brought over from the courthouse."

Johannes shook his head. "Even if that were possible, we'd need more than a few of your friends. And she would spend her whole life on the run. Is that what you want?"

"It's better than seeing her hang from the gallows."

Johannes took a deep breath. The picture that Kilian's words painted made him shudder.

"Who was the fellow that represented Madlen before? I've forgotten his name."

"Andreas von Balge. He studies law here in the university."

"I have to speak to him. Can you arrange it? And can we rely on him again?"

"I'm sure of it. He helped us distract the guards so that Madlen could escape from the city. The sheriff held us for days to find out where Madlen had gone. Finally, Andreas insisted on our rights and threatened to report his conduct to the count unless he released us immediately. He's done a great deal."

Johannes had to smile. Kilian had already told him how Madlen escaped the city. The plan was as absurd as it was simple. No wonder the sheriff had been so annoyed.

"Who has been given jurisdiction?"

"That is currently in question. The last hearing was led by the sheriff, and the members of the jury were noblemen. The ongoing city wars have weakened applicable judicial laws. Whoever wins and rules the Hanseatic League will create a council and award new political offices. The Bavarian dukes will more than likely prevail. But until then, we must contend with the sheriff and the noblemen again. Why?"

"It would be better if we could find a way to move the trial to Trier. I have influence there."

"Do you think that's possible?" Agathe asked, sounding hopeful.

Johannes shrugged. "We should try anyway. The archbishop could be convinced to take on this matter, of that I'm sure. Do you think that you can convince the sheriff to dispose of the matter?"

Kilian shook his head. "No. He thinks Madlen deceived him."

Johannes pressed his lips together. "I'll send a message to the archbishop and hope that it gets there in time. But I don't want to give you too much hope; he wants to punish the secret healer, too."

"For healing, yes, not for a murder she didn't commit."

"That's exactly what we need to prove." Johannes rubbed his chin. "Kilian, bring this Andreas von Balge here as quickly as possible. And what was the name of the witness at that time, the maid?"

"Barbara? She's terrified of her master. We can't expect any help from her."

"We have to speak to her nevertheless. We must leave no stone unturned."

"What can I do?" Agathe asked. "I would like to help."

"You can. Try to get permission to see Madlen. You can say that you want to examine her because of her pregnancy; they won't deny you that."

"Good. And what should I tell her?"

Johannes looked at Agathe intently. "Don't promise her anything that we might not be able to do. But tell her that we're doing everything we can. Encourage her so she doesn't lose all hope." He looked at Kilian. "Be sure to make it clear to her that we're all in this together. Tell her that I love her."

"I will." Agathe stood up. "She must be dying from fright."

The thought was hard for Johannes to bear. He sincerely hoped that on top of everything Matthias Trauenstein hadn't beaten her, too. He clenched his hand into a fist. If this cur laid a hand on her, his life wouldn't be worth a pfennig; Johannes would take out that bastard himself.

"What's the matter?" Agathe looked at him worriedly.

"Nothing. Absolutely nothing. I just want her out of there as quickly as possible."

Agathe touched his hand. "That's what we all want. Don't lose faith." With that, she said good-bye and left the tavern.

Shortly after she left, Kilian went to find Andreas von Balge, and Johannes went to his room to write the archbishop. Then Johannes hired a messenger to bring the message to Trier as quickly as possible and promised to double his fee if the messenger went straight through without stopping. The messenger took the letter and set out immediately. Hopefully, he'd reach the archbishop before it was too late.

Although Madlen heard somebody open her cell door, she didn't move a muscle and kept her eyes closed. Agathe stepped in closer. "Madlen, my dear. Are you awake?"

She opened her eyes with effort and blinked several times. "Agathe?"

"Yes, it's me."

"Agathe." Madlen stood up. "It's really you." She stumbled slightly before falling into her aunt's arms.

"Oh, my sweet Madlen." Agathe hugged her niece tightly and kissed her tenderly on her forehead. "Everything's going to be all right, my child. It's all right."

Tears poured down Madlen's cheeks; she sobbed as her legs gave way. Agathe managed to catch her and bring her over to the bed before she crumpled all the way to the floor.

"You're all right," Madlen whispered as she put her head on her aunt's shoulder.

"Kilian is doing well, and so is Johannes."

Madlen sat up. "Johannes?"

"Yes. He knows the whole story. He asked me to let you know that he will do all he can to get you out of here. And"—she held Madlen's chin—"that he loves you."

Madlen broke out in tears again. "He loves me? Did he say that?"

"Yes, he said that."

"But what about Worms? And the healing?"

"He wants to try to convince the archbishop of your innocence."

"The archbishop? But what about the sheriff? I'm here on murder charges."

"Johannes is going to talk to Andreas to find out exactly what happened."

"It will come to nothing." Madlen sighed. "I saw the sheriff's face. To him, I'm guilty no matter who represents me."

"You must have faith." Agathe tenderly stroked Madlen's back. She took a deep breath to prepare herself for the next question. "Did Matthias do anything to you?"

Madlen shook her head slowly. "He didn't touch a hair on my head."

"Thank God!" Agathe sighed with relief.

A guard walked past the cell, glanced at the women, and disappeared from sight.

"I'm afraid for my child." Madlen laid her hand on her stomach. "There won't be much time until the court passes judgment. My child will never breathe, laugh, or cry. It will die, without ever having done anything wrong."

"You also haven't done anything wrong," Agathe reminded her. "And you shouldn't give up hope. Johannes loves you more than anything, and he's a lawyer. Working with Andreas, he'll think of something."

"Time's up," a deep voice said outside the cell door. The women flinched.

The guard held the key in his hand, unlocked the door, and pointed at Agathe to come with him. She nodded.

"Never give up hope, my child. We're doing what we can to prove your innocence. Stay strong." She hugged her niece, and Madlen clung desperately to her aunt.

"That's enough now," the guard called out harshly.

Agathe let go and stood up. "I'll be back." She bent over and kissed Madlen on the forehead. "We're all going through this together." She straightened up, fixed her dress, and walked to the cell door. She heard Madlen whimpering softly, but she didn't turn around. She knew that the sight of her niece crying would break her heart.

"What made the sheriff and the members of the jury believe you?" Johannes looked at Andreas von Balge intently.

"It was the maid, this Barbara," the advocate explained. "Everyone could see that she said exactly what her master ordered her to say. The web of deceit became more and more tangled until she was backed into a corner."

The two legal experts sat with Kilian at a table in the tavern. Johannes had Andreas tell him everything. Every little detail counted, including every word of each witness's testimony. Thoughtfully, Johannes stroked his chin. "I think that might be the key to everything."

"I don't follow, my lord," Andreas said.

"Call me Johannes." He stroked his chin again.

"And please call me Andreas."

Johannes nodded absentmindedly; he was completely lost in thought. "You will take over her defense by yourself." He looked at Andreas, a smile playing on his lips.

"But why?"

"You just answered the question yourself. The court wasn't convinced by intercession on your part or Madlen's testimony, but by the witness's contradictions."

"Yes, that's right. But why can't you represent Madlen?"

"Because I will act as a prosecutor on behalf of the archbishop." He smirked. "And you, my dear Andreas, will bring me to my knees."

Chapter Thirty-One

Johannes waited a full day before he went to the sheriff and introduced himself as the Church's lawyer, sent by the archbishop. The sheriff was shocked, unaware of the archbishop's investigation. Johannes enlightened him about her crimes as a secret healer.

"Would you consider having the case transferred to Trier?" Johannes noticed the sheriff's interest.

"What? Why?"

"Well, so that the charges can be tried at the same time."

The sheriff seemed to think it over; Johannes believed he already knew what his answer would be.

"Would you have anything against having both offenses being tried here?"

Johannes was surprised. "I had not thought of that," he lied. "But you're right. Whether the trial is set in Trier or in Heidelberg, it doesn't matter. The main thing is for her to be tried for her crimes."

The sheriff nodded. "Your insight speaks volumes."

"I'll send a message to the archbishop that you here in Heidelberg are in the position to try the secret healer. When do you intend to begin the process?"

"Well, as quickly as possible. Why?"

"If the trials occurs here instead, I'll need some time to prepare my case. I'll have to ensure that the witnesses can come here to testify on the woman's activities. In addition, we should wait for an answer from the archbishop to ensure he agrees with our approach."

"I agree with you. How long do you need?"

"Five days should be enough."

"I'll give you six. Seven days from today, the trial will begin."

Johannes bowed politely. "Thank you. I'll send you the indictment on behalf of the archbishop in the next few days."

"Where can I find you if there are any questions?"

"I'm staying at the tavern. But I will only be there today; I'll leave early tomorrow to gather witnesses."

"I hope your trip is successful."

Johannes nodded. "As soon as I'm back in Heidelberg, I'll contact you. Farewell, Sheriff."

"Farewell, prosecutor."

Johannes left the sheriff's office feeling conflicted. He had to be clever to keep this game a secret. Above all, time was of the essence. First thing in the morning, he would head out to Worms. The messenger he'd sent to the archbishop would be unable to find him upon his return. Johannes sincerely hoped that the archbishop would feel compelled to come to Heidelberg once he got the message. This was the only way that Johannes could succeed in getting all the charges against Madlen tried in one procedure. He'd never experienced fear at the thought of failure. His self-confidence had always held him in good stead. But now, fear for Madlen and their child threatened to crush him; she must be exonerated at all costs. He took a deep breath as he left the house and walked onto the street. There were six days remaining to think through even the smallest detail; he had to anticipate his opponent's each and every step. He said a silent prayer to God for help. There was no way he would allow himself to fail; his wife and unborn child depended on him.

***

The next day, Johannes headed out before dawn. He'd met with Andreas von Balge the day before to discuss everything. He wanted to speak with Barbara, the maid, but both of them were doubtful that he could get through to her at all. She was the only one besides Madlen and Matthias that knew what had actually happened the night that Adelhaid Trauenstein died. They didn't even know the guard's name. In fact, nobody seemed to know the man; Johannes and Andreas doubted whether he was even one of Trauenstein's guards. He may have even been a paid thug who'd been sent away by Matthias after doing his dirty work. However, he was crucial for the defense, but only if he could be persuaded to tell the truth.

Johannes reached Worms in the afternoon. He rode to his parents' house, got off his horse, and knocked on the door impatiently. The guard had barely opened the door when he stormed in. "Is my mother here?"

"My lord, Johannes, greetings to you!" The guard bowed. "Your mother's in the office."

"And my father?"

"Him, too."

"Good. Fetch my mother. Tell her that it's Otilia."

"Otilia?" repeated the guard.

"That's correct."

The guard nodded and left; a few minutes later, he came back with Elsbeth. She rushed over and hugged Johannes. "I'm so relieved to see you," she whispered so that her husband, still in the office, couldn't hear them.

"Come." Johannes led her into the dining room.

"Did you find her?" Elsbeth sat down and looked at Johannes expectantly.

"Yes. And there's much more to the story than I first thought." He explained it all, starting with his wife's real name.

Elsbeth listened attentively, nodding and asking questions. "But then she hasn't done anything wrong," she said, shaking her head.

"And that's exactly why I have to do everything to get her out of there."

"What's your plan?"

"Well, what would you expect a lawyer to do when his wife is on trial?"

"Defend her," Elsbeth stated.

Johannes nodded in affirmation. "And that's why I'm going to do the opposite."

"What do you mean?"

"I'll prosecute her. Everyone will feel the hatred I have for her. And then I will leave room for doubt. Doubt about what I can actually prove. Doubt that she is a bad person, doubt about the alleged crimes that she'd been accused of. I sincerely hope that the archbishop comes to Heidelberg and takes part in the trial. He will see how I, as a lawyer, tried everything and yet failed miserably. Everyone will be convinced of Madlen's innocence."

"But your reputation." Elsbeth pressed her lips together. "You'll destroy everything that you've built over so many years."

He shrugged. "Possibly. But I'll save the lives of my wife and child."

Elsbeth didn't know what to say. She grabbed Johannes's hand and embraced him tenderly. "What can I do to help you?"

"I'm so glad you asked. Can you go see Otilia?"

"What shall I tell her?"

Johannes flushed. "Well, because of the way I acted on my last visit, I doubt that she'd be willing to speak to me. But she'll listen to you.

To help Madlen, we need Otilia, Roswitha, and Sander. And we have to locate anyone else we can find who Madlen healed of the cough."

"You want to summon these witnesses to help Madlen, right?"

"Exactly. I doubt they would even agree to speak to me when they hear I'm the prosecutor. I need you to convince them. If they show up in court without being summoned by me, no one will suspect anything."

"A good idea. But what if they refuse? After all, Heidelberg is a good piece away, and the people have to work to earn their daily bread."

"These people"—Johannes held up his finger—"wouldn't be alive today if Madlen hadn't helped them."

"I'll do everything I can, Johannes, but I can't make any promises."

"You can be very convincing if you want to be. And you want to be, right?"

"Of course. How can you ask me that?"

"Forgive me." Johannes plopped down on one of the chairs, exhausted. "You're right. I'm just so afraid for her life."

"I'm pleased to hear that we weren't deceived by Maria, uh, by Madlen. She's the woman you love." She smiled. "The woman we all love."

"I have to save her, Mother. Otherwise, my life will be ruined."

"I know." She touched his hand. "But even if you successfully defend her against the accusations that she's a miracle healer, there's still the issue of the murdered woman in Heidelberg. How do you plan to defend her against that?"

"I don't know," Johannes confessed. "Not yet, anyway. But I'll come up with something. I must succeed."

"I'll stand by you, son. We'll leave no stone unturned."

"You can start right now by going to Otilia and talking to Roswitha. She'll be suspicious, but if you send her to Heidelberg, she'll see Agathe. She trusts Agathe."

"I won't just send her." Elsbeth lifted her head proudly. "I'll bring her there myself, along with as many healed citizens of Worms as I can find."

"Oh, Mother." He kissed her forehead. "Then there's nothing more I can do here."

"What are you thinking?"

"I'll ride back to Heidelberg immediately."

"At least stay here tonight and ride out first thing in the morning. It won't help anybody if you fall victim to highwaymen in the middle of the night."

He wanted to argue but thought better of it. "You're right. I'll ride tomorrow."

"Now I'll tell Helene to prepare something for us to eat and inform your father that you're here." She looked at him thoughtfully. "I haven't said a word to him."

"Let's leave it like that until the trial is over."

Elsbeth stood up. "I'm going to Otilia's. Wait here."

She gave her son's hand an encouraging squeeze. "It's going to be all right."

By the time Johannes left the next morning, his newfound confidence had waned a bit. After several hours, Elsbeth returned, giving him little hope that she could convince Roswitha to go to Heidelberg. She was too suspicious. Elsbeth also told him that she'd spoken to Otilia and her daughter, Reni. She told Elsbeth that they would think it over. When Elsbeth asked them whether they knew other citizens who had been healed of the cough, they replied evasively and wouldn't give Elsbeth any names.

During dinner the previous night, Peter Goldmann had chatted amicably, but the conversation was one-sided; Elsbeth and Johannes replied tersely. They were too caught up in their own world.

Johannes reached Heidelberg at noon. His first order of business was to speak to Andreas.

"So you're not sure whether anyone will testify on Madlen's behalf?" Andreas said wearily.

Johannes shook his head slowly. "I hold very little hope."

"Then we have to find other people willing to testify." Andreas tapped his finger on his lips. "Like the women Madlen helped with their births."

"We would have their testimonies but also the accusations that they were healed in the name of the devil."

"We at least need someone who's been healed of the cough."

"As far as I know, that only happened in Worms."

For a moment, neither one said anything.

"You have to take care of that then," Andreas said finally. "I have to do everything I can to disprove these allegations of murder."

"What kind of approach are you planning on taking?"

Andreas shook his head. "I haven't been allowed to talk to this Barbara, though I've tried numerous times; Trauenstein's guard hasn't come forward, either."

"And Barbara's family or friends? What about other people who have something to do with Trauenstein's house?"

"That's just it. No one seems willing to step forward. I've talked with Kilian about it. He says that Barbara once trusted Irma unconditionally."

"Who is Irma?"

"The young woman who wore Madlen's bloodstained dress and helped her escape from the city. She and Kilian are together. But Barbara has become more and more withdrawn since she entered into service as the Trauensteins' maid."

"Do you believe that Matthias has been violent with her?"

Andreas nodded. "Kilian suggested there was some evidence of that."

"But then she must certainly want to press charges against Trauenstein so that justice can be served."

"Unfortunately, that does not look likely; he's a nobleman and does whatever he pleases."

"Then we must focus on what it will take to convict him," Johannes said thoughtfully. "Are there more women in the Trauenstein house?"

Andreas shrugged. "I don't know. That could be a viable approach."

Johannes nodded. "Let's try to find out. I'll speak to Kilian so that he can send this Irma to Barbara. She might be able to find her."

Andreas felt hopeless. He hadn't heard from Barbara in a long time. Most importantly, he didn't know how Matthias Trauenstein had treated her after she'd testified in court. He regretted never looking into Barbara's well-being after her court appearance. He briefly wondered whether she was even alive.

"What are you thinking?" Johannes asked.

Andreas pressed his lips together. "I didn't look into how Barbara fared. She was quite distraught when she was forced to testify in court. I saw it. Terror was written all over her face; she was deathly afraid when she looked at Matthias. But I didn't follow up. When we won the case, Madlen was exonerated. After that, Madlen escaped, then I just left."

"And now you blame yourself?"

Andreas nodded.

"It was your responsibility to defend your client, and you did just that."

"But it was my responsibility as a person not to abandon Barbara; I should have offered to help."

Johannes shook his head. "I have years more experience than you do. Believe me, this will not be the last time you doubt yourself. We're lawyers. We stand for justice. But what is justice?"

"Doing the right thing?" Andreas replied.

"I'll prosecute Madlen and you will defend her. Ostensibly, we'll be on different sides, though secretly we want to accomplish the same things. We'll craft clever, convincing speeches, but in reality, we're noth-ing but jugglers trying to manipulate the system and the minds of the people. And if we do our jobs well, we'll get what we want in the end."

"Has this profession made you cynical?" Andreas asked.

"Maybe, but I have never felt it like I do now. The entire prosecu-tion, which took weeks for me to prepare, the investigators I hired, the many leads I had to follow up on . . . I was completely convinced that I was hunting for a woman in whose body the devil himself resided," Johannes said, shaking his head sadly. "I was completely sure of myself. Then I met with Madlen and found out what she'd been accused of. The law, which we have both sworn to uphold, hunted down this wonderful woman and made her suffer. Is it any wonder that I feel cynical?"

Andreas nodded. "At the end of the day, we can only do what's within our power, in order to do the right thing in accordance with the law."

"Well said." Johannes smiled. "Let's try to make everything right and save Madlen's life."

Chapter Thirty-Two

Elsbeth was desperate. She didn't know what to do if her plan failed. She'd asked all over Worms, trying to find those who'd been healed by Madlen when sick with the cough. But everybody just shook their heads. She tried to convince Roswitha two more times without success. Roswitha was much more willing to believe that she was being forced to testify against her friend; she remained resolutely silent about what had happened when she was a servant in Agathe's household. Elsbeth had also spoken with Sander, but he hardly said a word, either, despite Elsbeth's vows that she only wanted the best for Madlen.

Now Elsbeth resorted to announcing throughout Worms that those who would come forward to testify that evening at St. Paul's Church would be able to earn quick money; it didn't matter if it was a lowly servant or a lofty member of the high council. It was a last desperate attempt; she had even confided in her husband. Peter Goldmann could only shake his head sadly over the latest developments. As she had expected, he didn't think her efforts carried much weight; he was the type that would rather just let things go, exactly as he always did.

People flocked to the church and were greeted at the entrance by Brother Simon, who welcomed each and every one into the house of the Lord. The monk had only agreed to this gathering because Elsbeth had made a generous donation. But he seemed pleased that, due to his benevolence, the house of the Lord was being used for the good of mankind. Elsbeth had kept her composure despite this seemingly holy man's greed. Surely, not even one-third of her donation would be applied to the good of the church's congregation; more than likely, most of the money would be used for worldly pleasures strictly forbidden by doctrine. But Elsbeth could not fight the cleric's odious behavior on top of everything else.

She was nervous and rubbed her cold hands together. More and more people came in and crowded together in the church pews. Would this project succeed? She waited a while until everyone settled down, and Brother Simon closed the door. When he gave her a sign, Elsbeth stood, then went to the front of the church; her knees trembled as she faced the crowd.

"Dear friends." She cleared her throat and held up her hands to ask for quiet, waiting until the church was dead silent. "Dear citizens of Worms," she began again, this time with a louder and clearer voice. "I've asked you all to come here today because I have something important, something vitally important, to say."

The crowd looked at her in anticipation.

"We all know what has been said about the secret healer." She raised her hands again to calm down the crowd's obvious uneasiness. "I know that you're afraid," she continued. "You're afraid of being punished because you let this woman help you." The crowd became uneasy again, and Elsbeth feared they would get up and go. She had to explain things quickly so they would listen. "The secret healer needs your help now." She let her words hang in the air. "She saved your life. Say what you want, but this woman has never done anything wrong."

The crowd whispered to one another, but their mood seemed to change. They listened with a degree of reluctance, but were still interested in hearing her out.

"Some people say that she has no right to heal."

"And that's true!" The city physician jumped up.

"And why not?" Elsbeth shot back.

"She gave people false hope."

"She," Elsbeth said, enunciating carefully, "never promised anybody anything. She simply helped people to be healthy again."

"Elsbeth Goldmann, how dare you!" The physician's face was red as a beet.

"How dare you speak so poorly about a woman who never charged a penny for saving the lives of many who sit here with us today! She did it out of compassion and not for profit, as you have."

The color of his face changed from dark scarlet to blue. "It's my job. Everybody takes money for his work."

"That's true. This is not meant as a condemnation of anyone here. I'm simply stating that the healer did not get paid."

"Because she shouldn't have been. She's no doctor." He slammed his fist down on a pew.

"That's correct. However, she was able to do what you could not. And in exchange, she got nothing more than eternal thanks from those she was able to save."

The physician started to speak, but Elsbeth held up her hand and looked at him angrily. "But now I ask you politely to hold your tongue or leave the church, my lord."

He gasped. The crowd craned their necks to look at him. "This is blasphemy," he spewed out.

Elsbeth laughed aloud. "Blasphemy? Just who do you think you are? God?"

"Be gone, Doctor," a voice bellowed. "We want to hear what she has to say."

"Yes, you couldn't help anybody," a woman roared.

"You'll be sorry for this," the doctor threatened as he pushed his way toward the exit. Brother Simon readily opened the large wooden door for him so he could leave once and for all. As the door closed, all eyes were once again upon Elsbeth.

"Now, let me tell you dear people why I've asked you here today. Some of you know the secret healer as Maria, but in reality her name is Madlen. She is being brought to trial in Heidelberg. She will soon be convicted for helping so many of us."

"But why?" a woman cried out.

"Why?" Elsbeth repeated. The question had surprised her. "You've heard the doctor. No one is allowed to heal for the welfare of the people alone. Especially a woman." She spit out the last few words contemptuously. "You all know that the healer was able to accomplish what the doctor, with all his knowledge, couldn't."

"My Georg died anyway," called one woman. "She couldn't help him."

"She's just a human being," Elsbeth shot back. "A person, with no magical powers."

"What should we do?"

"I need you. If any of you has been cured by the secret healer, I beseech you to go to Heidelberg and testify on her behalf in front of the court."

"In front of the court? So that they can lock us up because we put ourselves in her hands?" The crowd murmured uneasily.

"No one will be punished!" she assured them, though she didn't sound terribly convincing. No wonder, as she wasn't even sure of that herself; much depended on who presided over the court proceedings.

"She saved your lives!" Elsbeth called out as loudly as possible.

A few people stood to leave.

"Stop! I offer five guilders to the first ten to come with me to testify."

The crowd considered this.

"Stop!" Otilia suddenly roared; she'd been sitting to the side and following the events closely. She walked to the front and stood next to Elsbeth. Otilia glanced up at her before speaking.

"If this woman pays you to appear in front of the court, your testimony will be worthless." She lifted her head proudly. "Fellow citizens of Worms, you should be ashamed to accept money to save the life of a woman who has already saved yours or the life of a loved one." She let her gaze wander over the crowd. "Do you really have so little honor? Is that how we think in this city?" She turned to Elsbeth. "My daughter, Reni, had the cough. She was so terribly ill that I had no hope for her survival. But I went to the healer. She didn't want to risk it, but her compassion for others was stronger than her own instinct for self-preservation, and she came with me." Otilia's eyes welled up with tears. "She came and helped my Reni. She gave her back her life, which had almost slipped through my fingers. I'll never be able to thank her enough, and as I live and breathe, I will head out first thing tomorrow morning to Heidelberg." She turned again to the crowd, holding up her head. "I will not allow this woman to be punished. She helped my Reni as though she were merely doing her duty as a humble servant of the Lord." Otilia's voice grew louder. "She cares nothing for social standing or class. She never thinks about her own advantage or about money."

The people started cheering. "You're right!" a man's deep voice resonated above the crowd. "We'll help her!" a woman called from the other side.

"We will stand together as one people, one voice, one city, and one soul and revolt against the injustice of the authorities who want to hang our healer!" Otilia cried out as loud as she could. "She is our healer, and we will save her."

"She's a saint with the most merciful of hearts!" a voice echoed across the church.

"Tomorrow morning, let us all stand together as one and go to Heidelberg!" Elsbeth called out. "We will save my daughter-in-law! We will save our secret healer!"

The crowd roared as people embraced each other. They called out Madlen's name, and it echoed against the church walls. The atmosphere was electric with emotion. Elsbeth and Otilia held each other happily. She had succeeded. Would this incredible feeling hold out through the long night? She hoped desperately that it wasn't just a straw fire that burned bright for a moment and died out just as quickly.

"Go back to your homes, and tomorrow at dawn, gather in front of the church. We will head out together!" Elsbeth hoped that her voice could still be heard above the jubilation. Soon the last people shuffled out of the hallowed hall, and Brother Simon turned the key in the lock.

"That was unbelievable!" Brother Simon praised. "I've never seen the town so enthusiastic, so taken in."

"I won't be able to sleep a wink tonight."

"Try anyway," he advised. "I'll walk you home."

"Thank you."

They both took the short walk home, caught up in their thoughts. As they reached the Goldmann estate, Elsbeth stopped. "I thank you, Brother Simon."

"I'll see you tomorrow morning," he announced.

"Did she heal you, too?"

"No, but it has always been quite clear to me who the secret healer was. I taught her how to read and write. And if I can do nothing but sit in the courtroom and pray for her, that's exactly what I'll do. She needs all the support she can get."

Elsbeth smiled. "I wish you a good night. Pray that at least some remember the promises they made in the church this evening."

"I'm sure they will," Brother Simon replied. "Good night."

He waited until Elsbeth was safely back at home. Then he went back to the rectory. He imagined Madlen, a woman who was no longer a mystery to him, and smiled at the thought of seeing her again in a few days. If he weren't a monk, she would be the woman that he would want to have by his side. He said a long, fervent prayer in hopes that tomorrow morning more than just a handful of people came back to the church.

Although Elsbeth knew that she would need the strength, she could hardly force one bite of breakfast down her throat. She had tossed and turned half the night, staring off into the darkness, repeatedly praying to the Lord for help. She got up to drink something because her throat was dry and she was much too hot. A moment later, she pulled her blanket up to her neck because she was suddenly freezing. Just before dawn, she'd fallen fast asleep; Helene had to shake her gently awake.

Now she sat in front of her food, gnawing on a piece of bread. The sight of the wheat mash made her sick and she pushed the bowl away. She could barely choke down the few bites of bread and ham. This day would play the most decisive role in Madlen's journey. Had Elsbeth really convinced the crowd? She sickened at the thought that she would go to the church and, except for two or three people wanting to be paid for their efforts, there would be no one there.

Helene had already packed up some clothing for her. She had offered to accompany her mistress, but Elsbeth had shook her head. Her husband would stay in the city. It was out of the question; he wouldn't agree to leave Worms to support his daughter-in-law. Helene would need to take care of Peter until Elsbeth came back home. She sincerely hoped that Madlen and Johannes would be by her side upon her return.

Peter Goldmann was in the office when Elsbeth bade him farewell. He did not disguise his displeasure at his wife's foolishness. But he didn't want to forbid it. After all, the prospect of several days without her gave him certain freedoms. And even better, he liked the fact that Helene would be there. If Elsbeth wanted to wage a war against the authorities in Heidelberg, it was all the same to him, as long as she remained committed to her duties in Worms.

Elsbeth bent over slightly and kissed her husband on the cheek. Then she walked out of the house, her heart beating wildly. The closer she got to the church, the more intently she listened for voices coming from afar. As she turned the final corner, she put her hands over her mouth. She would have never believed that so many Worms citizens would show up. The whole city seemed ready to go with her to Heidelberg. Elsbeth was speechless; she finally spotted Otilia amid the teeming throng and went to her. Some people noticed Elsbeth had arrived and began to applaud and cheer. Elsbeth embraced Otilia. "My prayers have been answered. I never dared hope that this many would come."

Otilia winked at her. "You've started something. Let's pray that together we can bring Madlen safely home."

Elsbeth took a deep breath, then made her way through the crowd, hopping up on the steps in front of the church. She raised her arms to quiet them. "My good citizens of Worms. Let me thank you all. Today is a happy day. Together we will fight against injustice and corruption!"

"Against injustice and corruption!" the crowd echoed.

"And for our healer!" Elsbeth replied.

"For our healer, for our healer," they began to chant, and Elsbeth gestured for all to head out. She herself walked ahead with Otilia, Reni, Roswitha, Sander, and Brother Simon; those citizens that could not accompany them lined the streets on either side, cheering them on. Their chants could still be heard echoing far beyond the city gates. It seemed to Elsbeth as if their voices carried the travelers along.

The guards standing watch on the Neckar River bridge were astounded; their jaws dropped as hordes of people crossed the bridge.

"What's that?" the guard asked his colleagues as he shaded his eyes.

"I haven't the slightest idea," his colleague replied as they stared at the crowd.

The citizens of Worms marched decisively, waving at the men amiably as they crossed over the bridge.

"What is it that you want?"

"We are friendly people; our only desire is to take our seats at the trial," Elsbeth called out.

"All of you?"

"Why not?" She gave him her most charming smile.

"You can go, but we don't want any trouble."

"We don't want any trouble, either," Elsbeth assured them.

"So many people for a trial?" The guard scratched his head.

A man from the crowd shouted, "We want to bring back our healer. You Heidelbergers haven't been good to her. But we Worms citizens will take her off your hands." With that he continued to walk, singing a happy tune, which his companions took up as well.

Chapter Thirty-Three

"Mother?" Johannes couldn't believe his eyes.

Elsbeth hugged him and kissed his forehead. "I found out immediately where the archbishop's legal counsel was staying." She smiled at him.

"Were you able to find a witness?"

"One witness?" She beamed at him. "Go to the door, and you'll see what people really think of your wife."

Outside, Johannes immediately took a step back. "That's . . . it can't be . . ."

"At a loss for words?" she teased. "You?"

"How in the world did you do this?" His words poured out quickly.

"I didn't do it. Madlen did. She helped many people."

"But she could never have cured all these people."

"No, of course not. But all of them want to speak on her behalf."

"I'm overwhelmed." Johannes caught sight of Roswitha in the crowd and nodded. She returned the gesture with a smile.

"You were able to convince Roswitha?"

"Truth be told, Otilia did." Elsbeth moved aside, and Johannes and Otilia greeted each other. "We're here to support Madlen. Now you must use your legal skills to save her life."

"Indeed, I will."

It proved quite difficult to accommodate so many out-of-towners in Heidelberg. Some well-to-do gentlemen stayed in taverns, and some stayed in private houses, for which they paid a pretty penny. Most of the people went to the meadow right below the castle, where they settled down in the evening, eating and drinking and trying to outdo each other with outrageous tales of adventure. Tomorrow morning, the trial would begin.

Earlier in the day, the man arrived whose presence Johannes hadn't dared to hope for: Archbishop Werner III, the archbishop and prince-elector of Trier, who took over the office from his great-uncle Kuno II von Falkenstein. He was accompanied by an entourage of a dozen men riding into Heidelberg. He'd been consecrated a couple months prior, but Johannes had been introduced to him shortly before his duties as a Church lawyer had been conferred to him. Johannes didn't know whether Werner shared his great-uncle's determination to convict a supposed wonder healer. He sincerely hoped that he could steer this man away from such a desire, but he certainly didn't want to tarnish the memory of the archbishop's deceased relatives. Werner III von Falkenstein was famous for his many feuds. As far as Johannes knew, he'd successfully repelled the claims of other surviving Falkenstein relatives in line to inherit the family fortune. Only time would tell what he could get past him. At least for now, it seemed that the new archbishop was a firm believer in Johannes's abilities. Whether he was clever would remain to be seen.

Johannes had done everything possible to accommodate the archbishop's men in an appropriate manner. The archbishop himself felt at home in the church's magnificent building, where six of his security guards stayed. In the meantime, Johannes had met with Andreas every day. When it came to Adelhaid's murder, they were, as always, standing on shaky ground. Barbara had disappeared, and Matthias's cook was a gray-haired, surly hag who had dismissed Andreas's request to testify in court with a flick of her hand. Whatever kind of person Matthias was, Andreas didn't believe for one moment that he'd done anything untoward to the cook. Even if Matthias tried to get close, Johannes guessed that she would sooner clobber him with a big fat wooden spoon than let him lay one hand on her.

Trying to get in touch with the guards in the Trauenstein household had been futile. There wasn't a single guard or servant that had worked for him longer than a week. Evidently, Matthias had thought of everything; he'd replaced his entire domestic staff. Initially, Andreas thought that former employees might be angry at Matthias and would be only too willing to give information about what had played out between Adelhaid and her husband. But none of the former servants seemed to live in Heidelberg anymore. Andreas had been unable to track any of them down.

"I have no idea how we're going to be able to refute this murder charge," he said to Johannes, who had come to visit him at the university. They were careful not to be seen together in public. Their only public meeting had been at the tavern, but no one could fault them for that. It was common for defense attorneys and prosecutors to speak about defendants and the charges against them; no one would suspect any kind of conspiracy over one public meeting.

"Kilian was there when the guard came and asked Madlen to come to Adelhaid." Johannes rubbed his tired eyes.

"Yes, but Kilian is her brother and wants to save her life," Andreas asserted.

"That's what the court will think. Nevertheless, you should let Kilian speak."

"I will. But his testimony won't carry much weight."

"We'll see. What motive would Madlen have for killing Adelhaid?"

"Madlen wanted to silence her before she testified in court about losing her child."

"The trial was over. The sheriff decided that interrogating Adelhaid was no longer necessary."

"Some might argue that Madlen could have still been terrified that the truth could come to light."

"The truth." Johannes spit out the words with bitterness. "If only Adelhaid could have appeared in court to tell the truth, the whole truth."

Andreas nodded. "Maybe she could . . . ," he muttered. "At least in spirit."

"What do you mean?"

"We've spent a great deal of time trying to find witnesses who could exonerate Madlen."

"Yes. So?"

"We need to put our entire attention on Matthias." Andreas attempted to remember the trial. "Matthias and the sheriff."

"Why the sheriff?"

"When Madlen was acquitted, the sheriff said that he would interview Matthias to explain his wife's injuries, which ultimately led to the death of their child."

Johannes didn't understand. "But it's not about the child's death at all."

"No, but why did the sheriff drop the matter?"

"When Adelhaid was killed, Matthias became the poor widower." Johannes completed the thought.

"Exactly. But it was the sheriff's job to investigate the beatings that may have led to the death of Adelhaid's child. Madlen had been acquitted of all charges. Matthias, however, had every reason to get his wife out of the way. After all, the sheriff had announced there would be an investigation. Matthias could have brutalized his wife further, but he still would have run the risk that she would open her mouth and he would be convicted for his crimes. The rapes and beatings weren't all; a child was killed and an innocent woman accused. Other charges against Matthias should have been pursued."

"You really want to attack the sheriff? And you want to do it as he presides over the trial?"

"That's exactly what I want to do." Andreas nodded. "What can we expect from the archbishop's side? Will he intervene?"

"No. I've already talked to him. He's only here as an observer. However, I'm hoping his presence will ensure that no one will want to show their ignorance."

"What do you think he'll do?"

"I don't know. He's power hungry. Since he took over office, much has changed."

"So you had been working on behalf of the old archbishop?"

"Yes, four months before Archbishop Kuno replaced himself with his great-nephew. But both men were united on taking action against the secret healer."

"We'll see whether he's holding tightly to those views or whether we can do something to convince him to rethink everything." Andreas stood up. "I need to go see Madlen for one last conversation before the trial begins."

"How I would love to be by her side." Johannes pressed his lips together. "I miss her so much sometimes I can barely breathe."

"I'll tell her you're thinking of her. But when you see each other in court tomorrow, you have to hide your true feelings. Imagine that you're talking to Matthias Trauenstein when you question her. If the court or the archbishop gets wind of your relationship, all will be lost."

"I know. I'll conceal my emotion."

"Good-bye, my friend." Andreas left the room. To eliminate any danger of being seen together on the street, Johannes waited until Andreas was far enough from the building before he left.

"Is this the dress you'll be wearing tomorrow?" Andreas pointed to the gown draped over the back of the chair.

Madlen nodded. "Agathe brought it over for me. She thinks it will be most suitable." She placed the gown over her belly. "It will only fit for a short time longer."

"Despite the jail food, you still seem to have some meat on your bones."

"Agathe's been bringing me something to eat every single day."

"And the guards allowed this?"

Madlen smiled. "You don't know Agathe. She not only brought food for the guards, she slipped them a couple of bottles of schnapps, too."

"Schnapps instead of money." Andreas smirked. "Women certainly know how to make men do their bidding."

"She's such a warm person with such a good heart. I'd like to be more like her."

"Half of Worms is coming to support you, and you'd like to be a better person?"

"How are . . ." She hesitated. "The others?"

Andreas smiled. "Your brother and Irma are doing well." He went to the door to see whether anyone was listening. But the guards were somewhere else. "Kilian and I"—he winked at her—"will do everything we can to get you out of here."

"Please don't tell Agathe or the others that I've lost all hope."

"Madlen, you must believe with all your might that it will be all right."

"You know," she said pensively, "even though I'm still young, I have the feeling I've seen it all. I've experienced generosity and warmth as much as I've known hate and lies. I've found true love and lost it again."

"You haven't lost your true love. Your husband is waiting for your release."

She shook her head. "He won't be able to get me out of here. Not this time."

Andreas wanted to try to convince her otherwise, but the right words eluded him. Was it some awful premonition that led her to say this?

"Can you remember what I told you at the first trial?"

She looked puzzled.

"Smile. You need to smile when you come into the courtroom tomorrow to acknowledge all those who came to support you."

"I don't believe that I can do that."

"You have to do everything in your power to save your life." Andreas looked at her intently.

Tears welled up in Madlen's eyes. "Please, don't tell anyone, but I'm afraid that my baby's not doing well."

"Do you need a doctor?"

"No, he couldn't do anything anyway."

"Why? What do you need?"

"I've been bleeding."

"And you tell me so calmly? We have to get help."

"No." She sounded harsh. "I'll stand trial tomorrow and accept my conviction with dignity. If I'm executed, then let it happen while I'm carrying my child in my womb."

Ice-cold shivers went up and down Andreas's spine. Madlen's voice had an air of finality to it. He sincerely hoped that she was wrong.

Chapter Thirty-Four

There was no courtroom in all of Heidelberg remotely large enough to accommodate so many people. The decision was made to move the trial to St. Peter's Church, but there were still concerns that there wouldn't be enough seats.

Johannes had submitted a long list of Worms citizens available to testify in court. He explained to the court that with the help of these witnesses, he would be able to uncover the activities of the secret healer. The sheriff took a peek at the list with a satisfied nod.

Madlen wouldn't be able to wiggle her way out of this one. He was still annoyed that he'd allowed himself to be deceived at the last trial. He had believed her. He had seen Adelhaid with his own eyes. She was weak and had left her bed briefly when the sheriff told the guard that he wanted to speak to her. Her dress covered most of her body, but the sheriff could see obvious signs of physical abuse on her face and neck. Of course, she could have taken a bad fall down the steps, but the sheriff didn't believe it. Still, the most telling thing was the general impression that Adelhaid had made on him. She was a very frightened woman who had given up all hope. Although the miscarriage had occurred a few days before, the sheriff didn't believe that her fall was the only reason for it. Her end was profoundly cruel and deeply repugnant. But Matthias couldn't be responsible here, of that the sheriff was absolutely sure. Too many witnesses had seen Madlen flee the house in a blood-smeared dress. No, that wasn't Matthias's work, and the sheriff would make sure that justice would be served for Adelhaid Trauenstein.

In front, chairs were set up for the spectators. Agathe sat in the first row. She wanted to be as close as possible to Madlen. Kilian sat on her left, and on her right sat Elsbeth. The Wormsers on the witness list that Johannes presented to the court had to wait outside. Guards were posted around them to protect them from curious stares. No one was allowed to speak to the witnesses before they made their statement in court.

The archbishop was the last to enter the church; he walked down the center aisle, graciously nodding to the people on either side. With great ado, he took a place especially reserved for him, away from the spectators.

The sheriff and the members of the jury sat in a row in front of the spectators. On the left stood a table for Matthias Trauenstein and, a bit farther, a second one for Johannes Goldmann. In the middle was the witness seat. Madlen sat at a table with Andreas at a table on the right.

The sheriff stood and held up both his hands so he could be heard. Almost instantly, the people ceased their whispering.

"Greetings to all! I want to urge you to behave as you would at any trial," he warned them as he raised his finger. "Otherwise, I will be forced to throw you out of the courtroom and prevent you from taking further part."

Very few whispered; most took the threat seriously. Nobody wanted to miss whatever was going to happen in the courtroom today. The sheriff glanced at the jury for a moment. These were the same men who had presided over the first trial.

"And I must make all aware of another peculiarity. There are two different indictments, proffered by different men. Both charges will be handled here at this trial, one after another."

Many of the spectators nodded; most seemed to understand the procedure.

"I urge both the prosecution and the defense to speak as loudly and clearly as possible so that even the last rows can understand." With that, he sat in his place and turned to Johannes. "Prosecuting Counsel Goldmann, please take the floor."

Johannes nodded, stood up, and walked around the table. "Honorable Heidelbergers. The defendant is being charged with a heinous crime. You all know what's at stake. This one here"—he pointed at Madlen—"is a liar of the worst sort."

Otilia elbowed Elsbeth's side and looked at her questioningly. Elsbeth smiled knowingly, though she understood Otilia's concern over Johannes's threatening tone.

"She may have the face of an angel, but inside this woman is the playmate of the devil. I will prove it to you." He grimaced contemptuously then gave Madlen a cold, hard stare. Mortified, she looked at the floor.

Johannes took a step forward, until he stood in front of the rows of spectators. It was difficult for him to find the right words to say next. "From the beginning, I'll demonstrate to you the extent of her vile lies." He lifted his head and looked at Madlen again with disdain. "She fooled so many people, but not as much as she fooled me." He stomped over to the table where Madlen sat, and bent over, his face inches from hers. "I married this she-devil," he roared as Madlen flinched.

"Kindly keep your distance from my client," Andreas snapped as he jumped up. "If you are not in the condition to conduct yourself properly in this trial, then you should let a colleague do so." The two men faced each other antagonistically. Finally, Johannes turned away from him abruptly. "I apologize to the court." He nodded in deference to the archbishop. "My hatred for the defendant is not as large as my will to represent the case for the prosecution"—he turned and pointed at Madlen—"to prove that this woman has committed these heinous crimes beyond a shadow of a doubt."

"I didn't know that this was your wife." The sheriff looked at the jury members; all of them shook their heads.

"Believe me when I say that I'm not proud of it." Johannes took a deep breath. "But for me, all is not lost. I was lied to and betrayed and will do everything I must to annul this marriage."

"She has a souvenir from you, too," Matthias Trauenstein added contemptuously.

"You were so unaware when you married her that you didn't know she's the exact woman you were looking for on behalf of the archbishop?" asked the sheriff.

"No." Johannes shook his head helplessly. "I had no idea; she blinded me. You can imagine the shame I felt once I figured it all out."

"All this does not bring us any further," the sheriff stated. "We've come to understand that you are charging the defendant with a heinous crime. Please present it to the court."

It took Johannes considerable effort to gather himself. "Yes, may it please the court." He took a look at the document. "I would like to describe what happened and what the defendant is accused of." He sat on the edge of the table. "Many months ago, it came to the attention of the late Archbishop Kuno II that there was a secret healer in our land who worked with the devil. Because my family lived in Worms, he gave me this task, which was later confirmed by our revered new archbishop." He nodded deferentially to the archbishop. "So I returned to Worms and started hearing stories. I didn't want to believe these stories at first." He pushed himself away from the table and walked toward the first row of spectators. "Unfortunately, I can't say with certainty whether the defendant deliberately sought to distract me from my actual purpose or whether she simply intended to hide out in the home of a respected citizen."

"Could we please get to the point, or must we endure your entire life story today?" Andreas von Balge said sarcastically.

"Has she also put you under her evil spell?" Johannes spit back. "Is the child she's carrying actually yours?"

"I beg your pardon, sir," Andreas said indignantly.

"Gentlemen, please," the sheriff intervened. "This matter is not relevant to our proceedings." He pointed to Johannes. "Please, Master Goldmann, tell us what concrete charges you have against the defendant."

Johannes exhaled audibly. "In the name of Archbishop Werner III, prince-elector of Trier, I charge this woman with healing in the name of the devil." He waved his hand. "I will prove that she took advantage of people's fears and forced them to take part in unspeakable deeds. And this wasn't the first time she did such things. She also called the dark powers to her side here in Heidelberg."

"Many words but very little to say," Andreas commented.

Madlen lifted her head; her eyes met Johannes's. He looked at her angrily, full of hate and scorn. Had Andreas deceived her? Was Johannes waiting for her final death knell? She was shattered.

"What is this?" Otilia hissed in Elsbeth's ear.

"Believe me, I know my son. He knows exactly what he's doing."

"Shall we start with the first witness?" the sheriff asked.

"Yes, may it please the court. I have tracked down people who can confirm that she is the secret healer. The list lies before you." Johannes seemed exhausted as he went back to the table and sat in his chair.

"Will the maid Roswitha be the first to take her place as witness?" the sheriff called out to the guards next to the doors. A woman walked past them and entered the church. Roswitha went up the entire length of the aisle shyly, her head lowered.

"Please, come to the front and take a seat." The sheriff gestured.

Roswitha followed his orders, nodded to Madlen, then sat down.

Johannes stood up and went around the table again. "Roswitha. We know each other, isn't that right?"

"Yes, my lord."

"In whose service are you?"

"I was Agathe's maid." She turned and pointed at Madlen's aunt. "But now, I serve my lady, Otilia."

"In Worms, that might mean something to people. They are only names here. Tell me, what is the relationship between Agathe and the defendant?"

"I thought that Agathe was a friend of her mother's. Now I know that Agathe is her aunt."

"So, the defendant lied to you."

Roswitha turned red. "I might have misunderstood."

Johannes lifted an eyebrow. "Roswitha, back there"—he pointed—"is where the archbishop is sitting. Think about what you say very carefully. Let's try this again. Did the defendant lie?"

"Yes, my lord."

"Good. What kind of work did the defendant do?"

"She was a seamstress, just like my mistress."

"A seamstress? And did she do anything else?"

Roswitha looked over at Madlen, who kept her head down.

"Don't look at the defendant, look at me," Johannes ordered harshly. "Now answer the question."

"Could the prosecutor please clarify?" Andreas said as he stood.

"If it so pleases the defense." He looked at Andreas arrogantly. "Roswitha, to your knowledge, did the defendant work at something else besides sewing?"

"No, my lord."

"No? You must tell the truth."

"She didn't do any other work," she insisted.

"Didn't she also heal people?"

Roswitha looked over at Madlen as she bit her lower lip.

"Well, I'll make it a little easier for you," Johannes said. "Who is Sander?"

"He's . . . he's my husband."

He sounded condescending. "And your husband was sick?"

Roswitha kneaded her hands together. "Yes, my lord. He had a terrible cough. There was hardly a family in Worms that was spared."

"And did people die?"

"Yes, many."

"But Sander was healed?"

"Yes, my lord."

"And how did that come about?"

"Please, my lord, don't force me."

Johannes stepped toward her. "Answer the question."

"Madlen helped him," she whispered.

"Speak loud so that the people in the last rows can hear."

"Madlen helped him," she repeated loudly.

A murmur went through the crowd.

"Roswitha," Johannes said in a soothing tone, "it's obvious that you don't want to testify. But you must. Tell us in your own words."

Roswitha swallowed hard and looked over at Madlen, who at this exact instant returned her gaze. She smiled weakly and nodded. Roswitha's eyes welled up with tears.

"Agathe, my mistress, got sick first. She also had the cough. Madlen gathered some herbs, and I picked up frankincense. It took several days, but in the end, Agathe was cured. I was so relieved. And then Sander got sick."

"What happened then?"

"At first, Madlen only gave me the herbs. I tried everything. But his life hung by a thread. Then Madlen came, and from that point on, he got better. Now he's perfectly healthy."

"What did Madlen do that you couldn't?"

She kneaded her fingers together nervously. "She calmed him."

"How?"

Roswitha needed a moment. Then she described how Madlen swayed the candle to and fro and sang hymns and recited psalms and prayer. The spectators' uneasiness was palpable. The scene she described confused them.

"Roswitha, what did the defendant get in return?"

"She didn't get anything."

"Nothing? But why did she do it?"

"Why did she help him though he couldn't offer her anything in return?" Roswitha shrugged. "I don't know. She's simply a good person."

Johannes smiled joylessly. "You don't really believe that, do you? Did the defendant heal other people?"

"Yes, she healed other people. Many."

"And what did she get for this?"

"She did it out of the goodness of her heart."

He shook his head. "I have no further questions at the moment. Your witness, Master von Balge." He nodded at Andreas, then he went back to his table and took his place.

"Thank you." Andreas stood. "And how is Sander now?"

"He's doing very well, my lord."

"My lady, let me explain to you what my colleague was getting at with his questions about payment." He addressed the simple maid formally. "Sander didn't have to pay for help from my client?"

"That is correct, my lord."

"But she helped him anyway?"

"Yes, she saved his life. I'm eternally grateful to her."

"How wonderful is it that people like my client exist in this world?" He opened his arms up wide and looked at the crowd of spectators.

"Yes, my lord, it's a true blessing."

The spectators whispered to each other.

"The reason my colleague asked is simple: he wants to prove that she acted in the name of the devil and was rewarded with the souls of the healed."

Johannes jumped up. "You cannot put words in my mouth."

"So, that is not what you meant to imply?"

Johannes laughed scornfully. "The witness is sitting there in front of you, esteemed colleague. You should ask her, not me." He wanted to say something else, but the sheriff held up his hand.

"Sit down immediately and wait until it's your turn to take the floor."

Johannes let himself fall back into his seat angrily.

"Please continue, Master von Balge." The sheriff nodded at Andreas.

"Thank you." He turned to the witness again. "Now, Roswitha, my lady, you said that at the beginning, my client only gave your husband herbs and sent them with you, so that you could help him yourself."

"Yes, my lord. Sander wasn't my husband yet, but that's true. She didn't want to come with me."

"And did she demand something from you in exchange for her herbs?"

"No, my lord."

"And how did it come about that my client took over the treatment?"

"Well, this happened at the time that I served Agathe as a maid. Agathe knew that I could care for Sander until he was healthy again or until it was all over."

"And what did my client have to do with that?"

"I think she just wanted to see whether he was getting better. Or she came to check on me. I hadn't returned to my mistress's house after several days. I'd been taking care of Sander the whole time."

"Was there no one else who could have helped you?"

Roswitha shook her head. "Sander has a sister; her name is Mechthild. But she'd lost all hope and could not stay away from work any longer. She left me alone with him."

"His only sibling?" Andreas lifted an eyebrow.

"Yes, my lord."

"And then what happened?"

Roswitha took a deep breath. Even now, the memory of that time was hard for her. "I prepared the herbal brew the way Madlen had showed me. But he got worse and worse. I ran out of frankincense. I had no more strength, and Sander's cough wasn't getting any better. He had a convulsion because his fever was so high; I imagine his internal organs were burning up."

"Probably because the devil's soul was mixed in with the herbs," Johannes cried.

Andreas just looked at him. "Are you done now, or would you like to entertain us with another unsubstantiated anecdote?" Johannes lowered his head.

"Let us continue. You just told the court that he had convulsions and a high fever?" Andreas turned to Johannes again, as if he wanted to be sure that he wasn't going to make another outburst. But the lawyer sat silently.

"Yes, my lord."

"And what happened then?"

"At some point, Madlen came in. Sander had another convulsion and couldn't breathe. Madlen told me to get some frankincense and prepare some fresh herbal brew, so that's what I did."

"And did you leave the room?"

"Yes, my lord."

"And when you came back in, did you see what you described to my colleague earlier—Madlen swaying the candle back and forth?"

"Yes, my lord."

"What did you think?"

"I . . . I don't know. I was amazed."

"And were you also scared?"

"Yes, a little. I didn't know what Madlen was doing."

"Did it seem threatening to you at all?"

"No, my lord."

"But . . . ?"

"Well, it was just foreign to me. But I saw that it helped Sander calm down. And"—she held up her finger—"Madlen was reciting psalms and passages from the Bible. I've often heard the priest say them during Mass."

"During Mass? Did you get the impression that she was reciting these psalms in some sort of blasphemous way?"

"No, my lord. Exactly the opposite. She sounded like our priest. It calmed my Sander. And it calmed me, too."

"When you think back on that moment, how would you describe the feeling that my client gave you?"

Roswitha pondered a moment; she seemed to want to remember it exactly. "Peaceful. A feeling of peace came over me."

"And Sander?"

"She can't know how he felt," Johannes objected.

"Good. I'll reword the question: After my client used the candlelight, similar to that which surrounds us here in this beautiful church, and recited the same psalms and prayers that are recited here in the house of the Lord, did Sander seem to get better?"

"Yes, my lord. He did get better."

"Thank you, Roswitha. I have no further questions for you at the moment." He turned to Johannes. "Psalms and prayers from the Holy Bible are now works of the devil? I do believe that you might be a bit confused, my lord."

With that, he went back to his seat, sat down, and winked at Madlen.

"Do you have any further questions for the witness?" the sheriff asked.

"She should keep herself available," Johannes replied. "I might very well have questions for her later."

Andreas shrugged impassively. "If my colleague questions the witness again, I reserve the right to question her, too. Although I do not believe that anything will come up that will support the prosecution's untenable charges."

"Though you may believe that we could just as well end the trial now, I consider myself just at the beginning," Johannes shot back.

"And you seem to be doing well indeed," Andreas said sarcastically. The audience laughed.

The sheriff ignored the banter and turned to Roswitha. "You can go now."

"Yes, my lord." Roswitha stood and walked out of the church.

The sheriff looked at the parchment that lay before him. "Now the court would like to call up the next witness," he announced and sighed. This was going to be a very, very long trial.

Chapter Thirty-Five

By noon, fourteen Wormsers had testified about being treated by Madlen for the deadly cough. Among them was Reni, Otilia's daughter, who could confirm that it was Madlen, the defendant, who had cured her. All the others could only report that they'd been treated by a woman with a cloth over her face. But the treatment had been exactly as described by Roswitha each time.

"We can speed things up," Andreas said. "I'm sure we can all acknowledge and agree that it was my client that cured these people."

"Have you any objections to dispensing with the questioning of further witnesses, Prosecutor?" The sheriff seemed exhausted.

"If the rapid conviction of the accused is so important to opposing counsel, I have no objection," Johannes said.

"Conviction for what?" Andreas shot back. "For giving people back their health with no remuneration whatsoever?"

"She's not a doctor!" Johannes spit.

"No, and she never claimed to be. You heard it from some of your own witnesses. There were also people that she couldn't help."

"Because the devil failed when these desperate wretched souls resisted him!"

"The only failure here lies in your complete lack of faith," Andreas shot back. "How you can presume to credit such power to Lucifer while your God, our God in fact, you credit as weak and helpless, unable to give a woman, one of his flock, the help she needs to cure another?"

"How dare you!" Johannes smacked his hand loudly on the table. "How dare you suggest that God gave her the gift of healing!"

Andreas stood, turned away from Johannes, and gazed at the spectators. "Was this prosecutor listening? I can hardly believe it! Here is a young woman, just like you, eager to learn about the rich diversity of herbs that the dear Lord grows among us so that she can use this knowledge along with the Holy Scriptures to bring about healing. But that man there"—he turned around to face Johannes—"talks of Lucifer? Tell me, is this man in his right mind? I can't believe that you would freely admit to such a delusion in front of your archbishop." Andreas shook his head as he sat back down in his seat.

Johannes remained rooted to his seat, struggling for words.

"We will break for lunch," the sheriff announced. "The trial will continue in exactly one hour." He stood and indicated that the members of the jury should rise.

Matthias Trauenstein left his table and walked over to Johannes. "I thought you would be better at this, but even if you cannot convict her on this charge, in the end she'll hang for murder. You can be quite sure of that. The little bastard that sprang from your loins will bring no shame to you. Just like his whore of a mother, he's as good as dead." Matthias left.

Johannes glanced furtively over at Madlen, who sat behind two guards posted to ensure she did not escape. She spoke with Andreas, but seemed to notice her husband looking over at her. She met his gaze. Johannes's heart broke. He was overwhelmed by the desire to walk over to her and hold her in his arms. But that wasn't going to happen right now. She looked at him uncertainly. Could she really believe that he had not meant even one word of what he said during the trial when he dragged her through the muck? At the moment that his lips formed words, the guards indicated that she needed to come with them. Andreas nodded, as she followed the guards through one of the side doors of the church. Andreas gathered his papers together and briefly looked over at Johannes. Their shared look betrayed the mutual agreement between them. Andreas went outside, too.

"Do you really know what you're doing?" Agathe went to Andreas's side as he left the church. She guided him firmly out from the middle of the crowd to avoid prying ears.

"Johannes seems to want to see Madlen hang." Agathe looked worried.

"And that's exactly the impression we want to create so that no one gets suspicious. We know exactly what we're doing."

"Good." She sounded relieved. "If I didn't know better, I would think that Johannes hates Madlen so deeply that he can't wait to see her swing from the gallows."

"He's much more persuasive than I thought he'd be, I've got to admit." He smirked. "It's fun when he makes assertions I can rip apart. I'm enjoying this trial."

"What's going to happen next?"

"Frankly, I don't know. I've never attended a double trial." He made no mention at all of Madlen's first trial. "As it currently stands, I believe we can cease questioning the witnesses in regard to the so-called devil healing. Then the hard part begins."

"Defending Madlen against the charges of murdering Adelhaid Trauenstein?"

"Correct. Matthias is on a mission to see Madlen hang. As far as I know from Kilian, it's not really about the death of his wife. He wants a position on the city council when the city wars settle. To be awarded this kind of political office would be of great benefit to him, quite apart from the status and recognition."

"And do you know how you'll fight these allegations?"

"It's going to be difficult," he said evasively. He didn't want to admit that he had few ideas on how to effectively defend Madlen in this regard. He hoped for a way to prove that Matthias Trauenstein was lying, as he'd done with great success in the first trial. But the evidence against Madlen was overwhelming; of this he was all too aware. "If only I could find the maid, Barbara."

"That doesn't sound good to me," Agathe confessed. "But I know you'll do your best."

"Of that I can assure you, my lady. And now, if you'll please excuse me. I would like to get something to eat and prepare myself for what's next."

"Thank you for everything." Agathe nodded. After Andreas left, a feeling of hopelessness overwhelmed her. What did he say? If only he could find this maid, Barbara? She decided to speak to Kilian again. She would leave no stone unturned.

"Believe me, we've done everything to find her," Kilian replied, every word tinged with despair. "It's as if she disappeared from the face of the earth."

"That might have been exactly what happened."

"What do you mean?"

"From what I heard of the first trial, Matthias was furious with her."

"Yes." Kilian still rued the day that he'd followed his father's orders to work in the woodshop rather than support Madlen in the courtroom. "Matthias must have been beside himself with rage."

"Do you believe he could have done something to the maid?"

"He would be quite capable of doing so." He thought about it. "That evening, Barbara was still at the Trauensteins' house. Madlen said she was in the same room where Adelhaid lay dead in her bed."

"Has anyone seen her since then?"

"I don't know. We all had our hands full ensuring that Madlen escaped from the city safely."

"Damn!" Agathe winced at her own curse. "I'm sorry. It just angers me to not have thought of this earlier."

"What exactly?"

"Think about it. Barbara incurred the wrath of her master during the trial. Hours later, he forced her to be there when he entrapped Madlen. What if he doubted that Barbara would be able to testify without falling apart again? He couldn't risk it."

"So you think . . ." Kilian didn't finish his sentence.

Agathe nodded. "Matthias knew that Barbara might say something wrong that could cast a bad light on him and end up costing him his own head. He killed her."

Kilian swallowed hard. The idea had occurred to him recently; she'd disappeared without a trace. Even Irma and her friends had asked about Barbara's whereabouts again and again; unfortunately, all their efforts to find her had been in vain.

"What was it like here in Heidelberg after the incident with Adelhaid and Madlen?" Agathe asked, pulling him away from his thoughts.

"The whole city was searching for Madlen. That's why we had to get her out of Heidelberg."

"So Matthias wouldn't have been able to get Barbara's body out of the city at that time, right?"

Kilian got a lump in his throat thinking of the woman's corpse; he'd known Barbara since childhood. "Correct," he confirmed. "Matthias wouldn't have risked it."

"Of course, later, when everything had calmed down again, the opportunity to do so could have presented itself." Agathe thought about it. "But I don't believe that's what happened. I think he buried her somewhere." She moistened her lips with the tip of her tongue. "If you had been in his place, where in Heidelberg would you hide a body?"

"I don't know." He squinted his eyes in thought. "Maybe in the forest near the castle?"

"Could he have brought her there unnoticed?"

Kilian shook his head. "On the day of the murder, that would have been impossible. But it's been many months."

"Matthias is the type of man who wants to control everything. He wouldn't risk the possibility that the maid's body could be found."

"What if he threw her in the Neckar?" Kilian suggested.

Agathe shook her head. "The corpse would eventually surface. It would have to be a place that he knew well and where he could be sure that no one would ever discover it."

They both thought it over, then lifted their heads at the same time. "His house?" Kilian asked.

"That's exactly what I thought. Are you familiar with it?"

"Yes, of course. It's made from stone."

"What does this Trauenstein do exactly?"

"He's a merchant."

"A merchant, yes," Agathe repeated thoughtfully. "So he had an office?"

"I believe so, yes."

"It was probably in his cellar, where he puts products that have to be kept cool."

"Of course. But wouldn't the servants notice a corpse?"

"Who knows? This Trauenstein is a devious, cunning man. I'm sure it's not the first time that he had to make someone disappear."

"We have to get inside that house," Kilian said with renewed determination.

"Exactly. How lovely that we know that Matthias is in court right now."

"But there will be guards there," Kilian argued.

"Of course." Agathe's eyes lit up. "I think I have an idea."

"This could be very dangerous," Kilian warned.

"I know. But we have to try. Madlen's life depends on it."

"Where is Agathe?" Elsbeth whispered to Otilia as the seat between them remained empty.

"I don't know. She's probably been held up somehow."

"But the trial's resuming soon."

Suddenly, Agathe appeared out of nowhere. "Don't ask why, just come with me."

Elsbeth and Otilia followed her outside, confused, as the spectators looked on and whispered. As soon as they left the church, the sheriff and the jury members came back in. Shortly thereafter, the defendant was led in through the side door. Her gaze fell on the empty places in the first row, where her aunt, mother-in-law, and Otilia had been sitting. She felt uneasy, but she couldn't think about that now; she had to focus on saving her life.

"Before we continue, I would like to make an announcement," the sheriff said. "We've already heard the testimonies of many Wormsers who all said the same thing. If no one objects, I would like to propose that we waive the examination of the remaining witnesses."

"I have no objection," Johannes said after he stood up. "The plethora of testimonies that have already been given before the court gives a clear enough picture of the defendant's activities."

Andreas stood up, too. "The defense has no objection."

"Good, good." The sheriff looked up to see Otilia coming into the church, running up the middle aisle toward Andreas.

"Who are you and what do you want, my lady?" the sheriff asked indignantly.

"I ask the court for a moment of patience." Andreas leaned over toward Otilia, to better hear what she had to say. He nodded several times as she whispered something in his ear. Not even Madlen, who sat right next to him, could make out the words.

"My apologies to the court." Andreas nodded to Otilia, who mumbled an apology and immediately left the church. "I believe that it is now of the utmost importance that we hear from more witnesses."

"But didn't you just agree not to?" The sheriff seemed visibly upset.

"There's new evidence," Andreas replied, stalling for time.

"New evidence? What kind?"

"I'm not at liberty to reveal the exact nature of the evidence in open court at this time," Andreas said.

Johannes stood up. "In order to abide with the rule of law, the prosecution does not object. The defendant can bring in as many witnesses as she cares to. It will do her no good. No one will be able to say that we didn't honor the letter of the law." Johannes sat down again.

"What are you doing?" Matthias hissed as he jumped up, glaring at Johannes. "It's already been decided. How can you allow this man"—he pointed at Andreas—"to carry out this travesty of justice? It seems to me that no one here, not even the prosecutor, wants to have this whole thing over and done with."

Johannes stood up again. "My good man! I understand your desire to see that justice is quickly served, but you are not a lawyer. We must undeniably establish that the trial is conducted in the manner prescribed by law, so that this woman"—he nodded in Madlen's direction—"cannot say that she did not get a fair trial. For this reason, the prosecution sees no reason to rush through these proceedings. It's far more important that guilt is firmly established beyond a shadow of a doubt. Whether we have to take another day or two is of no consequence." Johannes smiled and took his seat again.

"Thank you for your comments, Prosecutor," said the sheriff. He waited until Matthias had taken his seat again. "So, defense counsel, call your next witness."

"The name is there on the list," Andreas explained amiably. "Please, let's hear each witness, one after the other, as listed there."

"What? You don't have any new witnesses except for what's here on the list?"

"That is correct, my lord. As you've just said: justice must be served by following the letter of the law." He smiled earnestly, keeping his gaze firmly on the sheriff, who bristled with hostility.

"If that is your wish," he grumbled.

"It is, indeed," Andreas confirmed as he looked briefly over at Johannes, who he could tell was trying as hard as he could to suppress a grin.

"Where did you say he is?"

"In church. The whole town of Heidelberg is there."

"You're here."

"Then everyone except for me," the guard responded irritably.

"What is your master doing at the church?"

"He's in court."

"So which is it then? Is he in church or in court?"

"You're making me crazy, wench."

"Me? Why? I only asked you a simple question."

The guard was readying his response when his attention was drawn elsewhere.

"Oh, there you are, Mother. I've been looking for you everywhere."

"Reni, my dear. I've been having such a nice conversation with the guard here."

"Yes, I can believe that." Reni looked at the guard. "May I join in?"

"Our pleasure, my child. Or do you have some sort of objection?"

The guard looked from Otilia to Agathe to Elsbeth, and then back at Reni. He seemed completely overwhelmed. "I, uh, well . . . I guess that would be all right."

"That's what I thought. You look like a very clever man. Can you tell me, kind sir, when you expect your master to return?" Otilia asked sweetly.

The man's attention stuck on Reni, who tugged on the neckline of her dress.

"Doesn't it seem to be terribly warm today?" Reni said, fanning herself as she undid one of the loops on her dress. "I can barely breathe." She picked up her long hair, cocked her head to the side, and kept on fanning herself, as if desperate to cool down. The bodice of her dress gaped open a little wider. The guard stared at her, spellbound. "I'm going to faint any second. Mother, I need some water." Reni grabbed at her chest. "I'm so hot. I am so . . ." She laid her hand on her forehead and then tugged violently on the bodice of her dress. "What is happening to me?"

The guard stared blatantly at her breasts.

"Oh my goodness, my dear child. What is the matter?" Otilia supported her, so she wouldn't fall to the ground. "Water, please, quickly. I beg of you."

The guard gazed at Reni, who grimaced in pain.

"It's the heat," he affirmed. "Let's bring her into the house. It'll be much cooler."

"What a fine man you are." Otilia nodded thankfully. She grabbed the seemingly semiconscious Reni with Agathe and Elsbeth's help. The guard wanted to intervene, but Otilia shook her head. "We've got her. A chair, my good man, we need a chair."

He rushed across the hall and brought one back from an adjacent room. The woman picked Reni up and let her settle into the chair. "Water, my good man, we need water."

To everyone's surprise, he called out a name, and immediately an old, fat, surly woman came in.

"What's going on here?"

"She's not doing well," the guard explained. "She needs water."

"It's the heat," Otilia explained.

"And why here?" The old hag scrutinized the visitors suspiciously.

"Water, please, if you would be so kind," Elsbeth pleaded, hoping that the woman would go back into the kitchen as quickly as possible. She hadn't counted on her.

The old lady eyed them critically but turned around to go get some water.

"We need another chair," Elsbeth said. "We have to put her legs up. Please, hurry."

The guard jumped up, then hurried to another room. Elsbeth watched him go. There wasn't much time. She ran over to the door, opened it, and let Kilian and Irma in. She immediately closed it again and pointed toward an alcove underneath the stairs. She held her breath as she knelt in front of Reni, and the guard came back with another chair.

"I thank you, kind sir." Elsbeth carefully lifted Reni's legs onto the chair as Agathe and Otilia unceasingly fanned her face. The cook came back with a jug filled with water, which Agathe took gratefully. She let Reni take small sips of the water as both the guard and the cook looked on. Elsbeth wondered how she could get the two to go away.

Reni moaned a few times, as she seemed to struggle to regain consciousness. "Where am I?" she asked weakly.

"You weren't well, my dear. The heat outside is simply horrible. You can stay here until you're feeling better."

Agathe looked at the guard. "Right?"

He shrugged. "Of course."

"But you can't stay too long," the cook remarked. "My master Matthias doesn't like it when something goes on in his house when he isn't here." She shot the guard an angry look.

"Should I have simply let them stay outside?"

"Oh." The cook waved him off. "This skinny bag of bones of a girl has nothing in reserve," she bleated. "I have to get back to my work now. And you"—she tapped a gnarled finger against the guard's chest—"you make sure that they disappear from here as soon as possible."

"Of course," he said sulkily. Then the old woman disappeared.

"So." He knelt down to make eye contact with Reni. "Are you feeling better?"

"A little." She smiled at him. "This must all seem quite silly to you. Please forgive me; it was not my intention to cause you any trouble."

"But it's no trouble at all," he said amiably.

"May I ask what your name is, kind sir?"

"Ditz. People call me Ditz."

"Ditz?" Reni took her legs off the chair and sat straight up. "What a fine-sounding name. And you're the guard here in this house?"

"Yes, I am."

"Who else do you work for? A man of your imposing stature must be in great demand as a guard."

He smiled, somewhat embarrassed. "Oh, well. There are many people like me."

"What? Surely you jest. I can't think of anyone who is as tall as you are."

"Really?"

"No. The men in Worms are so . . ." She realized that she had just told him the name of her city; she gazed at him wide-eyed, hoping he would think nothing of the blunder.

"Worms? You say you're from Worms?"

"Yes," Agathe added, as casually as possible. "A wonderful town, situated directly on the Rhine. Have you ever been there?"

"If you're from Worms, you're here because of the trial," the guard realized. "When you were in front of the door earlier, you acted as if you knew nothing about the trial." He gazed quickly at each of the women. "What kind of game are you playing?"

Before the women could say anything, he grabbed Reni roughly by the arm. "Out with you! Immediately! Out, I say!" He pulled the writhing woman over to the door. Elsbeth, Agathe, and Otilia followed quickly.

"Let her go immediately, or you'll be sorry!" Otilia roared at him.

"You'll be sorry if you don't get out of this house right now." He opened the door and shoved Reni out. The other three followed and turned around to face him.

"I never want to see you here again," he roared before slamming and locking the door with a loud bang.

"That was my fault. I'm so sorry," Reni said.

"Don't worry about it. It's going to be all right," Agathe said, trying to calm her down. She looked at the Trauenstein house, her heart pounding. Kilian and Irma were now locked in there by themselves.

The four women stayed close, but neither Kilian nor Irma came out.

"We have to do something," Elsbeth said, when she couldn't bear it any longer. "They've already been in there much too long."

"You're right," Agathe agreed. "But we have to be clever about this."

"What should we do?" Otilia asked.

"Get the constables," Elsbeth decided.

"The constables? And deliver Kilian and Irma to them, after they illegally gained entry to Matthias Trauenstein's house?" Agathe's eyes lit up.

"No. We're all witnesses. We all heard it, didn't we?"

"What?"

"The screams. The desperate cries of a woman. Certainly, there must be a woman being held there against her will. It's our duty to report this."

Agathe smiled and Reni's face brightened.

"I'll go get the constables," Reni stated as she pointed to her still-untied bodice.

"A good idea," Otilia agreed. "Go alone, but say your piece very quickly."

Agathe didn't like the idea. "No. I'm going with her. I don't trust anyone, especially around an open bodice like that. I'll accompany you. Come on."

For a brief moment, memories long suppressed burst forth into Agathe's mind. There was no way she would allow a young, innocent woman to fall into the hands of unscrupulous men. She knew all too well the suffering that such an experience could bring.

Chapter Thirty-Six

"How much longer must this go on?" Matthias Trauenstein shook his head. "We've heard the same story over and over again from different mouths. Law or no law, it makes no sense to continue this way in a respectable trial."

"Are you exhausted?" Andreas asked with seeming concern. "Do you need a break? We can do that any time—"

"No," the sheriff interrupted. "The prosecution is right. We've heard enough."

Andreas didn't know what to say at this point. "I only wanted justice to be served in such a way so that in the end there would be no open questions."

"You already said that," the sheriff shot back.

Johannes stood up. "I also think that enough of my witnesses have been heard. For me, the defendant's guilt is quite clear."

"The guilt of bringing the sick back to life, yes," Andreas agreed.

"No, no, no." The sheriff struck the palm of his hand on the table. "Not that same argument again. You two have been disputing this same issue for hours now."

Johannes and Andreas looked at each other, amazed by the sheriff's violent reaction.

"Please excuse me," Johannes said apologetically. "You're right. And I agree with the other prosecutor, Lord Trauenstein. The trial has exhausted me quite thoroughly; I would ask now to be allowed to collect my thoughts for a short while."

"The defense agrees," Andreas added immediately.

"Well, there seems to be agreement about this. How wonderful," the sheriff replied cynically. "We'll gather here again in one hour and will then immediately"—he raised his finger—"continue the trial without ever hearing from another witness for either side. We will move forward to the next charge: the murder of Adelhaid Trauenstein."

All parties nodded.

"In one hour. For now, I need a cold beer." With that, the sheriff left without another word.

"Where are Agathe and Kilian?" Andreas asked Madlen as softly as possible.

"I don't know. Elsbeth and Otilia aren't there, either. Did something happen? What did Otilia say to you before the trial resumed this afternoon?"

"I'm trying to buy us some more time. They have an idea that could prove your innocence."

"But now they're not here." Madlen's heartbeat quickened.

"Stay calm," Andreas said, trying to reassure her as he put his hand on Madlen's shoulder.

"Follow me, please." The guard bent over Madlen.

"Of course." She stood up right away. "But," she said before she left, "I'm worried. Please. Find them." She let the guard lead her away.

Andreas asked everywhere, but he could locate neither the women nor Kilian. Finally, it was time to return to the church and resume the trial. But the seats in the front row were still empty. Madlen was led over to the defendant's table; she immediately took her seat, then looked at Andreas. "What's happening?"

Andreas shook his head slowly. "I don't know. I didn't find them."

Madlen chewed on her lower lip nervously. "I couldn't bear it if . . ." She broke off her sentence.

"Don't think of it," Andreas warned.

Madlen nodded mutely.

Johannes came in and noted the depressed atmosphere at the defense table. He wanted to ask them about it. After all, he could easily invent an excuse. But he held back. Everything depended on him convincingly taking on the role of the angry, embittered husband who worked tirelessly to obtain a conviction. A brief moment of doubt by any one of the parties involved could invalidate all their efforts. He sat down and waited to make eye contact with Andreas. When he finally looked over at him, he lifted up his eyebrow questioningly. Andreas checked to make sure no one was watching him. Then he pointed his chin in the direction of the empty seats once occupied by Elsbeth, Agathe, and Otilia. Johannes looked at him helplessly. Andreas shook his head in frustration.

Matthias Trauenstein came back in and let himself fall into his chair. The man reeked of alcohol, the smell wafting over to where Johannes was sitting.

"Well, now, have you taken care to prepare your case?" Johannes asked.

"I was sitting with the honorable citizens of Heidelberg in our wonderful tavern. And what can I tell you: they asked me whether I want to be a member of the council. What do you think about that?"

"I congratulate you. Indeed, a high position."

"It's the highest position!" He stabbed the air with his index finger.

"Well, you must be quite satisfied then."

"Indeed I am, my good man. Indeed I am."

Johannes noted that Matthias slurred his words.

"And as soon as that one over there is dangling from the gallows, I can take my place among Heidelberg's most revered citizens. And I"—he pointed at himself—"will be at the very head of the council."

"Congratulations once more. You will have reached the pinnacle of success."

"Yes," Matthias said, a wide grin across his face. "Finally."

The sheriff entered the church along with the members of the jury; shortly afterward, the archbishop entered, assured of the veneration of all those present. He glided over to his place gracefully, not, however, without Johannes nodding at him deferentially.

The sheriff waited until the archbishop had settled into his seat. "After listening to several witnesses at length"—he threw a brief sideways glance at Andreas—"we can very well put together a picture of what occurred. Now, we shall focus on the charges brought against the defendant for the treacherous murder of the noblewoman, Adelhaid Trauenstein. The prosecutor for this charge will call himself as witness." He nodded at Matthias, who stood, grinning smugly.

"My good citizens of Heidelberg. You all know me. Whether this woman there"—he pointed to Madlen—"healed the sick or not makes no difference to me. The last time she did so in Heidelberg, as everybody here knows, was when she ripped my son out of my wife's womb." He slurred again.

"Not only that, but she committed an even more heinous act, for which she will hang from the gallows. With malice, she plunged her knife into my wife's already frail body, mortally stabbing her again and again." He clung to the table so as not to lose his balance.

"Tell me, are you feeling ill?" the sheriff asked.

"I've never been better," he replied exuberantly; Matthias realized immediately how inappropriate his last words were, so he added hastily, "Finally, my poor wife will be avenged, her murderer punished so that I can finally find peace of mind."

"I think we've understood what charges you're referring to here," the sheriff reminded Trauenstein.

"Fine," he replied and plopped down with a thump onto the chair.

"If you're not feeling well, we can continue the trial tomorrow."

"No!" Matthias shouted. "Thanks," he added quickly. "I'm fine."

"I'll ask you, counsel for the defense, how does the defendant plead?"

Madlen got up immediately, exactly as Andreas had taught her to do. "Not guilty," she said, her voice loud and confident. These were the first words she had said to the jury all day.

The spectators became restless again, murmuring and whispering to one another.

"Order in the court," the sheriff thundered, immediately silencing the voices.

"Good. Thank you. You can sit down now."

Madlen took her seat again.

"Now, Matthias Trauenstein, I ask you to call your first witness."

"You have the document. I've forgotten the name."

Some people laughed; the sheriff gave the spectators a stern look.

"Well." He scanned the document and called the first witness. The guard opened the door and passed on the witness's name. A young man entered the church; Andreas had seen him often in various taverns in Heidelberg.

"Tell us your name, young fellow," the sheriff ordered.

"They call me Jasper," he answered. "I work for Siegmund, the barrel maker."

"Good. Your witness, Prosecutor."

"Thank you." Matthias Trauenstein got up, and Johannes watched him closely. He was not as drunk as he'd appeared to be earlier. Was he playing some sort of game? Johannes doubted that. After all, the Heidelberger had no reason to distrust Johannes.

"What exactly did you see the day my wife was murdered?"

"I was in the tavern on the other side of the street," Jasper began. "Kilian, Madlen's brother, was sitting with me at a table. All of a sudden, we heard loud yelling and screaming coming from outside."

"What was being shouted?" Matthias asked as he gestured impatiently.

"That someone had been killed."

"And what happened then?"

"We all ran out of the tavern to take a look."

"And what did you and the others see?"

"The Trauensteins' front door opened up suddenly . . ." He looked over at Madlen briefly.

"And?" Matthias made another impatient hand movement.

"The defendant came out and ran by us."

"Where was she running to?"

"Where? I don't know that."

"And what did she look like?"

"She was bloody."

"What do you mean by that?"

"Her dress. It was covered in blood."

"What happened next?"

"You came out and shouted that she had murdered your wife."

Matthias nodded approvingly.

"I have no more questions."

"If it so pleases the court, I would like to question the witness." The sheriff nodded as Andreas walked over to the young man. "Tell me, Jasper, kind sir, were you talking with my client's brother before you heard yelling outside?" He addressed the simple lad formally.

"Yes, my lord."

"And what, sir, were you talking about?"

"Kilian said that his sister was at the Trauensteins'; he wanted to drink a beer with us while he waited for her."

"He told everyone at the table that Madlen was at the Trauensteins'?"

"Yes, he did."

"Hmm," Andreas said. "That seems rather strange. The brother of the accused, whom he had accompanied to the house in which she wanted to commit murder. Her brother tells you about it, casually drinks a beer, and waits calmly until she's ready to go?" He looked at the row of spectators. "Does that seem incredible only to me?"

"Are you trying to say that my witness is lying?" Matthias asked.

"No, not at all. I'm just saying the defendant's brother acted the exact opposite of what would be expected under the circumstances. Doesn't it seem that way to you, my good man?"

"Yes," Jasper said tersely.

"The man who initially called out that a murder had just occurred. Did you ever see him?"

"No, my lord. Or maybe. I think I did."

"Yes?"

"He was a very big man. Kilian told me he was one of Adelhaid Trauenstein's guards, who had come to his cottage to bring Madlen and her brother back to the Trauensteins'."

"A guard tried to convince the siblings to go to the Trauensteins' home?"

Matthias snorted in disgust. "Just because this Kilian told him that doesn't mean that's what actually happened."

"The witness is telling us about that evening. Not more, not less," Andreas shot back, then turned back to Jasper. "Please continue. You said that Kilian had been waiting for his sister?"

"Yes, that's correct."

"And Kilian explained to you why my client decided she had to go to Adelhaid Trauenstein's house?"

"*Allegedly* said she had to go," Matthias threw in.

"Would it please the court to instruct the prosecutor to refrain from interrupting my examination of his witness?" Andreas requested as he looked at the sheriff.

"Defense counsel is correct. Please hold your questions until it is your turn to speak."

"Thank you." Andreas nodded at the sheriff. "Now, where were we? Oh, yes, I had just asked you whether Kilian told you why my client had come to see Adelhaid Trauenstein."

"Yes, he said that the guard had come on behalf of his mistress because she wanted to apologize."

"Apologize for what?"

"For having put her through the trial; for the baby. Kilian told us that Adelhaid most likely hadn't even been aware of it till that day."

"Sheriff, you must allow me to intervene here," Matthias demanded.

"Why, if I may ask?" The sheriff cocked his head to the side.

"Well, because these are all lies. Lies, lies, nothing but lies."

"You're accusing your own witness of lying?"

Matthias clenched his hands into fists. "The defendant was covered in my wife's blood. There is nothing more to know."

"Oh, I see!" Andreas looked at Matthias, then the sheriff, then each member of the jury. "So the nobleman Lord Trauenstein would like that." His tone was mocking, derisive. "He wants witnesses to say what he wants and conceal what he wants concealed. And then my client can be convicted. Am I understanding this correctly?"

"Shut your trap, you pompous ass!" Matthias snapped.

"I beg your pardon," the sheriff exclaimed indignantly. "What are you thinking? Do you really believe that this kind of behavior is acceptable in a court of law?"

"Yes, I do, Sheriff. And if you want to keep your position in the future, then you should be very nice to me."

The spectators erupted, their voices abuzz as they whispered and murmured.

"Well, this is just getting better and better," Johannes jumped in. "Without wanting to offend you, Sheriff, everyone here has heard the complainant not only try to influence the witness but, you, too, who must make the final verdict along with the members of the jury."

"I agree. I've never come across such insolence before."

Matthias Trauenstein muttered underneath his breath. At this moment, the church door opened and a guard hurried up the aisle, passing Andreas and the witness, and went directly to the sheriff, who leaned forward.

"We need to interrupt the trial," the sheriff announced after a moment. "There has been an incident at your home, Matthias Trauenstein."

"What?" he asked as he stood up. "What happened?"

The sheriff glanced over at Madlen, who wasn't sure how to interpret his look. "Come with me," he said to Matthias.

"If it has something to do with the case, I should come, too," Andreas said.

"I'm not sure yet whether it has something to do with it or not," the sheriff said, thinking aloud. "But yes, I think you should come, Master von Balge."

"And me?" Johannes asked.

"I don't think it matters if one more or less comes now. Come with me. We'll resume the trial early tomorrow morning. All can go for today." He turned his head quickly. "Except for you," he added as he looked at Madlen.

Matthias's eyes widened. "Why is my front door wide open?" He stepped quickly up the steps to his house.

The sheriff, Andreas, and Johannes followed him along with eight guards.

"What happened?" Matthias shouted as he stormed inside the house and confronted a throng of mostly unfamiliar faces.

Ellin Carsta

"That's what I would like to know, too." The sheriff looked to a constable.

"These women here"—the constable pointed at Agathe and Reni—"contacted us because they claim to have heard a woman screaming."

Andreas and Johannes looked at each other, puzzled.

"And those two there"—the constable pointed at Elsbeth and Otilia—"were waiting in front of the house when we arrived."

"There was no woman screaming here because, except for the cook, there are no women living in this house," Matthias snapped. "Your people entered without my consent and without grounds."

"Not without grounds," the constable asserted and pointed at Kilian, who the sheriff, Johannes, and Andreas hadn't yet noticed because he stood behind one of the other officers.

"What happened to him?" Andreas went over to Kilian; his face was red, bloody, and swollen. His left eye was so bruised and puffy that he couldn't see through it.

"I had every right to do it," Matthias's guard, Ditz, declared. "He snuck into the house."

"And that's why you beat him half to death?" Andreas snapped. "As I live and breathe, you will pay for this."

"No, he won't," Matthias asserted. "Mangy low-life thieves deserve to be beaten. The best thing would be for him to hang right along with his sister, so we can be rid of this sort once and for all."

"Curb your tongue, sir," the sheriff shot back.

"And you?" He looked at the women. "Who are you, and what are you doing here?"

"They helped him get into the house," the guard said.

"Is that true?"

Andreas stepped up. "You ladies don't have to answer any more questions." He looked at Kilian. "And you, either."

346

"For the life of me, I can't fathom what's happened here," the sheriff said. "But you've all heard the lawyer. There's nothing to do but sort out the whole thing in court."

"So that's it? This gang breaks into my house and you don't have anything to say except that we'll have to figure it out?"

"You heard von Balge. The way I see it, he is the defense attorney for"—the sheriff swept his arm out—"well, all of them. It's their right to be questioned in court."

"Heidelberg has degenerated into a city of rogues and do-nothing public officials. And you, Sheriff, will be one of the first who will soon not have a say here." Matthias approached him threateningly.

The sheriff was just about to snap back when his gaze fell past Matthias onto a young woman who was shaking and pale as she entered the rear part of the house. Her eyes were glassy, and it looked as though she might collapse at any moment.

"What is this?" The sheriff hurried over to her as she dropped like a stone.

"Where did you come from?" Matthias snapped.

"I found her," Irma whispered, her teeth chattering.

"What? What did you say? Who did you find?" Andreas asked.

"Barbara," Irma continued. "The barrels in the basement . . . her hair and dress. She's there." Then she fainted.

Chapter Thirty-Seven

The seat at the prosecutor's table where Matthias Trauenstein had been sitting yesterday was empty. The sheriff, the members of the jury, Andreas, and Johannes all agreed that every moment the defendant was incarcerated was simply an additional undeserved punishment. They even included the archbishop in their deliberations to dismiss the charges of healing in the name of the devil. But Andreas insisted on getting an acquittal from the court on this matter. He didn't want the faintest shadow of a doubt to loom over Madlen ever again.

In the matter of the murder of Adelhaid Trauenstein, all were now convinced that Madlen had consistently told the truth, and it had been brought to trial only because Matthias was guilty of committing multiple murders. He was a vile and devious criminal, devoid of remorse or concern for anybody else's skin but his own.

So the spectators witnessed the sheriff as he reported the capture of Matthias Trauenstein, who would be tried for the murder of Adelhaid Trauenstein, a crime evidently solely committed by her husband and no one else. Everyone was convinced that Madlen was only a scapegoat to cover up Matthias's crime. As to the murder of the maid, Barbara—or what was left of her—was discovered in a barrel filled with liquid in the cellar of the Trauensteins' house. Her remains would be buried the next day. Matthias would also face charges for Barbara's gruesome death.

With that, Johannes Goldman took the floor; he asked forgiveness from the defendant, and went so far as to thank her for her devotion. A glimpse of the archbishop revealed to Johannes that he welcomed the conciliatory gesture, especially since Johannes stressed that he was not acting completely on his own accord, but was greatly influenced by the wishes and encouragement of the archbishop to make a public apology.

Then Andreas was given the floor. He cautioned both the court and the spectators that this trial should be a warning to all who too easily believed in the guilt of innocent parties based on unsubstantiated claims.

"Do you have anything you care to say, defendant? You have the right to a final word."

Madlen arose slowly, shaking at the knees. She cleared her throat, unsure that her voice would be heard. She was still soaking in all the events of the past few days. Her gaze fell upon Kilian, who smiled despite the injuries on his bruised and battered face.

"There isn't much more to say," Madlen began. "But I would like to speak nevertheless since there are so many citizens, both from a high social standing as well as the simple folk who have gathered here today, and I very much appreciate the presence of the archbishop." She took a deep breath. "It's true that I suffered much injustice. But I think of Adelhaid and Barbara, who lost their lives simply because that's what this repulsive man so desired. I wish I could have done more for them. As I stand in front of you in this church today, I promise I will no longer stand by passively when I encounter a woman beaten and abused by her husband; I will do everything in my power to help her. I bid you, Sheriff, to pledge your help as well when encountering such situations in the future." She lifted her head.

"You have my word, Madlen, and that of all my officers."

"You have our word, too," someone shouted from the spectator stands, and others murmured their assent.

"We citizens of Heidelberg, Worms, as well as Trier"—she nodded at the archbishop—"will no longer tolerate such brutes in our midst. We women bear your children. Honor us for that, as we honor you." She looked at the spectators, who hung on to her every word. This was something Madlen would have never dared to believe until now. "I'm a woman, and yet I wish nothing more than to heal, like a doctor. I want to learn, I want to do everything. Let me heal, and I swear by the Lord God Almighty, who's always been by my side, that I will only do good things for the people as long as I shall live." She bowed her head.

A single pair of hands clapped, and Madlen lifted her head. She looked the archbishop straight in the eye as he applauded. Next, the sheriff joined, then the members of the jury, and finally the spectators, who rose from their seats.

Tears of joy fell from Madlen's eyes. At that moment, she felt her child kick for the first time. She laughed and cried, unable to suppress her feelings any longer. Andreas briefly put his arm around her shoulders.

"Esteemed colleague," he called loudly over to Johannes, "it is your privilege to embrace your wife."

Johannes's chair fell over when he stood. He walked over, tenderly pulled Madlen close to him, and kissed her as if they were alone, not surrounded by hundreds of people. They held each other as if they never wanted to let each other go. Finally, they broke away when the sheriff cleared his throat loudly.

"We still must announce the verdict," he said apologetically as Johannes went back and took his place. Gradually, the spectators sat down again.

"A very lively trial, wasn't it?" the sheriff noted with a twinkle in his eye. He cleared his throat again. "The High Court of Heidelberg acquits the defendant of all charges. In light of her proven innocence, she shall be set free immediately. In addition, the court notes how proud we Heidelbergers are to have you in our midst." He raised his arms. "There will be few here who will quickly despair due to ill health," he joked, and the crowd laughed. "Defendant," he said seriously, "I cannot make amends for the injustice that has been perpetrated upon you. You have my commitment, of course, and you should never be afraid to come to me, when you believe that a woman has been abused. We will no longer tolerate such atrocities here in our midst. I pray that the Lord continues to stand faithfully by your side, and I hope that what has been said here also reaches the king's ears. The archbishop has already heard you. One day, perhaps women like you will be able to attend our wonderful university. Go now with your husband, have a healthy baby, and live a full life. I will pray for you." He choked up, but continued. "The court has spoken."

The holy archbishop himself said good-bye to Madlen and Johannes. When he got on his horse, he waved to Johannes to come closer. "I didn't believe your little charade for one moment."

Johannes looked up in shock, but the archbishop grinned broadly. Once again, he signaled for Johannes to lean in. "Take a little time with your wife to recover from all this. Have your child and enjoy being together. And then come to Trier with your family. A lawyer like you is exactly what I want by my side."

"Thank you." Johannes bowed. "We shall come, Your Grace."

"Yes, I'll be expecting you."

Johannes took a step back as the archbishop mounted his horse. "Take care of yourselves. I'll see you in Trier." Then he rode along with his entourage.

"In Trier?" Madlen asked.

"Yes, he would like me to remain in his service as a lawyer."

"Although, you did lose the trial," she noted.

"You are quite impudent, wife." Johannes pulled her close and kissed her tenderly.

"This is unbearable." Kilian rolled his eyes.

"You're just envious," Johannes joked.

Kilian shook his head. "Nope. Not envious," he asserted. "I have my Irma. Eventually, she will recover from the shock of that cellar and laugh again."

"Does that mean you want to marry her?" Madlen inquired. "What about distant lands and beautiful women?"

"So much has become clearer to me now."

"And that would be?"

"In distant lands, I am, after all, a lonely stranger. And Irma is beautiful. Maybe not like the women there, but she's the one I love, and she loves me. I see the same thing in both of you. This is what's truly important."

"How wonderful." Madlen kissed her brother on the cheek.

"What's next now for you two?"

Madlen looked questioningly at Johannes. "I don't know. First, we'll return to Worms. Elsbeth and Agathe are already fighting over who will be allowed to spoil our child the most. And someday, we'll move to Trier, so that Johannes can take up his work there."

"We don't necessarily have to live in Trier to work for the archbishop."

"No?"

"No. And Worms is not far. The citizens championed for your freedom so valiantly there. I think it only right to raise our daughter in their midst."

"Or our son," Madlen added.

"First a daughter, then a son?" Johannes suggested.

"Why not? If it's the Lord's will."

"Good. And then again, another daughter . . . or no, rather just two. Then again, another son . . ."

Madlen kissed his lips tenderly. "Yes, that would be fine with me," she whispered.

"I must go," Kilian said. "Father has work for me, of course."

Madlen touched his arm. "Have you thought about coming to Worms? Of course, you'd be able to find a place there for you and Irma."

"No, why should I?"

"He is our father, yes, but believe me, he doesn't do either of us any good. Just promise me you'll think about it."

"I promise." He tenderly stroked his sister's cheek and went on his way.

Hours later, it was time for the citizens of Worms to gather at the church and make their way back together. Many Heidelbergers came to say good-bye to their out-of-town guests. The trial seemed to unite the two cities in a unique way.

"Greetings to the people on the Rhine, and come back to visit us any time," a Heidelberger called out, as the group of Wormsers approached the bridge over the Neckar River. Madlen enjoyed every moment. Johannes led his horse next to her as she walked because she refused to ride. She had ridden here, and it had caused her to bleed. In the meantime, everything seemed to have calmed down again, and the only thing she felt was the kick of a small foot, which didn't hurt at all; instead, it triggered a feeling of happiness that flowed from the top of her head to the tip of her toes.

"Did you say good-bye to your father?" asked Agathe, walking next to Elsbeth.

"Yes, but only briefly. He seemed indifferent."

"That sounds like your father," Agathe stated. "Don't let it bother you."

"I won't," Madlen affirmed. "The last weeks and months have changed me."

"How?"

"I've resolved to deal only with people who look out for my best interests."

"A wise decision," Agathe said.

"Then I should hope that you take up your reading and writing lessons again."

"Brother Simon?" Madlen looked at him questioningly. "I didn't know you were here at all. Why didn't you inform me?"

"It proved next to impossible to get anywhere near you. So I ministered to some of the other prisoners instead."

"It's nice to see you again."

"So nice that you'll want to resume your lessons again?"

"It would be my pleasure. I must improve my reading and writing if I ever want to study at the university."

"What? I didn't think you still wanted to do that," Johannes said.

"Does it bother you?" Madlen said hesitantly.

"On the contrary. I've even thought about what we could do together so as not to rely solely on the goodwill of the archbishop or the king."

"And? Have you come up with an idea yet?"

"Not yet. But I'm a lawyer. Just because I haven't come up with something yet doesn't mean that I'll quit before I find one."

"You really think that one day it could be possible?" Madlen's eyes lit up.

"Yes," replied Johannes, after thinking about it for a moment. "I'll be your lawyer. Even the archbishop praised me for my exceptional talent." He grinned. "But first"—he touched Madlen's stomach—"we'll have our child, for the sake of those two." He nodded to Elsbeth and Agathe. "And then I'll study the Scriptures to search for where it's written that a woman cannot attend university."

"Even if it's not written, it doesn't mean that it won't take a long time to—"

"Please, let that be my concern. I don't tell you what herbs to use on your sick, so don't you get yourself mixed up with my interpretation of the law."

"You're right." She leaned her head against his shoulder, and he put his arm around her. "All that will come in good time. First, I just want to get back to Worms."

"And then?"

"Then I want to be happy." She gazed at him. "I want to live happily with all my friends and family but most especially, with you."

About the Author

Born in 1970, Ellin Carsta is a successful German author who publishes under various pseudonyms. She is married with three children, ages twenty, eighteen, and sixteen. Although writing books is her passion, she also enjoys sports, especially jogging and cross-training.

About the Translator

Terry Laster is a musician, singer, and former music teacher who sang, studied, and worked in Germany for many years. Terry is also a writer, currently working on her long-overdue historical novel. She lives with her tiny Chihuahua in Los Angeles, California, where the youngest of her four sons plays water polo for UCLA.